Penguin Books
Vintage Wodehouse

P. G. Wodehouse was born in Guildford in 1881 and educated at Dulwich College. After working in London for the Hong Kong and Shanghai Bank for two years, he left to earn his living as a journalist and storywriter, writing the 'By the Way' column in the old *Globe*. He also contributed a series of school stories to a magazine for boys, the *Captain*, in one of which Psmith made his first appearance. Going to America before the First World War, he sold a serial to the *Saturday Evening Post* and for the next twenty-five years almost all his books appeared first in this magazine. He was part author, and writer of the lyrics, of eighteen musical comedies including *Kissing Time*; he married in 1914 and in 1955 took American, in addition to his British, citizenship. He wrote over ninety books and his work has won world-wide acclaim, being translated into many languages. *The Times* hailed him as 'a comic genius recognized in his lifetime as a classic and an old master of farce'.

P. G. Wodehouse said 'I believe there are two ways of writing novels. One is mine, making a sort of musical comedy without music and ignoring real life altogether; the other is going right deep down into life and not caring a damn . . .' He was created a Knight of the British Empire in the New Year's Honours List in 1975. In a B.B.C. interview he said that he had no ambitions left, now that he had been knighted and there was a waxwork of him in Madame Tussaud's. He died on St Valentine's Day in 1975 at the age of ninety-three.

Vintage
Wodehouse

edited by Richard Usborne

Penguin Books

PENGUIN BOOKS

Published by the Penguin Group
27 Wrights Lane, London W8 5TZ, England
Viking Penguin Inc., 40 West 23rd Street, New York, New York 10010, USA
Penguin Books Australia Ltd, Ringwood, Victoria, Australia
Penguin Books Canada Ltd, 2801 John Street, Markham, Ontario, Canada L3R 1B4
Penguin Books (NZ) Ltd, 182–190 Wairau Road, Auckland 10, New Zealand

Penguin Books Ltd, Registered Offices: Harmondsworth, Middlesex, England

First published by Barrie & Jenkins 1977
Published in Penguin Books 1979
Reprinted 1981, 1983, 1987, 1988

Made and printed in Great Britain by
Hazell Watson & Viney Limited
Member of BPCC plc
Aylesbury, Bucks, England
Set in Times Roman

Contents

Contents

Foreword
by Richard Usborne

P. G. Wodehouse – or Sir Pelham Wodehouse, to give him his long overdue title – was a professional writer for seventy-odd years, had notched up more than ninety books (say five million words) and had a nearly finished new Blandings novel in typescript on the table in the hospital when he died.

The publishers have given me a target of one hundred and eighty thousand words for the anthology. That's the equivalent of eighteen of the short stories. Well, *The World of Jeeves* omnibus alone contains thirty-four short stories. So that, admittedly substantial, book is already twice my target length. And Blandings, Mr Mulliner, Golf, Ukridge, Psmith, Uncle Fred, Bingo Little, Freddie Widgeon and others of the Drones Club lot ... shelves of novels and short stories ... still to come.

It's an embarrassment of choice. I have just managed to leave out 'The Great Sermon Handicap'. But I can't leave out Gussie presenting the prizes, or 'The Clicking of Cuthbert', even though they have appeared in so many anthologies. And there's so much stuff, newer stuff, in the same class. Those talks Wodehouse gave on the German radio to America from Berlin in 1941 ... it's about time they got a proper airing. But I have only been able to give bits of them here.

Anyway, the longer I go on, the less room there is for Wodehouse. So ...

Boxing Final

What follows is the first chapter of the first book Wodehouse published, a public school novel. He had been a good school boxer at Dulwich.

'Where *have* I seen that face before?' said a voice. Tony Graham looked up from his bag.

'Hullo, Allen,' he said, 'what the dickens are you up here for?'

'I was rather thinking of doing a little boxing. If you've no objection, of course.'

'But you ought to be on a bed of sickness, and that sort of thing. I heard you'd crocked yourself.'

'So I did. Nothing much, though. Trod on myself during a game of fives, and twisted my ankle a bit.'

'In for the middles, of course?'

'Yes.'

'So am I.'

'Yes, so I saw in the *Sportsman*. It says you weigh eleven-three.'

'Bit more, really, I believe. Shan't be able to have any lunch, or I shall have to go in for the heavies. What are you?'

'Just eleven. Well, let's hope we meet in the final.'

'Rather,' said Tony.

It was at Aldershot – to be more exact, in the dressing-room of the Queen's Avenue Gymnasium at Aldershot – that the conversation took place. From East and West, and North and South, from Dan even unto Beersheba, the representatives of the Public Schools had assembled to box, fence, and perform gymnastic prodigies for fame and silver medals. The room was

9

full of all sorts and sizes of them, heavy-weights looking ponderous and muscular, feather-weights diminutive but wiry, light-weights, middle-weights, fencers, and gymnasts in scores, some wearing the unmistakable air of the veteran, for whom Aldershot has no mysteries, others nervous, and wishing themselves back again at school.

Tony Graham had chosen a corner near the door. This was his first appearance at Aldershot. St Austin's was his school, and he was by far the best middle-weight there. But his doubts as to his ability to hold his own against all-comers were extreme, nor were they lessened by the knowledge that his cousin, Allen Thomson, was to be one of his opponents. Indeed, if he had not been a man of mettle, he might well have thought that with Allen's advent his chances were at an end.

Allen was at Rugby. He was the son of a baronet who owned many acres in Wiltshire, and held fixed opinions on the subject of the whole duty of man, who, he held, should be before anything else a sportsman. Both the Thomsons – Allen's brother Jim was at St Austin's in the same House as Tony – were good at most forms of sport. Jim, however, had never taken to the art of boxing very kindly, but, by way of compensation, Allen had enough skill for two. He was a splendid boxer, quick, neat, scientific. He had been up to Aldershot three times, once as a feather-weight and twice as a light-weight, and each time he had returned with the silver medal.

As for Tony, he was more a fighter than a sparrer. When he paid a visit to his uncle's house he boxed with Allen daily, and invariably got the worst of it. Allen was too quick for him. But he was clever with his hands. His supply of pluck was inexhaustible, and physically he was as hard as nails.

'Is your ankle all right again, now?' he asked.

'Pretty well. It wasn't much of a sprain. Interfered with my training a good bit, though. I ought by rights to be well under eleven stone. You're all right, I suppose?'

'Not bad. Boxing takes it out of you more than footer or a race. I was in good footer training long before I started to get fit for Aldershot. But I think I ought to get along fairly well. Any idea who's in against us?'

'Harrow, Felsted, Wellington. That's all, I think.'

'St Paul's?'

'No.'

'Good. Well, I hope your first man mops you up. I've a con-scientious objection to scrapping with you.'

Allen laughed. 'You'd be all right,' he said, 'if you weren't so beastly slow with your guard. Why don't you wake up? You hit like blazes.'

'I think I shall start guarding two seconds before you lead. By the way, don't have any false delicacy about spoiling my aristo-cratic features. On the ground of relationship, you know.'

'Rather not. Let auld acquaintance be forgot. I'm not Thom-son for the present. I'm Rugby.'

'Just so, and I'm St Austin's. Personally, I'm going for the knock-out. You won't feel hurt?'

This was in the days before the Headmasters' conference had abolished the knock-out blow, and a boxer might still pay at-tention to the points of his opponent's jaw with an easy con-science.

'I probably shall if it comes off,' said Allen. 'I say, it occurs to me that we shall be weighing-in in a couple of minutes, and I haven't started to change yet. Good, I've not brought evening dress or somebody else's footer clothes, as usually happens on these festive occasions.'

He was just pulling on his last boot when a Gymnasium official appeared in the doorway.

'Will all those who are entering for the boxing get ready for the weighing-in, please?' he said, and a general exodus ensued.

The weighing-in at the Public Schools' Boxing Competition is something in the nature of a religious ceremony, but even religious ceremonies come to an end, and after a quarter of an hour or so Tony was weighed in the balance and found correct. He strolled off on a tour of inspection.

After a time he lighted upon the St Austin's Gym Instructor, whom he had not seen since they had parted that morning, the one on his way to the dressing-room, the other to the refresh-ment-bar for a modest quencher.

'Well, Mr Graham?'

'Hullo, Dawkins. What times does this show start? Do you know when the middle-weights come on?'

'Well, you can't say for certain. They may keep 'em back a bit or they may make a start with 'em first thing. No, the light-weights are going to start. What number did you draw, sir?'

'One.'

'Then you'll be in the first middle-weight pair. That'll be after these two gentlemen.'

'These two gentlemen,' the first of the light-weights, were by this time in the middle of a warmish opening round. Tony watched them with interest and envy. 'How beastly nippy they are,' he said.

'Wish I could duck like that,' he added.

'Well, the 'ole thing there is you 'ave to watch the other man's eyes. But light-weights is always quicker at the duck than what heavier men are. You get the best boxing in the light-weights, though the feathers spar quicker.'

Soon afterwards the contest finished, amidst volleys of applause. It had been a spirited battle, and an exceedingly close thing. The umpires disagreed. After a short consultation, the referee gave it as his opinion that on the whole R. Cloverdale, of Bedford, had had a shade the worse of the exchanges, and that in consequence J. Robinson, of St Paul's, was the victor. This was what he meant. What he said was, 'Robinson wins,' in a sharp voice, as if somebody were arguing about it. The pair then shook hands and retired.

'First bout, middle-weights,' shrilled the M.C. 'W. P. Ross (Wellington) and A. C. R. Graham (St Austin's).'

Tony and his opponent retired for a moment to the changing-room, and then made their way amidst applause on to the raised stage on which the ring was pitched. Mr W. P. Ross proceeded to the farther corner of the ring, where he sat down and was vigorously massaged by his two seconds. Tony took the opposite corner and submitted himself to the same process. It is a very cheering thing at any time to have one's arms and legs kneaded like bread, and it is especially pleasant if one is at all nervous. Like somebody's something it is both grateful and comforting.

Tony's seconds were curious specimens of humanity. One was a gigantic soldier, very gruff and taciturn, and with decided leanings towards pessimism. The other was also a soldier. He was in every way his colleague's opposite. He was half his size, had red hair, and was bubbling over with conversation. The other could not interfere with his hair or his size, but he could with his conversation, and whenever he attempted a remark, he was promptly silenced, much to his disgust.

'Plenty o' moosle 'ere, Fred,' he began, as he rubbed Tony's left arm.

'Moosle ain't everything,' said the other, gloomily, and there was silence again.

'Are you ready? Seconds away,' said the referee.

'Time!'

The two stood up to one another.

The Wellington representative was a plucky boxer, but he was not in the same class as Tony. After a few exchanges, the latter got to work, and after that there was only one man in the ring. In the middle of the second round the referee stopped the fight, and gave it to Tony, who came away as fresh as he had started, and a great deal happier and more confident.

'Did us proud, Fred,' began the garrulous man.

'Yes, but that 'un ain't nothing. You wait until he meets young Thomson. I've seen 'im box 'ere three years, and never bin beat yet. Three bloomin' years. Yus.'

This might have depressed anybody else, but as Tony already knew all there was to be known about Allen's skill with the gloves, it had no effect upon him.

A sanguinary heavy-weight encounter was followed by the first bout of the feathers and the second of the light-weights, and then it was Allen's turn to fight the Harrow representative.

It was not a very exciting bout. Allen took things very easily. He knew his training was by no means all it should have been, and it was not his game to take it out of himself with any fire-work business in the trial heats. He could reserve that for the

13

final. So he sparred three gentle rounds with the Harrow sportsman, just doing sufficient to keep the lead and obtain the verdict after the last round. He finished without having turned a hair. He had only received one really hard blow, and that had done no damage. After this came a long series of fights. The heavy-weights shed their blood in gallons for name and fame. The feather-weights gave excellent exhibitions of science, and the light-weight pairs were fought off until there remained only the final to be decided, Robinson, of St Paul's, against a Charterhouse boxer.

In the middle-weights there were three competitors still in the running, Allen, Tony, and a Felsted man. They drew lots, and the bye fell to Tony, who put up an uninteresting three rounds with one of the soldiers, neither fatiguing himself very much. Henderson, of Felsted, proved a much tougher nut to crack than Allen's first opponent. He was a rushing boxer, and in the first round had, if anything, the best of it. In the last two, however, Allen gradually forged ahead, gaining many points by his perfect style alone. He was declared the winner, but he felt much more tired than he had done after his first fight.

By the time he was required again, however, he had had plenty of breathing space. The final of the light-weights had been decided, and Robinson, of St Paul's, after the custom of Paulines, had set the crown upon his afternoon's work by fighting the Carthusian to a standstill in the first round. There only remained now the finals of the heavies and middles.

It was decided to take the latter first.

Tony had his former seconds, and Dawkins had come to his corner to see him through the ordeal.

'The 'ole thing 'ere,' he kept repeating, 'is to keep goin' 'ard all the time and wear 'im out. He's too quick for you to try any sparrin' with.'

'Yes,' said Tony.

'The 'ole thing,' continued the expert, 'is to feint with your left and 'it with your right.' This was excellent in theory, no doubt, but Tony felt when he came to put it into practice Allen might have other schemes on hand and bring them off first.

'Are you ready? Seconds out of the ring . . . Time!'

'Go in, sir, 'ard,' whispered the red-haired man as Tony rose from his place.

Allen came up looking pleased with matters in general. He gave Tony a cousinly grin as they shook hands. Tony did not respond. He was feeling serious, and wondering if he could bring off his knock-out before the three rounds were over. He had his doubts.

The fight opened slowly. Both were cautious, for each knew the other's powers. Suddenly, just as Tony was thinking of leading, Allen came in like a flash. A straight left between the eyes, a right on the side of the head, and a second left on the exact tip of the nose, and he was out again, leaving Tony with a helpless feeling of impotence and disgust.

Then followed more sparring. Tony could never get in exactly the right position for a rush. Allen circled round him with an occasional feint. Then he hit out with the left. Tony ducked. Again he hit, and again Tony ducked, but this time the left stopped halfway, and his right caught Tony on the cheek just as he swayed to one side. It staggered him, and before he could recover himself, in darted Allen again with another trio of blows, ducked a belated left counter, got in two stinging hits on the ribs, and finished with a left drive which took Tony clean off his feet and deposited him on the floor beside the ropes.

'Silence, *please*,' said the referee, as a burst of applause greeted this feat.

Tony was up again in a moment. He began to feel savage. He had expected something like this, but that gave him no consolation. He made up his mind that he really would rush this time, but just as he was coming in, Allen came in instead. It seemed to Tony for the next half-minute that his cousin's fists were never out of his face. He looked on the world through a brown haze of boxing glove. Occasionally his hand met something solid which he took to be Allen, but this was seldom, and, whenever it happened, it only seemed to bring him back again like a boomerang. Just at the most exciting point, 'Time' was called.

The pessimist shook his head gloomily as he sponged Tony's face.

'You must lead if you want to 'it 'im,' said the garrulous man. 'You're too slow. Go in at 'im, sir, wiv both 'ands, an' you'll be all right. Won't 'e, Fred?'

'I said 'ow it 'ud be,' was the only reply Fred would vouchsafe.

Tony was half afraid the referee would give the fight against him without another round, but to his joy 'Time' was duly called. He came up to the scratch as game as ever, though his head was singing. He meant to go in for all he was worth this round.

And go in he did. Allen had managed, in performing a complicated manoeuvre, to place himself in a corner, and Tony rushed. He was sent out again with a flush hit on the face. He rushed again, and again met Allen's left. Then he got past, and in the confined space had it all his own way. Science did not tell here. Strength was the thing that scored, hard half-arm smashes, left and right, at face and body, and the guard could look after itself.

Allen upper-cut him twice, but after that he was nowhere. Tony went in with both hands. There was a prolonged rally, and it was not until 'Time' had been called that Allen was able to extricate himself. Tony's blows had been mostly body blows, and very warm ones at that.

'That's right, sir,' was the comment of the red-headed second. 'Keep 'em both goin' hard, and you'll win yet. You 'ad 'im proper then. 'Adn't 'e, Fred?'

And even the pessimist was obliged to admit that Tony could fight, even if he was not quick with his guard.

Allen took the ring slowly. His want of training had begun to tell on him, and some of Tony's blows had landed in very tender spots. He knew that he could win if his wind held out, but he had misgivings. The gloves seemed to weigh down his hands. Tony opened the ball with a tremendous rush. Allen stopped him neatly. There was an interval while the two sparred for an opening. Then Allen feinted and dashed in. Tony did not hit him once. It was the first round over again. Left right, left right, and, finally, as had happened before, a tremendously hot shot which sent him under the ropes. He got up, and again Allen darted in. Tony met him with a straight left. A rapid exchange of blows, and the end came. Allen lashed out with his left. Tony ducked sharply, and brought his right across with every ounce of his weight behind it, fairly on to the point of the jaw. The right cross-counter is distinctly one of those things which it is more blessed to give than to receive. Allen collapsed.

'... nine ... ten.'

The time-keeper closed his watch.

'Graham wins,' said the referee, 'look after that man there.'

The Pothunters (1902)

Mike Meets Psmith

*Mike Jackson, the star schoolboy cricketer, has been removed,
for not working, from Wrykyn by his father and sent, for his
last term at public school, to Sedleigh, which has a reputation
for making boys work. A new boy in his last term, he meets
another new boy, recently removed from Eton by a father with
thoughts similar to Mike's father's.*

Mike strayed about, finding his bearings, and finally came to a
room which he took to be the equivalent of the senior day-room
at a Wrykyn house. Everywhere else he had found nothing but
emptiness. Evidently he had come by an earlier train than was
usual. But this room was occupied.

A very long, thin youth, with a solemn face and immaculate
clothes, was leaning against the mantelpiece. As Mike entered
he fumbled in his top left waistcoat pocket, produced an eyeglass attached to a cord, and fixed it in his right eye. With the
help of this aid to vision he inspected Mike in silence for a
while, then, having flicked an invisible speck of dust from the
left sleeve of his coat, he spoke.

'Hullo,' he said.

He spoke in a tired voice.

'Hullo,' said Mike.

'Take a seat,' said the immaculate one. 'If you don't mind
dirtying your bags, that's to say. Personally, I don't see any
prospect of ever sitting down in this place. It looks to me as if
they meant to use these chairs as mustard-and-cress beds. A
Nursery Garden in the Home. That sort of idea. My name,' he
added pensively, 'is Smith. What's yours?'

'Jackson,' said Mike.

'Are you the Bully, the Pride of the School, or the Boy who

18

is Led Astray and takes to Drink in Chapter Sixteen?'

'The last for choice,' said Mike, 'but I've only just arrived, so I don't know.'

'The boy – what will he become? Are you new here, too, then?'

'Yes! Why, are you new?'

'Do I look as if I belonged here? I'm the latest import. Sit down on yonder settee, and I will tell you the painful story of my life. By the way, before I start, there's just one thing. If you ever have occasion to write to me, would you mind sticking a P at the beginning of my name? P-s-m-i-t-h see?' There are too many Smiths, and I don't care for Smythe. My father's content to worry along in the old-fashioned way, but I've decided to strike out a fresh line. I shall found a new dynasty. The resolve came to me unexpectedly this morning. I jotted it down on the back of an envelope. In conversation you may address me as Rupert (though I hope you won't), or simply Smith, the P not being sounded. Cp. the name Zbysco, in which the Z is given a similar miss-in-baulk. See?'

Mike said he saw. Psmith thanked him with a certain stately old-world courtesy.

'Let us start at the beginning,' he resumed. 'My infancy. When I was but a babe, my eldest sister was bribed with a shilling an hour by my nurse to keep an eye on me, and see that I did not raise Cain. At the end of the first day she struck for one-and-six, and got it. We now pass to my boyhood. At an early age, I was sent to Eton, everybody predicting a bright career for me. But,' said Psmith solemnly, fixing an owl-like gaze on Mike through the eyeglass, 'it was not to be.'

'No?' said Mike.

'No. I was superannuated last term.'

'Bad luck.'

'For Eton, yes. But what Eton loses, Sedleigh gains.'

'But why Sedleigh, of all places?'

'This is the most painful part of my narrative. It seems that a certain scug in the next village to ours happened last year to collar a Balliol –'

'Not Barlitt!' exclaimed Mike.

'That was the man. The son of the vicar. The vicar told the curate, who told our curate, who told our vicar, who told my father, who sent me off here to get a Balliol too. Do *you* know Barlitt?'

'His father's vicar in our village. It was because his son got a Balliol that I was sent here.'

'Do you come from Crofton?'

'Yes.'

'I've lived at Lower Benford all my life. We are practically long-lost brothers. Cheer a little, will you?'

Mike felt as Robinson Crusoe felt when he met Friday. Here was a fellow human being in this desert place. He could almost have embraced Psmith. The very sound of the name Lower Benford was heartening. His dislike for his new school was not diminished, but now he felt that life here might at least be tolerable.

'Where were you before you came here?' asked Psmith. 'You have heard my painful story. Now tell me yours.'

'Wrykyn. My father took me away because I got such a lot of bad reports.'

'My reports from Eton were simply scurrilous. There's a libel action in every sentence. How do you like this place from what you've seen of it?'

'Rotten.'

'I am with you, Comrade Jackson. You won't mind my calling you Comrade, will you? I've just become a Socialist. It's a great scheme. You ought to be one. You work for the equal distribution of property and start by collaring all you can and sitting on it. We must stick together. We are companions in misfortune. Lost lambs. Sheep that have gone astray. Divided, we fall, together we may worry through. Have you seen Professor Radium yet? I should say Mr Outwood. What do you think of him?'

'He doesn't seem a bad sort of chap. Bit off his nut.'

Mike (1909)

The Clicking of Cuthbert

*Wodehouse was never much better than a 'goof' golfer. He tried
to reach the green in one shot from any distance up to 500
yards.*

The young man came into the smoking-room of the club-house,
and flung his bag with a clatter on the floor. He sank moodily
into an arm-chair and pressed the bell.

'Waiter!'

'Sir?'

The young man pointed at the bag with every evidence of
distaste.

'You may have these clubs,' he said. 'Take them away. If you
don't want them yourself, give them to one of the caddies.'

Across the room the Oldest Member gazed at him with a
grave sadness through the smoke of his pipe. His eye was deep
and dreamy, – the eye of a man who, as the poet says, has seen
Golf steadily and seen it whole.

'You are giving up golf?' he said.

He was not altogether unprepared for such an attitude on the
young man's part: for from his eyrie on the terrace above the
ninth green he had observed him start out on the afternoon's
round and had seen him lose a couple of balls in the lake at the
second hole after taking seven strokes at the first.

'Yes!' cried the young man fiercely. 'For ever, dammit!
Footling game! Blanked infernal fat-headed silly ass of a
game! Nothing but a waste of time.'

The Sage winced.

'Don't say that, my boy.'

'But I do say it. What earthly good is golf? Life is stern and life is earnest. We live in a practical age. All round us we see foreign competition making itself unpleasant. And we spend our time playing golf! What do we get out of it? Is golf any use? That's what I'm asking you. Can you name me a single case where devotion to this pestilential pastime has done a man any practical good?'

The Sage smiled gently.

'I could name a thousand.'

'One will do.'

'I will select,' said the Sage, 'from the innumerable memories that rush to my mind, the story of Cuthbert Banks.'

'Never heard of him.'

'Be of good cheer,' said the Oldest Member. 'You are going to hear of him now.'

It was in the picturesque little settlement of Wood Hills (said the Oldest Member) that the incidents occurred which I am about to relate. Even if you have never been in Wood Hills, that suburban paradise is probably familiar to you by name. Situated at a convenient distance from the city, it combines in a notable manner the advantages of town life with the pleasant surroundings and healthful air of the country. Its inhabitants live in commodious houses, standing in their own grounds, and enjoy so many luxuries – such as gravel soil, main drainage, electric light, telephone, baths (h. and c.), and company's own water, that you might be pardoned for imagining life to be so ideal for them that no possible improvement could be added to their lot. Mrs Willoughby Smethurst was under no such delusion. What Wood Hills needed to make it perfect, she realized, was Culture. Material comforts are all very well, but, if the *summum bonum* is to be achieved, the Soul also demands a look in, and it was Mrs Smethurst's unfaltering resolve that never while she had her strength should the Soul be handed the loser's end. It was her intention to make Wood Hills a centre of all that was most cultivated and refined, and, golly! how she had succeeded. Under her presidency the Wood Hills Literary and Debating Society had tripled its membership.

But there is always a fly in the ointment, a caterpillar in the salad. The local golf club, an institution to which Mrs Smethurst strongly objected, had also tripled its membership; and the division of the community into two rival camps, the Golfers and the Cultured, had become more marked than ever. This division, always acute, had attained now to the dimensions of a Schism. The rival sects treated one another with a cold hostility.

Unfortunate episodes came to widen the breach. Mrs Smethurst's house adjoined the links, standing to the right of the fourth tee: and, as the Literary Society was in the habit of entertaining visiting lecturers, many a golfer had foozled his drive owing to sudden loud outbursts of applause coinciding with his down-swing. And not long before this story opens a sliced ball, whizzing in at the open window, had come within an ace of incapacitating Raymond Parsloe Devine, the rising young novelist (who rose at that moment a clear foot and a half) from any further exercise of his art. Two inches, indeed, to the right and Raymond must inevitably have handed in his dinner-pail.

To make matters worse, a ring at the front door-bell followed almost immediately, and the maid ushered in a young man of pleasing appearance in a sweater and baggy knickerbockers who apologetically but firmly insisted on playing his ball where it lay, and what with the shock of the lecturer's narrow escape and the spectacle of the intruder standing on the table and working away with a niblick, the afternoon's session had to be classed as a complete frost. Mr Devine's determination, from which no argument could swerve him, to deliver the rest of his lecture in the coal-cellar gave the meeting a jolt from which it never recovered.

I have dwelt upon this incident, because it was the means of introducing Cuthbert Banks to Mrs Smethurst's niece, Adeline. As Cuthbert, for it was he who had so nearly reduced the muster-roll of rising novelists by one, hopped down from the table after his stroke, he was suddenly aware that a beautiful girl was looking at him intently. As a matter of fact, everyone in the room was looking at him intently, none more so than Raymond Parsloe Devine, but none of the others were beautiful girls. Long as the members of Wood Hills Literary Society were on brain, they were short on looks, and, to Cuthbert's excited eye, Adeline Smethurst stood out like a jewel in a pile of coke.

He had never seen her before, for she had only arrived at her aunt's house on the previous day, but he was perfectly certain that life, even when lived in the midst of gravel soil, main drainage, and company's own water, was going to be a pretty poor affair if he did not see her again. Yes, Cuthbert was in love: and it is interesting to record, as showing the effect of the tender emotion on a man's game, that twenty minutes after he had met Adeline he did the short eleventh in one, and as near as a toucher got a three on the four-hundred-yard twelfth.

I will skip lightly over the intermediate stages of Cuthbert's courtship and come to the moment when – at the annual ball in aid of the local Cottage Hospital, the only occasion during the year on which the lion, so to speak, lay down with the lamb, and the Golfers and the Cultured met on terms of easy comradeship, their differences temporarily laid aside – he proposed to Adeline and was badly stymied.

That fair, soulful girl could not see him with a spy-glass.

'Mr Banks,' she said, 'I will speak frankly.'

'Charge right ahead,' assented Cuthbert.

'Deeply sensible as I am of –'

'I know. Of the honour and the compliment and all that. But, passing lightly over all that guff, what seems to be the trouble? I love you to distraction –'

'Love is not everything.'

'You're wrong,' said Cuthbert earnestly. 'You're right off it. Love –' And he was about to dilate on the theme when she interrupted him.

'I am a girl of ambition.'

'And very nice, too,' said Cuthbert.

'I am a girl of ambition,' repeated Adeline, 'and I realize that the fulfilment of my ambitions must come through my husband. I am very ordinary myself –'

'What!' cried Cuthbert. 'You ordinary? Why, you are a pearl among women, the queen of your sex. You can't have been looking in a glass lately. You stand alone. Simply alone. You make the rest look like battered repaints.'

'Well,' said Adeline, softening a trifle, 'I believe I am fairly good-looking –'

'Anybody who was content to call you fairly good-looking would describe the Taj Mahal as a pretty nifty tomb.'

'But that is not the point. What I mean is, if I marry a nonentity I shall be a nonentity myself for ever. And I would sooner die than be a nonentity.'

'And, if I follow your reasoning, you think that let's *me* out?'

'Well, really, Mr Banks, *have* you done anything, or are you likely ever to do anything worth while?'

Cuthbert hesitated.

'It's true,' he said, 'I didn't finish in the first ten in the Open, and I was knocked out in the semi-final of the Amateur, but I won the French Open last year.'

'The – what?'

'The French Open Golf Championship. Golf, you know.'

'Golf! You waste all your time playing golf. I admire a man who is more spiritual, more intellectual.'

A pang of jealousy rent Cuthbert's bosom.

'Like What's-his-name Devine?' he said, sullenly.

'Mr Devine,' replied Adeline, blushing faintly, 'is going to be a great man. Already he has achieved much. The critics say that he is more Russian than any other young English writer.'

'And is that good?'

'Of course it's good.'

'I should have thought the wheeze would be to be more English than any other young English writer.'

'Nonsense! Who wants an English writer to be English? You've got to be Russian or Spanish or something to be a real success. The mantle of the great Russians has descended on Mr Devine.'

'From what I've heard of Russians, I should hate to have that happen to *me*.'

'There is no danger of that,' said Adeline, scornfully.

'Oh! Well, let me tell you that there is a lot more in me than you think.'

'That might easily be so.'

'You think I'm not spiritual and intellectual,' said Cuthbert deeply moved. 'Very well. Tomorrow I join the Literary Society.'

Even as he spoke the words his leg was itching to kick himself for being such a chump, but the sudden expression of pleasure on Adeline's face soothed him; and he went home that night with the feeling that he had taken on something rather attractive. It was only in the cold, grey light of the morning that he realized what he had let himself in for.

I do not know if you have had any experience of suburban literary societies, but the one that flourished under the eye of Mrs Willoughby Smethurst at Wood Hills was rather more so than the average. With my feeble powers of narrative, I cannot hope to make clear to you all that Cuthbert Banks endured in the next few weeks. And, even if I could, I doubt if I should do so. It is all very well to excite pity and terror, as Aristotle re-recommends, but there are limits. In the ancient Greek tragedies it was an ironclad rule that all the real rough stuff should take place off-stage, and I shall follow this admirable principle. It will suffice if I say merely that J. Cuthbert Banks had a thin time. After attending eleven debates and fourteen lectures on *vers libre* Poetry, the Seventeenth-Century Essayists, the Neo-Scandinavian Movement in Portuguese Literature, and other subjects of a similar nature, he grew so enfeebled that, on the rare occasions when he had time for a visit to the links, he had to take a full iron for his mashie shots.

It was not simply the oppressive nature of the debates and lectures that sapped his vitality. What really got right in amongst him was the torture of seeing Adeline's adoration of Raymond Parsloe Devine. The man seemed to have made the deepest possible impression upon her plastic emotions. When he spoke, she leaned forward with parted lips and looked at him. When he was not speaking – which was seldom – she leaned back and looked at him. And when he happened to take the next seat to her, she leaned sideways and looked at him. One glance at Mr Devine would have been more than enough for Cuthbert; but Adeline found him a spectacle that never palled. She could not have gazed at him with a more rapturous intensity if she had been a small child and he a saucer of ice-cream. All this Cuthbert had to witness while still endeavouring to retain the possession of his faculties sufficiently to enable him to duck and back away if somebody suddenly asked him what he thought of the sombre realism of Vladimir Brusiloff. It is little wonder that he tossed in bed, picking at the coverlet, through sleepless nights, and had to have all his waistcoats taken in three inches to keep them from sagging.

This Vladimir Brusiloff to whom I have referred was the famous Russian novelist, and, owing to the fact of his being in the country on a lecturing tour at the moment there had been something of a boom in his works. The Wood Hills Literary Society had been studying them for weeks, and never since his first entrance into the intellectual circles had Cuthbert Banks come nearer to throwing in the towel. Vladimir specialized in grey studies of hopeless misery, where nothing happened till page three hundred and eighty, when the moujik decided to commit suicide. It was tough going for a man whose deepest reading hitherto had been Vardon on the Push-shot, and there can be no greater proof of the magic of love than the fact that Cuthbert stuck it without a cry. But the strain was terrible and I am inclined to think that he must have cracked, had it not been for the daily reports in the papers of the internecine strife which was proceeding so briskly in Russia. Cuthbert was an optimist at heart, and it seemed to him that, at the rate at which the inhabitants of that interesting country were murdering one another, the supply of Russian novelists must eventually give out.

One morning, as he tottered down the road for a short walk which was now almost the only exercise to which he was equal, Cuthbert met Adeline. A spasm of anguish flitted through all his nerve-centres as he saw that she was accompanied by Raymond Parsloe Devine.

'Good morning, Mr Banks,' said Adeline.

'Good morning,' said Cuthbert, hollowly.

'Such good news about Vladimir Brusiloff.'

'Dead?' said Cuthbert, with a touch of hope.

'Dead? Of course not. Why should he be? No, Aunt Emily

27

met his manager after his lecture at Queen's Hall yesterday, and he has promised that Mr Brusiloff shall come to her next Wednesday reception.'

'Oh, ah!' said Cuthbert dully.

'I don't know how she managed it. I think she must have told him that Mr Devine would be there to meet him.'

'But you said he was coming,' argued Cuthbert.

'I shall be very glad,' said Raymond Devine, 'of the opportunity of meeting Brusiloff.'

'I'm sure,' said Adeline, 'he will be very glad of the opportunity of meeting you.'

'Possibly,' said Mr Devine. 'Possibly. Competent critics have said that my work closely resembles that of the great Russian Masters.'

'Your psychology is so deep.'

'Yes, yes.'

'And your atmosphere.'

'Quite.'

Cuthbert in a perfect agony of spirit prepared to withdraw from this love-feast. The sun was shining brightly, but the world was black to him. Birds sang in the tree-tops, but he did not hear them. He might have been a moujik for all the pleasure he found in life.

'You will be there, Mr Banks?' said Adeline, as he turned away.

'Oh, all right,' said Cuthbert.

When Cuthbert had entered the drawing-room on the following Wednesday and had taken his usual place in a distant corner where, while able to feast his gaze on Adeline, he had a sporting chance of being overlooked or mistaken for a piece of furniture, he perceived the great Russian thinker seated in the midst of a circle of admiring females. Raymond Parsloe Devine had not yet arrived.

His first glance at the novelist surprised Cuthbert. Doubtless with the best motives, Vladimir Brusiloff had permitted his face to become almost entirely concealed behind a dense zareba of hair, but his eyes were visible through the undergrowth, and it seemed to Cuthbert that there was an expression in them not un-like that of a cat in a strange backyard surrounded by small boys. The man looked forlorn and hopeless, and Cuthbert won-dered whether he had had bad news from home.

This was not the case. The latest news which Vladimir Brusi-loff had had from Russia had been particularly cheering. Three of his principal creditors had perished in the last massacre of the *bourgeoisie*, and a man whom he owed for five years for a samo-var and a pair of overshoes had fled the country, and had not been heard of since. It was not bad news from home that was depressing Vladimir. What was wrong with him was the fact that this was the eighty-second suburban literary reception he had been compelled to attend since he had landed in the country on his lecturing tour, and he was sick to death of it. When his agent had first suggested the trip, he had signed on the dotted line without an instant's hesitation. Worked out in roubles, the fees offered had seemed just about right. But now, as he peered through the brushwood at the faces around him, and realized that eight out of ten of those present had manuscripts of some sort concealed on their persons, and were only waiting for an opportunity to whip them out and start reading, he wished that he had stayed at his quiet home in Nijni-Novgorod, where the worst thing that could happen to a fellow was a brace of bombs coming in through the window and mixing themselves up with his breakfast egg.

At this point in his meditations he was aware that his hostess was looming up before him with a pale young man in horn-rimmed spectacles at her side. There was in Mrs Smethurst's de-meanour something of the unction of the master-of-ceremonies at the big fight who introduces the earnest gentleman who wishes to challenge the winner.

'Oh, Mr Brusiloff,' said Mrs Smethurst, 'I do want you to meet Mr Raymond Parsloe Devine, whose work I expect you know. He is one of our younger novelists.'

The distinguished visitor peered in a wary and defensive man-ner through the shrubbery, but did not speak. Inwardly he was thinking how exactly like Mr Devine was to the eighty-one other younger novelists to whom he had been introduced at various hamlets throughout the country. Raymond Parsloe Devine bowed courteously, while Cuthbert, wedged into his corner, glowered at him.

'The critics,' said Mr Devine, 'have been kind enough to say that my poor efforts contain a good deal of the Russian spirit. I owe much to the great Russians. I have been greatly influenced by Sovietski.'

Down in the forest something stirred. It was Vladimir's mouth opening, as he prepared to speak. He was not a man who prattled readily, especially in a foreign tongue. He gave the impression that each word was excavated from his interior by some up-to-date process of mining. He glared bleakly at Mr Devine, and allowed three words to drop out of him.

'Sovietski no good!'

He paused for a moment, set the machinery working again, and delivered five more at the pithead.

'I spit me of Sovietski!'

There was a painful sensation. The lot of a popular idol is in many ways an enviable one, but it has the drawback of uncertainty. Here today and gone tomorrow. Until this moment Raymond Parsloe Devine's stock had stood at something considerably over par in Wood Hills intellectual circles, but now there was a rapid slump. Hitherto he had been greatly admired for being influenced by Sovietski, but it appeared now that this was not a good thing to be. It was evidently a rotten thing to be. The law could not touch you for being influenced by Sovietski, but there is an ethical as well as a legal code, and this it was obvious that Raymond Parsloe Devine had transgressed. Women drew away from him slightly, holding their skirts. Men looked at him censoriously. Adeline Smethurst started violently, and dropped a tea-cup. And Cuthbert Banks, doing his popular imitation of a sardine in his corner, felt for the first time that life held something of sunshine.

Raymond Parsloe Devine was plainly shaken, but he made an adroit attempt to recover his lost prestige.

'When I say I have been influenced by Sovietski, I mean, of

course, that I was once under his spell. A young writer commits many follies. I have long since passed through that phase. The false glamour of Sovietski has ceased to dazzle me. I now belong whole-heartedly to the school of Nastikoff.'

There was another reaction. People nodded at one another sympathetically. After all, we cannot expect old heads on young shoulders, and a lapse at the outset of one's career should not be held against one who has eventually seen the light.

'Nastikoff no good,' said Vladimir Brusiloff, coldly. He paused, listening to the machinery.

'Nastikoff worse than Sovietski.'

He paused again.

'I spit me of Nastikoff!' he said.

This time there was no doubt about it. The bottom had dropped out of the market, and Raymond Parsloe Devine Preferred were down in the cellar with no takers. It was clear to the entire assembled company that they had been all wrong about Raymond Parsloe Devine. They had allowed him to play on their innocence and sell them a pup. They had taken him at his own valuation, and had been cheated into admiring him as a man who amounted to something, and all the while he had belonged to the school of Nastikoff. You can never tell. Mrs Smethurst's guests were well-bred, and there was consequently no violent demonstration, but you could see by their faces what they felt. Those nearest Raymond Parsloe jostled to get further away. Mrs Smethurst eyed him stonily through a raised lorgnette. One or two low hisses were heard, and over at the other end of the room somebody opened the window in a marked manner.

Raymond Parsloe Devine hesitated for a moment, then, realizing his situation, turned and slunk to the door. There was an audible sigh of relief as it closed behind him.

Vladimir Brusiloff proceeded to sum up.

'No novelist any good except me. Sovietski – yah! Nastikoff – bah! I spit me of zem all. No novelist anywhere any good except me. P. G. Wodehouse and Tolstoi not bad. Not good, but not bad. No novelist any good except me.'

And, having uttered this dictum, he removed a slab of cake from a near-by plate, steered it through the jungle, and began to champ.

It is too much to say that there was a dead silence. There could never be that in any room in which Vladimir Brusiloff was eating cake. But certainly what you might call the general chit-chat was pretty well down and out. Nobody liked to be the first to speak. The members of the Wood Hills Literary Society looked at one another timidly. Cuthbert, for his part, gazed at Adeline; and Adeline gazed into space. It was plain that the girl was deeply stirred. Her eyes were opened wide, a faint flush crimsoned her cheeks, and her breath was coming quickly.

Adeline's mind was in a whirl. She felt as if she had been walking gaily along a pleasant path and had stopped suddenly on the very brink of a precipice. It would be idle to deny that Raymond Parsloe Devine had attracted her extraordinarily. She had taken him at his own valuation as an extremely hot potato and her hero-worship had gradually been turning into love. And now her hero had been shown to have feet of clay. It was hard, I consider, on Raymond Parsloe Devine, but that is how it goes in this world. You get a following as a celebrity, and then you run up against another bigger celebrity and your admirers desert you. One could moralize on this at considerable length, but better not, perhaps. Enough to say that the glamour of Raymond Devine ceased abruptly in that moment for Adeline, and her most coherent thought at this juncture was the resolve, as soon as she got up to her room, to burn the three signed photographs he had sent her and to give the autographed presentation set of his books to the grocer's boy.

Mrs Smethurst, meanwhile, having rallied somewhat, was endeavouring to set the feast of reason and flow of soul going again.

'And how do you like England, Mr Brusiloff?' she asked.

The celebrity paused in the act of lowering another segment of cake.

'Dam good,' he replied, cordially.

'You said it,' agreed the Thinker.

'I suppose you have travelled all over the country by this time?'

'Have you met many of our great public men?'

'Yais – Yais – Quite a few of the nibs – Lloyid Gorge, I meet him. But –' Beneath the matting a discontented expression came into his face, and his voice took on a peevish note. 'But I not meet your *réal* great men – your Arbmishel, your Arreevadon – I not meet them. That's what gives me to pipovitch. Have *you* ever met Arbmishel and Arreevadon?'

A strained, anguished look came into Mrs Smethurst's face and was reflected in the faces of the other members of the circle. The eminent Russian had sprung two entirely new ones on them, and they felt that their ignorance was about to be exposed. What would Vladimir Brusiloff think of the Wood Hills Literary Society? The reputation of the Wood Hills Literary Society was at stake, trembling in the balance, and coming up for the third time. In dumb agony Mrs Smethurst rolled her eyes about the room searching for someone capable of coming to the rescue. She drew blank.

And then, from a distant corner, there sounded a deprecating cough, and those nearest Cuthbert Banks saw that he had stopped twisting his right foot round his left leg and his left foot round his right ankle and was sitting up with a light of almost human intelligence in his eyes.

'Er –' said Cuthbert, blushing as every eye in the room seemed to fix itself on him, 'I think he means Abe Mitchell and Harry Vardon.'

'Abe Mitchell and Harry Vardon?' repeated Mrs Smethurst, blankly. 'I've never heard of –'

'Yais! Yais! Most! Very!' shouted Vladimir Brusiloff, enthusiastically. 'Arbmishel and Arreevadon. You know them, yes, what, no, perhaps?'

'I've played with Abe Mitchell often, and I was partnered with Harry Vardon in last year's Open.'

The great Russian uttered a cry that shook the chandelier.

'You play in ze Open? Why,' he demanded reproachfully of

Mrs Smethurst, 'was I not introduced to this young man who play in opens?'

'Well, really,' faltered Mrs Smethurst. 'Well, the fact is, Mr Brusiloff –'

She broke off. She was unequal to the task of explaining, without hurting anyone's feelings, that she had always regarded Cuthbert as a piece of cheese and a blot on the landscape.

'Introduce me!' thundered the Celebrity.

'Why, certainly, certainly, of course. This is Mr –.' She looked appealingly at Cuthbert.

'Banks,' prompted Cuthbert.

'Banks!' cried Vladimir Brusiloff. 'Not Cootaboot Banks?'

'*Is* your name Cootaboot?' asked Mrs Smethurst, faintly.

'Well, it's Cuthbert.'

'Yais! Yais! Cootaboot!' There was a rush and swirl, as the effervescent Muscovite burst his way through the throng and rushed to where Cuthbert sat. He stood for a moment eyeing him excitedly, then, stooping swiftly, kissed him on both cheeks before Cuthbert could get his guard up. 'My dear young man, I saw you win ze French Open. Great! Great! Grand! Superb! Hot stuff, and you can say I said so! Will you permit one who is but eighteen at Nijni-Novgorod to salute you once more?'

And he kissed Cuthbert again. Then, brushing aside one or two who were in the way, he dragged up a chair and sat down.

'You are a great man!' he said.

'Oh, no,' said Cuthbert modestly.

'Yais! Great. Most! Very! The way you lay your approach-putts dead from anywhere!'

'Oh, I don't know.'

Mr Brusiloff drew his chair closer.

'Let me tell you one vairy funny story about putting. It was one day I play at Nijni-Novgorod with the pro. against Lenin and Trotsky, and Trotsky had a two-inch putt for the hole. But, just as he addresses the ball, someone in the crowd he tries to assassinate Lenin with a rewolwer – you know that is our great national sport, trying to assassinate Lenin with rewolwers – and the bang puts Trotsky off his stroke and he goes five yards past the hole, and then Lenin, who is rather shaken, you understand, he misses again himself, and we win the hole and match and I clean up three hundred and ninety-six thousand roubles, or fifteen shillings in your money. Some gameovitch! And now let me tell you one other vairy funny story –'

Desultory conversation had begun in murmurs over the rest of the room, as the Wood Hills intellectuals politely endeavoured to conceal the fact that they realized that they were about as much out of it at this re-union of twin souls as cats at a dogshow. From time to time they started as Vladimir Brusiloff's laugh boomed out. Perhaps it was a consolation to them to know that he was enjoying himself.

As for Adeline, how shall I describe her emotions? She was stunned. Before her very eyes the stone which the builders had rejected had become the main thing, the hundred-to-one shot had walked away with the race. A rush of tender admiration for Cuthbert Banks flooded her heart. She saw that she had been all wrong. Cuthbert, whom she had always treated with a patronizing superiority, was really a man to be looked up to and worshipped. A deep, dreamy sigh shook Adeline's fragile form.

Half an hour later Vladimir and Cuthbert Banks rose.

'Goot-a-bye, Mrs Smeth-thirst,' said the Celebrity. 'Zank you for a most charming visit. My friend Cootaboot and me we go now to shoot a few holes. You will lend me clobs, friend Cootaboot?'

'Any you want.'

'The niblicksky is what I use most. Goot-a-bye, Mrs Smeth-thirst.'

They were moving to the door, when Cuthbert felt a light touch on his arm. Adeline was looking up at him tenderly.

'May I come, too, and walk round with you?'

Cuthbert's bosom heaved.

'Oh,' he said, with a tremor in his voice, 'that you would walk round with me for life!'

Her eyes met his.

'Perhaps,' she whispered, softly, 'it could be arranged.'

*

'And so,' (concluded the Oldest Member), 'you see that golf can be of the greatest practical assistance to a man in Life's struggle. Raymond Parsloe Devine, who was no player, had to move out of the neighbourhood immediately, and is now, I believe, writing scenarios out in California for the Flicker Film Company. Adeline is married to Cuthbert, and it was only his earnest pleading which prevented her from having their eldest son christened Abe Mitchell Ribbed-Faced Mashie Banks, for she is now as keen a devotee of the great game as her husband. Those who know them say that theirs is a union so devoted, so –'

The Sage broke off abruptly, for the young man had rushed to the door and out into the passage. Through the open door he could hear him crying passionately to the waiter to bring back his clubs.

The Clicking of Cuthbert (1922)

Boyhood Memories

Wodehouse and Guy Bolton, needing to work uninterrupted on Oh Kay, *a show that would be starring Gertrude Lawrence, settled into a quiet house in quiet Droitwich. One day they drove to*

the minute hamlet of Stableford, seven miles outside the town of Bridgnorth, where Plum had lived as a young man.

'Pretty remote sort of spot,' said Guy, studying the old home through the window of the car.

'Yes, quite remote,' Plum agreed. 'I loved it. I've never found a better place for work. At the age of twenty I once wrote fourteen short stories there in ten days. They were never printed, which was a break for the reading public, but I wrote 'em.'

'Had you any neighbours in this grim solitude?'

'One family about a mile away. We quarrelled with them two days after we arrived and never spoke to them again. It was milk that caused the rift. At least, they said it was milk when they sold it to us, and we said it was skim-milk. Harsh words and dirty looks passed to and fro, and the thing culminated in us cutting them or them cutting us, we never quite made out which. That always happens in rural England. It's pure routine. Directly you have moved in and got your trunks unpacked, you have a hell of a row with the nearest neighbours about milk. Make a note of that.'

'I will.'

'Father sorts out his things, has a wash and brush-up, and looks in on Mother. "All set?" he asks. "All set," says Mother. "Fine," says Father. 'Then let's go and beat the stuffing out of those swindling crooks down the road who've been selling us that so-called milk." And off they go. Father with his Roget's *Thesaurus* under his arm in case he runs short of adjectives.'

'It sounds a jolly life.'

'Oh, it was. Though my mother didn't like it much. She found it a little on the lonely side. My father had seen this house advertised in one of the papers, and he and she went down to take a look at it. As they were driving away, my mother said "Well, thank goodness I shall never see that awful place again." "Eh?" said my father. "I was saying that it was a relief to me to think I should never see that frightful house again." "Oh, the house?" said my father. "You are speaking of the house. I was meaning to tell you about that. I've signed a twenty-years' lease on it." Victorian husbands were like that. Men of steel.'

'I'd like to see you springing that sort of surprise on Ethel.'

Plum shivered.

'Don't say such things, even in fun. But, as I was saying, I loved the place. The only thing I didn't like in my formative, or Stableford, period was the social stuff. Owners of big estates round about would keep inviting me for the week-end.'

'*You?*'

'I don't wonder you're surprised. Even today I'm about as pronounced an oaf as ever went around with his lower jaw drooping and a glassy look in his eyes, but you have literally no conception what I was like in my early twenties. Do you remember what Brichoux said about the chambermaid in the third act of *The Girl Behind the Gun*?'

' "She was a nice girl, but she had no conversation".'

'That was me. I completely inarticulate. Picture to yourself a Trappist monk with large feet and a tendency to upset tables with priceless china on them, and you will have the young Wodehouse. The solution of the mystery of my mixing with the County is that my brother Armine was very popular. He played the piano like a Gershwin and could converse pleasantly on any subject you cared to bring up, and I suppose what happened was that one of these territorial magnates would run into Mother at a garden-party or somewhere and say "I do wish you would persuade your son to come to us for the week-end."

"Why, of course," Mother would reply. "My sons will be there with their hair in a braid." The magnate would start like a man seeing a serpent in his path.

' "Did you say *sons*?"

' "Yes, I have two – Armine and Pelham."

' "Oh? ... Well, of course, we were rather thinking of Armine, but if Pelham can come as well, we shall be charmed ... that is to say ... oh, yes, charmed."

'And he would totter off and tell his wife that the curse had come upon them and she had better put the best china away till I had blown over.'

Bring On The Girls (1954)

Dark Deeds at Blandings Castle

*Baxter is Lord Emsworth's secretary, suspicious of everybody
already, but a more sympathetic character than in later books.
He suspects Ashe Marson of intent to steal the scarab. What
scarab? Well, Ashe is acting valet to Mr Peters, a dyspeptic
American scarab-collector. Lord Emsworth has dreamily
pocketed, for his museum, a priceless scarab Mr Peters was
showing him, and Ashe is trying to get it back into its rightful
owner's hands. Mr Peters is dieting, and Ashe has been reading
him to sleep from what are now his favourite books, of cookery
recipes. Mr Peters's daughter Aline – also a guest at the Castle –
is trying to encourage her father by herself dieting. George
Emerson is in love with Aline and hates the thought of her
going hungry. He has bought food and wine and is going to
leave it, when the Castle is asleep, chastely outside his beloved's
bedroom door.*

It is long past midnight . . .

In the gallery which ran above the hall, there was a large chair,
situated a few paces from the great staircase. On this, in an
overcoat – for the nights were chilly – and rubber-soled shoes,
the Efficient Baxter had sat, without missing a single night, from
one in the morning till daybreak, waiting, waiting, waiting,
waiting. It had been an ordeal to try the stoutest determination.
Nature had never intended Baxter for a night-bird. He loved
his bed. He knew that doctors held that insufficient sleep made
a man pale and sallow, and he had always aimed at the peach-
bloom complexion which comes from a sensible eight hours
between the sheets. One of the Georges – I forget which – once
said that a certain number of hours' sleep each night – I cannot

recall at the moment how many – made a man something, which for the time being has slipped my memory. Baxter agreed with him. It went against all his instincts to sit up in this fashion, but it was his duty and he did it.

A little sigh came from the bed.

' "Way of Preparing: Wipe the tenderloins with a damp cloth. With a sharp knife make a deep pocket lengthwise in each tenderloin. Cut your pork into long thin strips, and with a needle lard each tenderloin. Melt the butter in the water, add the seasoning and the cracker crumbs, combining all thoroughly. Now fill each pocket in the tenderloin with this stuffing, place the tenderloins –" '

A snore sounded from the pillows, punctuating the recital like a mark of exclamation. Ashe laid down the book and peered into the darkness beyond the rays of the bed-lamp. His employer slept.

Ashe switched off the light and crept to the door. Out in the passage he stopped and listened. All was still.

He stole downstairs.

George Emerson looked at his watch. It was nearly two. By this time the house must be asleep.

He gathered up the tongue, the bread, the knife, the fork, the salt, the corkscrew, and the bottle of white wine, and left the room.

All was still. He stole downstairs.

Baxter awoke to a sound of tumult and crashing. For a moment he hovered between dreaming and waking, and then sleep passed from him, and he was aware that something noisy and exciting was in progress in the Hall below.

Coming down to first causes, the only reason why collisions of any kind occur is because two bodies defy Nature's law that a given spot on a given plane shall at a given moment of time be occupied by only one body. There was a certain spot near the foot of the great staircase which Ashe, coming downstairs, and George Emerson coming up, had to pass on their respective routes. George reached it at one minute and three seconds after two a.m., moving silently but swiftly, and Ashe, also maintaining a good rate of speed, arrived there at one minute and four seconds after the hour, when he ceased to walk and began to fly, accompanied by George Emerson, now coming down. His arms were round George's neck, and George was clinging to his waist. In due season they reached the foot of the stairs and a small table covered with occasional china and photographs in frames which lay adjacent to the foot of the stairs.

That, especially the occasional china, was what Baxter had heard.

George Emerson thought it was a burglar. Ashe did not know what it was, but he knew he wanted to shake it off, so he insinuated a hand beneath George's chin and pushed upwards. George, by this time parted for ever from the tongue, the bread, the knife, the fork, the salt, the corkscrew, and the bottle of white wine, and having both hands free for the work of the moment, held Ashe with the left and punched him in the ribs with the right. Ashe, removing his left arm from George's neck, brought it up as a reinforcement to his right, and used both as a means of throttling George. This led George, now permanently underneath, to grasp Ashe's ears firmly and twist them, relieving the pressure on his throat and causing Ashe to utter the first vocal sound of the evening, other than the explosive '*Ugh*' which both had emitted at the instant of impact. Ashe dislodged George's hands from his ears, and hit George in the ribs with his elbow. George kicked Ashe on the left ankle. Ashe rediscovered George's throat and began to squeeze it afresh, and a pleasant time was being had by all, when the Efficient Baxter, whizzing down the stairs, tripped over Ashe's legs, shot forward, and cannoned into another table, also covered with occasional china and photographs in frames. The hall at Blandings Castle was more an extra drawing-room than a hall, and, when not nursing a sick headache in her bedroom, Lady Anne

Warblington would dispense afternoon tea there to her guests. Consequently it was dotted pretty freely with small tables. There were, indeed, no fewer than five or more in various spots waiting to be bumped into and smashed.

But the bumping into and smashing of small tables is a task that calls for plenty of time, a leisured pursuit, and neither George nor Ashe, a third party having added to their little affair, felt a desire to stay on and do the thing properly. Ashe was strongly opposed to being discovered and called upon to account for his presence there at that hour, and George, conscious of the tongue and its adjuncts now strewn about the hall, had a similar prejudice against the tedious explanations which detection must involve. As if by mutual consent each relaxed his grip. They stood panting for an instant, then, Ashe in the direction where he supposed the green-baize door of the servants' quarters to be, George to the staircase which led to his bedroom, they went away from that place.

They had hardly done so, when Baxter, having dissociated himself from the contents of the table which he had upset, began to grope his way towards the electric light switch, the same being situated near the foot of the main staircase. He went on all fours, as a safer method of locomotion, if slower, than the one which he had attempted before.

Noises began to make themselves heard on the floors above. Roused by the merry crackle of occasional china, the house-party was bestirring itself to investigate. Voices sounded muffled and inquiring.

Baxter, meanwhile, crawled steadily on his hands and knees towards the light switch. He was in much the same condition as one White Hope of the ring is after he has put his chin in the way of the fist of a rival member of the Truck-drivers' Union. He knew that he was still alive. More he could not say. The mists of sleep which still shrouded his brain and the shaking-up he had had from his encounter with the table, a corner of which he had rammed with the top of his head, combined to produce a dream-like state.

And so the Efficient Baxter crawled on, and as he crawled his hand, advancing cautiously, fell on a Something – a something that was not alive, something clammy and icy-cold, the touch of which filled him with a nameless horror.

To say that Baxter's heart stood still would be medically inexact. The heart does not stand still. Whatever the emotions of its owners, it goes on beating. It would be more accurate to say that Baxter felt like a man taking his first stride in an express elevator who has outstripped his vital organs by several floors and sees no immediate prospect of their ever catching up with him again. There was a great cold void where the more intimate parts of his body should have been. His throat was dry and contracted. The flesh of his back crawled. For he knew what it was that he had touched.

Painful and absorbing as had been his encounter with the table, Baxter had never lost sight of the fact that close beside him a furious battle between unseen forces was in progress. He had heard the bumping and the thumping and the tense breathing even as he picked occasional china from his person. Such a combat, he had felt, could hardly fail to result in personal injury to either the party of the first part or the party of the second part, or both. He knew now that worse than mere injury had happened, and that he knelt in the presence of death.

There was no doubt that the man was dead. Insensibility alone could never have produced this icy chill.

He raised his head in the darkness, and cried aloud, to those approaching.

He meant to cry, 'Help! Murder!' but fear prevented clear articulation.

What he shouted was, 'Heh! Mer!'

Upon which from the neighbourhood of the staircase, someone began to fire off a revolver.

The Earl of Emsworth had been sleeping a sound and peaceful sleep when the imbroglio began downstairs. He sat up and listened. Yes, undoubtedly burglars. He switched on his light and jumped out of bed. He took a pistol from the drawer, and thus armed, went to look into the matter. The dreamy peer was no poltroon.

It was quite dark when he arrived on the scene of the conflict in the van of a mixed bevy of pyjamaed and dressing-gowned relations. He was in the van because meeting those relations in the passage above, he had said to them, 'Let me go first. I have a pistol.' And they let him go first. They were, indeed, awfully nice about it, not thrusting themselves forward or jostling or anything, but behaving in a modest and self-effacing manner which was pretty to watch. When Lord Emsworth said, 'Let me go first,' young Algernon Wooster, who was on the very point of leaping to the fore, said, 'Yes, by Jove, sound scheme, by Gad!' and withdrew into the background, and the Bishop of Godalming said, 'By all means Clarence, undoubtedly, most certainly precede us.'

When his sense of touch told him that he had reached the foot of the stairs, Lord Emsworth paused. The Hall was very dark, and the burglars seemed to have suspended activities. And then one of them, a man with a ruffianly grating voice, spoke. What it was he said, Lord Emsworth could not understand. It sounded like 'Heh! Mer!' Probably some secret signal to his confederate. Lord Emsworth raised his revolver and emptied it in the direction of the sound.

Extremely fortunate for him, the Efficient Baxter had not changed his all-fours attitude. This undoubtedly saved Lord Emsworth the worry of engaging a new secretary. The shots sang above Baxter's head, one after the other, six in all, and found themselves billets other than his person. They disposed themselves as follows. The first shot broke a window and whistled out into the night. The second shot hit the dinner-gong and made a perfectly extraordinary noise like the Last Trump. The third, fourth and fifth shots embedded themselves in the wall. The sixth and final shot hit a life-size picture of his lordship's maternal grandmother in the face and improved it out of all knowledge. One thinks no worse of Lord Emsworth's maternal grandmother because she looked like George Robey, and had allowed herself to be painted, after the heavy Classical manner of some of the portraits of a hundred years ago, in the character of Venus (suitably draped, of course) rising from the sea; but it was beyond the possibility of denial that her grandson's bullet permanently removed one of Blandings Castle's most prominent eyesores.

Having emptied his revolver, Lord Emsworth said, 'Who is there? Speak!' in rather an aggrieved tone, as if he felt he had done his part in breaking the ice and it was now for the intruder to exert himself and bear his share of the social amenities.

The Efficient Baxter did not reply. Nothing in the world would have induced him to speak at that moment or to make any sound whatsoever that might betray his position to a dangerous maniac who might at any instant reload his pistol and resume the fusillade. Explanations, in his opinion, could be deferred till somebody had the presence of mind to switch on the lights. He flattened himself on the carpet, and hoped for better things. His cheek touched the corpse beside him, but, though he winced and shuddered, he made no outcry. After those six shots he was through with outcries.

A voice from above – the Bishop's voice – said, 'I think you have killed him, Clarence.'

Another voice – that of Colonel Horace Mant – said, 'Switch on those dashed lights, why doesn't someone dash it?'

The whole strength of the company began to demand light.

When the lights came on it was from the other side of the Hall. Six revolver shots, fired at a quarter-past two in the morning, will rouse even sleeping domestics. The servants' quarters were buzzing like a hive. Shrill feminine screams were puncturing the air. Mr Beach, the butler, in a suit of pink silk pyjamas of which no one would have suspected him, was leading a party of men-servants down the stairs, not so much because he wanted to lead them as because they pushed him. The passage beyond the green-baize door became congested, and there were cries for Mr Beach to open it, and look through and see what was the matter, but Mr Beach was smarter than that, and wriggled back so that he no longer headed the procession.

This done, he shouted. 'Open the door there, open that door. Look and see what the matter is.'

Ashe opened the door. Since his escape from the Hall he had been lurking in the neighbourhood of the green-baize, and had been engulfed by the swirling throng. Finding himself with elbow room for the first time, he pushed through, swung the door open, and switched on the lights.

They shone on a collection of semi-dressed figures, crowding the staircase, on a hall littered with china and glass, on a dented dinner-gong, on an edited and improved portrait of the late Countess of Emsworth and on the Efficient Baxter, in an overcoat and rubber-soled shoes, lying beside a cold tongue.

At no great distance lay a number of other objects – a knife, a fork, some bread, salt, a corkscrew, and a bottle of white wine.

Using the word in the sense of saying something coherent, the Earl of Emsworth was the first to speak. He peered down at his recumbent secretary and said, 'Baxter! My dear fellow, what the devil?'

The feeling of the company was one of profound disappointment. They were disgusted at the anti-climax. For an instant, when the Efficient one did not move, hope began to stir, but as soon as it was seen that he was not even injured, gloom reigned. One or two things would have satisfied them – either a burglar or a corpse. A burglar would have been welcome, dead or alive, but if Baxter proposed to fill the part adequately, it was imperative that he be dead. He had disappointed them deeply by turning out to be the object of their quest. That he should not have been even grazed was too much.

There was a cold silence as he slowly raised himself from the floor.

As his eyes fell on the tongue, he started, and remained gazing fixedly at it. Surprise paralysed him.

Lord Emsworth was also looking at the tongue, and he leaped to a not unreasonable conclusion. He spoke coldly and haughtily, for he was not only annoyed like the others at the anti-climax, but offended. He knew that he was not one of your energetic hosts who exert themselves unceasingly to supply their guests with entertainment, but there was one thing on which, as a host, he did pride himself. In the material matters of life he did his guests well. He kept an admirable table.

'My dear Baxter,' he said in the tones which usually he

reserved for the correction of his son Freddie, 'if your hunger is so great that you are unable to wait for breakfast and have to raid my larder in the middle of the night, I wish to goodness you would contrive to make less noise about it. I do not grudge you the food – help yourself when you please – but do remember that people who have not such keen appetites as yourself, like to sleep during the night. A far better plan, my dear fellow, would be to have sandwiches – or buns – whatever you consider most sustaining sent up to your bedroom.'

Not even the bullets had disordered Baxter's faculties so much as this monstrous accusation. Explanations pushed and jostled one another in his fermenting brain, but he could not utter them. On every side he met gravely reproachful eyes. George Emerson was looking at him in pained disgust. Ashe Marson's face was the face of one who could never have believed this had he not seen it with his own eyes. The scrutiny of the knife-and-shoe boy was unendurable.

He stammered. Words began to proceed from him, tripping and stumbling over each other.

Lord Emsworth's frigid disapproval did not relax.

'Pray do not apologize, Baxter. The desire for food is human. It is your boisterous mode of securing and conveying it that I deprecate. Let us all go to bed.'

'But, Lord Emsworth –!'

'To bed,' repeated his lordship firmly.

The company began to stream moodily upstairs. The lights were switched off. The Efficient Baxter dragged himself away.

From the darkness in the direction of the servants' door a voice spoke.

'Greedy pig!' said the voice scornfully.

It sounded like the fresh young voice of the knife-and-shoe boy, but Baxter was too broken to investigate. He continued his retreat without pausing.

'Stuffin' of 'isself at all hours!' said the voice.

There was a murmur of approval from the unseen throng of domestics.

Something Fresh (1915)

Dedications

*Of the English editions of Wodehouse's books, twenty-two
have dedications – to his wife ('bless her'), his father, his
mother, his brother Dick, Denis Mackail, Edgar Wallace, the
Earl of Oxford and Asquith (a great admirer of the books),
Ian Hay, Phillips Oppenheim, Douglas Fairbanks (Sr), George
Grossmith and others. 'Old Bill Townend, my friend from
boyhood's days' got three dedications, in* Love Among the
Chickens *and* Ukridge *because Townend in a long letter has
described a real-life ne'er-do-well that Wodehouse could refine
and build into Stanley Featherstonehaugh Ukridge, and in*
A Prefect's Uncle.

Right Ho, Jeeves *is dedicated 'To Raymond Needham, K.C.,
with affection and admiration', a toning down from the first
draft on the advice of the eminent dedicatee himself. Needham
told me the story. Wodehouse in the early 1930s was in the bad
books of the Inland Revenue. He enjoyed earning the stuff 'in
sackfuls'. But his wife Ethel was supposed to be in charge of the
family finances. As a boy Wodehouse had heard his parents
quarrelling about money, and he had then determined that
when he was married, he would elect his wife as chancellor of
the exchequer, to spend, hoard, invest, gamble, pay income
tax, pay the bills, buy houses or horses … whatever she
fancied, so long as she didn't bother him.*

*Eventually the Inland Revenue summoned Wodehouse to
court for a matter of £25,000 or so that they said he owed
them. There was one particular senior Inland Revenue
Inspector – call him Smith – who had been in charge of the
Wodehouse file for years, and now Smith thought he had got
his quarry cornered and cold. Wodehouse's solicitors thought*

49

so too, but (said Raymond Needham, K.C., to me modestly)
they came to him, the topmost Income Tax K.C., in the hope
he might get their client a settlement a few thousands less than
Smith was claiming. Needham took the brief and found that
his old friend Smith (often a client, often an opponent in
previous tax litigations) had made a bit of a howler in his
presentation of the Inland Revenue case. Needham based his
rebuttal on this point and got the case dismissed . . . nothing to
pay except taxi fares and Needham's own bill.

Smith was furious when he heard the judgment and told
Needham he would appeal against it damn quick. Needham
said, 'Well, anyway, come and have lunch with us now.' 'Us?
Who else?' said Smith. 'My client, P. G. Wodehouse,' said
Needham. 'Savoy Grill at one.' Grinding a tooth or two, as
Needham's client might have described it, Smith finally and
grudgingly accepted and (Needham told me) Smith and
Wodehouse came out from lunch arm in arm and smoking one
cigar. It had transpired that they had played rugger against
each other for their schools, Wodehouse for Dulwich, Smith
for Bedford, in the late 1890s. For whatever reason, the Inland
Revenue didn't, in fact, appeal the judgment, and Wodehouse
was £25,000 (barring taxi fares and legal costs) better off than
he had feared.

When Wodehouse had finished his next book, Right Ho,
Jeeves, *he asked Needham for permission to dedicate it to him*
in words (Needham couldn't remember them exactly)
something like

> To Raymond Needham, K.C., who put the tax-
> gatherers to flight when they had their feet
> on my neck and their hands on my wallet.

Needham had said, 'Plum, don't be an ass. If you say that, it
will infuriate Smith. He'll open your file again and will give
you no peace. He'll get you into court and probably brief me
for his side against you.' So the dedication of Right Ho, Jeeves
now, and for always, reads discreetly as revised.

Four other Wodehouse dedications are:
In *The Indiscretions of Archie*:

To
B. W. KING-HALL

My dear Buddy,

   We have been friends for eighteen years. A considerable portion of my books were written under your hospitable roof. And yet I have never dedicated one to you. What will be the verdict of Posterity on this? The fact is, I have become rather superstitious about dedications. No sooner do you label a book with a legend:

To
MY BEST FRIEND
X

than X cuts you in Piccadilly, or you bring a lawsuit against him. There is a fatality about it. However, I can't imagine anyone quarrelling with you, and I am getting more attractive all the time, so let's take a chance.

Yours ever
P. G. WODEHOUSE

In *The Clicking of Cuthbert* (the first collection of golf stories):

TO THE
IMMORTAL MEMORY
OF
JOHN HENRIE AND PAT ROGIE
WHO
AT EDINBURGH, IN THE YEAR 1593 A.D.
WERE IMPRISONED FOR
'PLAYING OF THE GOWFF ON THE LINKS OF LEITH
EVERY SABBATH THE TIME OF THE SERMONSES,'

ALSO OF
ROBERT ROBERTSON
WHO GOT IT IN THE NECK IN 1604 A.D.
FOR THE SAME REASON

In *Louder and Funnier*:

To
GEORGE BLAKE
A Splendid Fellow
and
Very Sound on Pekes*

*But he should guard against the tendency to claim that his Peke fights Alsatians. Mine is the only one that does this.

And in *The Heart of a Goof*:

TO
MY DAUGHTER
LEONORA
WITHOUT WHOSE NEVER-FAILING
SYMPATHY AND ENCOURAGEMENT
THIS BOOK
WOULD HAVE BEEN FINISHED
IN
HALF THE TIME

Ukridge's Accident Syndicate

*Stanley Featherstonehaugh Ukridge was always cooking up
schemes, generally dishonest, generally disastrous, for making
himself enormously rich.*

'Half a minute, laddie,' said Ukridge. And, gripping my arm,
he brought me to a halt on the outskirts of the little crowd
which had collected about the church door.

It was a crowd such as may be seen any morning during the
London mating-season outside any of the churches which nestle
in the quiet squares between Hyde Park and the King's Road,
Chelsea.

It consisted of five women of cooklike aspect, four nurse-
maids, half a dozen men of the non-producing class who had
torn themselves away for the moment from their normal task
of propping up the wall of the Bunch of Grapes public-house
on the corner, a costermonger with a barrow of vegetables,
divers small boys, eleven dogs, and two or three purposeful-
looking young fellows with cameras slung over their shoulders.
It was plain that a wedding was in progress – and, arguing from
the presence of the camera-men and the line of smart motor-
cars along the kerb, a fairly fashionable wedding. What was
not plain – to me – was why Ukridge, sternest of bachelors, had
desired to add himself to the spectators.

'What,' I enquired, 'is the thought behind this? Why are we
interrupting our walk to attend the obsequies of some perfect
stranger?'

Ukridge did not reply for a moment. He seemed plunged in
thought. Then he uttered a hollow, mirthless laugh – a dreadful
sound like the last gargle of a dying moose.

53

'Perfect stranger, my number eleven foot!' he responded, in a coarse way. 'Do you know who it is who's getting hitched up in there?'

'Who?'

'Teddy Weeks.'

'Teddy Weeks? Teddy Weeks? Good Lord!' I exclaimed. 'Not really?'

And five years rolled away.

It was at Barolini's Italian restaurant in Beak Street that Ukridge evolved his great scheme. Barolini's was a favourite resort of our little group of earnest strugglers in the days when the philanthropic restaurateurs of Soho used to supply four courses and coffee for a shilling and sixpence; and there were present that night, besides Ukridge and myself, the following men-about-town: Teddy Weeks, the actor, fresh from a six-weeks' tour with the Number Three 'Only a Shop-Girl' Company; Victor Beamish, the artist, the man who drew that picture of the O-So-Eesi Piano-Player in the advertisement pages of the *Piccadilly Magazine*; Bertram Fox, author of *Ashes of Remorse*, and other unproduced motion-picture scenarios; and Robert Dunhill, who, being employed at a salary of eighty pounds per annum by the New Asiatic Bank, represented the sober, hard-headed commercial element. As usual, Teddy Weeks had collared the conversation, and was telling us once again how good he was and how hardly treated by a malignant fate.

There is no need to describe Teddy Weeks. Under another and a more euphonious name he has long since made his personal appearance dreadfully familiar to all who read the illustrated weekly papers. He was then, as now, a sickeningly handsome young man, possessing precisely the same melting eyes, mobile mouth, and corrugated hair so esteemed by the theatre-going public today. And yet, at this period of his career he was wasting himself on minor touring companies of the kind which open at Barrow-in-Furness and jump to Bootle for the second half of the week. He attributed this, as Ukridge was so apt to attribute his own difficulties, to lack of capital.

'I have everything,' he said, querulously, emphasizing his remarks with a coffee-spoon. 'Looks, talent, personality, a beautiful speaking voice – everything. All I need is a chance. And I can't get that because I have no clothes fit to wear. These managers are all the same, they never look below the surface, they never bother to find out if a man has genius. All they go by are his clothes. If I could afford to buy a couple of suits from a Cork Street tailor, if I could have my boots made to order by Moykoff instead of getting them ready-made and second-hand at Moses Brothers', if I could once contrive to own a decent hat, a really good pair of spats, and a gold cigarette-case, all at the same time, I could walk into any manager's office in London and sign up for a West-end production tomorrow.'

It was at this point that Freddie Lunt came in. Freddie, like Robert Dunhill, was a financial magnate in the making and an assiduous frequenter of Barolini's; and it suddenly occurred to us that a considerable time had passed since we had last seen him in the place. We enquired the reason for this aloofness.

'I've been in bed,' said Freddie, 'for over a fortnight.'

The statement incurred Ukridge's stern disapproval. That great man made a practice of never rising before noon, and on one occasion, when a carelessly-thrown match had burned a hole in his only pair of trousers, had gone so far as to remain between the sheets for forty-eight hours, but sloth on so majestic a scale as this shocked him.

'Lazy young devil,' he commented severely. 'Letting the golden hours of youth slip by like that when you ought to have been bustling about and making a name for yourself.'

Freddie protested himself wronged by the imputation.

'I had an accident,' he explained. 'Fell off my bicycle and sprained my ankle.'

'Tough luck,' was our verdict.

'Oh, I don't know,' said Freddie. 'It wasn't bad fun getting a rest. And of course there was the fiver.'

'What fiver?'

'I got a fiver from the *Weekly Cyclist* for getting my ankle sprained.'

55

'You – *what*?' cried Ukridge, profoundly stirred – as ever – by a tale of easy money. 'Do you mean to sit there and tell me that some dashed paper paid you five quid simply because you sprained your ankle? Pull yourself together, old horse. Things like that don't happen.'

'It's quite true.'

'Can you show me the fiver?'

'No; because if I did you would try to borrow it.'

Ukridge ignored this slur in dignified silence.

'Would they pay a fiver to *anyone* who sprained his ankle?' he asked, sticking to the main point.

'Yes. If he was a subscriber.'

'I knew there was a catch in it,' said Ukridge, moodily.

'Lots of weekly papers are starting this wheeze,' proceeded Freddie. 'You pay a year's subscription and that entitles you to accident insurance.'

We were interested. This was in the days before every daily paper in London was competing madly against its rivals in the matter of insurance and offering princely bribes to the citizens to make a fortune by breaking their necks. Nowadays papers are paying as high as two thousand pounds for a genuine corpse and five pounds a week for a mere dislocated spine; but at that time the idea was new and it had an attractive appeal.

'How many of these rags are doing this?' asked Ukridge. You could tell from the gleam in his eyes that that great brain was whirring like a dynamo. 'As many as ten?'

'Yes, I should think so. Quite ten.'

'Then a fellow who subscribed to them all and then sprained his ankle would get fifty quid?' said Ukridge, reasoning acutely.

'More if the injury was more serious,' said Freddie, the expert. 'They have a regular tariff. So much for a broken arm, so much for a broken leg, and so forth.'

Ukridge's collar leaped off its stud and his pince-nez wobbled drunkenly as he turned to us.

'How much money can you blokes raise?' he demanded.

'What do you want it for?' asked Robert Dunhill, with a banker's caution.

'My dear old horse, can't you see? Why, my gosh, I've got the idea of the century. Upon my Sam, this is the giltest-edged scheme that was ever hatched. We'll get together enough money and take out a year's subscription for every one of these dashed papers.'

'What's the good of that?' said Dunhill, coldly unenthusiastic.

They train bank clerks to stifle emotions, so that they will be able to refuse overdrafts when they become managers. 'The odds are we should none of us have an accident of any kind, and then the money would be chucked away.'

'Good heavens, ass,' snorted Ukridge, 'you don't suppose I'm suggesting that we should leave it to chance, do you? Listen! Here's the scheme. We take out subscriptions for all these papers, then we draw lots, and the fellow who gets the fatal card or whatever it is goes out and breaks his leg and draws the loot, and we split up between us and live on it in luxury. It ought to run into hundreds of pounds.'

A long silence followed. Then Dunhill spoke again. His was a solid rather than a nimble mind.

'Suppose he couldn't break his leg?'

'My gosh!' cried Ukridge, exasperated. 'Here we are in the twentieth century, with every resource of modern civilization at our disposal, with opportunities for getting our legs broken opening about us on every side – and you ask a silly question like that! Of course he could break his leg. Any ass can break a leg. It's a little hard! We're all infernally broke – personally, unless Freddie can lend me a bit of that fiver till Saturday, I'm going to have a difficult job pulling through. We all need money like the dickens, and yet, when I point out this marvellous scheme for collecting a bit, instead of fawning on me for my ready intelligence you sit and make objections. It isn't the right spirit. It isn't the spirit that wins.'

'If you're as hard up as that,' objected Dunhill, 'how are you going to put in your share of the pool?'

A pained, almost a stunned, look came into Ukridge's eyes. He gazed at Dunhill through a lop-sided pince-nez as one who speculates as to whether his hearing has deceived him.

'Me?' he cried. 'Me? I like that! Upon my Sam, that's rich! Why, damme, if there's any justice in the world, if there's a spark of decency and good feeling in your bally bosoms, I should think you would let me in free for suggesting the idea. It's a little hard! I supply the brains and you want me to cough up cash as well. My gosh, I didn't expect this. This hurts me, by George! If anybody had told me that an old pal would –'

'Oh, all right,' said Robert Dunhill. 'All right, all right, all right. But I'll tell you one thing. If you draw the lot it'll be the happiest day of my life.'

'I shan't,' said Ukridge. 'Something tells me that I shan't.'

Nor did he. When, in a solemn silence broken only by the sound of a distant waiter quarrelling with the cook down a speaking-tube, we had completed the drawing, the man of destiny was Teddy Weeks.

I suppose that even in the springtime of Youth, when broken limbs seem a lighter matter than they become later in life, it can never be an unmixedly agreeable thing to have to go out into the public highways and try to make an accident happen to one. In such circumstances the reflection that you are thereby benefiting your friends can bring but slight balm. To Teddy Weeks it appeared to bring no balm at all. That he was experiencing a certain disinclination to sacrifice himself for the public good became more and more evident as the days went by and found him still intact. Ukridge, when he called upon me to discuss the matter, was visibly perturbed. He sank into a chair beside the table at which I was beginning my modest morning meal, and, having drunk half my coffee, sighed deeply.

'Upon my Sam,' he moaned, 'it's a little disheartening. I strain my brain to think up schemes for getting us all a bit of money just at the moment when we are all needing it most, and when I hit on what is probably the simplest and yet ripest notion of our time, this blighter Weeks goes and lets me down by shirking his plain duty. It's just my luck that a fellow like that should have drawn the lot. And the worst of it is, laddie, that now we've started with him, we've got to keep on. We can't possibly raise enough money to pay yearly subscriptions for anybody else. It's Weeks or nobody.'

'I suppose we must give him time.'

'That's what he says,' grunted Ukridge, morosely, helping himself to toast. 'He says he doesn't know how to start about it. To listen to him, you'd think that going and having a trifling accident was the sort of delicate and intricate job that required years of study and special preparation. Why, a child of six could do it on his head at five minutes' notice. The man's so infernally particular. You make helpful suggestions, and instead of accepting them in a broad, reasonable spirit of co-operation he comes back at you every time with some frivolous objection. He's so dashed fastidious. When we were out last night, we came on a couple of navvies scrapping. Good hefty fellows, either of them capable of putting him in hospital for a month. I told him to jump in and start separating them, and he said no; it was a private dispute which was none of his business, and he didn't feel justified in interfering. Finicky, I call it. I tell you, laddie, this blighter is a broken reed. He has got cold feet. We did wrong to let him into the drawing at all. We might have known that a fellow like that would never give results. No conscience. No sense of esprit de corps. No notion of putting himself out to the most trifling extent for the benefit of the community. Haven't you any more marmalade, laddie?'

'I have not.'

'Then I'll be going,' said Ukridge, moodily. 'I suppose,' he added, pausing at the door, 'you couldn't lend me five bob?'

'How did you guess?'

'Then I'll tell you what,' said Ukridge, ever fair and reasonable; 'you can stand me dinner tonight.' He seemed cheered up for the moment by this happy compromise, but gloom descended on him again. His face clouded. 'When I think,' he said, 'of all the money that's locked up in that poor faint-hearted fish, just waiting to be released, I could sob. Sob, laddie, like a little child. I never liked that man – he has a bad eye and waves his hair. Never trust a man who waves his hair, old horse.'

Ukridge's pessimism was not confined to himself. By the end of a fortnight, nothing having happened to Teddy Weeks worse than a slight cold which he shook off in a couple of days, the general consensus of opinion among his apprehensive colleagues in the Syndicate was that the situation had become desperate. There were no signs whatever of any return on the vast capital which was laid out, and meanwhile meals had to be bought, landladies paid, and a reasonable supply of tobacco acquired. It was a melancholy task in these circumstances to read one's paper of a morning.

All over the inhabited globe, so the well-informed sheet gave one to understand, every kind of accident was happening every day to practically everybody in existence except Teddy Weeks. Farmers in Minnesota were getting mixed up with reaping-machines; peasants in India were being bisected by crocodiles; iron girders from skyscrapers were falling hourly on the heads of citizens in every town from Philadelphia to San Francisco; and the only people who were not down with ptomaine poisoning were those who had walked over cliffs, driven motors into walls, tripped over manholes, or assumed on too slight evidence that the gun was not loaded. In a crippled world, it seemed, Teddy Weeks walked alone, whole and glowing with health. It was one of those grim, ironical, hopeless, grey, despairful situations which the Russian novelists love to write about, and I could not find it in me to blame Ukridge for taking direct action in this crisis. My only regret was that bad luck caused so excellent a plan to miscarry.

My first intimation that he had been trying to hurry matters on came when he and I were walking along the King's Road one evening, and he drew me into Markham Square, a dismal backwater where he had once had rooms.

'What's the idea?' I asked, for I disliked the place.

'Teddy Weeks lives here,' said Ukridge. 'In my old rooms.' I could not see that this lent any fascination to the place. Every day and in every way I was feeling sorrier and sorrier that I had been foolish enough to put money which I could ill spare into a venture which had all the earmarks of a wash-out, and my sentiments towards Teddy Weeks were cold and hostile.

'I want to inquire after him.'

'Inquire after him? Why?'

'Well, the fact is, laddie, I have an idea that he has been bitten by a dog.'

'What makes you think that?'

'Oh, I don't know,' said Ukridge, dreamily. 'I've just got the idea. You know how one gets ideas.'

The mere contemplation of this beautiful event was so inspiring that for awhile it held me silent. In each of the ten journals in which we had invested dog-bites were specifically recommended as things which every subscriber ought to have. They came about half-way up the list of lucrative accidents, inferior to a broken rib or a fractured fibula, but better value than an ingrowing toe-nail. I was gloating happily over the picture conjured up by Ukridge's words when an exclamation brought me back with a start to the realities of life. A revolting sight met my eyes. Down the street came ambling the familiar figure of Teddy Weeks, and one glance at his elegant person was enough to tell us that our hopes had been built on sand. Not even a toy Pomeranian had chewed this man.

'Hallo, you fellows!' said Teddy Weeks.

'Hallo!' we responded, dully.

'Can't stop,' said Teddy Weeks. 'I've got to fetch a doctor.'

'A doctor?'

'Yes. Poor Victor Beamish. He's been bitten by a dog.'

Ukridge and I exchanged weary glances. It seemed as if Fate was going out of its way to have sport with us. What was the good of a dog biting Victor Beamish? What was the good of a hundred dogs biting Victor Beamish? A dog-bitten Victor Beamish had no market value whatever.

'You know that fierce brute that belongs to my landlady,' said Teddy Weeks. 'The one that always dashes out into the area and barks at people who come to the front door.' I remembered. A large mongrel with wild eyes and flashing fangs, badly in need of a haircut. I had encountered it once in the street, when visiting Ukridge, and only the presence of the latter, who knew it well and to whom all dogs were as brothers, had saved me from the doom of Victor Beamish. 'Somehow or other he got into my bedroom this evening. He was waiting there when I came home. I had brought Beamish back with me, and the animal pinned him by the leg the moment I opened the door.'

'Why didn't he pin you?' asked Ukridge, aggrieved.

'What I can't make out,' said Teddy Weeks, 'is how on earth the brute came to be in my room. Somebody must have put him there. The whole thing is very mysterious.'

'Why didn't he pin you?' demanded Ukridge again.

'Oh, I managed to climb on to the top of the wardrobe while he was biting Beamish,' said Teddy Weeks. 'And then the landlady came and took him away. But I can't stop here talking. I must go and get that doctor.'

We gazed after him in silence as he tripped down the street. We noted the careful manner in which he paused at the corner to eye the traffic before crossing the road, the wary way in which he drew back to allow a truck to rattle past.

'You heard that?' said Ukridge, tensely. 'He climbed on to the top of the wardrobe!'

'Yes.'

'And you saw the way he dodged that excellent truck?'

'Yes.'

'Something's got to be done,' said Ukridge, firmly. 'The man has got to be awakened to a sense of his responsibilities.'

Next day a deputation waited on Teddy Weeks.

Ukridge was our spokesman, and he came to the point with admirable directness.

'How about it?' asked Ukridge.

'How about what?' replied Teddy Weeks, nervously, avoiding his accusing eye.

'When do we get action?'

'Oh, you mean that accident business?'

'Yes.'

'I've been thinking about that,' said Teddy Weeks.

Ukridge drew the mackintosh which he wore indoors and out of doors and in all weathers more closely around him. There was in the action something suggestive of a member of the Roman Senate about to denounce an enemy of the State. In just such a manner must Cicero have swished his toga as he took a deep breath preparatory to assailing Clodius. He toyed for a moment with the ginger-beer wire which held his pince-nez in place, and endeavoured without success to button his collar at the back. In moments of emotion Ukridge's collar always took on a sort of temperamental jumpiness which no stud could restrain.

'And about time you *were* thinking about it,' he boomed, sternly.

We shifted appreciatively in our seats, all except Victor Beamish, who had declined a chair and was standing by the mantelpiece. 'Upon my Sam, it's about time you were thinking about it. Do you realize that we've invested an enormous sum of money in you on the distinct understanding that we could rely on you to do your duty and get immediate results? Are we to be forced to the conclusion that you are so yellow and few in the pod as to want to evade your honourable obligations? We thought better of you, Weeks. Upon my Sam, we thought better of you. We took you for a two-fisted, enterprising, big-souled, one hundred-per-cent he-man who would stand by his friends to the finish.'

'Yes, but –'

'Any bloke with a sense of loyalty and an appreciation of what it meant to the rest of us would have rushed out and found some means of fulfilling his duty long ago. You don't even grasp at the opportunities that come your way. Only yesterday I saw you draw back when a single step into the road would have had a truck bumping into you.'

'Well, it's not easy to let a truck bump into you.'

'Nonsense. It only requires a little ordinary resolution. Use your imagination, man. Try to think that a child has fallen down in the street – a little golden-haired child,' said Ukridge, deeply affected. 'And a dashed great cab or something comes rolling up. The kid's mother is standing on the pavement, helpless, her hands clasped in agony. "Dammit," she cries, "will no one save my darling?" "Yes, by George," you shout, "*I* will." And out you jump and the thing's over in half a second. I don't know what you're making such a fuss about.'

'Yes, but –' said Teddy Weeks.

'I'm told what's more, it isn't a bit painful. A sort of dull shock, that's all.'

'Who told you that?'

'I forget. Someone.'

'Well, you can tell him from me that he's an ass,' said Teddy Weeks, with asperity.

'All right. If you object to being run over by a truck there are lots of other ways. But, upon my Sam, it's pretty hopeless suggesting them. You seem to have no enterprise at all. Yesterday, after I went to all the trouble to put a dog in your room, a dog which would have done all the work for him – all you had to do was stand still and let him use his own judgement – what happened? You climbed on to –'

Victor Beamish interrupted, speaking in a voice husky with emotion.

'Was it you who put that damned dog in the room?'

'Eh?' said Ukridge. 'Why, yes. But we can have a good talk about all that later on,' he proceeded, hastily. 'The point at the moment is how the dickens we're going to persuade this poor worm to collect our insurance money for us. Why, damme, I should have thought you would have –'

'All I can say –' began Victor Beamish, heatedly.

'Yes, yes,' said Ukridge; 'some other time. Must stick to business now, laddie. I was saying,' he resumed, 'that I should have thought you would have been as keen as mustard to put the job through for your own sake. You're always beefing that you haven't any clothes to impress managers with. Think of all you can buy with your share of the swag once you have summoned up a little ordinary determination and seen the thing through. Think of the suits, the boots, the hats, the spats. You're always talking about your dashed career, and how all you need to land you in a West-end production is good clothes. Well, here's your chance to get them.'

His eloquence was not wasted. A wistful look came into Teddy Weeks's eye, such a look as must have come into the eye of Moses on the summit of Pisgah. He breathed heavily! You could see that the man was mentally walking along Cork Street, weighing the merits of one famous tailor against another.

'I'll tell you what I'll do,' he said, suddenly. 'It's no use asking me to put this thing through in cold blood. I simply can't do it. I haven't the nerve. But if you fellows will give me a dinner tonight with lots of champagne I think it will key me up to it.'

A heavy silence fell upon the room. Champagne! The word was like a knell.

'How on earth are we going to afford champagne?' said Victor Beamish.

'Well, there it is,' said Teddy Weeks. 'Take it or leave it.'

'Gentlemen,' said Ukridge, 'it would seem that the company requires more capital. How about it, old horses? Let's get together in a frank, business-like cards-on-the-table spirit, and see what can be done. I can raise ten bob.'

'What!' cried the entire assembled company, amazed. 'How?'

'I'll pawn a banjo.'

'You haven't got a banjo.'

'No, but George Tupper has, and I know where he keeps it.'

Started in this spirited way, the subscriptions came pouring in. I contributed a cigarette-case, Bertram Fox thought his landlady would let him owe for another week, Robert Dunhill had an uncle in Kensington who, he fancied, if tactfully approached, would be good for a quid, and Victor Beamish said that if the advertisement-manager of the O-So-Eesi Piano-Player was churlish enough to refuse an advance of five shillings against future work he misjudged him sadly. Within a few minutes, in short, the Lightning Drive had produced the impressive total of two pounds six shillings, and we asked Teddy Weeks if he thought that he could get adequately keyed up within the limits of that sum.

'I'll try,' said Teddy Weeks.

So, not unmindful of the fact that the excellent hostelry supplied champagne at eight shillings the quart bottle, we fixed the meeting for seven o'clock at Barolini's.

Considered as a social affair, Teddy Weeks's keying-up dinner was not a success. Almost from the start I think we all found it trying. It was not so much the fact that he was drinking deeply of Barolini's eight-shilling champagne while we, from lack of funds, were compelled to confine ourselves to meaner beverages; what really marred the pleasantness of the function was the extraordinary effect the stuff had on Teddy. What was actually in the champagne supplied to Barolini and purveyed by him to the public, such as were reckless enough to drink it, at eight shillings the bottle remains a secret between its maker and his Maker; but three glasses of it were enough to convert Teddy Weeks from a mild and rather oily young man into a truculent swashbuckler.

He quarrelled with us. With the soup he was tilting at Victor Beamish's theories of Art; the fish found him ridiculing Bertram Fox's views on the future of the motion-picture; and by the time the leg of chicken with dandelion salad arrived – or, as some held, string salad – opinions varied on this point – the hell-brew had so wrought on him that he had begun to lecture Ukridge on his mis-spent life and was urging him in accents audible across the street to go out and get a job and thus acquire sufficient self-respect to enable him to look himself in the face in a mirror without wincing. Not, added Teddy Weeks with what we all thought uncalled-for offensiveness, that any amount of self-respect was likely to do that. Having said which, he called imperiously for another eight bobs'-worth.

We gazed at one another wanly. However excellent the end towards which all this was tending, there was no denying that it was hard to bear. But policy kept us silent. We recognized that this was Teddy Weeks's evening and that he must be humoured. Victor Beamish said meekly that Teddy had cleared up a lot of points which had been troubling him for a long time. Bertram Fox agreed that there was much in what Teddy had said about the future of the close-up. And even Ukridge, though his haughty soul was seared to its foundations by the latter's personal remarks, promised to take his homily to heart and act upon it at the earliest possible moment.

'You'd better!' said Teddy Weeks, belligerently, biting off the end of one of Barolini's best cigars. 'And there's another thing – don't let me hear of your coming and sneaking people's socks again.'

'Very well, laddie,' said Ukridge, humbly.

'If there is one person in the world that I despise,' said Teddy, bending a red-eyed gaze on the offender, 'it's a snock-seeker – a seek-snocker – a – well, you know what I mean.'

We hastened to assure him that we knew what he meant and he relapsed into a lengthy stupor, from which he emerged three-quarters of an hour later to announce that he didn't know what we intended to do, but that he was going. We said that we were going too, and we paid the bill and did so.

Teddy Weeks's indignation on discovering us gathered about him upon the pavement outside the restaurant was intense, and he expressed it freely. Among other things, he said – which was not true – that he had a reputation to keep up in Soho.

'It's all right, Teddy, old horse,' said Ukridge, soothingly. 'We just thought you would like to have all your pals round you when you did it.'

'Did it? Did what?'

'Why, had the accident.'

Teddy Weeks glared at him truculently. Then his mood seemed to change abruptly, and he burst into a loud and hearty laugh.

'Well, of all the silly ideas!' he cried, amusedly. 'I'm not going to have an accident. You don't suppose I ever seriously intended to have an accident, do you? It was just my fun.' Then, with another sudden change of mood, he seemed to become a victim to an acute unhappiness. He stroked Ukridge's arm affectionately, and a tear rolled down his cheek. 'Just my fun,' he repeated. 'You don't mind my fun, do you?' he asked, pleadingly. 'You like my fun, don't you? All my fun. Never meant to have an accident at all. Just wanted dinner.' The gay humour of it all overcame his sorrow once more. 'Funniest thing ever heard,' he said cordially. 'Didn't want accident, wanted dinner. Dinner daxident, danner dixident,' he added, driving home his point. 'Well, good night all,' he said, cheerily. And, stepping off the kerb on to a banana-skin, was instantly knocked ten feet by a passing lorry.

'Two ribs and an arm,' said the doctor five minutes later,

superintending the removal proceedings. 'Gently with that stretcher.'

It was two weeks before we were informed by the authorities of Charing Cross Hospital that the patient was in a condition to receive visitors. A whip-round secured the price of a basket of fruit, and Ukridge and I were deputed by the shareholders to deliver it with their compliments and kind inquiries.

'Hallo!' we said in a hushed, bedside manner when finally admitted to his presence.

'Sit down, gentlemen,' replied the invalid.

I must confess even in that first moment to having experienced a slight feeling of surprise. It was not like Teddy Weeks to call us gentlemen. Ukridge, however, seemed to notice nothing amiss.

'Well, well, well,' he said buoyantly. 'And how are you, laddie? We've brought you a few fragments of fruit.'

'I'm getting along capitally,' replied Teddy Weeks, still in that odd precise way which had made his opening words strike me as curious. 'And I should like to say that in my opinion England has reason to be proud of the alertness and enterprise of her great journals. The excellence of their reading-matter, the ingenuity of their various competitions, and above all, the go-ahead spirit which has resulted in this accident insurance scheme are beyond praise. Have you got that down?' he inquired.

Ukridge and I looked at each other. We had been told that Teddy was practically normal again, but this sounded like delirium.

'Have we got what down, old horse?' asked Ukridge, gently.

Teddy Weeks seemed surprised.

'Aren't you reporters?'

'How do you mean, reporters?'

'I thought you had come from one of these weekly papers that have been paying me insurance money, to interview me,' said Teddy Weeks.

Ukridge and I exchanged another glance. An uneasy glance this time. I think that already a grim foreboding had begun to cast its shadow over us.

'Surely you remember me, Teddy, old horse?' said Ukridge, anxiously.

Teddy Weeks knit his brow, concentrating painfully.

'Why, of course,' he said at last. 'You're Ukridge, aren't you?'

'That's right. Ukridge.'

'Of course. Ukridge.'

'Yes. Ukridge. Funny your forgetting me!'

'Yes,' said Teddy Weeks. 'It's the effect of the shock I got when that thing bowled me over. I must have been struck on the head, I suppose. It has had the effect of rendering my memory rather uncertain. The doctors here are very interested. They say it is a most unusual case. I can remember some things perfectly, but in some ways my memory is a complete blank.'

'Oh, but I say, old horse,' quavered Ukridge. 'I suppose you haven't forgotten about that insurance, have you?'

'Oh, no, I remember that.'

Ukridge breathed a relieved sigh.

'I was a subscriber to a number of weekly papers,' went on Teddy Weeks. 'They are paying me insurance money now.'

'Yes, yes, old horse,' cried Ukridge. 'But what I mean is you remember the Syndicate, don't you?'

Terry Weeks raised his eyebrows.

'Syndicate? What Syndicate?'

'Why, when we all got together and put up the money to pay for the subscriptions to these papers and drew lots, to choose which of us should go out and have an accident and collect the money. And you drew it, don't you remember?'

Utter astonishment, and a shocked astonishment at that, spread itself over Teddy Weeks's countenance. The man seemed outraged.

'I certainly remember nothing of the kind,' he said severely. 'I cannot imagine myself for a moment consenting to become a party to what from your own account would appear to have been a criminal conspiracy to obtain money under false pretences from a number of weekly papers.'

'But, laddie –'

'However,' said Teddy Weeks, 'if there is any truth in this story, no doubt you have documentary evidence to support it.'

Ukridge looked at me. I looked at Ukridge. There was a long silence.

'Shift-ho, old horse?' said Ukridge, sadly. 'No use staying on here.'

'No,' I replied, with equal gloom. 'May as well go.'

'Glad to have seen you,' said Teddy Weeks, 'and thanks for the fruit.'

The next time I saw the man he was coming out of a manager's office in the Haymarket. He had on a new Homburg hat of a delicate pearl grey, spats to match, and a new blue flannel suit, beautifully cut, with an invisible red twill. He was looking jubilant, and, as I passed him, he drew from his pocket a gold cigarette-case.

It was shortly after that, if you remember, that he made a big hit as the juvenile lead in that piece at the Apollo and started on his sensational career as a *matinée* idol.

Inside the church the organ had swelled into the familiar music of the Wedding March. A verger came out and opened the doors. The five cooks ceased their reminiscences of other and smarter weddings at which they had participated. The camera-men unshipped their cameras. The costermonger moved his barrow of vegetables a pace forward. A dishevelled and unshaven man at my side uttered a disapproving growl.

'Idle rich!' said the dishevelled man.

Out of the church came a beauteous being, leading attached to his arm another being, somewhat less beauteous.

There was no denying the spectacular effect of Teddy Weeks. He was handsomer than ever. His sleek hair, gorgeously waved, shone in the sun, his eyes were large and bright; his lissome frame, garbed in faultless morning-coat and trousers, was that of an Apollo. But his bride gave the impression that Teddy had married money. They paused in the doorway, and the cameramen became active and fussy.

'Have you got a shilling, laddie?' said Ukridge in a low, level voice.

'Why do you want a shilling?'

'Old horse,' said Ukridge, tensely, 'it is of the utmost vital importance that I have a shilling here and now.'

I passed it over. Ukridge turned to the dishevelled man, and I perceived that he held in his hand a large rich tomato of juicy and over-ripe appearance.

'Would you like to earn a bob?' Ukridge said.

'Would I!' replied the dishevelled man.

Ukridge sank his voice to a hoarse whisper.

The camera-men had finished their preparations. Teddy Weeks, his head thrown back in that gallant way which has endeared him to so many female hearts, was exhibiting his celebrated teeth. The cooks, in undertones, were making adverse comments on the appearance of the bride.

'Now, please,' said one of the camera-men.

Over the heads of the crowd, well and truly aimed, whizzed a large juicy tomato. It burst like a shell full between Teddy Weeks's expressive eyes, obliterating them in scarlet ruin. It spattered Teddy Weeks's collar, it dripped on Teddy Weeks's morning-coat. And the dishevelled man turned abruptly and raced off down the street.

Ukridge grasped my arm. There was a look of deep content in his eyes.

Arm-in-arm, we strolled off in the pleasant June sunshine.

Ukridge (1924)

Grand Hotel

Barribault's in Mayfair is a rendezvous in several of the later books.

It is the boast of Barribault's Hotel, which caters principally to American millionaires and visiting maharajahs, that it can make the wrong sort of client feel more like a piece of cheese – and a cheap yellow piece of cheese at that – than any other similar establishment in the world. The personnel of its staff are selected primarily for their ability to curl the upper lip and raise the eyebrows just that extra quarter of an inch which makes all the difference.

Full Moon (1947)

Jeeves and the Yule-Tide Spirit

Bobbie Wickham is one of Wodehouse's best fizzy girls, a danger to everybody. She recurs in several stories and books. So does Sir Roderick Glossop, the loony-doctor.

The letter arrived on the morning of the sixteenth. I was pushing a bit of breakfast into the Wooster face at the moment and, feeling fairly well fortified with coffee and kippers, I decided to break the news to Jeeves without delay. As Shakespeare says, if you're going to do a thing you might as well pop right at it and get it over. The man would be disappointed, of course, and possibly even chagrined: but, dash it all, a splash of disappointment here and there does a fellow good. Makes him realize that life is stern and life is earnest.

'Oh, Jeeves,' I said.

'Sir?'

'We have here a communication from Lady Wickham. She has written inviting me to Skeldings for Christmas. So you will see about bunging the necessaries together. We repair thither on the twenty-third. Plenty of white ties, Jeeves, also a few hearty country suits for use in the daytime. We shall be there some little time, I expect.'

There was a pause. I could feel he was directing a frosty gaze at me, but I dug into the marmalade and refused to meet it.

'I thought I understood you to say, sir, that you proposed to visit Monte Carlo immediately after Christmas.'

'I know. But that's all off. Plans changed.'

'Very good, sir.'

At this point the telephone bell rang, tiding over nicely what

73

had threatened to be an awkward moment. Jeeves unhooked the receiver.

'Yes? ... Yes, madam ... Very good, madam. Here is Mr Wooster.' He handed me the instrument. 'Mrs Spenser Gregson, sir.'

You know, every now and then I can't help feeling that Jeeves is losing his grip. In his prime it would have been with him the work of a moment to have told Aunt Agatha that I was not at home. I gave him one of those reproachful glances and took the machine.

'Hullo?' I said. 'Yes? Hullo? Hullo? Bertie speaking. Hullo? Hullo? Hullo?'

'Don't keep on saying Hullo,' yipped the old relative in her customary curt manner. 'You're not a parrot. Sometimes I wish you were, because then you might have a little sense.'

Quite the wrong sort of tone to adopt towards a fellow in the early morning, of course, but what can one do?

'Bertie, Lady Wickham tells me she has invited you to Skeldings for Christmas. Are you going?'

'Rather!'

'Well, mind you behave yourself. Lady Wickham is an old friend of mine.'

I was in no mood for this sort of thing over the telephone. Face to face, I'm not saying, but at the end of a wire, no.

'I shall naturally endeavour, Aunt Agatha,' I replied stiffly, 'to conduct myself in a manner befitting an English gentleman paying a visit –'

'What did you say? Speak up. I can't hear.'

'I said Right-ho.'

'Oh? Well, mind you do. And there's another reason why I particularly wish you to be as little of an imbecile as you can manage while at Skeldings. Sir Roderick Glossop will be there.'

'What!'

'Don't bellow like that. You nearly deafened me.'

'Did you say Sir Roderick Glossop?'

'I did.'

'You don't mean Tuppy Glossop?'

'I mean Sir Roderick Glossop. Which was my reason for saying Sir Roderick Glossop. Now, Bertie, I want you to listen to me attentively. Are you there?'

'Yes. Still here.'

'Well, then, listen. I have at last succeeded, after incredible difficulty, and in face of all the evidence, in almost persuading Sir Roderick that you are not actually insane. He is prepared to suspend judgement until he has seen you once more. On your behaviour at Skeldings, there –'

But I had hung up the receiver. Shaken. That's what I was. S. to the core.

Stop me if I've told you this before: but, in case you don't know, let me just mention the facts in the matter of this Glossop. He was a formidable old bird with a bald head and out-size eyebrows, by profession a loony-doctor. How it happened, I couldn't tell you to this day, but I once got engaged to his daughter, Honoria, a ghastly dynamic exhibit who read Nietzsche and had a laugh like waves breaking on a stern and rock-bound coast. The fixture was scratched owing to events occurring which convinced the old boy that I was off my napper; and since then he has always had my name at the top of his list of 'Loonies I have Lunched With.'

It seemed to me that even at Christmas time, with all the peace on earth and goodwill towards men that there is knocking about at that season, a reunion with this bloke was likely to be tough going. If I hadn't had more than one particularly good reason for wanting to go to Skeldings, I'd have called the thing off.

'Jeeves,' I said, all of a twitter: 'Do you know what? Sir Roderick Glossop is going to be at Lady Wickham's.'

'Very good, sir. If you have finished breakfast, I will clear away.'

Cold and haughty. No symp. None of the rallying-round spirit which one likes to see. As I had anticipated, the information that we were not going to Monte Carlo had got in amongst him. There is a keen sporting streak in Jeeves and I knew he had been looking forward to a little flutter at the tables.

We Woosters can wear the mask. I ignored his lack of decent feeling.

'Do so, Jeeves,' I said proudly, 'and with all convenient speed.'

Relations continued pretty fairly strained all through the rest of the week. There was a frigid detachment in the way the man brought me my dollop of tea in the mornings. Going down to Skeldings in the car on the afternoon of the twenty-third, he was aloof and reserved. And before dinner on the first night of my visit he put the studs in my dress-shirt in what I can only call a marked manner. The whole thing was extremely painful, and it seemed to me, as I lay in bed on the morning of the twenty-fourth, that the only step to take was to put the whole facts of the case before him and trust to his native good sense to effect an understanding. I was feeling considerably in the pink that morning. Everything had gone like a breeze. My hostess, Lady Wickham, was a beaky female built far too closely on the lines of my Aunt Agatha for comfort, but she had seemed matey enough on my arrival. Her daughter, Roberta, had welcomed me with a warmth which, I'm bound to say, had set the old heart-strings fluttering a bit. And Sir Roderick, in the brief moment we had had together, appeared to have let the Yule-tide spirit soak into him to the most amazing extent. When he saw me, his mouth sort of flickered at one corner, which I took to be his idea of smiling, and he said 'Ha, young man!' Not particularly chummily, but he said it: and my view was that it practically amounted to the lion lying down with the lamb.

So, all in all, life at this juncture seemed pretty well all to the mustard, and I decided to tell Jeeves exactly how matters stood.

'Jeeves,' I said, as he appeared with the steaming.

'Sir?'

'Touching on this business of our being here, I would like to say a few words of explanation. I consider that you have a right to the facts.'

'Sir?'

'I'm afraid scratching that Monte Carlo trip has been a bit of a jar for you, Jeeves.'

'Not at all, sir.'

'Oh, yes, it has. The heart was set on wintering in the world's good old Plague Spot, I know. I saw your eye light up when I said we were due for a visit there. You snorted a bit and your fingers twitched. I know, I know. And now that there has been a change of programme the iron has entered into your soul.'

'Not at all, sir.'

'Oh, yes, it has. I've seen it. Very well, then, what I wish to impress upon you, Jeeves, is that I have not been actuated in this matter by any mere idle whim. It was through no light and airy caprice that I accepted this invitation to Lady Wickham's. I have been angling for it for weeks, prompted by many considerations. In the first place, does one get the Yule-tide spirit at a spot like Monte Carlo?'

'Does one desire the Yule-tide spirit, sir?'

'Certainly one does. I am all for it. Well, that's one thing. Now here's another. It was imperative that I should come to Skeldings for Christmas, Jeeves, because I knew that young Tuppy Glossop was going to be here.'

'Sir Roderick Glossop, sir?'

'His nephew. You may have observed hanging about the place a fellow with light hair and a Cheshire-cat grin. That is Tuppy, and I have been anxious for some time to get to grips with him. I have it in for that man of wrath. Listen to the facts, Jeeves, and tell me if I am not justified in planning a hideous vengeance.' I took a sip of tea, for the mere memory of my wrongs had shaken me. 'In spite of the fact that young Tuppy is the nephew of Sir Roderick Glossop, at whose hands, Jeeves, as you are aware, I have suffered much, I fraternized with him freely, both at the Drones Club and elsewhere. I said to myself that a man is not blamed for his relations, and that I would hate to have my pals hold my Aunt Agatha, for instance, against me. Broad-minded, Jeeves, I think?'

'Extremely, sir.'

'Well, then, as I say, I sought this Tuppy out, Jeeves, and hobnobbed, and what do you think he did?'

'I could not say, sir.'

'I will tell you. One night after dinner at the Drones he betted me I wouldn't swing myself across the swimming-bath by the ropes and rings. I took him on and was buzzing along in great style until I came to the last ring. And then I found that this fiend in human shape had looped it back against the rail, thus leaving me hanging in the void with no means of getting ashore to my home and loved ones. There was nothing for it but to drop into the water. He told me that he had often caught fellows that way: and what I maintain, Jeeves, is that, if I can't get back at him somehow at Skeldings – with all the vast resources which a country house affords at my disposal – I am not the man I was.'

'I see, sir.'

There was still something in his manner which told me that even now he lacked complete sympathy and understanding, so, delicate though the subject was, I decided to put all my cards an the table.

'And now, Jeeves, we come to the most important reason why I had to spend Christmas at Skeldings. Jeeves,' I said, diving into the old cup once more for a moment and bringing myself out wreathed in blushes, 'the fact of the matter is, I'm in love.'

'Indeed, sir?'

'You've seen Miss Roberta Wickham?'

'Yes, sir.'

'Very well, then.'

There was a pause, while I let it sink in.

'During your stay here, Jeeves,' I said, 'you will, no doubt, be thrown a good deal together with Miss Wickham's maid. On such occasions, pitch it strong.'

'Sir?'

'You know what I mean. Tell her I'm rather a good chap. Mention my hidden depths. These things get round. Dwell on the fact that I had a kind heart and was runner-up in the Squash Handicap at the Drones this year. A boost is never wasted, Jeeves.'

'Very good, sir. But –'

'But what?'

'Well, sir –'

'I wish you wouldn't say "Well, sir" in that soupy tone of voice. I have had to speak of this before. The habit is one that is growing upon you. Check it. What's on your mind?'

'I hardly like to take the liberty –'

'Carry on, Jeeves. We are always glad to hear from you, always.'

'What I was about to remark, if you will excuse me, sir, was that I would scarcely have thought Miss Wickham a suitable –'

'Jeeves,' I said coldly, 'if you have anything to say against that lady, it had better not be said in my presence.'

'Very good, sir.'

'Or anywhere else, for that matter. What is your kick against Miss Wickham?'

'Oh, really, sir!'

'Jeeves, I insist. This is a time for plain speaking. You have beefed about Miss Wickham. I wish to know why.'

'It merely crossed my mind, sir, that for a gentleman of your description Miss Wickham is not a suitable mate.'

'What do you mean by a gentleman of my description?'

'Well, sir –'

'Jeeves!'

'I beg your pardon, sir. The expression escaped me inadvertently. I was about to observe that I can only asseverate –'

'Only what?'

'I can only say that, as you have invited my opinion –'

'But I didn't.'

'I was under the impression that you desired to canvass my views on the matter, sir.'

'Oh? Well, let's have them, anyway.'

'Very good, sir. Then briefly, if I may say so, sir, though Miss Wickham is a charming young lady –'

'There, Jeeves, you spoke an imperial quart. What eyes!'

'Yes, sir.'

'What hair!'

'Very true, sir.'

'And what *espièglerie*, if that's the word I want.'

79

'The exact word, sir.'

'All right, then. Carry on.'

'I grant Miss Wickham the possession of all these desirable qualities, sir. Nevertheless, considered as a matrimonial prospect for a gentleman of your description, I cannot look upon her as suitable. In my opinion Miss Wickham lacks seriousness, sir. She is too volatile and frivolous. To qualify as Miss Wickham's husband, a gentleman would need to possess a commanding personality and considerable strength of character.'

'Exactly!'

'I would always hesitate to recommend as a life's companion a young lady with quite such a vivid shade of red hair. Red hair, in my opinion, is dangerous.'

I eyed the blighter squarely.

'Jeeves,' I said, 'you're talking rot.'

'Very good, sir.'

'Absolute drivel.'

'Very good, sir.'

'Pure mashed potatoes.'

'Very good, sir.'

'Very good, sir – I mean very good Jeeves, that will be all,' I said.

And I drank a modicum of tea, with a good deal of hauteur.

It isn't often that I find myself able to prove Jeeves in the wrong, but by dinner-time that night I was in a position to do so, and I did it without delay.

'Touching on that matter we were touching on, Jeeves,' I said, coming in from the bath and tackling him as he studded the shirt, 'I should be glad if you would give me your careful attention for a moment, I warn you that what I am about to say is going to make you look pretty silly.'

'Indeed, sir?'

'Yes, Jeeves. Pretty dashed silly it's going to make you look. It may lead you to be rather more careful in future about broadcasting these estimates of yours of people's character. This morning, if I remember rightly, you stated that Miss Wickham was volatile, frivolous and lacking in seriousness. Am I correct?'

'Quite correct, sir.'

'Then what I have to tell you may cause you to alter that opinion. I went for a walk with Miss Wickham this afternoon; and, as we walked, I told her about what young Tuppy Glossop did to me in the swimming-bath at the Drones. She hung upon my words, Jeeves, and was full of sympathy.'

'Indeed, sir?'

'Dripping with it. And that's not all. Almost before I had finished, she was suggesting the ripest, fruitiest, brainiest scheme for bringing young Tuppy's grey hairs in sorrow to the grave that anyone could possibly imagine.'

'That is very gratifying, sir.'

'Gratifying is the word. It appears that at the girls' school where Miss Wickham was educated, Jeeves, it used to become necessary from time to time for the right-thinking element of the community to slip it across certain of the baser sort. Do you know what they did, Jeeves?'

'No, sir.'

'They took a long stick, Jeeves, and – follow me closely here – they tied a darning-needle to the end of it. Then at dead of night, it appears, they sneaked privily into the party of the second part's cubicle and shoved the needle through the bed-clothes and punctured her hot-water bottle. Girls are much subtler in these matters than boys, Jeeves. At my old school one would occasionally heave a jug of water over another bloke during the night-watches, but we never thought of effecting the same result in this particularly neat and scientific manner. Well, Jeeves, that was the scheme which Miss Wickham suggested I should work on young Tuppy, and that is the girl you call frivolous and lacking in seriousness. Any girl who can think up a wheeze like that is my idea of a helpmeet. I shall be glad, Jeeves, if by the time I come to bed tonight you have waiting for me in this room a stout stick with a good sharp darning needle attached.'

'Well, sir –'

v.w.—5

I raised my hand.

'Jeeves,' I said. 'Not another word. Stick, one, and needle, darning, good, sharp, one, without fail in this room at eleven-thirty tonight.'

'Very good sir.'

'Have you any idea where young Tuppy sleeps?'

'I could ascertain, sir.'

'Do so, Jeeves.'

In a few minutes he was back with the necessary informash.

'Mr Glossop is established in the Moat Room, sir.'

'Where's that?'

'The second door on the floor below this, sir.'

'Right-ho, Jeeves. Are the studs in my shirt?'

'Yes, sir.'

'And the links also?'

'Yes, sir.'

'Then push me into it.'

The more I thought about this enterprise which a sense of duty and good citizenship had thrust upon me, the better it seemed to me. I am not a vindictive man, but I felt, as anybody would have felt in my place, that if fellows like young Tuppy are allowed to get away with it the whole fabric of Society and Civilization must inevitably crumble. The task to which I had set myself was one that involved hardship and discomfort, for it meant sitting up till well into the small hours and then padding down a cold corridor, but I did not shrink from it. After all, there is a lot to be said for family tradition. We Woosters did our bit in the Crusades.

It being Christmas Eve, there was, as I had foreseen, a good deal of revelry and what not. First, the village choir surged round and sang carols outside the front door, and then somebody suggested a dance, and after that we hung around chatting of this and that, so that it wasn't till past one that I got to my room. Allowing for everything, it didn't seem that it was going to be safe to start my little expedition till half-past two at the earliest: and I'm bound to say that it was only the utmost resolution that kept me from snuggling into the sheets and calling it a day. I'm not much of a lad now for late hours.

However, by half-past two everything appeared to be quiet. I shook off the mists of sleep, grabbed the good old stick-and-needle, and off along the corridor. And presently, pausing outside the Moat Room, I turned the handle, found the door wasn't locked, and went in.

I suppose a burglar – I mean a real professional who works at the job six nights a week all the year round – gets so that finding himself standing in the dark in somebody else's bedroom means absolutely nothing to him. But for a bird like me, who has had no previous experience, there's a lot to be said in favour of washing the whole thing out and closing the door gently and popping back to bed again. It was only by summoning up all the old bull-dog courage of the Woosters, and reminding myself that, if I let this opportunity slip another might never occur, that I managed to stick out what you might call the initial minute of the binge. Then the weakness passed, and Bertram was himself again.

At first when I beetled in, the room had seemed as black as a coal-cellar: but after a bit things began to lighten. The curtains weren't quite drawn over the window and I could see a trifle of the scenery here and there. The bed was opposite the window, with the head against the wall and the end where the feet were jutting out towards where I stood, thus rendering it possible after one had sown the seed, so to speak, to make a quick getaway. There only remained now the rather tricky problem of locating the old hot-water bottle. I mean to say, the one thing you can't do if you want to carry a job like this through with secrecy and dispatch is to stand at the end of a fellow's bed, jabbing the blankets at random with a darning needle. Before proceeding to anything in the nature of definite steps, it is imperative that you locate the bot.

I was a good deal cheered at this juncture to hear a fruity snore from the direction of the pillows. Reason told me that a bloke who could snore like that wasn't going to be awakened by a trifle. I edged forward and ran a hand in a gingerly sort of

way over the coverlet. A moment later I had found the bulge. I
steered the good old darning-needle on to it, gripped the stick,
and shoved. Then, pulling out the weapon, I sidled towards the
door, and in another moment would have been outside, buzzing
for home and the good night's rest, when suddenly there was a
crash that sent my spine shooting up through the top of my
head and the contents of the bed sat up like a jack-in-the-box
and said:

'Who's that?'

It just shows how your most careful strategic moves can be
the very ones that dish your campaign. In order to facilitate the
orderly retreat according to plan I had left the door open, and
the beastly thing had slammed like a bomb.

But I wasn't giving much thought to the causes of the explosion, having other things to occupy my mind. What was disturbing me was the discovery that, whoever else the bloke in the
bed might be, he was not young Tuppy. Tuppy has one of those
high, squeaky voices that sound like the tenor of the village
choir failing to hit a high note. This one was something in between the Last Trump and a tiger calling for breakfast after
being on a diet for a day or two. It was the sort of nasty, rasp-
ing voice you hear shouting 'Fore!' when you're one of a slow
foursome on the links and are holding up a couple of retired
colonels. Among the qualities it lacked were kindliness, suavity
and that sort of dove-like cooing note which makes a fellow
feel he has found a friend.

I did not linger. Getting swiftly off the mark, I dived for the
door-handle and was off and away, banging the door behind
me. I may be a chump in many ways, as my Aunt Agatha will
freely attest, but I know when and when not to be among those
present.

And I was just about to do the stretch of corridor leading to
the stairs in a split second under the record time for the course,
when something brought me up with a sudden jar. One moment I was all dash and fire and speed; the next, an irresistible
force had checked me in my stride and was holding me straining
at the leash, as it were.

You know, sometimes it seems to me as if Fate were going out of its way to such an extent to snooter you that you wonder if it's worth while continuing to struggle. The night being a trifle chillier than the dickens, I had donned for this expedition a dressing-gown. It was the tail of this infernal garment that had caught in the door and pipped me at the eleventh hour.

The next moment the door had opened, light streaming through it, and the bloke with the voice had grabbed me by the arm.

It was Sir Roderick Glossop.

The next thing that happened was a bit of a lull in the proceedings. For about three and a quarter seconds or possibly more we just stood there, drinking each other in, so to speak, the old boy still attached with a limpet-like grip to my elbow. If I hadn't been in a dressing-gown and he in pink pyjamas with a blue stripe, and if he hadn't been glaring quite so much as if he were shortly going to commit a murder, the tableau would have looked rather like one of those advertisements you see in magazines, where the experienced elder is patting the young man's arm, and saying to him: 'My boy, if you subscribe to the Mutt-Jeff Correspondence School of Oswego, Kan., as I did, you may some day, like me, become Third Assistant Vice-President of the Schenectady Consolidated Nail-File and Eye-brow Tweezer Corporation.'

'You!' said Sir Roderick finally. And in this connection I want to state that it's all rot to say you can't hiss a word that hasn't an 's' in it. The way he pushed out that 'You!' sounded like an angry cobra, and I am betraying no secrets when I mention that it did me no good whatsoever.

By rights, I suppose, at this point I ought to have said something. The best I could manage, however, was a faint, soft bleating sound. Even on ordinary social occasions, when meeting this bloke as man to man and with a clear conscience, I could never be completely at my ease: and now those eyebrows seemed to pierce me like a knife.

'Come in here,' he said, lugging me into the room. 'We don't want to wake the whole house. Now,' he said, depositing me on the carpet, and closing the door and doing a bit of eyebrow work, 'kindly inform me what is this latest manifestation of insanity?'

It seemed to me that a light and cheery laugh might help the thing along. So I had a pop at one.

'Don't gibber!' said my genial host. And I'm bound to admit that the light and cheery hadn't come out quite as I'd intended.

I pulled myself together with a strong effort.

'Awfully sorry about all this,' I said in a hearty sort of voice. 'The fact is, I thought you were Tuppy.'

'Kindly refrain from inflicting your idiotic slang on me. What do you mean by the adjective "tuppy"?'

'It isn't so much an adjective, don't you know. More of a noun, I should think, if you examine it squarely. What I mean to say is, I thought you were your nephew.'

'You thought I was my nephew? Why should I be my nephew?'

'What I'm driving at is, I thought this was his room.'

'My nephew and I changed rooms. I have a great dislike for sleeping on an upper floor. I am nervous about fire.'

For the first time since this interview had started, I braced up a trifle. The injustice of the whole thing stirred me to such an extent that for a moment I lost that sense of being a toad under the harrow which had been cramping my style up till now. I even went so far as to eye this pink-pyjamaed poltroon with a good deal of contempt and loathing. Just because he had this craven fear of fire and this selfish preference for letting Tuppy be cooked instead of himself should the emergency occur, my nicely-reasoned plans had gone up the spout. I gave him a look, and I think I may even have snorted a bit.

'I should have thought that your man-servant would have informed you,' said Sir Roderick, 'that we contemplated making this change. I met him shortly before luncheon and told him to tell you.'

I reeled. Yes, it is not too much to say that I reeled. This extraordinary statement had taken me amidships without any preparation, and it staggered me. That Jeeves had been aware all along that this old crumb would be the occupant of the bed which I was proposing to prod with darning-needles and had let me rush upon my doom without a word of warning was almost beyond belief. You might say I was aghast. Yes, practically aghast.

'You told Jeeves that you were going to sleep in this room?' I gasped.

'I did. I was aware that you and my nephew were on terms of intimacy, and I wished to spare myself the possibility of a visit from you. I confess that it never occurred to me that such a visit was to be anticipated at three o'clock in the morning. What the devil do you mean,' he barked, suddenly hotting up, 'by prowling about the house at this hour? And what is that thing in your hand?'

I looked down, and found that I was still grasping the stick. I give you my honest word that, what with the maelstrom of emotions into which his revelation about Jeeves had cast me, the discovery came as an absolute surprise.

'This?' I said, 'Oh, yes.'

'What do you mean, Oh yes? What is it?'

'Well, it's a long story –'

'We have the night before us.'

'It's this way. I will ask you to picture me some weeks ago, perfectly peaceful and inoffensive, after dinner at the Drones, smoking a thoughtful cigarette and –'

I broke off. The man wasn't listening. He was goggling in a rapt sort of way at the end of the bed, from which there had now begun to drip on to the carpet a series of drops.

'Good heavens!'

'–thoughtful cigarette and chatting pleasantly of this and that –'

I broke off again. He had lifted the sheets and was gazing at the corpse of the hot-water bottle.

'Did you do this?' he said in a low, strangled sort of voice.

'Er – yes. As a matter of fact, yes. I was just going to tell you –'

'And your aunt tried to persuade me that you were not insane!'

'I'm not. Absolutely not. If you'll just let me explain.'

'I will do nothing of the kind.'

'It all began –'

'Silence!'

'Right-ho.'

He did some deep-breathing exercises through the nose.

'My bed is drenched!'

'The way it all began –'

'Be quiet!' He heaved somewhat for awhile. 'You wretched, miserable idiot,' he said, 'kindly inform me which bedroom you are supposed to be occupying?'

'It's on the floor above. The Clock Room.'

'Thank you. I will find it.'

'Eh?'

He gave me the eyebrow.

'I propose,' he said, 'to pass the remainder of the night in your room where, I presume, there is a bed in a condition to be slept in. You may bestow yourself as comfortably as you can here. I will wish you good night.'

He buzzed off, leaving me flat.

Well, we Woosters are old campaigners. We can take the rough with the smooth. But to say that I liked the prospect now before me would be paltering with the truth. One glance at the bed told me that any idea of sleeping there was out. A goldfish could have done it, but not Bertram. After a bit of a look round, I decided that the best chance of getting a sort of night's rest was to doss as well as I could in the arm-chair. I pinched a couple of pillows off the bed, shoved the hearth-rug over my knees, and sat down and started counting sheep.

But it wasn't any good. The old lemon was sizzling much too much to admit of anything in the nature of slumber. This hideous revelation of the blackness of Jeeves's treachery kept coming back to me every time I nearly succeeded in dropping off: and, what's more it seemed to get colder and colder as the long night wore on. I was just wondering if I could ever get to sleep again in this world when a voice at my elbow said 'Good morning, sir,' and I sat up with a jerk.

I could have sworn I hadn't so much as dozed off for even a minute, but apparently I had. For the curtains were drawn and daylight was coming in through the window and there was Jeeves standing beside me with a cup of tea on a tray.

'Merry Christmas, sir!'

I reached out a feeble hand for the restoring brew. I swallowed a mouthful or two, and felt a little better. I was aching in every limb and the dome felt like lead, but I was now able to think with a certain amount of clearness, and I fixed the man with a stony eye and prepared to let him have it.

'You think so, do you?' I said. 'Much, let me tell you, depends on what you mean by the adjective "merry". If, moreover, you suppose that it is going to be merry for you, correct that impression. Jeeves,' I said, taking another half-oz. of tea and speaking in a cold, measured voice, 'I wish to ask you one question. Did you or did you not know that Sir Roderick Glossop was sleeping in this room last night?'

'Yes, sir.'

'You admit it!'

'Yes, sir.'

'And you didn't tell me!'

'No, sir. I thought it would be more judicious not to do so.'

'Jeeves –'

'If you will allow me to explain, sir.'

'Explain!'

'I was aware that my silence might lead to something in the nature of an embarrassing contretemps, sir –'

'You thought that, did you?'

'Yes, sir.'

'You were a good guesser,' I said, sucking down further Bohea.

'But it seemed to me, sir, that whatever might occur was all for the best.'

I would have put in a crisp word or two here, but he carried on without giving me the opp.

'I thought that possibly, on reflection, sir, your views being what they are, you would prefer your relations with Sir Roderick Glossop and his family to be distant rather than cordial.'

'My views? What do you mean, my views?'

'As regards a matrimonial alliance with Miss Honoria Glossop, sir.'

Something like an electric shock seemed to zip through me. The man had opened up a new line of thought. I suddenly saw what he was driving at, and realized all in a flash that I had been wronging this faithful fellow. All the while I supposed he had been landing me in the soup, he had really been steering me away from it. It was like those stories one used to read as a kid about the traveller going along on a dark night and his dog grabs him by the leg of his trousers and he says 'Down, sir! What are you doing, Rover?' and the dog hangs on and he gets rather hot under the collar and curses a bit but the dog won't let him go and then suddenly the moon shines through the clouds and he finds he's been standing on the edge of a precipice and one more step would have – well anyway, you get the idea: and what I'm driving at is that much the same sort of thing seemed to have been happening now.

It's perfectly amazing how a fellow will let himself get off his guard and ignore the perils which surround him. I give you my honest word, it had never struck me till this moment that my Aunt Agatha had been scheming to get me in right with Sir Roderick so that I should eventually be received back into the fold, if you see what I mean, and subsequently pushed off on Honoria.

'My God, Jeeves!' I said, paling.

'Precisely, sir.'

'You think there was a risk?'

'I do, sir. A very grave risk.'

A disturbing thought struck me.

'But, Jeeves, on calm reflection, won't Sir Roderick have gathered by now that my objective was young Tuppy and that puncturing his hot-water bottle was just one of those things that occur when the Yule-tide spirit is abroad – one of those things that have to be overlooked and taken with the indulgent smile and the fatherly shake of the head? I mean to say, Young Blood and all that sort of thing? What I mean is he'll realize that I wasn't trying to snooter him, and then all the good work will have been wasted.'

'No, sir. I fancy not. That might possibly have been Sir Roderick's mental reaction, had it not been for the second incident.'

'The second incident?'

'During the night, sir, while Sir Roderick was occupying your bed, somebody entered the room, pierced his hot-water bottle with some sharp insrument, and vanished in the darkness.'

I could make nothing of this.

'What! Do you think I walked in my sleep?'

'No, sir. It was young Mr Glossop who did it. I encountered him this morning, sir, shortly before I came here. He was in cheerful spirits and inquired of me how you were feeling about the incident. Not being aware that his victim had been Sir Roderick.'

'But, Jeeves, what an amazing coincidence!'

'Sir?'

'Why, young Tuppy getting exactly the same idea as I did. Or, rather, as Miss Wickham did. You can't say that's not rummy. A miracle, I call it.'

'Not altogether, sir. It appears that he received the suggestion from the young lady.'

'From Miss Wickham?'

'Yes, sir.'

'You mean to say that, after she had put me up to the scheme of puncturing Tuppy's hot-water bottle, she went away and tipped Tuppy off to puncturing mine?'

'Precisely, sir. She is a young lady with a keen sense of humour, sir.'

I sat there, you might say stunned. When I thought how near I had come to offering the heart and hand to a girl capable of double-crossing a strong man's honest love like that, I shivered.

'Are you cold, sir?'

'No, Jeeves. Just shuddering.'

'The occurrence, if I may take the liberty of saying so, sir, will perhaps lend colour to the view which I put forward yesterday that Miss Wickham, though in many respects a charming young lady –'

I raised the hand.

'Say no more, Jeeves,' I replied. 'Love is dead.'

'Very good, sir.'

I brooded for a while.

'You've seen Sir Roderick this morning, then?'

'Yes, sir.'

'How did he seem?'

'A trifle feverish, sir.'

'Feverish?'

'A little emotional, sir. He expressed a strong desire to meet you, sir.'

'What would you advise?'

'If you were to slip out by the back entrance as soon as you are dressed, sir, it would be possible for you to make your way across the field without being observed and reach the village, where you could hire an automobile to take you to London. I could bring on your effects later in your own car.'

'But London, Jeeves? Is any man safe? My Aunt Agatha is in London.'

'Yes, sir.'

'Well, then?'

He regarded me for a moment with fathomless eye.

'I think the best plan, sir, would be for you to leave England, which is not pleasant at this time of the year, for some little while. I would not take the liberty of dictating your movements, sir, but as you already have accommodation engaged on the Blue Train for Monte Carlo for the day after tomorrow –'

'But you cancelled the booking?'

'No, sir.'

'I thought you had.'

'No, sir.'

'I told you to.'

'Yes, sir. It was remiss of me, but the matter slipped my mind.'

'Oh?'

'Yes, sir.'

'All right, Jeeves. Monte Carlo ho, then.'

'Very good, sir.'

'It's lucky, as things have turned out, that you forgot to cancel that booking.'

'Very fortunate indeed, sir. If you will wait here, sir, I will return to your room and procure a suit of clothes.'

Very Good, Jeeves (1930)

Franglais

Wodehouse lived in France, on and off, for years. He took French lessons there, but, though he could read the language, he couldn't, or wouldn't, speak it.

Into the face of the young man who sat on the terrace of the Hotel Magnifique at Cannes there had crept a look of furtive shame, the shifty, hangdog look which announces that an Englishman is about to talk French. One of the things which Gertrude Butterwick had impressed upon Monty Bodkin when he left for this holiday on the Riviera was that he must be sure to practise his French, and Gertrude's word was law. So now, though he knew that it was going to make his nose tickle, he said:

'Er, garçon.'

'M'sieur?'

'Er, garçon, esker-vous avez un spot de l'encre et une pièce de papier – notepapier, vous savez – et une enveloppe et une plume?'

'Ben, m'sieur.'

The strain was too great. Monty relapsed into his native tongue.

'I want to write a letter,' he said. And having, like all lovers, rather a tendency to share his romance with the world, he would probably have added 'to the sweetest girl on earth', had not the waiter already bounded off like a retriever, to return a few moments later with the fixings.

'V'là, sir! Zere you are, sir,' said the waiter. He was engaged to a girl in Paris who had told him that when on the Riviera he must be sure to practise his English. 'Eenk – pin – pipper – enveloppe – and a liddle bit of bloddin-pipper.'

'Oh, merci,' said Monty, well pleased at this efficiency. 'Thanks. Right-ho.'

'Right-ho, m'sieur,' said the waiter.

The Luck of the Bodkins (1935)

Anselm Gets His Chance

*Wodehouse on the Anglican Church – its ministers, their ladies,
their pets (Bottles and Webster) and their sermons – is
Wodehouse at his benign best.*

The summer Sunday was drawing to a close. Twilight had fallen
on the little garden of the Anglers' Rest, and the air was fragrant with the sweet scent of jasmine and tobacco plant. Stars
were peeping out. Blackbirds sang drowsily in the shrubberies.
Bats wheeled through the shadows, and a gentle breeze played
fitfully among the hollyhocks. It was, in short, as a customer
who had looked in for a gin and tonic rather happily put it, a
nice evening.

Nevertheless, to Mr Mulliner and the group assembled in the
bar parlour of the inn there was a sense of something missing.
It was due to the fact that Miss Postlethwaite, the efficient barmaid, was absent. Some forty minutes had elapsed before she
arrived and took over from the pot-boy. When she did so, the
quiet splendour of her costume and the devout manner in which
she pulled the beer handle told their own story.

'You've been to church,' said a penetrating Sherry and
Angostura.

Miss Postlethwaite said Yes, she had, and it had been
lovely.

'Beautiful in every sense of the word,' said Miss Postlethwaite, filling an order for a pint of bitter. 'I do adore evening
service in the summer. It sort of does something to you, what
I mean. All that stilly hush and what not.'

'The vicar preached the sermon, I suppose?' said Mr Mulliner.

'Yes,' said Miss Poslethwaite, adding that it had been extremely moving.

Mr Mulliner took a thoughtful sip of his hot Scotch and lemon.

'The old, old story,' he said, a touch of sadness in his voice. 'I do not know if you gentlemen were aware of it, but in the rural districts of England vicars always preach the evening sermon during the summer months, and this causes a great deal of discontent to seethe among curates. It exasperates the young fellows, and one can understand their feelings. As Miss Poslethwaite rightly says, there is something about the atmosphere of evensong in a village church that induces a receptive frame of mind in a congregation, and a preacher, preaching under such conditions, can scarcely fail to grip and stir. The curates, withheld from so preaching, naturally feel that they are being ground beneath the heel of an iron monopoly and chiselled out of their big chance.'

A Whisky and Splash said he had never thought of that.

'In that respect,' said Mr Mulliner, 'you differ from my cousin Rupert's younger son, Anselm. He thought of it a great deal. He was the curate of the parish of Rising Mattock in Hampshire, and when he was not dreaming fondly of Myrtle Jellaby, niece of Sir Leopold Jellaby, O.B.E., the local squire, you would generally find him chafing at his vicar's high-handed selfishness in always hogging the evening sermon from late April till well on in September. He told me once that it made him feel like a caged skylark.'

'Why did he dream fondly of Myrtle Jellaby?' asked a Stout and Mild, who was not very quick at the uptake.

'Because he loved her. And she loved him. She had, indeed, consented to become his wife.'

'They were engaged?' said the Stout and Mild, beginning to get it.

'Secretly. Anselm did not dare to inform her uncle of the position of affairs, because all he had to marry on was his meagre stipend. He feared the wrath of that millionaire philatelist.'

97

'Millionaire what?' asked a Small Bass.

'Sir Leopold,' explained Mr Mulliner, 'collected stamps.'

The Small Bass said that he had always thought that a philatelist was a man who was kind to animals.

'No,' said Mr Mulliner, 'a stamp collector. Though many philatelists are, I believe, also kind to animals. Sir Leopold Jellaby had been devoted to this hobby for many years, ever since he had retired from business as a promotor of companies in the City of London. His collection was famous.'

'And Anselm didn't like to tell him about Myrtle,' said the Stout and Mild.

'No. As I say, he lacked the courage. He pursued instead the cautious policy of lying low and hoping for the best. And one bright summer day the happy ending seemed to have arrived. Myrtle, calling at the vicarage at breakfast-time, found Anselm dancing round the table, in one hand a half-consumed piece of toast, in the other a letter, and learned from him that under the will of his late godfather, the recently deceased Mr J. G. Beenstock, he had benefited by an unexpected legacy – to wit, the stout stamp album which now lay beside the marmalade dish.'

The information caused the girl's face to light up (continued Mr Mulliner). A philatelist's niece, she knew how valuable these things could be.

'What's it worth?' she asked eagerly.

'It is insured, I understand, for no less a sum than five thousand pounds.'

'Golly!'

'Golly, indeed,' assented Anselm.

'Nice sugar!' said Myrtle.

'Exceedingly nice,' agreed Anselm.

'You must take care of it. Don't leave it lying about. We don't want somebody pinching it.'

A look of pain passed over Anselm's spiritual face.

'You are not suggesting that the vicar would stoop to such an act?'

'I was thinking more,' said Myrtle, 'of Joe Beamish.'

She was alluding to a member of her loved one's little flock who had at one time been a fairly prosperous burglar. Seeing the light after about sixteen prison sentences, he had given up his life-work and now raised vegetables and sang in the choir.

'Old Joe is supposed to have reformed and got away from it all, but, if you ask me, there's a lot of life in the old dog yet. If he gets to hear that there's a five-thousand-pound stamp collection lying around . . .'

'I think you wrong our worthy Joe, darling. However, I will take precautions. I shall place the album in a drawer in the desk in the vicar's study. It is provided with a stout lock. But before doing so, I thought I might take it round and show it to your uncle. It is possible that he may feel disposed to make an offer for the collection.'

'That's a thought,' agreed Myrtle. 'Soak him good.'

'I will assuredly omit no effort to that end,' said Anselm.

And, kissing Myrtle fondly, he went about his parochial duties.

It was towards evening that he called upon Sir Leopold, and the kindly old squire, learning the nature of his errand and realizing that he had not come to make a touch on behalf of the Church Organ Fund, lost the rather strained look which he had worn when his name was announced and greeted him warmly.

'Stamps?' he said. 'Yes, I am always ready to add to my collection, provided that what I am offered is of value and the price reasonable. Had you any figure in mind for these of yours, my dear Mulliner?'

Anselm said that he had been thinking of something in the neighbourhood of five thousand pounds, and Sir Leopold shook from stem to stern like a cat that had received half a brick in the short ribs. All his life the suggestion that he should part with large sums of money had shocked him.

'Oh?' he said. Then, seeming to master himself with a strong effort. 'Well, let me look at them.'

Ten minutes later, he had closed the volume and was eyeing Anselm compassionately.

'I am afraid you must be prepared for bad news, my boy,' he said.

A sickening feeling of apprehension gripped Anselm.

'You don't mean they are not valuable?'

Sir Leopold put the tips of his fingers together and leaned back in his chair in the rather pontifical manner which he had been accustomed to assume in the old days when addressing meetings of shareholders.

'The term "valuable", my dear fellow, is a relative one. To some people five pounds would be a large sum.'

'Five pounds!'

'That is what I am prepared to offer. Or, seeing that you are a personal friend, shall we say ten?'

'But they are insured for five thousand.'

Sir Leopold shook his head with a half-smile.

'My dear Mulliner, if you knew as much as I do about the vanity of stamp collectors, you would not set great store by that. Well, as I say, I don't mind giving you ten pounds for the lot. Think it over and let me know.'

On leaden feet Anselm left the room. His hopes were shattered. He felt like a man who, chasing rainbows, has had one of them suddenly turn and bite him in the leg.

'Well?' said Myrtle, who had been waiting the result of the conference in the passage.

Anselm broke the sad news. The girl was astounded.

'But you told me the thing was insured for –'

Anselm sighed.

'Your uncle appeared to attribute little or no importance to that. It seems that stamp collectors are in the habit of insuring their collections for fantastic sums, out of a spirit of vanity. I intend,' said Anselm broodingly, 'to preach a very strong sermon shortly on the subject of Vanity.'

There was silence.

'Ah, well,' said Anselm, 'these things are no doubt sent to try us. It is by accepting such blows in a meek and chastened spirit . . .'

'Meek and chastened spirit my left eyeball,' cried Myrtle who, like so many girls today, was apt to be unguarded in her speech. 'We've got to do something about this.'

'But what? I am not denying,' said Anselm, 'that the shock

has been a severe one, and I regret to confess that there was a moment when I was sorely tempted to utter one or two of the observations which I once heard the coach of my college boat at Oxford make to Number Five when he persisted in obtruding his abdomen as he swung his oar. It would have been wrong, but it would unquestionably have relieved my ...'

'I know!' cried Myrtle. 'Joe Beamish!'

Anselm stared at her.

'Joe Beamish? I do not understand you, dear.'

'Use your bean, boy, use your bean. You remember what I told you. All we've got to do is let old Joe know where those stamps are, and he will take over from there. And there we shall be with our nice little claim for five thousand of the best on the insurance company.'

'Myrtle!'

'It would be money for jam,' the enthusiastic girl continued. 'Just so much velvet. Go and see Joe at once.'

'Myrtle! I beg you, desist. You shock me inexpressibly.'

She gazed at him incredulously. 'You mean you won't do it?'

'I could never even contemplate such a course.'

'You won't unleash old Joe and set him acting for the best?'

'Certainly not. Most decidedly not. A thousand times, no.'

'But what's wrong with the idea?'

'The whole project is ethically unsound.'

There was a pause. For a moment it seemed as if the girl was about to express her chagrin in an angry outburst. A frown darkened her brow, and she kicked petulantly at a passing beetle. Then she appeared to get the better of her emotion. Her face cleared, and she smiled at him tenderly, like a mother at her fractious child.

'Oh, all right. Just as you say. Where are you off to now?'

'I have a Mothers' Meeting at six.'

'And I,' said Myrtle, 'have got to take a few pints of soup to the deserving poor. I'd better set about it. Amazing the way these bimbos absorb soup. Like sponges.'

They walked together as far as the Village Hall. Anselm went in to meet the Mothers. Myrtle, as soon as he was out of sight, turned and made her way to Joe Beamish's cosy cottage. The crooning of a hymn from within showing that its owner was at home, she walked through its honeysuckle-covered porch.

'Well, Joe, old top,' she said, 'how's everything?'

Joe Beamish was knitting a sock in the tiny living-room which smelled in equal proportions of mice, ex-burglars and shag tobacco, and Myrtle, as her gaze fell upon his rugged features, felt her heart leap within her like that of the poet Wordsworth when beholding a rainbow in the sky. His altered circumstances had not changed the erstwhile porch-climber's outward appearance. It remained that of one of those men for whom the police are always spreading drag-nets; and Myrtle, eyeing him, had the feeling that in supposing that in this pre-eminent plugugly there still lurked something of the Old Adam, she had called her shots correctly.

For some minutes after her entry, the conversation was confined to neutral topics – the weather, the sock and the mice behind the wainscoting. It was only when it turned to the decoration of the church for the forthcoming Harvest Festival – to which, she learned, her host would be in a position to contribute two cabbages and a pumpkin – that Myrtle saw her opportunity of approaching a more intimate subject.

'Mr Mulliner will be pleased about that,' she said. 'He's nuts on the Harvest Festival.'

'R,' said Joe Beamish. 'He's a good man, Mr Mulliner.'

'He's a lucky man,' said Myrtle. 'Have you heard what's just happened to him? Some sort of deceased Beenstock has gone and left him five thousand quid.'

'Coo! Is that right?'

'Well, it comes to the same thing. An album of stamps that's worth five thousand. You know how valuable stamps are. Why, my uncle's collection is worth ten times that. That's why we've got all those burglar alarms up at the Hall.'

A rather twisted expression came into Joe Beamish's face.

'I've heard there's a lot of burglar alarms up at the Hall,' he said.

'But there aren't any at the vicarage, and, between you and me, Joe, it's worrying me rather. Because, you see, that's where Mr Mulliner is keeping his stamps.'

'R,' said Joe Beamish, speaking now with a thoughtful intonation.

'I told him he ought to keep them at his bank.'

Joe Beamish started.

'Wot ever did you go and say a silly thing like that for?' he asked.

'It wasn't at all silly,' said Myrtle warmly. 'It was just ordinary common sense. I don't consider those stamps are safe, left lying in a drawer in the desk in the vicar's study, that little room on the ground floor to the right of the front door with its flimsy French windows that could so easily be forced with a chisel or something. They are locked up, of course, but what good are locks? I've seen these, and anybody could open them with a hairpin. I tell you, Joe, I'm worried.'

Joe Beamish bent over his socks, knitting and purling for a while in silence. When he spoke again, it was to talk of pumpkins and cabbages, and after that, for he was a man of limited ideas, of cabbages and pumpkins.

Anselm Mulliner, meanwhile, was passing through a day of no little spiritual anguish. At the moment when it had been made, Myrtle's proposal had shaken him to his foundations. He had not felt so utterly unmanned since the evening when he had been giving young Willie Purvis a boxing lesson at the Lads' Club, and Willie, by a happy accident, had got home squarely on the button.

This revelation of the character of the girl to whom he had given a curate's unspotted heart had stunned him. Myrtle, it seemed to him, appeared to have no notion whatsoever of the distinction between right and wrong. And while this would not have mattered, of course, had he been a gun-man and she his prospective moll, it made a great deal of difference to one who hoped later on to become a vicar and, in such event, would want his wife to look after the parish funds. He wondered what the prophet Isaiah would have had to say about it, had he been informed of her views on strategy and tactics.

All through the afternoon and evening he continued to brood on the thing. At supper that night he was distrait and preoccupied. Busy with his own reflections, he scarcely listened to the conversation of the Rev. Sidney Gooch, his vicar. And this was perhaps fortunate, for it was a Saturday and the vicar, as was his custom at Saturday suppers, harped a good deal on the subject of the sermon which he was proposing to deliver at evensong on the morrow. He said, not once but many times, that he confidently expected, if the fine weather held up, to knock his little flock cockeyed. The Rev. Sidney was a fine, upstanding specimen of the muscular Christian, but somewhat deficient in tact.

Towards nightfall, however, Anselm found a kindlier, mellower note creeping into his meditations. Possibly it was the excellent round of beef of which he had partaken, and the wholesome ale with which he had washed it down, that caused this softer mood. As he smoked his after-supper cigarette, he found himself beginning to relax in his austere attitude towards Myrtle's feminine weakness. He reminded himself that it must be placed to her credit that she had not been obdurate. On the contrary, the moment he had made plain his disapproval of her financial methods, conscience had awakened, her better self had prevailed and she had abandoned her dubious schemes. That was much.

Happy once more, he went to bed and, after dipping into a good book for half an hour, switched off the light and fell into a restful sleep.

But it seemed to him that he had scarcely done so when he was awakened by loud noises. He sat up, listening. Something in the nature of a free-for-all appeared to be in progress in the lower part of the house. His knowledge of the vicarage's topography suggested to him that the noises were proceeding from the study and, hastily donning a dressing-gown, he made his way thither.

The room was in darkness, but he found the switch and,

turning on the light, perceived that the odd, groaning sound which had greeted him as he approached the door proceeded from the Rev. Sidney Gooch. The vicar was sitting on the floor, a hand pressed to his left eye.

'A burglar!' he said, rising. 'A beastly bounder of a burglar.'

'He has injured you, I fear,' said Anselm commiseratingly.

'Of course he has injured me,' said the Rev. Sidney, with some testiness. 'Can a man take fire in his bosom and his clothes not be burned? Proverbs, six, twenty-seven. I heard a sound and came down and seized the fellow, and he struck me so violently that I was compelled to loosen my grip, and he made his escape through the window. Be so kind, Mulliner, as to look about and see if he has taken anything. There were some manuscript sermons which I should not care to lose.'

Anselm was standing beside the desk. He had to pause for a moment in order to control his voice.

'The only object that appears to have been removed,' he said, 'is an album of stamps belonging to myself.'

'The sermons are there?'

'Still there.'

'Bitter,' said the vicar. 'Bitter.'

'I beg your pardon?' said Anselm.

He turned. His superior of the cloth was standing before the mirror, regarding himself in it with a rueful stare.

'Bitter!' he repeated. 'I was thinking,' he explained, 'of the one I had planned to deliver at evensong tomorrow. A pippin, Mulliner, in the deepest and truest sense a pippin. I am not exaggerating when I say that I would have had them tearing up the pews. And now that dream is ended. I cannot possibly appear in the pulpit with a shiner like this. I would put wrong ideas into the heads of the congregation – always, in these rural communities, so prone to place the worst construction on such disfigurements. Tomorrow, Mulliner, I shall be confined to my bed with a slight chill, and you will conduct both matins and evensong. Bitter!' said the Rev. Sidney Gooch. 'Bitter!'

Anselm did not speak. His heart was too full for words.

*

In Anselm's deportment and behaviour on the following morning there was nothing to indicate that his soul was a maelstrom of seething emotions. Most curates who find themselves unexpectedly allowed to preach on Sunday evening in the summer time are like dogs let off the chain. They leap. They bound. They sing snatches of the more rollicking psalms. They rush about saying 'Good morning, good morning,' to everybody and patting children on the head. Not so Anselm. He knew that only by conserving his nervous energies would he be able to give of his best when the great moment came.

To those of the congregation who were still awake in the later stages of the service his sermon at Matins seemed dull and colourless. And so it was. He had no intention of frittering away eloquence on a morning service. He deliberately held himself back, concentrating every fibre of his being on the address which he was to deliver in the evening.

He had had it by him for months. Every curate throughout the English countryside keeps tucked away among his effects a special sermon designed to prevent him being caught short, if suddenly called upon to preach at evensong. And all through the afternoon he remained closeted in his room, working upon it. He pruned. He polished. He searched the Thesaurus for the telling adjective. By the time the church bells began to ring out over the fields and spinneys of Rising Mattock in the quiet gloaming, his masterpiece was perfected to the last comma.

Feeling more like a volcano than a curate, Anselm Mulliner pinned together the sheets of manuscript and set forth.

The conditions could not have been happier. By the end of the pre-sermon hymn the twilight was far advanced, and through the door of the little church there poured the scent of trees and flowers. All was still, save for the distant tinkling of sheep bells and the drowsy calling of rooks among the elms. With quiet confidence Anselm mounted the pulpit steps. He had been sucking throat pastilles all day and saying 'Mi-mi' to himself in an undertone throughout the service, and he knew that he would be in good voice.

For an instant he paused and gazed about him. He was rejoiced to see that he was playing to absolute capacity. Every pew was full. There, in the squire's highbacked stall, was Sir Leopold Jellaby, O.B.E., with Myrtle at his side. There, among the choir, looking indescribably foul in a surplice, sat Joe Beamish. There, in their respective places, were the butcher, the baker, the candlestick-maker and all the others who made up the personnel of the congregation. With a little sigh of rapture, Anselm cleared his throat and gave out the simple text of Brotherly Love.

I have been privileged (said Mr Mulliner) to read the script of this sermon of Anselm's, and it must, I can see, have been extremely powerful. Even in manuscript form, without the added attraction of the young man's beautifully modulated tenor voice, one can clearly sense its magic.

Beginning with a thoughtful excursus on Brotherly Love among the Hivites and Hittites, it came down through the Early Britons, the Middle Ages and the spacious days of Queen Elizabeth to these modern times of ours, and it was here that Anselm Mulliner really let himself go. It was at this point, if one may employ the phrase, that he – in the best and most reverent spirit of the words – reached for the accelerator and stepped on it.

Earnestly, in accents throbbing with emotion, he spoke of our duty to one another; of the task that lies clear before all of us to make this a better and a sweeter world for our fellows; of the joy that awaits those who give no thought to self but strain every nerve to do the square thing by one and all. And with each golden phrase he held his audience in an ever-tightening grip. Tradesmen who had been nodding somnolently woke up and sat with parted lips. Women dabbed at their eyes with handkerchiefs. Choir-boys who had been sucking acid drops swallowed them remorsefully and stopped shuffling their feet.

Even at a morning service, such a sermon would have been a smash hit. Delivered in the gloaming, with all its adventitious aids to success, it was a riot.

It was not immediately after the conclusion of the proceedings that Anselm was able to tear himself away from the crowd of admirers that surged round him in the vestry. There were churchwardens who wanted to shake his hand, other church- wardens who insisted on smacking him on the back. One even asked for his autograph. But eventually he laughingly shook himself free and made his way back to the vicarage. And scarcely had he passed through the garden gate when some- thing shot out at him from the scented darkness, and he found Myrtle Jellaby in his arms.

'Anselm!' she cried. 'My wonder-man! However did you do it? I never heard such a sermon in my life!'

'It got across, I think?' said Anselm modestly.

'It was terrific. Golly! When you admonish a congregation, it stays admonished. How you think of all these things beats me.'

'Oh, they come to one.'

'And another thing I can't understand is how you came to be preaching at all in the evening. I thought you told me the vicar always did.'

'The vicar,' began Anselm, 'has met with a slight ...'

And then it suddenly occurred to him that in the excitement of being allowed to preach at evensong he had quite forgotten to inform Myrtle of that other important happening, the theft of the stamp album.

'A rather extraordinary thing occurred last night, darling,' he said. 'The vicarage was burgled.'

Myrtle was amazed.

'Not really?'

'Yes. A marauder broke in through the study window.'

'Well, fancy that! Did he take anything?'

'He took my collection of stamps.'

Myrtle uttered a cry of ecstasy.

'Then we collect!'

Anselm did not speak for a moment.

'I wonder.'

'What do you mean, you wonder? Of course we collect. Shoot the claim in to the insurance people without a moment's delay.'

'But have you reflected, dearest? Am I justified in doing as you suggest?'

'Of course. Why ever not?'

'It seems to me a moot point. The collection, we know, is worthless. Can I justly demand of this firm – The London and Midland Counties Aid and Benefit Association is its name – that they pay me five thousand pounds for an album of stamps that is without value?'

'Of course you can. Old Beenstock paid the premiums, didn't he?'

'That is true. Yes. I had forgotten that.'

'It doesn't matter whether a thing's valuable or not. The point is what you insure it for. And it isn't as if it's going to hurt these Mutual Aid and Benefit birds to brass up. It's sinful the amount of money those insurance companies have. Must be jolly bad for them, if you ask me.'

Anselm had not thought of that. Examining the point now, it seemed to him that Myrtle, with her woman's intuition, had rather gone to the root of the matter and touched the spot.

Was there not, he asked himself, a great deal to be said for this theory of hers that insurance companies had much too much money and would be better, finer, more spiritual insurance companies if somebody came along occasionally and took a bit of the stuff off them? Unquestionably there was. His doubts were removed. He saw now that it was not only a pleasure, but a duty, to nick the London and Midland Counties Mutual Aid and Benefit Association for five thousand. It might prove the turning-point in the lives of its Board of Directors.

'Very well,' he said. 'I will send in the claim.'

'At-a-boy! And the instant we touch, we'll get married.'

'Myrtle!'

'Anselm!'

'Guv'nor,' said the voice of Joe Beamish at their side, 'could I 'ave a word with you?'

They drew apart with a start, and stared dumbly at the man.

'Guv'nor,' said Joe Beamish, and it was plain from the thickness of his utterance that he was in the grip of some strong

109

emotion, 'I want to thank, you, guv'nor, for that there sermon of yours. That there wonderful sermon.'

Anselm smiled. He had recovered from the shock of hearing this sudden voice in the night. It was a nuisance, of course, to be interrupted like this at such a moment, but one must, he felt, be courteous to the fans. No doubt he would have to expect a lot of this sort of thing from now on.

'I am rejoiced that my poor effort should have elicited so striking an encomium.'

'Wot say?'

'He says he's glad you liked it,' said Myrtle, a little irritably, for she was not feeling her most amiable. A young girl who is nestling in the arms of the man she loves resents having cracksmen popping up through traps at her elbow.

'R,' said Joe Beamish, enlightened. 'Yes, guv'nor, that was a sermon, that was. That was what I call a blinking sermon.'

'Thank you, Joe, thank you. It is nice to feel that you were pleased.'

'You're right, I was pleased, guv'nor. I've 'eard sermons in Pentonville, and I've 'eard sermons in Wormwood Scrubs, and I've 'eard sermons in Dartmoor, and very good sermons they were, but of all the sermons I've 'eard I never 'eard a sermon that could touch this 'ere sermon for class and pep and ...'

'Joe,' said Myrtle.

'Yes, lady?'

'Scram!'

'Pardon, lady?'

'Get out. Pop off. Buzz along. Can't you see you're not wanted? We're busy.'

'My dear,' said Anselm, with gentle reproach, 'is not your manner a little peremptory? I would not have the honest fellow feel ...'

'R,' interrupted Joe Beamish, and there was a suggestion of unshed tears in his voice, 'but I'm not an honest feller, guv'nor. There, if you don't mind me saying so, no offence meant and none, I 'ope, taken, is where you make your bloomin' error. I'm a poor sinner and backslider and evildoer and ...'

'Joe,' said Myrtle, with a certain menacing calm, 'if you get a thick ear, always remember that you asked for it. The same applies to a lump the size of an egg on top of your ugly head through coming into violent contact with the knob of my parasol. Will you or will you not,' she said, taking a firmer grip of the handle of the weapon to which she had alluded, 'push off?'

'Lady,' said Joe Beamish, not without a rough dignity, 'as soon as I've done what I come to do, I will withdraw. But first I got to do what I come to do. And what I come to do is 'and back in a meek and contrite spirit this 'ere album of stamps what I snitched last night, never thinking that I was to 'ear that there wonderful sermon and see the light. But 'avin' 'eard that there wonderful sermon and seen the light, I now 'ave great pleasure in doing what I come to do, namely,' said Joe Beamish, thrusting the late J. G. Beenstock's stamp collection into Anselm's hand, 'this 'ere. Lady ... Guv'nor ... With these few words, 'opin' that you are in the pink as it leaves me at present, I will now withdraw.'

'Stop!' cried Anselm.

'R?'

Anselm's face was strangely contorted. He spoke with difficulty.

'Joe ...'

'Yes, guv'nor?'

'Joe ... I would like ... I would prefer ... In a very real sense I do so feel ... In short, I would like you to keep this stamp album, Joe.'

The burglar shook his head

'No, guv'nor. It can't be done. When I think of that there wonderful sermon and all those beautiful things you said in that there wonderful sermon about the 'Ivites and the 'Ittites and doing the right thing by the neighbours and 'elping so far as in you lies to spread sweetness and light throughout the world, I can't keep no albums which 'ev come into my possession through gettin' in at other folks' french winders on account of not 'avin' seen the light. It don't belong to me, not

111

that album don't, and I now take much pleasure in 'anding it back with these few words. Goo' night, guv'nor. Goo' night, lady. Goo' night all. I will now withdraw.'

His footsteps died away, and there was silence in the quiet garden. Both Anselm and Myrtle were busy with their thoughts. Once more through Anselm's mind there was racing that pithy address which the coach of his college boat had delivered when trying to do justice to the spectacle of Number Five's obtrusive stomach: while Myrtle, on her side, was endeavouring not to give utterance to rough translation of something she had once heard a French taxi-driver say to a gendarme during her finishing-school days in Paris.

Anselm was the first to speak.

'This, dearest,' he said, 'calls for discussion. One does so feel that little or nothing can be accomplished without earnest thought and a frank round-table conference. Let us go indoors and thresh the whole matter out in as calm a spirit as we can achieve.'

He led the way to the study and seated himself moodily, his chin in his hands, his brow furrowed. A deep sigh escaped him.

'I understand now,' he said, 'why it is that curates are not permitted to preach on Sunday evenings during the summer months. It is not safe. It is like exploding a bomb in a public place. It upsets existing conditions too violently. When I reflect that, had our good vicar but been able to take evensong tonight, this distressing thing would not have occurred, I find myself saying in the words of the prophet Hosea to the children of Adullam . . .'

'Putting the prophet Hosea to one side for the moment and temporarily pigeon-holing the children of Adullam,' interrupted Myrtle, 'what are we going to do about this?'

Anselm sighed again.

'Alas, dearest, there you have me. I assume that it is no longer feasible to submit a claim to the London and Midland Counties Mutual Aid and Benefit Association.'

'So we lose five thousand of the best and brightest?'

Anselm winced. The lines deepened on his careworn face.

'It is not an agreeable thing to contemplate, I agree. One had been looking on the sum as one's little nest-egg. One did so want to see it safely in the bank, to be invested later in sound, income-bearing securities. I confess to feeling a little vexed with Joe Beamish.'

'I hope he chokes.'

'I would not go so far as that, darling,' said Anselm, with loving rebuke. 'But I must admit that if I heard that he had tripped over a loose shoelace and sprained his ankle, it would – in the deepest and truest sense – be all right with me. I deplore the man's tactless impulsiveness. "Officious" is the word that springs to the lips.'

Myrtle was musing.

'Listen,' she said. 'Why not play a little joke on these London and Midland bozos? Why tell them you've got the stamps back? Why not just sit tight and send in the claim and pouch their cheque? That would be a lot of fun.'

Again, for the second time in two days, Anselm found himself looking a little askance at his loved one. Then he reminded himself that she was scarcely to be blamed for her somewhat unconventional outlook. The niece of a prominent financier, she was perhaps entitled to be somewhat eccentric in her views. No doubt, her earliest childhood memories were of coming down to dessert and hearing her elders discuss over the nuts and wine some burgeoning scheme for trimming the investors.

He shook his head.

'I could hardly countenance such a policy, I fear. To me there seems something – I do not wish to hurt your feelings, dearest – something almost dishonest about what you suggest. Besides,' he added meditatively, 'when Joe Beamish handed back that album, he did it in the presence of witnesses.'

'Witnesses?'

'Yes, dearest. As we came into the house, I observed a shadowy figure. Whose it was, I cannot say, but of this I feel convinced – that this person, whoever he may have been, heard all.'

'You're sure?'

113

'Quite sure. He was standing beneath the cedar-tree, within easy earshot. And, as you know, our worthy Beamish's voice is of a robust and carrying timbre.'

He broke off. Unable to restrain her pent-up feelings any longer, Myrtle Jellaby had uttered the words which the taxi-driver had said to the gendarme, and there was that about them which might well have rendered a tougher curate than Anselm temporarily incapable of speech. A throbbing silence followed the ejaculation. And during this silence there came to their ears from the garden without a curious sound.

'Hark,' said Myrtle.

They listened. What they heard was unmistakably a human being sobbing.

'Some fellow creature in trouble,' said Anselm.

'Thank goodness,' said Myrtle.

'Should we go and ascertain the sufferer's identity?'

'Let's,' said Myrtle. 'I have an idea it may be Joe Beamish. In which case, what I am going to do to him with my parasol will be nobody's business.'

But the mourner was not Joe Beamish, who had long since gone off to the Goose and Grasshopper. To Anselm, who was short-sighted, the figure leaning against the cedar-tree, shaking with uncontrollable sobs, was indistinct and unrecognizable, but Myrtle, keener-eyed, uttered a cry of surprise.

'Uncle!'

'Uncle?' said Anselm, astonished.

'It is Uncle Leopold.'

'Yes,' said the O.B.E., choking down a groan and moving away from the tree, 'it is I. Is that Mulliner standing beside you, Myrtle?'

'Yes.'

'Mulliner,' said Sir Leopold Jellaby, 'you find me in tears. And why am I in tears? Because, my dear Mulliner, I am still overwhelmed by that wonderful sermon of yours on Brotherly Love and our duty to our neighbours.'

Anselm began to wonder if ever a curate had had notices like these.

'Oh, thanks,' he said, shuffling a foot. 'Awfully glad you liked it.'

' "Liked it", Mulliner, is a weak term. That sermon has revolutionized my entire outlook. It has made me a different man. I wonder, Mulliner, if you can find me pen and ink inside the house?'

'Pen and ink?'

'Precisely. I wish to write you a cheque for ten thousand pounds for that stamp collection of yours.'

'Ten thousand!'

'Come inside,' said Myrtle. 'Come right in.'

'You see,' said Sir Leopold, as they led him to the study and plied him with many an eager query as to whether he preferred a thick nib or a thin, 'when you showed me those stamps yesterday, I recognized their value immediately – they would fetch five thousand pounds anywhere – so I naturally told you they were worthless. It was one of those ordinary, routine business precautions which a man is bound to take. One of the first things I remember my dear father saying to me, when he sent me out to battle with the world, was "Never give a sucker an even break," and until now I have always striven not to do so. But your sermon tonight has made me see that there is something higher and nobler than a code of business ethics. Shall I cross the cheque?'

'If you please.'

'No,' said Myrtle. 'Make it open.'

'Just as you say, my dear. You appear,' said the kind old squire, smiling archly through his tears, 'to be showing considerable interest in the matter. Am I to infer –'

'I love Anselm. We are engaged.'

'Mulliner! Is this so?'

'Er – yes,' said Anselm. 'I was meaning to tell you about that.'

Sir Leopold patted him on the shoulder.

'I could wish her no better husband. There. There is your cheque, Mulliner. The collection, as I say, is worth five thousand pounds, but after that sermon, I give ten freely – freely!'

Anselm, like one in a dream, took the oblong slip of paper

115

and put it in his pocket. Silently, he handed the album to Sir Leopold.

'Thank you,' said the latter. 'And now, my dear fellow, I think I shall have to ask you for the loan of a clean pocket handkerchief. My own, as you see, is completely saturated.'

It was while Anselm was in his room, rummaging in the chest of drawers, that a light footstep caused him to turn. Myrtle was standing in the doorway, a finger on her lip.

'Anselm,' she whispered, 'have you a fountain pen?'

'Certainly, dearest. There should be one in this drawer. Yes, here it is. You wish to write something?'

'I wish you to write something. Endorse that cheque here and now, and give it to me, and I will motor to London tonight in my two-seater, so as to be at the bank the moment it opens and deposit. You see, I know Uncle Leopold. He might take it into his head, after he had slept on it and that sermon had worn off a bit, to 'phone and stop payment. You know how he feels about business precautions. This way we shall avoid all rannygazoo.'

Anselm kissed her fondly.

'You think of everything, dearest,' he said. 'How right you are. One does so wish, does one not, to avoid rannygazoo.'

Eggs, Beans and Crumpets (1940)

Militant Poet

Ricky, in addition to being a poet and a boxer, was also nephew of a Duke.

'Ricky said he was going to look in today and break my neck.'

'I didn't know poets broke people's necks.'

'Ricky does. He once took on three simultaneous coster-mongers in Covent Garden and cleaned them up in five minutes. He had gone there to get inspiration for a pastoral, and they started chi-iking him, and he sailed in and knocked them base over apex into a pile of Brussels sprouts.'

'How different from the home life of the late Lord Tennyson.'

Uncle Fred in the Springtime (1939)

Gussie Presents the Prizes

*For reasons too complicated to explain here, Gussie
Fink-Nottle, Bertie's newt-fancying and ('either through a
hereditary taint or because he had promised his mother he
wouldn't') teetotal friend, faces the prospect of presenting the
prizes at the end-of-term rally at Market Snodsbury Grammar
School, of which Bertie's good Aunt Dahlia, Mrs Tom Travers,
is a Governor. To add to his misery, Gussie has recently failed
in his attempt to propose to Madeline Bassett. Bertie, always
keen to solve other people's difficulties, thinks that alcohol,
surreptitiously laced into Gussie's orange juice, will make a
temporary man of him and help him to win through in both
directions. Jeeves isn't so keen on the idea as Bertie is.*

Everything was in train. Jeeves's morbid scruples about lacing
the chap's orange juice had put me to a good deal of trouble,
but I had surmounted every obstacle in the old Wooster way.
I had secured an abundance of the necessary spirit, and it was
now lying in its flask in the drawer of the dressing-table. I had
also ascertained that the jug, duly filled, would be standing on
a shelf in the butler's pantry round about the hour of one. To
remove it from that shelf, sneak it up to my room, and return
it, laced, in good time for the midday meal would be a task
calling, no doubt, for address, but in no sense an exacting one.

It was with something of the emotions of one preparing for
a treat for a deserving child that I finished my tea and rolled
over for that extra spot of sleep which just makes all the difference when there is man's work to be done and the brain must
be kept clear for it.

And when I came downstairs an hour or so later, I knew how

right I had been to formulate this scheme for Gussie's bucking up. I ran into him on the lawn, and I could see at a glance that if ever there was a man who needed a snappy stimulant, it was he. All nature, as I have indicated, was smiling, but not Augustus Fink-Nottle. He was walking round in circles, muttering something about not proposing to detain us long, but on this auspicious occasion feeling compelled to say a few words.

'Ah, Gussie,' I said, arresting him as he was about to start another lap. 'A lovely morning, is it not?'

Even if I had not been aware of it already, I could have divined from the abruptness with which he damned the lovely morning that he was not in merry mood. I addressed myself to the task of bringing the roses back into his cheeks.

'I've got good news for you, Gussie.'

He looked at me with a sudden sharp interest.

'Has Market Snodsbury Grammar School burned down?'

'Not that I know of.'

'Have mumps broken out? Is the place closed on account of measles?'

'No, no.'

'Then what do you mean you've got good news?'

I endeavoured to soothe.

'You mustn't take it so hard, Gussie. Why worry about a laughably simple job like distributing prizes at a school?'

'Laughably simple, eh? Do you realize I've been sweating for days and haven't been able to think of something to say yet, except that I won't detain them long. You bet I won't detain them long. I've been timing my speech, and it lasts five seconds. What the devil am I to say, Bertie? What do you say when you're distributing prizes?'

I considered. Once, at my private school, I had won a prize for Scripture knowledge, so I suppose I ought to have been full of inside stuff. But memory eluded me.

Then something emerged from the mists.

'You say the race is not always to the swift.'

'Why?'

'Well, it's a good gag. It generally gets a hand.'

'I mean, why isn't it? Why isn't the race to the swift?'

'Ah, there you have me. But the nibs say it isn't.'

'But what does it mean?'

'I take it it's supposed to console the chaps who haven't won prizes.'

'What's the good of that to me? I'm not worrying about them. It's the ones that have won prizes that I'm worrying about, the little blighters who will come up on the platform. Suppose they make faces at me.'

'They won't.'

'How do you know they won't? It's probably the first thing they'll think of. And even if they don't – Bertie, shall I tell you something?'

'What?'

'I've a good mind to take that tip of yours and have a drink.'

I smiled. He little knew, about summed up what I was thinking.

'Oh, you'll be all right,' I said.

He became fevered again.

'How do you know I'll be all right? I'm sure to blow up in my lines.'

'Tush!'

'Or drop a prize.'

'Tut!'

'Or something. I can feel it in my bones. As sure as I'm standing here, something is going to happen this afternoon which will make everybody laugh themselves sick at me. I can hear them now. Like hyenas . . . Bertie!'

'Hullo?'

'Do you remember that kids' school we went to before Eton?'

'Quite. It was there I won my Scripture prize.'

'Never mind about your Scripture prize. I'm not talking about your Scripture prize. Do you recollect the Bosher incident?'

I did, indeed. It was one of the high spots of my youth.

'Major-General Sir Wilfred Bosher came to distribute the

prizes at that school,' proceeded Gussie in a dull, toneless voice. 'He dropped a book. He stooped to pick it up. And, as he stooped, his trousers split up the back.'

'How we roared!'

Gussie's face twisted.

'We did, little swine that we were. Instead of remaining silent and exhibiting a decent sympathy for a gallant officer at a peculiarly embarrassing moment, we howled and yelled with mirth. I loudest of any. That is what will happen to me this afternoon, Bertie. It will be a judgement on me for laughing like that at Major-General Sir Wilfred Bosher.'

'No, no, Gussie, old man. Your trousers won't split.'

'How do you know they won't? Better men than I have split their trousers. General Bosher was a D.S.O., with a fine record of service on the north-western frontier of India, and his trousers split. I shall be a mockery and a scorn. I know it. And you, fully cognizant of what I am in for, babbling about good news. What news could possibly be good to me at this moment except the information that bubonic plague had broken out among the scholars of Market Snodsbury Grammar School, and that they were all confined to their beds with spots?'

The moment had come for me to speak. I laid a hand gently on his shoulder. He brushed it off. I laid it on again. He brushed it off once more. I was endeavouring to lay it on for the third time, when he moved aside and desired, with a certain petulance, to be informed if I thought I was a ruddy osteopath.

I found his manner trying, but one has to make allowances. I was telling myself that I should be seeing a very different Gussie after lunch.

'When I said I had good news, old man, I meant about Madeline Bassett.'

The febrile gleam died out of his eyes, to be replaced by a look of infinite sadness.

'You can't have good news about her. I've dished myself there completely.'

'Not at all. I am convinced that if you take another whack at her, all will be well.'

And, keeping it snappy, I related what had passed between the Bassett and myself on the previous night.

'So all you have to do is play a return date, and you cannot fail to swing the voting. You are her dream man.'

He shook his head.

'No.'

'What?'

'No use.'

'What do you mean?'

'Not a bit of good trying.'

'But I tell you she said so in so many words –'

'It doesn't make any difference. She may have loved me once. Last night will have killed all that.'

'Of course it won't.'

'It will. She despises me now.'

'Not a bit of it. She knows you simply got cold feet.'

'And I should get cold feet if I tried again. It's no good, Bertie. I'm hopeless, and there's an end of it. Fate made me the sort of chap who can't say "bo" to a goose.'

'It isn't a question of saying "bo" to a goose. The point doesn't arise at all. It is simply a matter of –'

'I know, I know. But it's no good. I can't do it. The whole thing is off. I am not going to risk a repetition of last night's fiasco. You talk in a light way of taking another whack at her, but you don't know what it means. You have not been through the experience of starting to ask the girl you love to marry you and then suddenly finding yourself talking about the plumlike external gills of the newly-born newt. It's not a thing you can do twice. No, I accept my destiny. It's all over. And now, Bertie, like a good chap, shove off. I want to compose my speech. I can't compose my speech with you mucking around. If you are going to continue to muck around, at least give me a couple of stories. The little hell hounds are sure to expect a story or two.'

'Do you know the one about –'

'No good. I don't want any of your off-colour stuff from the Drones' smoking-room. I need something clean. Something that will be a help to them in their after lives. Not that I care a damn about their after lives, except that I hope they'll all choke.'

'I heard a story the other day. I can't quite remember it, but it was about a chap who snored and disturbed the neighbours, and it ended, "It was his adenoids that adenoid them." '

He made a weary gesture.

'You expect me to work that in, do you, into a speech to be delivered to an audience of boys, every one of whom is probably riddled with adenoids? Damn it, they'd rush the platform. Leave me, Bertie. Push off. That's all I ask you to do. Push off ... Ladies and gentlemen,' said Gussie, in a low, soliloquizing sort of way, 'I do not propose to detain this auspicious occasion long –'

It was a thoughtful Wooster who walked away and left him at it. More than ever I was congratulating myself on having had the sterling good sense to make all my arrangements so that I could press a button and set the things moving at an instant's notice.

Until now, you see, I had rather entertained a sort of hope that when I had revealed to him the Bassett's mental attitude, Nature would have done the rest, bracing him up to such an extent that artificial stimulants would not be required. Because, naturally, a chap doesn't want to have to sprint about country houses lugging jugs of orange juice, unless it is absolutely essential.

But now I saw that I must carry on as planned. The total absence of pep, ginger, and the right spirit which the man had displayed during these conversational exchanges convinced me that the strongest measure would be necessary. Immediately upon leaving him, therefore, I proceeded to the pantry, waited till the butler had removed himself elsewhere, and nipped in and secured the vital jug. A few moments later, after a wary passage of the stairs, I was in my room. And the first thing I saw there was Jeeves, fooling about with trousers.

He gave the jug a look which – wrongly, as it was to turn out

– I diagnosed as censorious. I drew myself up a bit. I intended
to have no rot from the fellow.

'Yes, Jeeves?'

'Sir?'

'You have the air of one about to make a remark, Jeeves.'

'Oh, no, sir. I note that you are in possession of Mr Fink-
Nottle's orange juice. I was merely about to observe that in my
opinion it would be injudicious to add spirit to it.'

'That is a remark, Jeeves, and it is precisely –'

'Because I have already attended to the matter, sir.'

'What?'

'Yes, sir. I decided, after all, to acquiesce in your wishes.'

I stared at the man, astounded. I was deeply moved. Well, I
mean, wouldn't any chap who had been going about thinking
that the old feudal spirit was dead and then suddenly found it
wasn't, have been deeply moved?

'Jeeves,' I said, 'I am touched.'

'Thank you, sir.'

'Touched and gratified.'

'Thank you very much, sir.'

'But what caused this change of heart?'

'I chanced to encounter Mr Fink-Nottle in the garden, sir,
while you were still in bed, and we had a brief conversation.'

'And you came away feeling that he needed a bracer?'

'Very much so, sir. His attitude struck me as defeatist.'

I nodded.

'I felt the same. "Defeatist" sums it up to a nicety. Did you
tell him his attitude struck you as defeatist?'

'Yes, sir.'

'But it didn't do any good?'

'No, sir.'

'Very well, then, Jeeves. We must act. How much gin did you
put in the jug?'

'A liberal tumblerful, sir.'

'Would that be a normal dose for an adult defeatist, do you
think?'

'I fancy it should prove adequate, sir.'

'I wonder. We must not spoil the ship for a ha'porth of tar. I think I'll add just another fluid ounce or so.'

'I would not advocate it, sir. In the case of Lord Brancaster's parrot –'

'You are falling into your old error, Jeeves, of thinking that Gussie is a parrot. Fight against this. I shall add the oz.'

'Very good, sir.'

'And, by the way, Jeeves, Mr Fink-Nottle is in the market for bright, clean stories to use in his speech. Do you know any?'

'I know a story about two Irishmen, sir.'

'Pat and Mike?'

'Yes, sir.'

'Who were walking along Broadway?'

'Yes, sir.'

'Just what he wants. Any more?'

'No, sir.'

'Well, every little helps. You had better go and tell it to him.'

'Very good, sir.'

He passed from the room, and I unscrewed the flask and tilted into the jug a generous modicum of its contents. And scarcely had I done so, when there came to my ears the sound of footsteps without. I had only just time to shove the jug behind the photograph of Uncle Tom on the mantelpiece before the door opened and in came Gussie, curveting like a circus horse.

'What-ho, Bertie,' he said. 'What-ho, what-ho, what-ho, and again what-ho. What a beautiful world this is, Bertie. One of the nicest I ever met.'

I stared at him speechless. We Woosters are as quick as lightning, and I saw at once that something had happened.

I mean to say, I told you about him walking round in circles. I recorded what passed between us on the lawn. And if I portrayed the scene with anything like adequate skill, the picture you will have retained of this Fink-Nottle will have been that of a nervous wreck, sagging at the kneees, green about the gills, and picking feverishly at the lapels of his coat in an ecstasy of craven fear. In a word, defeatist. Gussie, during that interview,

125

had, in fine, exhibited all the earmarks of one licked to a custard.

Vastly different was the Gussie who stood before me now. Self-confidence seemed to ooze from the fellow's every pore. His face was flushed, there was a jovial light in his eyes, the lips were parted in a swashbuckling smile. And when with a genial hand he sloshed me on the back before I could sidestep, it was as if I had been kicked by a mule.

'Well, Bertie,' he proceeded, as blithely as a linnet without a thing on his mind, 'you will be glad to hear that you were right. Your theory has been tested and proved correct. I feel like a fighting cock.'

My brain ceased to reel. I saw all.

'Have you been having a drink?'

'I have. As you advised. Unpleasant stuff. Like medicine. Burns your throat, too, and makes one as thirsty as the dickens. How anyone can mop it up, as you do, for pleasure, beats me. Still, I would be the last to deny that it tunes up the system. I could bite a tiger.'

'What did you have?'

'Whisky. At least, that was the label on the decanter, and I have no reason to suppose that a woman like your aunt – staunch, true-blue, British – would deliberately deceive the public. If she labels her decanters Whisky, then I consider that we know where we are.'

'A whisky and soda, eh? You couldn't have done better.'

'Soda?' said Gussie thoughtfully. 'I knew there was something I had forgotten.'

'Didn't you put any soda in it?'

'It never occurred to me. I just nipped into the dining-room and drank out of the decanter.'

'How much?'

'Oh, about ten swallows. Twelve, maybe. Or fourteen. Say sixteen medium-sized gulps. Gosh, I'm thirsty.'

He moved over to the wash-stand and drank deeply out of the water bottle. I cast a covert glance at Uncle Tom's photograph behind his back. For the first time since it had come into my life, I was glad that it was so large. It hid its secret well. If Gussie had caught sight of that jug of orange juice, he would unquestionably have been on to it like a knife.

'Well, I'm glad you're feeling braced,' I said.

He moved buoyantly from the wash-stand, and endeavoured to slosh me on the back again. Foiled by my nimble footwork, he staggered to the bed and sat down upon it.

'Braced? Did I say I could bite a tiger?'

'You did.'

'Make it two tigers. I could chew holes in a steel door. What an ass you must have thought me out there in the garden. I see now you were laughing in your sleeve.'

'No, no.'

'Yes,' insisted Gussie. 'That very sleeve,' he said, pointing. 'And I don't blame you. I can't imagine why I made all that fuss about a potty job like distributing prizes at a rotten little country grammar school. Can you imagine, Bertie?'

'No.'

'Exactly. Nor can I imagine. There's simply nothing to it. I just shin up on the platform, drop a few gracious words, hand the little blighters their prizes, and hop down again, admired by all. Not a suggestion of split trousers from start to finish. I mean, why should anybody split his trousers? I can't imagine. Can you imagine?'

'No.'

'Nor can I imagine. I shall be a riot. I know just the sort of stuff that's needed – simple, manly, optimistic stuff straight from the shoulder. This shoulder,' said Gussie, tapping. 'Why I was so nervous this morning I can't imagine. For anything simpler than distributing a few footling books to a bunch of grimy-faced kids I can't imagine. Still, for some reason I can't imagine, I was feeling a little nervous, but now I feel fine, Bertie – fine, fine, fine – and I say this to you as an old friend. Because that's what you are, old man, when all the smoke has cleared away – an old friend. I don't think I've ever met an older friend. How long have you been an old friend of mine, Bertie?'

'Oh, years and years.'

'Imagine! Though, of course, there must have been a time when you were a new friend ... Hullo, the luncheon gong. Come on, old friend.'

And, rising from the bed like a performing flea, he made for the door.

I followed rather pensively. What had occurred was, of course, so much velvet, as you might say. I mean, I had wanted a braced Fink-Nottle – indeed, all my plans had had a braced Fink-Nottle as their end and aim – but I found myself wondering a little whether the Fink-Nottle now sliding down the banister wasn't, perhaps, a shade too braced. His demeanour seemed to me that of a man who might quite easily throw bread about at lunch.

Fortunately, however, the settled gloom of those around him exercised a restraining effect upon him at the table. It would have needed a far more plastered man to have been rollicking at such a gathering. I had told the Bassett that there were aching hearts in Brinkley Court, and it now looked probable that there would shortly be aching tummies. Anatole, I learned, had retired to his bed with a fit of the vapours, and the meal now before us had been cooked by the kitchen maid – as C3 a performer as ever wielded a skillet.

This, coming on top of their other troubles, induced in the company a pretty unanimous silence – a solemn silence, as you might say – which even Gussie did not seem prepared to break. Except, therefore, for one short snatch of song on his part, nothing untoward marked the occasion, and presently we rose, with instructions from Aunt Dahlia to put on festal raiment and be at Market Snodsbury not later than 3.30. This leaving me ample time to smoke a gasper or two in a shady bower beside the lake, I did so, repairing to my room round about the hour of three.

Jeeves was on the job, adding the final polish to the old topper, and I was about to appraise him of the latest developments in the matter of Gussie, when he forestalled me by observing that the latter had only just concluded an agreeable visit to the Wooster bed-chamber.

'I found Mr Fink-Nottle seated here when I arrived to lay out your clothes, sir.'

'Indeed, Jeeves? Gussie was in here, was he?'

'Yes, sir. He left only a few moments ago. He's driving to the school with Mr and Mrs Travers in the large car.'

'Did you give him your story of the two Irishmen?'

'Yes, sir. He laughed heartily.'

'Good. Had you any other contributions for him?'

'I ventured to suggest that he might mention to the young gentlemen that education is a drawing out, not a putting in. The late Lord Brancaster was much addicted to presenting prizes at schools, and he invariably employed this dictum.'

'And how did he react to that?'

'He laughed heartily, sir.'

'This surprised you, no doubt? This practically incessant merriment, I mean.'

'Yes, sir.'

'You thought it odd in one who, when you last saw him, was well up in Group A of the defeatists.'

'Yes, sir.'

'There is a ready explanation, Jeeves. Since you last saw him, Gussie has been on a bender. He's as tight as an owl.'

'Indeed, sir?'

'Absolutely. His nerve cracked under the strain, and he sneaked into the dining-room and started mopping the stuff up like a vacuum cleaner. Whisky would seem to be what he filled the radiator with. I gather that he used up most of the decanter. Golly, Jeeves, it's lucky he didn't get at that laced orange juice on top of that, what?'

'Extremely, sir.'

I eyed the jug. Uncle Tom's photograph had fallen into the fender, and it was standing there right out in the open, where Gussie couldn't have helped seeing it. Mercifully, it was empty now.

'It was a most prudent act on your part, if I may say so, sir, to dispose of the orange juice.'

I stared at the man.

129

'What? Didn't you?'

'No, sir.'

'Jeeves, let us get this clear. Was it not you who threw away that o.j.?'

'No, sir. I assumed, when I entered the room and found the pitcher empty, that you had done so.'

We looked at each other, awed. Two minds with but a single thought.

'I very much fear, sir –'

'So do I, Jeeves.'

'It would seem almost certain –'

'Quite certain. Weigh the facts. Sift the evidence. The jug was standing on the mantelpiece, for all eyes to behold. Gussie had been complaining of thirst. You found him in here, laughing heartily. I think that there can be little doubt, Jeeves, that the entire contents of that jug are at this moment reposing on top of the existing cargo in that already brilliantly lit man's interior. Disturbing, Jeeves.'

'Most disturbing, sir.'

'Let us face the position, forcing ourselves to be calm. You inserted in that jug – shall we say a tumblerful of the right stuff?'

'Fully a tumblerful, sir.'

'And I added of my plenty about the same amount.'

'Yes, sir.'

'And in two shakes of a duck's tail Gussie, with all that lapping about inside him, will be distributing the prizes at Market Snodsbury Grammar School before an audience of all that is fairest and most refined in the country.'

'Yes, sir.'

'It seems to me, Jeeves, that the ceremony may be one fraught with considerable interest.'

'Yes, sir.'

'What, in your opinion, will the harvest be?'

'One finds it difficult to hazard a conjecture, sir.'

'You mean imagination boggles?'

'Yes, sir.'

130

I inspected my imagination. He was right. It boggled.

'And yet, Jeeves,' I said, twiddling a thoughtful steering wheel, 'there is always the bright side.'

Some twenty minutes had elapsed, and having picked the honest fellow up outside the front door, I was driving in the two-seater to the picturesque town of Market Snodsbury. Since we had parted – he to go to his lair and fetch his hat, I to remain in my room and complete the formal costume – I had been doing some close thinking.

The results of this I now proceeded to hand on to him.

'However dark the prospect may be, Jeeves, however murkily the storm clouds may seem to gather, a keen eye can usually discern the blue bird. It is bad, no doubt, that Gussie should be going, some ten minutes from now, to distribute prizes in a state of advanced intoxication, but we must never forget that these things cut both ways.'

'You imply, sir –'

'Precisely. I am thinking of him in his capacity of wooer. All this ought to have put him in rare shape for offering his hand in marriage. I shall be vastly surprised if it won't turn him into a sort of caveman. Have you ever seen James Cagney in the movies?'

'Yes, sir.'

'Something on those lines.'

I heard him cough, and sniped him with a sideways glance. He was wearing that informative look of his.

'Then you have not heard, sir?'

'Eh?'

'You are not aware that a marriage has been arranged and will shortly take place between Mr Fink-Nottle and Miss Bassett?'

'What?'

'Yes, sir.'

'When did this happen?'

'Shortly after Mr Fink-Nottle had left your room, sir.'

'Ah! In the post-orange-juice era?'

131

'Yes, sir.'

'But are you sure of your facts? How do you know?'

'My informant was Mr Fink-Nottle himself, sir. He appeared anxious to confide in me. His story was somewhat incoherent, but I had no difficulty in apprehending its substance. Prefacing his remarks with the statement that this was a beautiful world, he laughed heartily and said that he became formally engaged.'

'No details?'

'No, sir.'

'But one can picture the scene.'

'Yes, sir.'

'I mean, imagination doesn't boggle.'

'No, sir.'

And it didn't. I could see exactly what must have happened. Insert a liberal dose of mixed spirits in a normally abstemious man, and he becomes a force. He does not stand around, twiddling his fingers and stammering. He acts. I had no doubt that Gussie must have reached for the Bassett and clasped her to him like a stevedore handling a sack of coals. And one could readily envisage the effect of that sort of thing on a girl of romantic mind.

'Well, well, well, Jeeves.'

'Yes, sir.'

'This is splendid news.'

'Yes, sir.'

'You see now how right I was.'

'Yes, sir.'

'It must have been rather an eye-opener for you, watching me handle this case.'

'Yes, sir.'

'The simple, direct method never fails.'

'No, sir.'

'Whereas the elaborate does.'

'Yes, sir.'

'Right-ho, Jeeves.'

We had arrived at Market Snodsbury Grammar School. It

had, I understood, been built somewhere in the year 1416, and as with so many of these ancient foundations, there still seemed to brood over its Great Hall, where the afternoon's festivities were to take place, not a little of the fug of the centuries. It was the hottest day of the summer, and though somebody had opened a tentative window or two, the atmosphere remained distinctive and individual.

In this hall the youth of Market Snodsbury had been eating its daily lunch for a matter of five hundred years, and the flavour lingered. The air was sort of heavy and languorous, if you know what I mean, with the scent of Young England and boiled beef and carrots.

Aunt Dahlia, who was sitting with a bevy of the local nibs in the second row, sighted me as I entered and waved to me to join her, but I was too smart for that. I wedged myself in among the standees at the back, leaning up against a chap who, from the aroma, might have been a corn chandler or something on that order. The essence of strategy on these occasions is to be as near the door as possible.

The hall was gaily decorated with flags and coloured paper, and the eye was further refreshed by the spectacle of a mixed drove of boys, parents, and what not, the former running a good deal to shiny faces and Eton collars, the latter stressing the black-satin note rather when female, and looking as if their coats were too tight, if male. And presently there was some applause – sporadic, Jeeves has since told me it was – and I saw Gussie being steered by a bearded bloke in a gown to a seat in the middle of the platform.

And I confess that as I beheld him and felt that there but for the grace of God went Bertram Wooster, a shudder ran through the frame. It all reminded me so vividly of the time I had addressed that girls' school.

Of course, looking at it dispassionately, you may say that for horror and peril there is no comparison between an almost human audience like the one before me and a mob of small girls with pig-tails down their backs, and this, I concede, is true. Nevertheless, the spectacle was enough to make me feel like a fellow watching a pal going over Niagara Falls in a barrel, and the thought of what I had escaped caused everything for a moment to go black and swim before my eyes.

When I was able to see clearly once more, I perceived that Gussie was now seated. He had his hands on his knees, with his elbows out at right angles, like a nigger minstrel of the old school about to ask Mr Bones why a chicken crosses the road, and he was staring before him with a smile so fixed and pebble-beached that I should have thought that anybody could have guessed that there sat one in whom the old familiar juice was plashing up against the back of the front teeth.

In fact, I saw Aunt Dahlia, who, having assisted at so many hunting dinners in her time, is second to none as a judge of the symptoms, give a start and gaze long and earnestly. And she was just saying something to Uncle Tom on her left when the bearded bloke stepped to the footlights and started making a speech. From the fact that he spoke as if he had a hot potato in his mouth without getting the raspberry from the lads in the ringside seats. I deduced that he must be the head master.

With his arrival in the spotlight, a sort of perspiring resigna-. tion seemed to settle on the audience. Personally, I snuggled up against the chandler and let my attention wander. The speech was on the subject of the doings of the school during the past term, and this part of a prize-giving is always apt to fail to grip the visiting stranger. I mean, you know how it is. You're told that J. B. Brewster has won an Exhibition for Classics at Cat's, Cambridge, and you feel that it's one of those stories where you can't see how funny it is unless you really know the fellow. And the same applies to G. Bullett being awarded the Lady Jane Wix Scholarship at the Birmingham College of Veterinary Science.

In fact, I and the corn chandler, who was looking a bit fagged I thought, as if he had had a hard morning chandling the corn, were beginning to doze lightly when things suddenly brisked up, bringing Gussie into the picture for the first time.

'Today,' said the bearded bloke, 'we are happy to welcome as the guest of the afternoon Mr Fitz-Wattle –'

At the beginning of the address, Gussie had subsided into a sort of daydream, with his mouth hanging open. About half-way through, faint signs of life had begun to show. And for the last few minutes he had been trying to cross one leg over the other and failing and having another shot and failing again. But only now did he exhibit any real animation. He sat up with a jerk.

'Fink-Nottle,' he said, opening his eyes.

'Fitz-Nottle.'

'Fink-Nottle.' .

'I should say Fink-Nottle.'

'Of course you should, you silly ass,' said Gussie genially. 'All right, get on with it.'

And closing his eyes, he began trying to cross his legs again.

I could see that this little spot of friction had rattled the bearded bloke a bit. He stood for a moment of fumbling at the fungus with a hesitating hand. But they make these head masters of tough stuff. The weakness passed. He came back nicely and carried on.

'We are all happy, I say, to welcome as the guest of the afternoon Mr Fink-Nottle, who has kindly consented to award the prizes. This task, as you know, is one that should have de-volved upon that well-beloved and vigorous member of our board of governors, the Rev. William Plomer, and we are all, I am sure, very sorry that illness at the last moment should have prevented him from being here today. But, if I may borrow a familiar metaphor from the – if I may employ a homely meta-phor familiar to you all – what we lose on the swings we gain on the roundabouts.'

He paused, and beamed rather freely, to show that this was comedy. I could have told the man it was no use. Not a ripple. The corn chandler leaned against me and muttered 'Whoddid-esay?' but that was all.

It's always a nasty jar to wait for the laugh and find that the gag hasn't got across. The bearded bloke was visibly discom-posed. At that, however, I think he would have got by, had he not, at this juncture, unfortunately stirred Gussie up again.

'In other words, though deprived of Mr Plomer, we have with us this afternoon Mr Fink-Nottle. I am sure Mr Fink-Nottle's name is one that needs no introduction to you. It is, I venture to assert, a name that is familiar to us all.'

'Not to you,' said Gussie.

And the next moment I saw what Jeeves had meant when he had described him as laughing heartily. 'Heartily' was absolutely the *mot juste*. It sounded like a gas explosion.

'You didn't seem to know it so dashed well, what, what?' said Gussie. And, reminded apparently by the word 'what' of the word 'Wattle,' he repeated the latter some sixteen times with a rising inflection.

'Wattle, Wattle, Wattle,' he concluded. 'Right-ho. Push on.'

But the bearded bloke had shot his bolt. He stood there, licked at last; and, watching him closely, I could see that he was now at the crossroads. I could spot what he was thinking as clearly as if he had confided it to my personal ear. He wanted to sit down and call it a day, I mean, but the thought that gave him pause was that, if he did, he must then either uncork Gussie or take the Fink-Nottle speech as read and get straight on to the actual prize-giving.

It was a dashed tricky thing, of course, to have to decide on the spur of the moment. I was reading in the paper the other day about those birds who are trying to split the atom, the nub being that they haven't the foggiest as to what will happen if they do. It may be all right. On the other hand, it may not be all right. And pretty silly a chap would feel, no doubt, if, having split the atom, he suddenly found the house going up in smoke and himself torn limb from limb.

So with the bearded bloke. Whether he was abreast of the inside facts in Gussie's case, I don't know, but it was obvious to him by this time that he had run into something pretty hot. Trial gallops had shown that Gussie had his own way of doing things. Those interruptions had been enough to prove to the perspicacious that here, seated on the platform at the big binge of the season, was one who, if pushed forward to make a speech, might let himself go in a rather epoch-making manner.

On the other hand, chain him up and put a green-baize cloth

over him, and where were you? The proceeding would be over about half an hour too soon.

It was, as I say, a difficult problem to have to solve, and, left to himself, I don't know what conclusion he would have come to. Personally, I think he would have played it safe. As it happened, however, the thing was taken out of his hands, for at this moment, Gussie, having stretched out his arms and yawned a bit, switched on that pebble-beached smile again and tacked down to the edge of the platform.

'Speech,' he said affably.

He then stood with his thumbs in the armholes of his waist-coat, waiting for the applause to die down.

It was some time before this happened, for he had got a very fine hand indeed. I suppose it wasn't often that the boys of Market Snodsbury Grammar Schoool came across a man public-spirited enough to call their head master a silly ass, and they showed their appreciation in no uncertain manner. Gussie may have been one over the eight, but as far as the majority of those present were concerned he was sitting on top of the world.

'Boys,' said Gussie, 'I mean ladies and gentlemen and boys, I do not detain you long, but I suppose on this occasion to feel compelled to say a few auspicious words. Ladies – and boys and gentlemen – we have all listened with interest to the remarks of our friend here who forgot to shave this morning – I don't know his name, but then he didn't know mine – Fitz-Wattle, I mean, absolutely absurd – which squares things up a bit – and we are all sorry that the Reverend What-ever-he-was-called should be dying of adenoids, but after all, here today, gone tomorrow, and all flesh is as grass, and what not, but that wasn't what I wanted to say. What I wanted to say was this – and I say it confidently – without fear of contradiction – I say, in short, I am happy to be here on this auspicious occasion and I take much pleasure in kindly awarding the prizes, consisting of the handsome books you see laid out on that table. As Shakespeare says, there are sermons in books, stones in the running brooks, or, rather, the other way about, and there you have it in a nut-shell.'

It went well, and I wasn't surprised. I couldn't quite follow some of it, but anybody could see that it was real ripe stuff, and I was amazed that even the course of treatment he had been taking could have rendered so normally tongue-tied a dumb brick as Gussie capable of it.

It just shows, what any member of Parliament will tell you, that if you want real oratory, the preliminary noggin is essential. Unless pie-eyed, you cannot hope to grip.

'Gentlemen,' said Gussie, 'I mean ladies and gentlemen and, of course, boys, what a beautiful world this is. A beautiful world, full of happiness on every side. Let me tell you a little story. Two Irishmen, Pat and Mike, were walking along Broadway, and one said to the other, 'Begorrah, the race is not always to the swift,'' and the other replied, ''Faith and begob, education is a drawing out, not a putting in.'' '

I must say it seemed to me the rottenest story I had ever heard, and I was surprised that Jeeves should have considered it worth while shoving into a speech. However, when I taxed him with this later, he said that Gussie had altered the plot a good deal, and I dare say that accounts for it.

At any rate, that was the *conte* as Gussie told it, and when I say that it got a very fair laugh, you will understand what a popular figure he had become with the multitude. There might be a bearded bloke or so on the platform and a small section in the second row who were wishing the speaker would conclude his remarks and resume his seat, but the audience as a whole was for him solidly.

There was applause, and a voice cried: 'Hear, hear!'

'Yes,' said Gussie, 'it is a beautiful world. The sky is blue, the birds are singing, there is optimism everywhere. And why not, boys and ladies and gentlemen? I'm happy, you're happy, we're all happy, even the meanest Irishman that walks along Broadway. Though, as I say, there were two of them – Pat and Mike, one drawing out, the other putting in. I should like you boys, taking the time from me, to give three cheers for this beautiful world. All together, now.'

Presently the dust settled down and the plaster stopped falling from the ceiling, and he went on.

'People who say it isn't a beautiful world don't know what they are talking about. Driving here in the car today to award the kind prizes, I was reluctantly compelled to tick off my host on this very point. Old Tom Travers. You will see him sitting there in the second row next to the large lady in beige.'

He pointed helpfully, and the hundred or so Market Snodsburyians who craned their necks in the direction indicated were able to observe Uncle Tom blushing prettily.

'I ticked him off properly, the poor fish. He expressed the opinion that the world was in a deplorable state. I said, "Don't talk rot, old Tom Travers." "I am not accustomed to talk rot," he said. "Then, for a beginner," I said, "you do it dashed well." And I think you will admit, boys and ladies and gentlemen, that was telling him.'

The audience seemed to agree with him. The point went big. The voice that had said, 'Hear, hear,' said 'Hear, hear' again, and my corn chandler hammered the floor vigorously with a large-size walking stick.

'Well, boys,' resumed Gussie, having shot his cuffs and smirked horribly, 'this is the end of the summer term, and many of you, no doubt, are leaving the school. And I don't blame you, because there's a froust in here you could cut with a knife. You are going out into the great world. Soon many of you will be walking along Broadway. And what I want to impress upon you is that, however much you may suffer from adenoids, you must all use every effort to prevent yourselves becoming pessimists and talking rot like old Tom Travers. There in the second row. The fellow with a face rather like a walnut.'

He paused to allow those wishing to do so to refresh themselves with another look at Uncle Tom, and I found myself musing in some little perplexity. Long association with the members of the Drones has put me pretty well in touch with the various ways in which an overdose of the blushful Hippocrene can take the individual, but I had never seen anyone react quite as Gussie was doing.

There was a snap about his work which I had never witnessed

139

before, even in Barmy Fotheringay-Phipps on New Year's Eve.

Jeeves, when I discussed the matter with him later, said it was something to do with inhibitions, if I caught the word correctly, and the suppression of, I think he said, the ego. What he meant, I gathered, was that, owing to the fact that Gussie had just completed a five years' stretch of blameless seclusion among the newts, all the goofiness which ought to have been spread out thin over those five years and had been bottled up during that period came to the surface on this occasion in a lump – or, if you prefer to put it that way, like a tidal wave.

There may be something in this. Jeeves generally knows.

Anyway, be that as it may, I was dashed glad I had had the shrewdness to keep out of that second row. It might be unworthy of the prestige of a Wooster to squash in among the proletariat in the standing-room-only section, but at least, I felt, I was out of the danger zone. So thoroughly had Gussie got it up his nose by now that it seemed to me that had he sighted me he might have become personal about even an old school friend.

'If there's one thing in the world I can't stand,' proceeded Gussie, 'it's a pessimist. Be optimists, boys. You all know the difference between an optimist and a pessimist. An optimist is a man who – well, take the case of two Irishmen, walking along Broadway. One is an optimist and one is a pessimist, just as one's name is Pat and the other Mike . . . Why, hullo, Bertie; I didn't know you were here.'

Too late, I endeavoured to go to earth behind the chandler, only to discover that there was no chandler there. Some appointment, suddenly remembered – possibly a promise to his wife that he would be home to tea – had caused him to ooze away while my attention was elsewhere, leaving me right out in the open.

Between me and Gussie, who was now pointing in an offensive manner, there was nothing but a sea of interested faces looking up at me.

'Now, there,' boomed Gussie, continuing to point, 'is an

instance of what I mean. Boys and ladies and gentlemen, take a good look at that object standing up there at the back – morning coat, trousers as worn, quiet grey tie, and carnation in button-hole – you can't miss him. Bertie Wooster, that is, and as foul a pessimist as ever bit a tiger. I tell you I despise that man. And why do I despise him? Because, boys and ladies and gentlemen, he is a pessimist. His attitude is defeatist. When I told him I was going to address you this afternoon, he tried to dissuade me. And do you know why he tried to dissuade me? Because he said my trousers would split up the back.'

The cheers that greeted this were the loudest yet. Anything about splitting trousers went straight to the simple hearts of the young scholars of Market Snodsbury Grammar School. Two in the row in front of me turned purple, and a small lad with freckles seated beside them asked me for my autograph.

'Let me tell you a story about Bertie Wooster.'

A Wooster can stand a good deal, but he cannot stand having his name bandied in a public place. Picking my feet up softly, I was in the very process of executing a quiet sneak for the door, when I perceived that the bearded bloke had at last decided to apply the closure.

Why he hadn't done so before is beyond me. Spell-bound, I take it. And, of course, when a chap is going like a breeze with the public, as Gussie had been, it's not so dashed easy to chip in. However, the prospect of hearing another of Gussie's anecdotes seemed to have done the trick. Rising rather as I had risen from my bench at the beginning of that painful scene with Tuppy in the twilight, he made a leap for the table, snatched up a book and came bearing down on the speaker.

He touched Gussie on the arm, and Gussie, turning sharply and seeing a large bloke with a beard apparently about to bean him with a book, sprang back in an attitude of self-defence.

'Perhaps, as time is getting on, Mr Fink-Nottle, we had better –'

'Oh, ah,' said Gussie, getting the trend. He relaxed. 'The prizes, eh? Of course, yes. Right-ho. Yes, might as well be shoving along with it. What's this one?'

'Spelling and dictation – P. K. Purvis,' announced the bearded bloke.

'Spelling and dictation – P. K. Purvis,' echoed Gussie, as if he were calling coals. 'Forward, P. K. Purvis.'

Now that the whistle had been blown on his speech, it seemed to me that there was no longer any need for the strategic retreat which I had been planning. I had no wish to tear myself away unless I had to. I mean, I had told Jeeves that this binge would be fraught with interest, and it was fraught with interest. There was a fascination about Gussie's methods which gripped and made one reluctant to pass the thing up provided personal innuendoes were steered clear of. I decided, accordingly, to remain, and presently there was musical squeaking and P. K. Purvis climbed the platform.

The spelling-and-dictation champ was about three foot six in his squeaking shoes, with a pink face and sandy hair. Gussie patted his hair. He seemed to have taken an immediate fancy to the lad.

'You P. K. Purvis?'

'Sir, yes, sir.'

'It's a beautiful world, P. K. Purvis.'

'Sir, yes, sir.'

'Ah, you've noticed it, have you? Good. You married, by any chance?'

'Sir, no, sir.'

'Get married, P. K. Purvis,' said Gussie earnestly. 'It's the only life . . . Well, here's your book. Looks rather bilge to me from a glance at the title page, but, such as it is, here you are.'

P. K. Purvis squeaked off amidst sporadic applause, but one could not fail to note that the sporadic was followed by a rather strained silence. It was evident that Gussie was striking something of a new note in Market Snodsbury scholastic circles. Looks were exchanged between parent and parent. The bearded bloke had the air of one who has drained the bitter cup. As for Aunt Dahlia, her demeanour now told only too clearly that her last doubts had been resolved and her verdict was in. I saw her whisper to the Bassett, who sat on her right, and the Bassett nodded sadly and looked like a fairy about to shed a tear and add another star to the Milky Way.

Gussie, after the departure of P. K. Purvis, had fallen into a sort of daydream and was standing with his mouth open and his hands in his pockets. Becoming abruptly aware that a fat kid in knickerbockers was at his elbow, he started violently.

'Hullo!' he said, visibly shaken. 'Who are you?'

'This,' said the bearded bloke, 'is R. V. Smethurst.'

'What's he doing here?' asked Gussie suspiciously.

'You are presenting him with the drawing prize, Mr Fink-Nottle.'

This apparently struck Gussie as a reasonable explanation. His face cleared.

'That's right, too,' he said ... 'Well, here it is, cocky. You off?' he said, as the kid prepared to withdraw.

'Sir, yes, sir.'

'Wait, R. V. Smethurst. Not so fast. Before you go, there is a question I wish to ask you.'

But the bearded bloke's aim now seemed to be to rush the ceremonies a bit. He hustled R. V. Smethurst off stage rather like a chucker-out in a pub regretfully ejecting an old and respected customer, and started paging G. G. Simmons. A moment later the latter was up and coming, and conceive my emotion when it was announced that the subject on which he had clicked was Scripture knowledge. One of us, I mean to say.

G. G. Simmons was an unpleasant, perky-looking stripling, mostly front teeth and spectacles, but I gave him a big hand. We Scripture-knowledge sharks stick together.

Gussie, I was sorry to see, didn't like him. There was in his manner, as he regarded G. G. Simmons, none of the chumminess which had marked it during his interview with P. K. Purvis or, in a somewhat lesser degree, with R. V. Smethurst. He was cold and distant.

'Well, G. G. Simmons.'

'Sir, yes, sir.'

'What do you mean – sir, yes, sir? Dashed silly thing to say.

143

So you've won the Scripture-knowledge prize, have you?'

'Sir, yes, sir.'

'Yes.' said Gussie, 'you look just the sort of little tick who would. And yet,' he said, pausing and eyeing the child keenly, 'how are we to know that this has all been open and above board? Let me test you, G. G. Simmons. What was What's-His-Name – the chap who begat Thingummy? Can you answer me that, Simmons?'

'Sir, no, sir.'

Gussie turned to the bearded bloke.

'Fishy,' he said. 'Very fishy. This boy appears to be totally lacking in Scripture knowledge.'

The bearded bloke passed a hand across his forehead.

'I can assure you, Mr Fink-Nottle, that every care was taken to ensure a correct marking and that Simmons outdistanced his competitors by a wide margin.'

'Well, if you say so,' said Gussie doubtfully. 'All right, G. G. Simmons, take your prize.'

'Sir, thank you, sir.'

'But let me tell you that there's nothing to stick on side about in winning a prize for Scripture knowledge. Bertie Wooster –'

I don't know when I've had a nastier shock. I had been going on the assumption that, now that they had stopped him making his speech, Gussie's fangs had been drawn, as you might say. To duck my head down and resume my edging toward the door was with me the work of a moment.

'Bertie Wooster won the Scripture-knowledge prize at a kids' school we were at together, and you know what he's like. But, of course, Bertie frankly cheated. He succeeded in scrounging that Scripture-knowledge trophy over the heads of better men by means of some of the rawest and most brazen swindling methods ever witnessed even at a school where such things were common. If that man's pockets, as he entered the examination-room, were not stuffed to bursting-point with lists of the kings of Judah –'

I heard no more. A moment later I was out in God's air, fumbling with a fevered foot at the self-starter of the old car.

The engine raced. The clutch slid into position. I tooted and drove off.

My ganglions were still vibrating as I ran the car into the stables of Brinkley Court, and it was a much shaken Bertram who tottered up to his room to change into something loose. Having donned flannels, I lay down on the bed for a bit, and I suppose I must have dozed off, for the next thing I remember is finding Jeeves at my side.

I sat up. 'My tea, Jeeves?'

'No, sir. It is nearly dinner-time.'

The mists cleared away.

'I must have been asleep.'

'Yes, sir.'

'Nature taking its toll of the exhausted frame.'

'Yes, sir.'

'And enough to make it.'

'Yes, sir.'

'And now it's nearly dinner-time, you say? All right. I am in no mood for dinner, but I suppose you had better lay out the clothes.'

'It will not be necessary, sir. The company will not be dressing tonight. A cold collation has been set out in the dining-room.'

There was a pause.

'Well, Jeeves,' I said, 'it was certainly one of those afternoons, what?'

'Yes, sir.'

'I cannot recall one more packed with incident. And I left before the finish.'

'Yes, sir. I observed your departure.'

'You couldn't blame me for withdrawing.'

'No, sir. Mr Fink-Nottle had undoubtedly become embarrassingly personal.'

'Was there much more of it after I went?'

'No, sir. The proceedings terminated very shortly. Mr Fink-Nottle's remarks with reference to Master G. G. Simmons brought about an early closure.'

'But he had finished his remarks about G. G. Simmons.'

145

'Only temporarily, sir. He resumed them immediately after your departure. If you recollect, sir, he had already proclaimed himself suspicious of Master Simmons's bona fides, and he now proceeded to deliver a violent verbal attack upon the young gentleman, asserting that it was impossible for him to have won the Scripture-knowledge prize without systematic cheating on an impressive scale. He went to far as to suggest that Master Simmons was well known to the police.'

'Golly, Jeeves!'

'Yes, sir. The words did create a considerable sensation. The reaction of those present to this accusation I should describe as mixed. The young students appeared pleased and applauded vigorously, but Master Simmons's mother rose from her seat and addressed Mr Fink-Nottle in terms of strong protest.

'Did Gussie seem taken aback? Did he recede from his position?'

'No, sir. He said that he could see it all now, and hinted at a guilty liaison between Master Simmons's mother and the head master, accusing the latter of having cooked the marks, as his expression was, in order to gain favour with the former.'

'You don't mean that?'

'Yes, sir.'

'Egad, Jeeves! And then–'

'They sang the national anthem, sir.'

'Surely not?'

'Yes, sir.'

'At a moment like that?'

'Yes, sir.'

'Well, you were there and you know, of course, but I should have thought the last thing Gussie and this woman would have done in the circs. would have been to start singing duets.'

'You misunderstand me, sir. It was the entire company who sang. The head master turned to the organist and said something to him in a low tone. Upon which the latter began to play the national anthem, and the proceedings terminated.'

'I see. About time, too.'

'Yes, sir. Mrs Simmons's attitude had become unquestionably menacing.'

I pondered. What I had heard was, of course, of a nature to excite pity and terror, not to mention alarm and despondency, and it would be paltering with the truth to say that I was pleased about it. On the other hand, it was all over now, and it seemed to me that the thing to do was not to mourn over the past but to fix the mind on the bright future. I mean to say, Gussie might have lowered the existing Worcestershire record for goofiness and definitely forfeited all chance of becoming Market Snodsbury's favourite son, but you can't get away from the fact that he had proposed to Madeline Bassett, and you had to admit that she had accepted him.

I put this to Jeeves.

'A frightful exhibition,' I said, 'and one which will very possibly ring down history's pages. But we mut not forget, Jeeves, that Gussie, though now doubtless looked upon in the neighbourhood as the world's worst freak, is all right otherwise.'

'No, sir.'

I did not quite get this.

'When you say "No, sir," do you mean "Yes, sir"?'

'No, sir. I mean "No, sir." '

'He is not all right otherwise?'

'No, sir.'

'But he's betrothed.'

'No longer, sir. Miss Bassett has severed the engagement.'

Right Ho, Jeeves (1934)

Debut of Young Barrister

Myrtle was Jeff's fiancée and she was not amused when she read the newspaper reports. But Jeff found a better girl and better career before the end of this book.

Jeff Miller stood leaning out of his third-floor window in Halsey Chambers, his eyes fixed on the entrance of the court. His air was one of anxiety and apprehension. Earlier in the day, he had received a telegram from Myrtle Shoesmith, announcing that she would be with him in the course of the afternoon. And if Myrtle had cut short her visit to her friends in the country and was rushing back to see him in this impetuous fashion, it could mean but one thing. She had been reading about the case of Pennefather *v.* Tarvin, in which Jeff, against his will, had been counsel for the plaintiff.

Full report of this had appeared that morning in all the brighter London journals, in some cases on the front page. Jeff would not have done it for pleasure, but he could, if called upon, have recited those newspaper reports verbatim. They were graven on his mind. An excerpt from one flashed before him now, in letters of flame.

COUNSEL: Is it not a fact, Green –
JUDGE: Mr Green, if you please, Mr Miller.
COUNSEL: Oh, sorry.
JUDGE: Not at all, Mr Miller. Pray continue.
COUNSEL: Right ho. Thanks. Is it not a fact, Mr Green ...
    Look at me, if you please, and not at the jury –
JUDGE: Witness is looking at you, Mr Miller.
COUNSEL: Oh, is he? Right ho. Is it not a fact, Mr Green,

that at school you were known as Stinker, and that we were given a half-holiday the day the news came out that you had had a bath?

WITNESS: Your worship!

JUDGE: It is more customary to address me as 'My Lord', Mr Green, or, alternatively, as 'Me lud'. However, I find your emotion intelligible. Have these references to witness's apparently misspent youth any bearing on the case now before us, Mr Miller?

COUNSEL: I'm shaking him, me lud – showing what a louse he is.

JUDGE: Do not use the word 'louse', Mr Miller.

COUNSEL: As your ludship pleases. Well, anyway, Stinker, putting aside for the moment the question of your niffiness, wasn't it notorious that you couldn't tell the truth without straining a ligament? What I'm driving at is that this story of yours about the blow or buffet being really a prod or tap is a tissue of lies from soup to nuts. Come on now, come clean, you unspeakable wart.

JUDGE: The expression 'wart', Mr Miller –

There had been quite a lot of this sort of thing, culminating in Counsel requesting the Learned Judge for heaven's sake not to keep interrupting all the time, and His Lordship, ceasing to be urbane, speaking of contempt of court and advising Counsel to lose no time in adopting some other walk in life, for he, His Lordship, could see no future for him at the Bar.

Money in The Bank (1946)

Rodney Has a Relapse

When Wodehouse was in trouble in 1941 (see page 399) his 'old friend' A. A. Milne sprang to his attack. Is there a memory of that in this story?

The Oldest Member, who had been in a reverie, came out of it abruptly and began to speak with the practised ease of a raconteur who does not require a cue to start him off on a story.

When William Bates came to me that afternoon with his tragic story (said the Oldest Member, as smoothly as if we had been discussing William Bates, whoever he might be, for hours), I felt no surprise that he should have selected me as a confidant. I have been sitting on the terrace of this golf club long enough to know that this is what I am here for. Everybody with a bit of bad news always brings it to me.

'I say,' said William Bates.

This William was a substantial young man constructed rather on the lines of a lorry, and as a rule he shared that vehicle's placid and unruffled outlook on life. He lived mainly on chops and beer, and few things were able to disturb him. Yet, as he stood before me now, I could see that he was all of a twitter, as far as a fourteen-stone-six man full of beer and chops can be all of a twitter.

'I say,' said William. 'You know Rodney?'

'Your brother-in-law, Rodney Spelvin?'

'Yes. I believe he's gone cuckoo.'

'What gives you that impression?'

'Well, look. Listen to this. We were playing our usual foursome this morning, Rodney and Anastatia and me and Jane, a bob a corner, nip and tuck all the way around, and at the eighteenth Jane and I were lying dead in four and Rodney had a simple chip to reach the green in three. You get the set-up?'

I said I got the set-up.

'Well, knowing my sister Anastatia's uncanny ability to hole out from anywhere within fifteen yards of the pin, I naturally thought the thing was in the bag for them. I said as much to Jane. "Jane," I said, "be ready with the stiff upper lip. They've dished us." And I had already started to feel in my pocket for my bob, when I suddenly saw that Rodney was picking up his ball.'

'Picking up his ball?'

'And what do you think his explanation was? His explanation was that in order to make his shot he would have had to crush a daisy. "I couldn't crush a daisy," he said. "The pixies would never forgive me." What do you make of it?'

I knew what I made of it, but I had not the heart to tell him. I passed it off by saying that Rodney was one of these genial clowns who will do anything for a laugh and, William being a simple soul, my efforts to soothe him were successful. But his story had left me uneasy and apprehensive. It seemed to me only too certain that Rodney Spelvin was in for another attack of poetry.

I have generally found, as I have gone through the world, that people are tolerant and ready to forgive, and in our little community it was never held against Rodney Spelvin that he had once been a poet and a very virulent one, too; the sort of man who would produce a slim volume of verse bound in squashy mauve leather at the drop of a hat, mostly on the subject of sunsets and pixies. He had said goodbye to all that directly he took up golf and announced his betrothal to William's sister Anastatia.

It was golf and the love of a good woman that saved Rodney Spelvin. The moment he had bought his bag of clubs and signed up Anastatia Bates as a partner for life's medal round, he was a different man. He now wrote mystery thrillers, and with such success that he and Anastatia and their child Timothy were enabled to live like fighting cocks. It was impossible not to be thrilled by Rodney Spelvin, and so skilful was the technique which he had developed that he was soon able to push out his couple of thousand words of wholesome blood-stained fiction each morning before breakfast, leaving the rest of the day for the normal fifty-four holes of golf.

At golf, too, he made steady progress. His wife, a scratch player who had once won the Ladies' Championship, guided him with loving care, and it was not long before he became a skilful twenty-one and was regarded in several knowledgeable quarters as a man to keep your eye on for the Rabbits Umbrella, a local competition open to those with a handicap of eighteen or over.

But smooth though the putting green of Anastatia Spelvin's happiness was to the casual glance, there lurked on it, I knew, a secret worm-cast. She could never forget that the man she loved was a man with a past. Deep down in her soul there was always the corroding fear lest at any moment a particularly fine sunset or the sight of a rose in bud might undo all the work she had done, sending Rodney hot-foot once more to his Thesaurus and rhyming dictionary. It was for this reason that she always hurried him indoors when the sun began to go down and refused to have rose trees in her garden. She was in the same position as a wife who has married a once heavy drinker and, though tolerably certain that he has reformed, nevertheless, feels it prudent to tear out the whisky advertisements before giving him his *Tatler*.

And now, after seven years, the blow was about to fall. Or so I felt justified in supposing. And I could see that Anastatia thought the same. There was a drawn look on her face, and she was watching her husband closely. Once when I was dining at her house and a tactless guest spoke of the June moon, she changed the subject hurriedly, but not before I had seen Rodney Spelvin start and throw his head up like a war horse at the sound of the bugle. He recovered himself quickly, but for an instant he had looked like a man who has suddenly awakened to the fact that 'June' rhymes with 'moon' and feels that steps of some sort ought to be taken.

A week later suspicion became certainty. I had strolled over to William's cottage after dinner, as I often did, and I found him and Anastatia in the morning-room. At a glance I could see that something was wrong. William was practising distrait swings with a number three iron, a moody frown on his face, while Anastatia in what seemed to me a feverish way sat knitting a sweater for her little nephew, Braid Bates, the son of William and Jane, at the moment away from home undergoing intensive instruction from a leading professional in preparation for the forthcoming contest for the Children's Cup. Both William and Jane rightly felt that the child could not start getting the competition spirit too soon.

Anastatia was looking pale, and William would have been, too, no doubt, if it had been possible for him to look pale. Years of incessant golf in all weathers had converted his cheeks into a substance resembling red leather.

'Lovely evening,' I said.

'Beautiful,' replied Anastatia wildly.

'Good weather for the crops.'

'Splendid,' gasped Anastatia.

'And where is Rodney?'

Anastatia quivered all over and dropped a stitch.

'He's out, I think,' she said in a strange strangled voice.

William's frown deepened. A plain, blunt man, he dislikes evasions.

'He is not out,' he said curtly. 'He is at home, writing poetry. Much better to tell him,' he added to Anastatia, who had uttered a wordless sound of protest. 'You can't keep the thing dark, and he will be able to handle it. He has white whiskers. A fellow with white whiskers is bound to be able to handle things better than a couple of birds like us who haven't white whiskers. Stands to reason.'

I assured them that they could rely on my secrecy and discretion and that I would do anything that lay in the power of myself and my whiskers to assist them in their distress.

'So Rodney is writing poetry?' I said. 'I feared that this might happen. Yes, I think I may say I saw it coming. About pixies, I suppose?'

Anastatia gave a quick sob and William a quick snort.

'About pixies, you suppose, do you?' he cried. 'Well, you're wrong. If pixies were all the trouble, I wouldn't have a word to say. Let Rodney Spelvin come in at the door and tell me he has written a poem about pixies, and I will clasp him in my arms. Yes,' said William, 'to my bosom. The thing has gone far, far beyond the pixie stage. Do you know where Rodney is at this moment? Up in the nursery, bending over his son Timothy's cot, gathering material for a poem about the unfortunate little rat when asleep. Some bolony, no doubt, about how he hugs his teddy bear and dreams of angels. Yes, that is what he is doing, writing poetry about Timothy. Horrible whimsical stuff that ... Well, when I tell you that he refers to him throughout as "Timothy Bobbin", you will appreciate what we are up against.'

I am not a weak man, but I confess that I shuddered.

'Timothy Bobbin?'

'Timothy by golly Bobbin. No less.'

I shuddered again. This was worse than I had feared. And yet, when you examined it, how inevitable it was. The poetry virus always seeks out the weak spot. Rodney Spelvin was a devoted father. It had long been his practice to converse with his offspring in baby talk, though hitherto always in prose. It was only to be expected that when he found verse welling up in him, the object on which he would decant it would be his unfortunate son.

'What it comes to,' said William, 'is that he is wantonly laying up a lifetime of shame and misery for the wretched little moppet. In the years to come, when he is playing in the National Amateur, the papers will print photographs of him with captions underneath explaining that he is the Timothy Bobbin of the well-known poems —'

'Rodney says he expects soon to have sufficient material for a slim volume,' put in Anastatia in a low voice.

'— and he will be put clean off his stroke. Misery, desolation and despair,' said William. 'That is the programme, as I see it.'

'Are these poems so very raw?'

'Read these and judge for yourself. I swiped them off his desk.'

The documents which he thrust upon me appeared to be in the nature of experimental drafts, intended at a later stage to be developed more fully; what one might perhaps describe as practice swings.

The first ran:

> Timothy Bobbin has a puppy,
> A dear little puppy that goes Bow-wow . . .

Beneath were the words:

> Woa! Wait a minute!

followed, as though the writer had realized in time that this 'uppy' rhyming scheme was going to present difficulties, by some scattered notes: –

> Safer to change to rabbit?
> (Habit . . . Grab it . . . Stab it . . . Babbitt)

> Rabbit looks tough, too. How about canary?
> (Airy, dairy, fairy, hairy, Mary, contrary, vary)

> Note: Canaries go tweet-tweet.
> (Beat, seat, feet, heat, meet, neat, repeat, sheet, complete, discreet).

> Yes, canary looks like goods.

> Timothy Bobbin has a canary.

> Gosh, this is pie.
> Timothy Bobbin has a canary.
> As regards its sex opinions vary.
> If it just goes tweet-tweet,
> We shall call it Pete,
> But if it lays an egg, we shall switch to Mary.

> *(Query: Sex motif too strongly stressed)*

That was all about canaries. The next was on a different theme:

> Timothy Bobbin has ten little toes.
> He takes them out walking wherever he goes.
> And if Timothy gets a cold in the head,
> His ten little toes stay with him in bed.

William saw me wince, and asked if that was the toes one. I said it was and hurried on to the third and last.

It ran:

> Timothy
>   Bobbin
>   Goes
>   Hoppity
>   Hoppity
>   Hoppity
>   Hoppity
>   Hop.

With this Rodney appeared to have been dissatisfied, for beneath it he had written the word

Reminiscent?

as though he feared that he might have been forestalled by some other poet, and there was a suggestion in the margin that instead of going Hoppity-hoppity-hop his hero might go Boppity-Boppity-bop. The alternative seemed to me equally melancholy, and it was with a grave face that I handed the papers back to William.

'Bad,' I said gravely.

'Bad is right.'

'Has this been going on long?'

'For days the fountain pen has hardly been out of his hand.'

I put the question which had been uppermost in my mind from the first.

'Has it affected his golf?'

'He says he is going to give up golf.'

'What! But the Rabbits Umbrella?'

'He intends to scratch.'

There seemed to be nothing more to be said. I left them. I wanted to be alone, to give this sad affair my undivided attention. As I made for the door, I saw that Anastatia had buried her face in her hands, while William, with brotherly solicitude, stood scratching the top of her head with the number three iron, no doubt in a well-meant effort to comfort and console.

For several days I brooded tensely on the problem, but it was all too soon borne in upon me that William had over-estimated the results-producing qualities of white whiskers. I think I may say with all modesty that mine are as white as the next man's, but they got me nowhere. If I had been a clean-shaven juvenile in the early twenties, I could not have made less progress towards a satisfactory settlement.

It was all very well, I felt rather bitterly at times, for William to tell me to 'handle it', but what could I do? What can any man do when he is confronted by these great natural forces? For years, it was evident, poetry had been banking up inside Rodney Spelvin, accumulating like steam in a boiler on the safety valve of which someone is sitting. And now that the explosion had come, its violence was such as to defy all ordinary methods of treatment. Does one argue with an erupting crater? Does one reason with a waterspout? When William in his airy way told me to 'handle it', it was as if someone had said to the young man who bore 'mid snow and ice the banner with the strange device Excelsior – 'Block that avalanche.'

I could see only one gleam of light in the whole murky affair. Rodney Spelvin had not given up golf. Yielding to his wife's prayers, he had entered for the competition for the Rabbits Umbrella, and had shown good form in the early rounds. Three of the local cripples had fallen victims to his prowess, leaving him a popular semi-finalist. It might be, then, that golf would work a cure.

It was as I was taking an afternoon nap a few days later that I was aroused by a sharp prod in the ribs and saw William's wife Jane standing beside me.

'Well?' she was saying.

I blinked, and sat up.

'Ah, Jane,' I said.

'Sleeping at a time like this,' she exclaimed, and I saw that she was regarding me censoriously. If Jane Bates has a fault, it is that she does not readily make allowances. 'But perhaps you are just taking a well-earned rest after doping out the scheme of a lifetime?'

I could not deceive her.

'I am sorry. No.'

'No scheme?'

'None.'

Jane Bates's face, like that of her husband, had been much worked upon by an open-air life, so she did not pale. But her nose twitched with sudden emotion, and she looked as if she had foozled a short putt for hole and match in an important contest. I saw her glance questioningly at my whiskers.

'Yes,' I said, interpreting her look, 'I know they are white, but I repeat: No scheme. I have no more ideas than a rabbit; indeed not so many.'

'But William said you would handle the thing.'

'It can't be handled.'

'It must be. Anastatia is going into a decline. Have you seen Timothy lately?'

'I saw him yesterday in the woods with his father. He was plucking a bluebell.'

'No, he wasn't.'

'He certainly had the air of one who is plucking a bluebell.'

'Well, he wasn't. He was talking into it. He said it was a fairy telephone and he was calling up the Fairy Queen to invite her to a party on his teddy bear's birthday. Rodney stood by, taking notes, and that evening wrote a poem about it.'

'Does Timothy often do that sort of thing?'

'All the time. The child has become a ham. He never ceases putting on an act. He can't eat his breakfast cereal without looking out of the corner of his eye to see how it's going with the audience. And when he says his prayers at night his eyes are ostensibly closed, but all the while he is peering through his fingers and counting the house. And that's not the worst of it. A wife and mother can put up with having an infant ham in the home, constantly popping out at her and being cute, provided that she is able to pay the household bills, but now Rodney says he is going to give up writing thrillers and devote himself entirely to poetry.'

'But his contracts?'

'He says he doesn't give a darn for any contracts. He says he wants to get away from it all and give his soul a chance. The way he talks about his soul and the raw deal it has had all these years, you would think it had been doing a stretch in Wormwood Scrubs. He says he is fed up with bloodstains and that the mere thought of bodies in the library with daggers of Oriental design in their backs makes him sick. He broke the news to his agent on the telephone last night, and I could hear the man's screams as plainly as if he had been in the next room.'

'But is he going to stop eating?'

'Practically. So is Anastatia. He says they can get along quite nicely on wholesome and inexpensive vegetables. He thinks it will help his poetry. He says look at Rabinadrath Tagore. Never wrapped himself around a T-bone steak in his life, and look where he fetched up. All done on rice, he said, with an occasional draft of cold water from the spring. I tell you my heart bleeds for Anastatia. A lunatic husband and a son who talks into bluebells, and she'll have to cope with them on Brussels sprouts. She certainly drew the short straw when she married the bard.'

She paused in order to snort, and suddenly, without warning, as so often happens, the solution came to me.

'Jane!' I said, 'I believe I see the way out.'

'You do?'

There flashed into her face a look which I had only once seen there before, on the occasion when the opponent who had fought her all the way to the twentieth hole in the final of the Ladies' Championship of the club was stung by a wasp while making the crucial putt. She kissed me between the whiskers and was good enough to say that she had known all along that I had it in me.

'When do you expect your son Braid back?'

'Some time tomorrow afternoon.'

'When he arrives, send him to me. I will outline the position of affairs to him, and I think we can be safe in assuming that he will immediately take over.'

'I don't understand.'

'You know what Braid is like. He has no reticences.'

I spoke feelingly. Braid Bates was one of those frank, un-inhibited children who are not afraid to speak their minds, and there had been certain passages between us in the not distant past in the course of which I had learned more about my personal appearance from two minutes of his conversation than I could have done from years of introspective study. At the time, I confess, I had been chagrined and had tried fruitlessly to get at him with a niblick, but now I found myself approving wholeheartedly of this trait in his character.

'Reflect. What will Braid's reaction be to the news that these poems are being written about Timothy? He will be revolted, and will say so, not mincing his words. Briefly, he will kid the pants off the young Spelvin, and it should not be long before the latter, instead of gloating obscenely, will be writhing in an agony of shame at the mention of Timothy Bobbin and begging Rodney to lay off. And surely even a poet cannot be deaf to the pleadings of the child he loves. Leave it to Braid. He will put everything right.'

Jane had grasped it now, and her face was aglow with the light of mother love.

'Why, of course!' she cried, clasping her hands in a sort of ecstasy. 'I ought to have thought of it myself. People may say what they like about my sweet Braid, but they can't deny that he is the rudest child this side of the Atlantic Ocean. I'll send him to you the moment he clocks in.'

Braid Bates at that time was a young plug-ugly of some nine summers, in appearance a miniature edition of William and in soul and temperament a combination of Dead End Kid and army mule; a freckled hard-boiled character with a sardonic eye and a mouth which, when not occupied in eating, had a cynical twist to it. He spoke little as a general thing, but when he did speak seldom failed to find a chink in the armour. The impact of such a personality on little Timothy must, I felt, be tremendous, and I was confident that we could not have placed the child in better hands.

I lost no time in showing him the poems about the Fairy Queen and the bluebell. He read it in silence, and when he had finished drew a deep breath.

'Is Timothy Bobbin Timothy?'

'He is.'

'The poem's all about Timothy?'

'Precisely.'

'Will it be printed in a book?'

'In a slim volume, yes. Together with others of the same type.'

I could see that he was deeply stirred, and felt that I had sown the good seed.

'You will probably have quite a good deal to say about this to Timothy at one time and another,' I said. 'Don't be afraid to speak out for fear of wounding his feelings. Remind yourself that it is all for his good. The expression "cruel to be kind" occurs to one.'

His manner, as I spoke, seemed absent, as if he were turning over in his mind a selection of good things to be said to his little cousin when they met, and shortly afterwards he left me, so moved that on my offering him a ginger ale and a slice of cake he appeared not to have heard me. I retired to rest that night with the gratifying feeling that I had done my day's good deed, and was on the verge of falling asleep when the telephone bell rang.

It was Jane Bates. Her voice was agitated.

'You and your schemes!' she said.

'I beg your pardon?'

'Do you know what has happened?'

'What?'

'William is writing poetry.'

It seemed to me that I could not have heard her correctly. 'William?'

'William.'

'You mean, Rodney –'

'I don't mean Rodney. Let me tell you in a few simple words what has happened. Braid returned from your house like one in a dream.'

'Yes, I thought he seemed impressed.'

'Please do not interrupt. It makes it difficult for me to control myself, and I have already bitten a semi-circle out of the mouthpiece. Like one in a dream, I was saying. For the rest of the evening he sat, apart, brooding and not answering when spoken to. At bedtime he came out of the silence. And how!'

'And what?'

'I said "And how!" He announced that that poem of Rodney's about the Fairy Queen was the snappiest thing he had ever read and he didn't see why, if Rodney could write poems about Timothy, William couldn't write poems about *him*. And when we told him not to talk nonsense, he delivered his ultimatum. He said that if William did not immediately come through, he would remove his name from the list of entrants for the Children's Cup. What did you say?'

'I said nothing. I was gasping.'

'You may well gasp. In fact, it will be all right with me if you choke. It was you who started all this. Of course, he had got us cold. It has been our dearest wish that he should win the Children's Cup, and we have spent money lavishly to have his short game polished up. Naturally, when he put it like that, we had no alternative. I kissed William, shook him by the hand, tied a wet towel around his head, gave him pencil and paper and locked him up in the morning-room with lots of hot coffee. When I asked him just now how he was making out, he said that he had had no inspiration so far but would keep on swinging. His voice sounded very hollow. I can picture the poor darling's agony. The only thing he has ever written before in his life was a stiff letter to the Greens Committee beefing about the new bunker on the fifth, and that took him four days and left him as limp as a rag.'

She then turned the conversation to what she described as my mischief-making meddling, and I thought it advisable to hang up.

A thing I have noticed frequently in the course of a long life, and it is one that makes for optimism, is that tragedy, while of course rife in this world of ours, is seldom universal. To give an instance of what I mean, while the barometer of William and Jane Bates pointed to 'Further Outlook Unsettled', with Anastasia Spelvin the weather conditions showed signs of improvement.

That William and his wife were in the depths there could be no question. I did not meet Jane, for after the trend of her telephone conversation I felt it more prudent not to, but I saw William a couple of times at luncheon at the club. He looked weary and haggard and was sticking cheese straws in his hair. I heard him ask the waiter if he knew any good rhymes, and when the waiter said 'To what?', William replied 'To anything'. He refused a second chop, and sighed a good deal.

Anastasia, on the other hand, whom I overtook on my way to the links to watch the final of the Rabbits Umbrella a few days later, I found her old cheerful self again. Rodney was one of the competitors in the struggle which was about to begin, and she took a rosy view of his chances. His opponent was Joe Stocker, and it appeared that Joe was suffering from one of his bouts of hay fever.

'Surely,' she said. 'Rodney can trim a man with hay fever? Of course, Mr Stocker is trying Sneezo, the sovereign remedy, but, after all, what is Sneezo?'

'A mere palliative.'

'They say he broke a large vase yesterday during one of his paroxysms. It flew across the room and was dashed to pieces against the wall.'

'That sounds promising.'

'Do you know,' said Anastasia, and I saw her eyes were

163

shining, 'I can't help feeling that if all goes well Rodney may turn the corner.'

'You mean that his better self will gain the upper hand, making him once again the Rodney we knew and loved?'

'Exactly. If he wins his final, I think he will be a changed man.'

I saw what she meant. A man who has won his first trophy, be it only a scarlet umbrella, has no room in his mind for anything but the improving of his game so that he can as soon as possible win another trophy. A Rodney Spelvin with the Rabbits Umbrella under his belt would have little leisure or inclination for writing poetry. Golf had been his salvation once. It might prove to be so again.

'You didn't watch the preliminary rounds, did you?' Anastasia went on. 'Well, at first Rodney was listless. The game plainly bored him. He had taken a notebook out with him, and he kept stopping to jot down ideas. And then suddenly, halfway through the semi-final, he seemed to change. His lips tightened. His face grew set. And on the tenth a particularly significant incident occurred. He was shaping for a brassie shot, when a wee little blue butterfly fluttered down and settled on his ball. And instead of faltering he clenched his teeth and swung at it with every ounce of weight and muscle. It had to make a quick jump to save its life. I have seldom seen a butterfly move more nippily. Don't you think that was promising?'

'Highly promising. And this brighter state of things continued?'

'All through the semi-final. The butterfly came back on the seventeenth and seemed about to settle on his ball again. But it took a look at his face and moved off. I feel so happy.'

I patted her on the shoulder, and we made our way to the first tee, where Rodney was spinning a coin for Joe Stocker to call. And presently Joe, having won the honour, drove off.

A word about this Stocker. A famous amateur wrestler in his youth, and now in middle age completely muscle bound, he made up for what he lacked in finesse by bringing to the links the rugged strength and directness of purpose which in other days had enabled him to pin one and all to the mat: and it had been well said of him as a golfer that you never knew what he was going to do next. It might be one thing, or it might be another. All you could say with certainty was that he would be in there, trying. I have seen him do the long fifteenth in two, and I have seen him do the short second in thirty-seven.

Today he made history immediately by holing out his opening drive. It is true that he holed it out on the sixteenth green, which lies some three hundred yards away and a good deal to the left of the first tee, but he holed it out, and a gasp went up from the spectators who had assembled to watch the match. If this was what Joseph Stocker did on the first, they said to one another, the imagination reeled stunned at the prospect of the heights to which he might soar in the course of eighteen holes.

But golf is an uncertain game. Taking a line through that majestic opening drive, one would have supposed that Joe Stocker's tee shot at the second would have beaned a lady, too far off to be identified, who was working in her garden about a quarter of a mile to the south-west. I had, indeed, shouted a warning 'Fore!'

So far from doing this, however, it took him in a classical curve straight for the pin, and he had no difficulty in shooting a pretty three. And as Rodney had the misfortune to sink a ball in the lake, they came to the third all square.

The third, fourth and fifth they halved. Rodney won the sixth, Stocker the seventh. At the eight I fancied that Rodney was about to take the lead again, for his opponent's third had left his ball entangled in a bush of considerable size, from which it seemed that it could be removed only with a pair of tweezers.

But it was at moments like this that you caught Joseph Stocker at his best. In some of the more scientific aspects of the game he might be forced to yield the palm to more skilful performers, but when it came to a straight issue of muscle and the will to win he stood alone. Here was where he could use his niblick, and Joe Stocker, armed with his niblick, was like King Arthur wielding his sword Excalibur. The next instant the ball, the bush, a last year's bird's nest and a family of caterpillars which had taken out squatter's rights were hurtling towards the green, and shortly after that Rodney was one down again.

And as they halved the ninth, it was in this unpleasant position that he came to the turn. Here Stocker, a chivalrous antagonist, courteously suggested a quick one at the bar before proceeding, and we repaired thither.

All through these nine gruelling holes, with their dramatic mutations of fortune, I had been watching Rodney carefully, and I had been well pleased with what I saw. There could be no doubt whatever that Anastatia had been right and that the game had gripped this backslider with all its old force. Here was no poet, pausing between shots to enter stray thoughts in a note-book, but something that looked like a Scotch pro in the last round of the National Open. What he had said to his caddy on the occasion of the lad cracking a nut just as he was putting had been music to my ears. It was plain that the stern struggle had brought out all that was best in Rodney Spelvin.

It seemed to me, too, an excellent sign that he was all impatience to renew the contest. He asked Stocker with some brusqueness if he proposed to spend the rest of the day in the bar, and Stocker hastily drained his second ginger ale and Sneezo and we went out.

As we were making our way to the tenth tee, little Timothy suddenly appeared from nowhere, gambolling up in an arch way like a miniature chorus-boy, and I saw at once what Jane had meant when she had spoken of him putting on an act. There was a sort of ghastly sprightliness about the child. He exuded whimsicality at every pore.

'Daddee,' he called, and Rodney looked round a little irritably, it seemed to me, like one interrupted while thinking of higher things.

'Daddee, I've made friends with such a nice beetle.'

It was a remark which a few days earlier would have had Rodney reaching for his note-book with a gleaming eye, but now he was plainly distrait. There was an absent look on his face, and watching him swing his driver one was reminded of a tiger of the jungle lashing its tail.

'Quite,' was all he said.

'It's green. I call it Mister Green Beetle.'

This idiotic statement – good, one would have thought, for at least a couple of stanzas – seemed to arouse little or no enthusiasm in Rodney. He merely nodded curtly and said 'Yes, yes, very sensible.'

'Run away and have a long talk with it,' he added.

'What about?'

'Why – er – other beetles.'

'Do you think Mister Green Beetle has some dear little brothers and sisters, Daddee?'

'Extremely likely. Good-bye. No doubt we shall meet later.'

'I wonder if the Fairy Queen uses beetles as horses, Daddee?'

'Very possibly, very possibly. Go and make inquiries. And you,' said Rodney, addressing his cowering caddy, 'if I hear one more hiccough out of you while I am shooting – just one – I shall give you two minutes to put your affairs in order and then I shall act. Come on, Stocker, come on, come on, come on. You have the honour.'

He looked at his opponent sourly, like one with a grievance, and I knew what was in his mind. He was wondering where this hay fever of Stocker's was, of which he had heard so much.

I could not blame him. A finalist in a golf tournament, playing against an antagonist who has been widely publicized as a victim to hay fever, is entitled to expect that the latter will give at least occasional evidence of his infirmity, and so far Joseph Stocker had done nothing of the kind. From the start of the proceedings he had failed to foozle a single shot owing to a sudden sneeze, and what Rodney was feeling was that while this could not perhaps actually be described as sharp practice, it was sailing very near the wind.

The fact of the matter was that the inventor of Sneezo knew

167

his stuff. A quick-working and harmless specific highly recommended by the medical fraternity and containing no deleterious drugs, it brought instant relief. Joe Stocker had been lowering it by the pailful since breakfast, and it was standing him in good stead. I have fairly keen ears, but up to now I had not heard him even sniffle. He played his shots dry-eyed and without convulsions, and whatever holes Rodney had won he had had to win by sheer unassisted merit.

There was no suggestion of the hay fever patient as he drove off now. He smote his ball firmly and truly, and it would unquestionably have travelled several hundred yards had it not chanced to strike the ladies' tee box and ricocheted into the rough. Encouraged by this, Rodney played a nice straight one down the middle and was able to square the match again.

A ding-dong struggle ensued, for both men were now on their mettle. First one would win a hole, then the other: and then, to increase the dramatic suspense, they would halve a couple. They arrived at the eighteenth all square.

The eighteenth was at that time one of those longish up-hill holes which present few difficulties if you can keep your drive straight, and it seemed after both men had driven that the issue would be settled on the green. But golf, as I said before, is an uncertain game. Rodney played a nice second to within fifty yards of the green, but Stocker, pressing, topped badly and with his next missed the globe altogether, tying himself in the process into a knot from which for an instant I thought it would be impossible to unravel him.

But he contrived to straighten himself out, and was collecting his faculties for another effort, when little Timothy came trotting up. He had a posy of wild flowers in his hand.

'Smell my pretty flowers, Mr Stocker,' he chirped. And with an arch gesture he thrust the blooms beneath Joseph Stocker's nose.

A hoarse cry sprang from the other's lips, and he recoiled as if the bouquet had contained a snake.

'Hey, look out for my hay fever!' he cried, and already I saw that he was beginning to heave and writhe. Under a direct frontal attack like this even Sneezo loses its power to protect.

'Don't bother the gentleman now dear,' said Rodney mildly. A glance at his face told me that he was saying to himself that this was something like family teamwork. 'Run along and wait for Daddy on the green.'

Little Timothy skipped off, and once more Stocker addressed his ball. It was plain that it was going to be a close thing. A sneeze of vast proportions was evidently coming to a head within him like some great tidal wave, and if he meant to forestall it he would have to cut his customary deliberate waggle to something short and sharp like George Duncan's. And I could see that he appreciated this.

But quickly though he waggled, he did not waggle quickly enough. The explosion came just as the club head descended on the ball.

The result was one of the most magnificent shots I have ever witnessed. It was as if the whole soul and essence of Joseph Stocker, poured into that colossal sneeze, had gone to the making of it. Straight and true, as if fired out of a gun, the ball flew up the hill and disappeared over the edge of the green.

It was with a thoughtful air that Rodney Spelvin prepared to play his chip shot. He had obviously been badly shaken by the miracle which he had just observed. But Anastatia had trained him well, and he made no mistake. He, too, was on the green and, as far as one could judge, very near the pin. Even supposing that Stocker was lying dead, he would still be in the enviable position of playing four as against the other's five. And he was a very accurate putter.

Only when we arrived on the green were we able to appreciate the full drama of the situation. Stocker's ball was nowhere to be seen, and it seemed for a moment as if it must have been snatched up to heaven. Then a careful search discovered it nestling in the hole.

'Ah,' said Joe Stocker, well satisfied. 'Thought for a moment I had missed it.'

There was good stuff in Rodney Spelvin. The best he could hope for now was to take his opponent on the nineteenth, but he did not quail. His ball was lying some four feet from the hole, never at any time an easy shot but at the crisis of a hard fought match calculated to unman the stoutest, and he addressed it with a quiet fortitude which I like to see.

Slowly he drew his club back, and brought it down. And as he did so, a clear childish voice broke the silence.

'Daddee!'

And Rodney, starting as if a red-hot iron had been placed against the bent seat of his knickerbockers, sent the ball scudding yards past the hole. Joseph Stocker was the winner of that year's Rabbits Umbrella.

Rodney Spelvin straightened himself. His face was pale and drawn.

'Daddee, are daisies little bits of the stars that have been chipped off by the angels?'

A deep sigh shook Rodney Spelvin. I saw his eyes. They were alight with a hideous menace. Quickly and silently, like an African leopard stalking its prey, he advanced on the child. An instant later the stillness was disturbed by a series of reports like pistol shots.

I looked at Anastatia. There was distress on her face, but mingled with the distress a sort of ecstasy. She mourned as a mother, but rejoiced as a wife.

Rodney Spelvin was himself again.

That night little Braid Bates, addressing his father, said:

'How's that poem coming along?'

William cast a hunted look at his helpmeet, and Jane took things in hand in her firm, capable way.

'That,' she said, 'will be all of that. Daddy isn't going to write any poem, and we shall want you out on the practice tee at seven sharp tomorrow, my lad.'

'But Uncle Rodney writes poems to Timothy.'

'No he doesn't. Not now.'

'But . . .'

Jane regarded him with quiet intentness.

'Does Mother's little chickabiddy want his nose pushed sideways?' she said. 'Very well, then.'

Nothing Serious (1950)

The Dreadful Duke

The Duke had once been engaged to Lord Emsworth's sister Constance, but had broken it off when her father wouldn't give her a sufficient (for the Duke) dowry.

Many people are fond of Dukes and place no obstacle in the way if the latter wish to fraternize with them, but few of those acquainted with Alaric, Duke of Dunstable, sought his society, Lord Emsworth least of all. He was an opinionated, arbitrary, autocratic man with an unpleasantly loud voice, bulging eyes and a walrus moustache which he was always blowing at and causing to leap like a rocketing pheasant, and he had never failed to affect Lord Emsworth unfavourably. Galahad, with his gift for the telling phrase, generally referred to the Duke as 'that stinker', and there was no question in Lord Emsworth's mind that he had hit on the right label.

A Pelican at Blandings (1969)

Uncle Fred Flits By

*This was the first – but mercifully not the last – appearance of
Frederick Altamont Cornwallis Twistleton, 5th Earl of
Ickenham.*

In order that they might enjoy their after-luncheon coffee in
peace, the Crumpet had taken the guest whom he was entertaining at the Drones Club to the smaller and less frequented of
the two smoking-rooms. In the other, he explained, though the
conversation always touched an exceptionally high level of
brilliance, there was apt to be a good deal of sugar thrown
about.

The guest said he understood.

'Young blood, eh?'

'That's right. Young blood.'

'And animal spirits.'

'And animal, as you say, spirits,' agreed the Crumpet. 'We
get a fairish amount of those here.'

'The complaint, however, is not, I observe, universal.'

'Eh?'

The other drew his host's attention to the doorway, where a
young man in form-fitting tweeds had just appeared. The aspect
of this young man was haggard. His eyes glared wildly and he
sucked at an empty cigarette-holder. If he had a mind, there
was something on it. When the Crumpet called to him to come
and join the party, he merely shook his head in a distraught sort
of way and disappeared, looking like a character out of a Greek
tragedy pursued by the Fates.

The Crumpet sighed.

'Poor old Pongo!'

172

'Pongo?'

'That was Pongo Twistleton. He's all broken up about his Uncle Fred.'

'Dead?'

'No such luck. Coming up to London again tomorrow. Pongo had a wire this morning.'

'And that upsets him?'

'Naturally. After what happened last time.'

'What was that?'

'Ah!' said the Crumpet.

'What happened last time?'

'You may well ask.'

'I do ask.'

'Ah!' said the Crumpet.

Poor old Pongo (said the Crumpet) has often discussed his Uncle Fred with me, and if there weren't tears in his eyes when he did so, I don't know a tear in the eye when I see one. In round numbers the Earl of Ickenham, of Ickenham Hall, Ickenham, Hants, he lives in the country most of the year, but from time to time has a nasty habit of slipping his collar and getting loose and descending upon Pongo at his flat in the Albany. And every time he does so, the unhappy young blighter is subjected to some soul-testing experience. Because the trouble with his uncle is that, although sixty if a day, he becomes on arriving in the metropolis as young as he feels – which is, apparently, a youngish twenty-two. I don't know if you happen to know what the word 'excesses' means, but those are what Pongo's Uncle Fred from the country, when in London, invariably commits.

It wouldn't so much matter, mind you, if he would confine his activities to the club's premises. We're pretty broad-minded here, and if you stop short of smashing the piano, there isn't much that you can do at the Drones that will cause the raised eyebrow and the sharp intake of breath. The snag is that he will insist on lugging Pongo out in the open and there, right in the public eye, proceeding to step high, wide and plentiful.

So when, on the occasion to which I allude, he stood pink and genial on Pongo's hearth-rug, bulging with Pongo's lunch and wreathed in the smoke of one of Pongo's cigars, and said: 'And now, my boy, for a pleasant and instructive afternoon,' you will readily understand why the unfortunate young clam gazed at him as he would have gazed at two-penn'orth of dynamite, had he discovered it lighting up in his presence.

'A what?' he said, giving at the knees and paling beneath the tan a bit.

'A pleasant and instructive afternoon,' repeated Lord Ickenham, rolling the words round his tongue. 'I propose that you place yourself in my hands and leave the programme entirely to me.'

Now, owing to Pongo's circumstances being such as to necessitate his getting into the aged relative's ribs at intervals and shaking him down for an occasional much-needed tenner or what not, he isn't in a position to use the iron hand with the old buster. But at these words he displayed a manly firmness.

'You aren't going to get me to the dog races again.'

'No, no.'

'You remember what happened last June.'

'Quite,' said Lord Ickenham, 'quite. Though I still think that a wiser magistrate would have been content with a mere reprimand.'

'And I won't –'

'Certainly not. Nothing of that kind at all. What I propose to do this afternoon is to take you to visit the home of your ancestors.'

Pongo did not get this.

'I thought Ickenham was the home of my ancestors.'

'It is one of the homes of your ancestors. They also resided rather nearer the heart of things, at a place called Mitching Hill.'

'Down in the suburbs, do you mean?'

'The neighbourhood is now surburban, true. It is many years since the meadows where I sported as a child were sold and cut up into building lots. But when I was a boy Mitching Hill was

174

open country. It was a vast, rolling estate belonging to your great-uncle, Marmaduke, a man with whiskers of a nature which you with your pure mind would scarcely credit, and I have long felt a sentimental urge to see what the hell the old place looks like now. Perfectly foul, I expect. Still, I think we should make the pious pilgrimage.'

Pongo absolutely-ed heartily. He was all for the scheme. A great weight seemed to have rolled off his mind. The way he looked at it was that even an uncle within a short jump of the loony-bin couldn't very well get into much trouble in a suburb. I mean, you know what suburbs are. They don't, as it were, offer the scope. One follows his reasoning, of course.

'Fine!' he said. 'Splendid! Topping!'

'Then put on your hat and rompers, my boy,' said Lord Ickenham, 'and let us be off. I fancy one gets there by omnibuses and things.'

Well, Pongo hadn't expected much in the way of mental uplift from the sight of Mitching Hill, and he didn't get it. Alighting from the bus, he tells me, you found yourself in the middle of rows and rows of semi-detached villas, all looking exactly alike, and you went on and you came to more semi-detached villas, and those all looked exactly alike, too. Nevertheless, he did not repine. It was one of those early spring days which suddenly change to mid-winter and he had come out without his overcoat, and it looked like rain and he hadn't an umbrella, but despite this his mood was one of sober ecstasy. The hours were passing and his uncle had not yet made a goat of himself. At the Dog Races the other had been in the hands of the constabulary in the first ten minutes.

It began to seem to Pongo that with any luck he might be able to keep the old blister pottering harmlessly about here till nightfall, when he could shoot a bit of dinner into him and put him to bed. And as Lord Ickenham had specifically stated that his wife, Pongo's Aunt Jane, had expressed her intention of scalping him with a blunt knife if he wasn't back at the Hall by lunch time on the morrow, it really looked as if he might get through this visit without perpetrating a single major outrage on the public weal. It is rather interesting to note that as he thought this Pongo smiled, because it was the last time he smiled that day.

All this while, I should mention, Lord Ickenham had been stopping at intervals like a pointing dog and saying that it must have been just about here that he plugged the gardener in the trousers seat with his bow and arrow and that over there he had been sick after his first cigar, and he now paused in front of a villa which for some unknown reason called itself The Cedars. His face was tender and wistful.

'On this very spot, if I am not mistaken,' he said, heaving a bit of a sigh, 'on this very spot, fifty years ago come Lammas Eve, I . . . Oh, blast it!'

The concluding remark had been caused by the fact that the rain, which had held off until now, suddenly began to buzz down like a shower-bath. With no further words, they leaped into the porch of the villa and there took shelter, exchanging glances with a grey parrot which hung in a cage in the window.

Not that you could really call it shelter. They were protected from above all right, but the moisture was now falling with a sort of swivel action, whipping in through the sides of the porch and tickling them up properly. And it was just after Pongo had turned up his collar and was huddling against the door that the door gave way. From the fact that a female of general-servant aspect was standing there he gathered that his uncle must have rung the bell.

This female wore a long mackintosh, and Lord Ickenham beamed upon her with a fairish spot af suavity.

'Good afternoon,' he said.

The female said good afternoon.

'The Cedars?'

The female said yes, it was The Cedars.

'Are the old folks at home?'

The female said there was nobody at home.

'Ah? Well, never mind. I have come,' said Lord Ickenham, edging in, 'to clip the parrot's claw. My assistant, Mr Walkinshaw, who applies the anaesthetic,' he added, indicating Pongo with a gesture.

'Are you from the bird shop?'

'A very happy guess.'

'Nobody told me you were coming.'

'They keep things from you, do they?' said Lord Ickenham, sympathetically. 'Too bad.'

Continuing to edge, he had got into the parlour by now, Pongo following in a sort of dream and the female following Pongo.

'Well, I suppose it's all right,' she said. 'I was just going out. It's my afternoon.'

'Go out,' said Lord Ickenham cordially. 'By all means go out. We will leave everything in order.'

And presently the female, though still a bit on the dubious side, pushed off, and Lord Ickenham lit the gas-fire and drew a chair up.

'So here we are my boy,' he said. 'A little tact, a little address, and here we are, snug and cosy and not catching our deaths of cold. You'll never go far wrong if you leave things to me.'

'But dash it, we can't stop here,' said Pongo.

Lord Ickenham raised his eyebrows.

'Not stop here? Are you suggesting that we go out into that rain? My dear lad, you are not aware of the grave issues involved. This morning, as I was leaving home, I had a rather painful disagreement with your aunt. She said the weather was treacherous and wished me to take my woolly muffler. I replied that the weather was not treacherous and that I would be dashed if I took my woolly muffler. Eventually, by the exercise of an iron will, I had my way, and I ask you, my dear boy, to envisage what will happen if I return with a cold in the head. I shall sink to the level of a fifth-class power. Next time I came to London, it would be a liver pad and a respirator. No! I shall remain here, toasting my toes at this really excellent fire. I had no idea that a gas-fire radiated such warmth. I feel all in a glow.'

So did Pongo. His brow was wet with honest sweat. He is reading for the Bar, and while he would be the first to admit that he hasn't yet got a complete toehold on the Law of Great Britain he had a sort of notion that oiling into a perfect stranger's semi-detached villa on the pretext of pruning the parrot was a tort or misdemeanour, if not actual barratry or soccage in fief or something like that. And apart from the legal aspect of the matter there was the embarrassment of the thing. Nobody is more of a whale on correctness and not doing what's not done than Pongo, and the situation in which he now found himself caused him to chew the lower lip and, as I say, perspire a goodish deal.

'But suppose the blighter who owns this ghastly house comes back?' he asked. 'Talking of envisaging things, try that one over on your pianola.'

And, sure enough, as he spoke, the front door bell rang.

'There!' said Pongo.

'Don't say "There!" my boy,' said Lord Ickenham reprovingly. 'It's the sort of thing your aunt says. I see no reason for alarm. Obviously this is some casual caller. A ratepayer would have used his latchkey. Glance cautiously out of the window and see if you can see anybody.'

'It's a pink chap,' said Pongo, having done so.

'How pink?'

'Pretty pink.'

'Well, there you are, then. I told you so. It can't be the big chief. The sort of fellows who own houses like this are pale and sallow, owing to working in offices all day. Go and see what he wants.'

'You go and see what he wants.'

'We'll both go and see what he wants,' said Lord Ickenham.

So they went and opened the front door, and there, as Pongo had said, was a pink chap. A small young pink chap, a bit moist about the shoulderblades.

'Pardon me,' said this pink chap, 'is Mr Roddis in?'

'No,' said Pongo.

'Yes,' said Lord Ickenham. 'Don't be silly, Douglas – of course I'm in. I am Mr Roddis,' he said to the pink chap. 'This, such as he is, is my son Douglas. And you?'

'Name of Robinson.'

'What about it?'

'My name's Robinson.'

'Oh, *your* name's Robinson? Now we've got it straight. Delighted to see you, Mr Robinson. Come right in and take your boots off.'

They all trickled back to the parlour, Lord Ickenham pointing out objects of interest by the wayside to the chap, Pongo gulping for air a bit and trying to get himself abreast of this new twist in the scenario. His heart was becoming more and more bowed down with weight of woe. He hadn't liked being Mr Walkinshaw, the anaesthetist, and he didn't like it any better being Roddis Junior. In was only too plain to him by now that his uncle had got it thoroughly up his nose and had settled down to one of his big afternoons, and he was asking himself, as he had so often asked himself before, what would the harvest be?

Arrived in the parlour, the pink chap proceeded to stand on one leg and look coy.

'Is Julia here?' he asked, simpering a bit, Pongo says.

'Is she?' said Lord Ickenham to Pongo.

'No,' said Pongo.

'No,' said Lord Ickenham.

'She wired me she was coming here today.'

'Ah, then we shall have a bridge four.'

The pink chap stood on the other leg.

'I don't suppose you've ever met Julia. Bit of trouble in the family, she gave me to understand.'

'It is often the way.'

'The Julia I mean is your niece Julia Parker. Or, rather, your wife's niece Julia Parker.'

'Any niece of my wife is a niece of mine,' said Lord Ickenham heartily. 'We share and share alike.'

'Julia and I want to get married.'

'Well, go ahead.'

'But they won't let us.'

'Who won't?'

'Her mother and father. And Uncle Charlie Parker and Uncle Henry Parker and the rest of them. They don't think I'm good enough.'

'The morality of the modern young men is notoriously lax.'

'Class enough, I mean. They're a haughty lot.'

'What makes them haughty? Are they earls?'

'No, they aren't earls.'

'Then why the devil,' said Lord Ickenham warmly, 'are they haughty? Only earls have a right to be haughty. Earls are hot stuff. When you get an earl, you've got something.'

'Besides, we've had words. Me and her father. One thing led to another, and in the end I called him a perishing old – Coo!' said the pink chap, breaking off suddenly.

He had been standing by the window, and he now leaped lissomely into the middle of the room, causing Pongo, whose nervous system was by this time definitely down among the wines and spirits and who hadn't been expecting this *adagio* stuff, to bite his tongue with some severity.

'They're on the doorstep! Julia and her mother and father. I didn't know they were all coming.'

'You do not wish to meet them?'

'No, I don't!'

'Then duck behind the settee, Mr Robinson,' said Lord Ickenham, and the pink chap, weighing the advice and finding it good, did so. And as he disappeared the door bell rang.

Once more, Lord Ickenham led Pongo out into the hall.

'I say!' said Pongo, and a close observer might have noted that he was quivering like an aspen.

'Say on, my dear boy.'

'I mean to say, what?'

'What?'

'You aren't going to let these bounders in, are you?'

'Certainly,' said Lord Ickenham. 'We Roddises keep open house. And as they are presumably aware that Mr Roddis has no son, I think we had better return to the old layout. You are the local vet, my boy, come to minister to my parrot. When I return, I should like to find you by the cage, staring at the bird in a scientific manner. Tap your teeth from time to time with a pencil and try to smell of iodoform. It will help to add conviction.'

So Pongo shifted back to the parrot's cage and stared so earnestly that it was only when a voice said 'Well!' that he became aware that there was anybody in the room. Turning, he perceived that Hampshire's leading curse had come back, bringing the gang.

It consisted of a stern, thin, middle-aged woman, a middle-aged man and a girl.

You can generally accept Pongo's estimate of girls, and when he says that this one was a pippin one knows that he uses the term in its most exact sense. She was about nineteen, he thinks, and she wore a black béret, a dark-green leather coat, a shortish tweed skirt, silk stockings and high-heeled shoes. Her eyes were large and lustrous and her face like a dewy rosebud at daybreak on a June morning. So Pongo tells me. Not that I suppose he has ever seen a rosebud at daybreak on a June morning, because it's generally as much as you can do to lug him out of bed in time for nine-thirty breakfast. Still, one gets the idea.

'Well,' said the woman, 'you don't know who I am, I'll be bound. I'm Laura's sister, Connie. This is Claude, my husband. And this is my daughter Julia. Is Laura in?'

'I regret to say, no,' said Lord Ickenham.

The woman was looking at him as if he didn't come up to her specifications.

'I thought you were younger,' she said.

'Younger than what?' said Lord Ickenham.

'Younger than you are.'

'You can't be younger than you are, worse luck,' said Lord Ickenham. 'Still, one does one's best, and I am bound to say that of recent years I have made a pretty good go of it.'

The woman caught sight of Pongo, and he didn't seem to please her, either.

'Who's that?'

'The local vet, clustering round my parrot.'

'I can't talk in front of him.'

'It is quite all right,' Lord Ickenham assured her. 'The poor fellow is stone deaf.'

And with an imperious gesture at Pongo, as much as to bid him stare less at girls and more at parrots, he got the company seated.

'Now, then,' he said.

There was silence for a moment, then a sort of muffled sob, which Pongo thinks proceeded from the girl. He couldn't see, of course, because his back was turned and he was looking at the parrot, which looked back at him – most offensively, he says, as parrots will, using one eye only for the purpose. It also asked him to have a nut.

The woman came into action again.

'Although,' she said, 'Laura never did me the honour to invite me to her wedding, for which reason I have not communicated with her for five years, necessity compels me to cross her threshold today. There comes a time when differences must be forgotten and relatives must stand shoulder to shoulder.'

'I see what you mean,' said Lord Ickenham. 'Like the boys of the old brigade.'

'What I say is, let bygones be bygones. I would not have intruded on you, but needs must. I disregard the past and appeal to your sense of pity.'

The thing began to look to Pongo like a touch, and he is convinced that the parrot thought so, too, for it winked and cleared its throat. But they were both wrong. The woman went on.

'I want you and Laura to take Julia into your home for a week or so, until I can make other arrangements for her. Julia is studying the piano, and she sits for her examination in two weeks' time, so until then she must remain in London. The trouble is, she has fallen in love. Or thinks she has.'

'I know I have,' said Julia.

Her voice was so attractive that Pongo was compelled to slew round and take another look at her. Her eyes, he says, were shining like twin stars and there was a sort of Soul's Awakening expression on her face, and what the dickens there was in a pink chap like the pink chap, who even as pink chaps go wasn't much of a pink chap, to make her look like that, was frankly, Pongo says, more than he could understand. The thing baffled him. He sought in vain for a solution.

'Yesterday, Claude and I arrived in London from our Bexhill home to give Julia a pleasant surprise. We stayed, naturally, in the boarding-house where she has been living for the past six weeks. And what do you think we discovered?'

'Insects?'

'Not insects. A letter. From a young man. I found to my horror that a young man of whom I knew nothing was arranging to marry my daughter. I sent for him immediately, and found him to be quite impossible. He jellies eels!'

'Does what?'

'He is an assistant at a jellied eel shop.'

'But surely,' said Lord Ickenham, 'that speaks well for him. The capacity to jelly an eel seems to me to argue intelligence of a high order. It isn't everybody who can do it, by any means. I know if someone came to me and said "Jelly this eel!" I should be nonplussed. And so, or I am very much mistaken, would Ramsay MacDonald and Winston Churchill.'

The woman did not seem to see eye to eye.

'Tchah!' she said. 'What do you suppose my husband's brother Charlie Parker would say if I allowed his niece to marry a man who jellies eels?'

'Ah!' said Claude, who, before we go any further, was a tall, drooping bird with a red soup-strainer moustache.

'Or my husband's brother, Henry Parker.'

'Ah!' said Claude. 'Or Cousin Alf Robbins, for that matter.'

'Exactly. Cousin Alfred would die of shame.'

The girl hiccoughed passionately, so much so that Pongo says it was all he could do to stop himself nipping across and taking her hand in his and patting it.

'I've told you a hundred times, mother, that Wilberforce is only jellying eels till he finds something better.'

'What is better than an eel?' asked Lord Ickenham, who had

been following this discussion with the close attention it deserved. 'For jellying purposes, I mean.'

'He is ambitious. It won't be long,' said the girl, 'before Wilberforce suddenly rises in the world.'

She never spoke a truer word. At this very moment, up he came from behind the settee like a leaping salmon.

'Julia!' he cried.

'Wilby!' yipped the girl.

And Pongo says he never saw anything more sickening in his life than the way she flung herself into the blighter's arms and clung there like the ivy on the old garden wall. It wasn't that he had anything specific against the pink chap, but this girl had made a deep impression on him and he resented her glueing herself to another in this manner.

Julia's mother, after just that brief moment which a woman needs in which to recover from her natural surprise at seeing eel-jelliers pop up from behind sofas, got moving and plucked her away like a referee breaking a couple of welter-weights.

'Julia Parker,' she said, 'I'm ashamed of you!'

'So am I,' said Claude.

'I blush for you.'

'Me, too,' said Claude. 'Hugging and kissing a man who called your father a perishing old bottle-nosed Gawd-help-us.'

'I think,' said Lord Ickenham, shoving his oar in, 'that before proceeding any further we ought to go into that point. If he called you a perishing old bottle-nosed Gawd-help-us, it seems to me that the first thing to do is to decide whether he was right, and frankly, in my opinion . . .'

'Wilberforce will apologize.'

'Certainly I'll apologize. It isn't fair to hold a remark passed in the heat of the moment against a chap . . .'

'Mr Robinson,' said the woman, 'you know perfectly well that whatever remarks you may have seen fit to pass don't matter one way or the other. If you were listening to what I was saying you will understand . . .'

'Oh, I know, I know. Uncle Charlie Parker and Uncle Henry Parker and Cousin Alf Robbins and all that. Pack of snobs!'

'What!'

'Haughty, stuck-up snobs. Them and their class distinctions. Think themselves everybody just because they've got money. I'd like to know how they got it.'

'What do you mean by that?'

'Never mind what I mean.'

'If you are insinuating –'

'Well, of course, you know, Connie,' said Lord Ickenham mildly, 'he's quite right. You can't get away from that.'

I don't know if you have ever seen a bull-terrier embarking on a scrap with an Airedale and just as it was getting down nicely to its work suddenly having an unexpected Kerry Blue sneak up behind it and bite it in the rear quarters. When this happens, it lets go of the Airedale and swivels round and fixes the butting-in animal with a pretty nasty eye. It was exactly the same with the woman Connie when Lord Ickenham spoke these words.

'What!'

'I was only wondering if you had forgotten how Charlie Parker made his pile.'

'What are you talking about?'

'I know it is painful,' said Lord Ickenham, 'and one doesn't mention it as a rule, but, as we are on the subject, you must admit that lending money at two hundred and fifty per cent interest is not done in the best circles. The judge, if you remember, said so at the trial.'

'I never knew that!' cried the girl Julia.

'Ah,' said Lord Ickenham. 'You kept it from the child? Quite right, quite right.'

'It's a lie!'

'And when Henry Parker had all that fuss with the bank it was touch and go they didn't send him to prison. Between ourselves, Connie, has a bank official, even a brother of your husband, any right to sneak fifty pounds from the till in order to put it on a hundred to one shot for the Grand National? Not quite playing the game, Connie. Not the straight bat. Henry, I grant you, won five thousand of the best and never looked back afterwards, but, though we applaud his judgement of form, we must surely look askance at his financial methods. As for cousin Alf Robbins . . .'

The woman was making rummy stuttering sounds. Pongo tells me he once had a Pommery Seven which used to express itself in much the same way if you tried to get it to take a hill on high. A sort of mixture of gurgles and explosions.

'There is not a word of truth in this,' she gasped at length, having managed to get the vocal cords disentangled. 'Not a single word. I think you must have gone mad.'

Lord Ickenham shrugged his shoulders.

'Have it your own way, Connie. I was only going to say that, while the jury were probably compelled on the evidence submitted to them to give Cousin Alf Robbins the benefit of the doubt when charged with smuggling dope, everybody knew that he had been doing it for years. I am not blaming him, mind you. If a man can smuggle cocaine and get away with it, good luck to him, say I. The only point I am trying to make is that we are hardly a family that can afford to put on dog and sneer at honest suitors for our daughters' hands. Speaking for myself, I consider that we are very lucky to have the chance of marrying even into eel-jellying circles.'

'So do I,' said Julia firmly.

'You don't believe what this man is saying?'

'I believe every word.'

'So do I,' said the pink chap.

The woman snorted. She seemed over-wrought.

'Well,' she said, 'goodness knows I have never liked Laura, but I would never have wished her a husband like you!'

'Husband?' said Lord Ickenham, puzzled. 'What gives you the impression that Laura and I are married?'

There was a weighty silence, during which the parrot threw out a general invitation to the company to join it in a nut. Then the girl Julia spoke.

'You'll have to let me marry Wilberforce now,' she said. 'He knows too much about us.'

'I was rather thinking that myself,' said Lord Ickenham. 'Seal his lips, I say.'

'You wouldn't mind marrying into a low family, would you, darling?' asked the girl, with a touch of anxiety.

'No family could be too low for me, dearest, if it was yours,' said the pink chap.

'After all, we needn't see them.'

'That's right.'

'It isn't one's relations that matter: it's oneselves.'

'That's right, too.'

'Wilby!'

'Julia!'

They repeated the old ivy on the garden wall act. Pongo says he didn't like it any better than the first time, but his distaste wasn't in it with the woman Connie's.

'And what, may I ask,' she said, 'do you propose to marry on?'

This seemed to cast a damper. They came apart. They looked at each other. The girl looked at the pink chap, and the pink chap looked at the girl. You could see that a jarring note had been struck.

'Wilberforce is going to be a very rich man some day.'

'Some day!'

'If I had a hundred pounds,' said the pink chap, 'I could buy a half-share in one of the best milk walks in South London tomorrow.'

'If!' said the woman.

'Ah!' said Claude.

'Where are you going to get it?'

'Ah!' said Claude.

'Where,' repeated the woman, plainly pleased with the snappy crack and loath to let it ride without an encore, 'are you going to get it?'

'That,' said Claude, 'is the point. Where are you going to get a hundred pounds?'

'Why, bless my soul,' said Lord Ickenham jovially, 'from me, of course. Where else?'

And before Pongo's bulging eyes he fished out from the recesses of his costume a crackling bundle of notes and handed it over. And the agony of realizing that the old bounder had

had all that stuff on him all this time and that he hadn't touched him for so much as a tithe of it was so keen, Pongo says, that before he knew what he was doing he had let out a sharp, whinnying cry which rang through the room like the yowl of a stepped-on puppy.

'Ah,' said Lord Ickenham. 'The vet wishes to speak to me. Yes, vet?'

This seemed to puzzle the cerise bloke a bit.

'I thought you said this chap was your son.'

'If I had a son,' said Lord Ickenham, a little hurt, 'he would be a good deal better-looking than that. No, this is the local veterinary surgeon. I may have said I *looked* on him as a son. Perhaps that was what confused you.'

He shifted across to Pongo and twiddled his hands enquiringly. Pongo gaped at him, and it was not until one of the hands caught him smartly in the lower ribs that he remembered he was deaf and started to twiddle back. Considering that he wasn't supposed to be dumb, I can't see why he should have twiddled, but no doubt there are moments when twiddling is about all a fellow feels himself equal to. For what seemed to him at least ten hours Pongo had been undergoing great mental stress, and one can't blame him for not being chatty. Anyway, be that as it may, he twiddled.

'I cannot quite understand what he says,' announced Lord Ickenham at length, 'because he sprained a finger this morning and that makes him stammer. But I gather that he wishes to have a word with me in private. Possibly my parrot has got something the matter with it which he is reluctant to mention even in sign language in front of a young unmarried girl. You know what parrots are. We will step outside.'

'*We* will step outside,' said Wilberforce.

'Yes,' said the girl Julia. 'I feel like a walk.'

'And you?' said Lord Ickenham to the woman Connie, who was looking like a female Napoleon at Moscow. 'Do you join the hikers?'

'I shall remain and make myself a cup of tea. You will not grudge us a cup of tea, I hope?'

'Far from it,' said Lord Ickenham cordially. 'This is Liberty Hall. Stick around and mop it up till your eyes bubble.'

Outside, the girl, looking more like a dewy rosebud than ever, fawned on the old buster pretty considerably.

'I don't know how to thank you!' she said. And the pink chap said he didn't, either.

'Not at all, my dear, not at all,' said Lord Ickenham.

'I think you're simply wonderful.'

'No, no.'

'You are. Perfectly marvellous.'

'Tut, tut,' said Lord Ickenham. 'Don't give the matter another thought.'

He kissed her on both cheeks, the chin, the forehead, the right eyebrow, and the tip of the nose, Pongo looking on the while in a baffled and discontented manner. Everybody seemed to be kissing this girl except him.

Eventually the degrading spectacle ceased and the girl and the pink chap shoved off, and Pongo was enabled to take up the matter of that hundred quid.

'Where,' he asked, 'did you get all that money?'

'Now, where did I?' mused Lord Ickenham. 'I know your aunt gave it to me for some purpose. But what? To pay some bill or other, I rather fancy.'

This cheered Pongo up slightly.

'She'll give you the devil when you get back,' he said, with not a little relish. 'I wouldn't be in your shoes for something. When you tell Aunt Jane,' he said, with confidence, for he knew his Aunt Jane's emotional nature, 'that you slipped her entire roll to a girl, and explain, as you will have to explain, that she was an extraordinarily pretty girl – a girl, in fine, who looked like something out of a beauty chorus of the better sort, I think she would pluck down one of the ancestral battleaxes from the wall and jolly well strike you on the mazzard.'

'Have no anxiety, my dear boy,' said Lord Ickenham. 'It is like your kind heart to be so concerned, but have no anxiety. I shall tell her that I was compelled to give the money to you to enable you to buy back some compromising letters from a

Spanish *demi-mondaine*. She will scarcely be able to blame me for rescuing a fondly-loved nephew from the clutches of an adventuress. It may be that she will feel a little vexed with you for a while, and that you may have to allow a certain time to elapse before you visit Ickenham again, but then I shan't be wanting you at Ickenham till the ratting season starts, so all is well.'

At this moment, there came toddling up to the gate of The Cedars a large red-faced man. He was just going in when Lord Ickenham hailed him.

'Mr Roddis?'

'Hey?'

'Am I addressing Mr Roddis?'

'That's me.'

'I am Mr J. G. Bulstrode from down the road,' said Lord Ickenham. 'This is my sister's husband's brother, Percy Frensham, in the lard and imported-butter business.'

The red-faced bird said he was pleased to meet them. He asked Pongo if things were brisk in the lard and imported-butter business, and Pongo said they were all right, and the red-faced bird said he was glad to hear it.

'We have never met, Mr Roddis,' said Lord Ickenham, 'but I think it would be only neighbourly to inform you that a short while ago I observed two suspicious-looking persons in your house.'

'In my house? How on earth did they get there?'

'No doubt through a window at the back. They looked to me like cat burglars. If you creep up, you may be able to see them.'

The red-faced bird crept, and came back not exactly foaming at the mouth but with the air of a man who for two pins would so foam.

'You're perfectly right. They're sitting in my parlour as cool as dammit, swigging my tea and buttered toast.'

'I thought as much.'

'And they've opened a pot of my raspberry jam.'

'Ah, then you will be able to catch them red-handed. I should fetch a policeman.'

'I will. Thank you, Mr Bulstrode.'

'Only too glad to have been able to render you this little service, Mr Roddis,' said Lord Ickenham. 'Well, I must be moving along. I have an appointment. Pleasant after the rain, is it not? Come, Percy.'

He lugged Pongo off.

'So that,' he said, with satisfaction, 'is that. On these visits of mine to the metropolis, my boy, I always make it my aim, if possible, to spread sweetness and light. I look about me, even in a foul hole like Mitching Hill, and I ask myself – How can I leave this foul hole a better and happier foul hole than I found it? And if I see a chance, I grab it. Here is our omnibus. Spring aboard, my boy, and on your way home we will be sketching out rough plans for the evening. If the old Leicester Grill is still in existence, we might look in there. It must be fully thirty-five years since I was last thrown out of the Leicester Grill. I wonder who is the bouncer there now.'

Such (concluded the Crumpet) is Pongo Twistleton's Uncle Fred from the country, and you will have gathered by now a rough notion of why it is that when a telegram comes announcing his impending arrival in the great city Pongo blenches to the core and calls for a couple of quick ones.

The whole situation, Pongo says, is very complex. Looking at it from one angle, it is fine that the man lives in the country most of the year. If he didn't he would have him in his midst all the time. On the other hand, by living in the country he generates, as it were, a store of loopiness which expends itself with frightful violence on his rare visits to the centre of things.

What it boils down to is this – Is it better to have a loopy uncle whose loopiness is perpetually on tap but spread out thin, so to speak, or one who lies low in distant Hants for three hundred and sixty days in the year and does himself proud in London for the other five? Dashed moot, of course, and Pongo has never been able to make up his mind on the point.

Naturally, the ideal thing would be if someone would chain the old hound up permanently and keep him from Jan. One to Dec. Thirty-one where he wouldn't do any harm – viz. among

Vintage Wodehouse

the spuds and tenantry. But this, Pongo admits, is a Utopian dream. Nobody could work harder to that end than his Aunt Jane, and she has never been able to manage it.

Young Men in Spats (1936)

Lottie Blossom of Hollywood

*Lottie and Ambrose were another of the many Anglo-American
couples to whom Anglo-American Wodehouse was godfather
in print.*

'Listen,' said Lottie, wasting no words on formal greetings, 'is
this true about Ikey firing Ambrose?'

'Quite.'

'But he can't go back on a contract.'

'There isn't any contract.'

'What!'

'No. Apparently it had to be signed at the New York office.'

'Well, there must have been a letter or something?'

'I gathered not.'

'You mean Ambrose hadn't a line in writing?'

'Not a syllable.'

Amazement held Lottie Blossom dumb for an instant. Then
she raged desperately.

'What chumps men are! Why couldn't the poor fish have
consulted me? I could have told him. Fancy selling up the farm
and starting off for Hollywood on the strength of Ikey Llew-
ellyn's word! Ikey's word! What a laugh that is. Why, if Ikey
had an only child and he promised her a doll on her birthday,
the first thing she would do, if she was a sensible kid, would be
to go to her lawyer and have a contract drawn up and signed,
with penalty clauses. Oh hell, oh hell, oh hell!' said Miss Blossom, for she was much stirred. 'Do you know what this means,
Reggie?'

'Means?'

'To me. Ambrose and I can't get married now.'

193

'Oh, come,' said Reggie, for his meditations on the deck had shown him that the situation, though sticky, was not so sticky as he had at first supposed. 'He may be broke, having given up his job at the Admiralty and all that, but you've enough for two, what?'

'I've enough for twenty. But what good is that? Ambrose won't live on my money. He wouldn't marry me on a bet now.'

'But, dash it, it's no different than marrying an heiress.'

'He wouldn't marry an heiress.'

'What!' cried Reggie, who would have married a dozen, had the law permitted it. 'Why not?'

'Because he's a darned ivory-domed, pig-headed son of an army mule,' cried Miss Blossom, the hot blood of the Hoboken Murphys boiling in her veins. 'Because he isn't human. Because he's like some actor in a play, doing the noble thing with one eye counting the house and the other on the gallery. No, he isn't,' she went on, with one of those swift transitions which made her character so interesting and which on the Superba-Llewellyn lot had so often sent overwrought directors groping blindly for the canteen to pull themselves together with frosted malted milk. 'He isn't anything of the kind. I admire his high principles. I think they're swell. It's a pity there aren't more men with this wonderful sense of honour and self-respect. I'm not going to have you saying a word against Ambrose. He's the finest man in the world, so if you want to sneer and jeer at him for refusing to live on my money, shoot ahead. Only remember that a cauliflower ear goes with it.'

The Luck of the Bodkins (1935)

Some Thoughts on Humorists

The New Yorker *did a most appreciative 'Profile' of Wodehouse in 1971, the year their 'burbling pixie' reached the age of 90.*

Well, time marched on, Winkler, and, pursuing the policy of writing a book, then another book, then another book, then another book and so on, while simultaneously short stories and musical comedies kept fluttering out of me like bats out of a barn, I was soon doing rather well as scriveners go. Twenty-one of my books were serialized in the *Saturday Evening Post*. For the second one they raised me to $5,000, for the third to $7,500, for the fourth to $10,000, for the fifth to $20,000. That was when I felt safe in becoming 'P. G. Wodehouse' again.

For the last twelve I got $40,000 per. Nice going, of course, and the stuff certainly came in handy, but I have always been alive to the fact that I am not one of the really big shots. Like Jeeves, I know my place, and that place is down at the far end of the table among the scurvy knaves and scullions.

I go in for what is known in the trade as 'light writing', and those who do that – humorists they are sometimes called – are looked down upon by the intelligentsia and sneered at. When I tell you that in a recent issue of the *New Yorker* I was referred to as 'that burbling pixie', you will see how far the evil has spread.

These things take their toll. You can't go calling a man a burbling pixie without lowering his morale. He frets. He refuses to eat his cereal. He goes about with his hands in his pockets and his lower lip jutting out, kicking stones. The next thing you know, he is writing thoughtful novels analysing social conditions, and you are short another humorist. With things going the way they are, it won't be long before the species dies out. Already what was once a full-throated chorus has faded into a few scattered chirps. You can still hear from the thicket the gay note of the Beachcomber, piping as the linnets do, but at any moment Lord Beaverbrook or somebody may be calling Beachcomber a burbling pixie and taking all the heart out of him, and then what will the harvest be?

These conditions are particularly noticeable in America. If as you walk along the streets of any city there you see a furtive-looking man who slinks past you like a cat in a strange alley which is momentarily expecting to receive a half brick in the short ribs, don't be misled into thinking it is Baby-Face Schultz, the racketeer for whom the police of thirty states are spreading a dragnet. He is probably a humorist.

I recently edited an anthology of the writings of American humorists of today, and was glad to do so, for I felt that such publications ought to be encouraged. Bring out an anthology of their writings, and you revive the poor drooping untouchables like watered flowers. The pleasant surprise of finding that somebody thinks they are also God's creatures makes them feel that it is not such a bad little world after all, and they pour their dose of strychnine back into the bottle and go out into the sunlit street through the door instead of, as they had planned, through the seventh-storey window. Being asked for contributions to the book I have mentioned was probably the only nice thing that had happened to these lepers since 1937. I am told that Frank Sullivan, to name but one, went about Saratoga singing like a lark.

Three suggestions as to why 'light writing' has almost ceased to be have been made – one by myself, one by the late Russell Maloney and one by Wolcott Gibbs of the *New Yorker*. Here is mine for what it is worth.

It is, in my opinion, the attitude of the boys with whom they mingle in their early days that discourages all but the most determined humorists. Arriving at their public school, they find themselves placed in one of two classes, both unpopular. If they merely talk amusingly, they are silly asses. ('You *are* a silly ass' is the formula.) If their conversation takes a mordant and satirical turn, they are 'funny swine'. ('You think you're a funny swine, don't you?') And whichever they are, they are scorned and despised and lucky not to get kicked. At least, it was so in my day. I got by somehow, possibly because I weighed twelve stone three and could box, but most of my contemporary pixies fell by the wayside and have not exercised their sense of humour since 1899 or thereabouts.

Russell Maloney's theory is that a humorist has always been a sort of comic dwarf, and it is quite true that in the Middle Ages the well-bred and well-to-do thought nothing so funny as a man who was considerably shorter than they were, or at least culti- vated a deceptive stoop. Anyone in those days who was fifty inches tall or less was *per se* a humorist. They gave him a comi- cal cap and a stick with little bells attached to it and told him to caper about and amuse them. And as it was not a hard life and the pickings were pretty good, he fell in with their wishes.

Today what amuses people, says Mr Maloney, is the mental dwarf or neurotic – the man unable to cross the street unes- corted, cash a cheque at the bank or stay sober for several hours at a time, and the reason there are so few humorists now- adays is that it is virtually impossible to remain neurotic when you have only to smoke any one of a dozen brands of cigarette to be in glowing health both physically and mentally.

Wolcott Gibbs thinks that the shortage is due to the fact that the modern tendency is to greet the humorist, when he dares to let out a blast, with a double whammy from a baseball bat. In order to be a humorist, you must see the world out of focus, and today, when the world is really out of focus, people insist that you see it straight. Humour implies ridicule of established insti- tution, and they want to keep their faith in the established order intact. In the past ten years, says Gibbs, the humorist has be- come increasingly harried and defensive, increasingly certain that the minute he raises his foolish head the hot-eyed crew will be after him, denouncing him as a fiddler while Rome burns.

197

Naturally after one or two experiences of this kind he learns sense and keeps quiet.

2

Gibbs, I think, is right. Humorists have been scared out of the business by the touchiness now prevailing in every section of the community. Wherever you look, on every shoulder there is a chip, in every eye a cold glitter warning you, if you know what is good for you, not to start anything.

'Never,' said one of the columnists the other day, 'have I heard such complaining as I have heard this last year. My last month's mail has contained outraged yelps on pieces I have written concerning dogs, diets, ulcers, cats and kings. I wrote a piece laughing at the modern tendency of singers to cry, and you would have thought I had assaulted womanhood.'

A few days before the heavyweight championship between Rocky Marciano and Roland La Starza, an Australian journalist who interviewed the latter was greatly struck by his replies to questions.

'Roland,' he wrote 'is a very intelligent young man. He has brains. Though it may be,' he added, 'that I merely think he has because I have been talking so much of late to tennis players. Tennis players are just one cut mentally above the wallaby.'

I have never met a wallaby, so cannot say from personal knowledge how abundantly – or poorly – equipped such animals are with the little grey cells, but of one thing I am sure and that is that letters poured in on the writer from Friends of The Wallaby, the International League for Promoting Fair Play for Wallabies and so on, protesting hotly against the injustice of classing them lower in the intellectual scale than tennis players. Pointing out, no doubt, that while the average run-of-the-mill wallaby is perhaps not an Einstein, it would never dream of bounding about the place shouting 'Forty love' and similar ill-balanced observations.

So there we are, and if you ask me what is to be done about it, I have no solution to suggest. It is what the French would call an impasse. In fact, it is what the French do call an impasse. Only they say amh-parrse. Silly, of course, but you know what Frenchmen are. (And now to await the flood of strongly protesting letters from Faure, Pinay, Maurice Chevalier, Mendès-France, Oo-Là-Là and Indignant Parisienne.)

3

They say it is possible even today to be funny about porcupines and remain unscathed, but I very much doubt it. Just try it and see how quickly you find your letter-box full of communications beginning:

Sir,
  With reference to your recent tasteless and uncalled-for comments on the porcupine ...

A writer in one of the papers was satirical the other day about oysters, and did he get jumped on! A letter half a column long next morning from Oyster Lover, full of the bitterest invective. And the same thing probably happened to the man who jocularly rebuked a trainer of performing fleas for his rashness in putting them through their paces while wearing a beard. Don't tell me there is not some league or society for the protection of bearded flea trainers, watching over their interests and defending them from ridicule.

There is certainly one watching over the interests of bearded swimming-pool attendants and evidently lobbying very vigorously, for it has just been ruled by the California State Labour Department that 'there is nothing inherently repulsive about a Vandyke beard'. It seems that a swimming-pool attendant in Los Angeles, who cultivated fungus of this type, was recently dismissed by his employer because the employer said, 'Shave that ghastly thing off. It depresses the customers,' and the swimming-pool attendant said he would be blowed if he would shave it off, and if the customers didn't like it let them eat cake. The State Labour Department (obviously under strong pressure from the League for the Protection of Bearded Swimming-Pool

Attendants) held that the employer's order 'constituted an un-warranted infringement upon the attendant's privilege as an individual in a free community to present such an appearance as he wished so long as it did not affect his duties adversely or tend to injure the employer in his business or reputation'. And then they went on to say that there is nothing inherently repulsive about a Vandyke beard.

Perfectly absurd, of course. There is. It looks frightful. A really vintage Vandyke beard, such as this swimming-pool attendant appears to have worn, seems to destroy one's view of Man as Nature's last word. If Vandyke thought he looked nice with that shrubbery on his chin, he must have been cockeyed.

And if the League for the Protection of Bearded Swimming-Pool Attendants and the Executors of the late Vandyke start writing me wounding letters, so be it. My head, though bloody, if you will pardon the expression, will continue unbowed. We light writers have learned to expect that sort of thing.

'What we need in America,' said Robert Benchley in one of his thoughtful essays, 'is fewer bridges and more fun.'

And how right he was, as always. America has the Tri-borough Bridge, the George Washington Bridge, the Fifty-Ninth Street Bridge, auction bridge, contract bridge, Senator Bridges and Bridgehampton, Long Island, but where's the fun?

When I first came to New York, everyone was gay and light-hearted. Each morning and evening paper had its team of humorists turning out daily masterpieces in prose and verse. Magazines published funny short stories, publishers humorous books. It was the golden age, and I think it ought to be brought back. I want to see an A. P. Herbert on every street corner, an Alex Atkinson in every local. It needs only a little resolution on the part of the young writers and a touch of the old broad-mindedness among editors.

And if any young writer with a gift for being funny has got the idea that there is something undignified and anti-social about making people laugh, let him read this from the *Talmud*, a book which, one may remind him, was written in an age just as grim as this one.

... And Elijah said to Berokah, 'These two will also share in the world to come.' Berokah then asked them, 'What is your occupation?' They replied, 'We are merrymakers. When we see a person who is downhearted we cheer him up.'

These two were among the very select few who would inherit the kingdom of Heaven.

Over Seventy (1957)

Lord Emsworth and the Girl Friend

Rudyard Kipling said that this was an example of the perfect short story.

The day was so warm, so fair, so magically a thing of sunshine and blue skies and bird-song that anyone acquainted with Clarence, ninth Earl of Emsworth, and aware of his liking for fine weather, would have pictured him going about the place on this summer morning with a beaming smile and an uplifted heart. Instead of which, humped over the breakfast table, he was directing at a blameless kippered herring a look of such intense bitterness that the fish seemed to sizzle beneath it. For it was August Bank Holiday, and Blandings Castle on August Bank Holiday became in his lordship's opinion, a miniature Inferno.

This was the day when his park and grounds broke out into a noisome rash of swings, roundabouts, marquees, toy balloons and paper bags; when a tidal wave of the peasantry and its squealing young engulfed those haunts of immemorial peace. On August Bank Holiday he was not allowed to potter pleasantly about his gardens in an old coat: forces beyond his control shoved him into a stiff collar and a top hat and told him to go out and be genial. And in the cool of the quiet evenfall they put him on a platform and made him make a speech. To a man with a day like that in front of him fine weather was a mockery.

His sister, Lady Constance Keeble, looked brightly at him over the coffee-pot.

'What a lovely morning!' she said.

Lord Emsworth's gloom deepened. He chafed at being called

upon – by this woman of all others – to behave as if everything was for the jolliest in the jolliest of all possible worlds. But for his sister Constance and her hawk-like vigilance, he might, he thought, have been able at least to dodge the top hat.

'Have you got your speech ready?'

'Yes.'

'Well, mind you learn it by heart this time and don't stammer and dodder as you did last year.'

Lord Emsworth pushed plate and kipper away. He had lost his desire for food.

'And don't forget you have to go to the village this morning to judge the cottage gardens.'

'All right, all right, all right,' said his lordship testily. 'I've not forgotten.'

'I think I will come to the village with you. There are a number of those Fresh Air London children staying there now, and I must warn them to behave properly when they come to the Fete this afternoon. You know what London children are. McAllister says he found one of them in the gardens the other day, picking his flowers.'

At any other time the news of this outrage would, no doubt, have affected Lord Emsworth profoundly. But now, so intense was his self-pity, he did not even shudder. He drank coffee with the air of a man who regretted that it was not hemlock.

'By the way, McAllister was speaking to me again last night about that gravel path through the yew alley. He seems very keen on it.'

'Glug!' said Lord Emsworth – which, as any philologist will tell you, is the sound which peers of the realm make when stricken to the soul while drinking coffee.

Concerning Glasgow, that great commercial and manufacturing city in the county of Lanarkshire in Scotland, much has been written. So lyrically does the Encyclopaedia Britannica deal with the place that it covers twenty-seven pages before it can tear itself away and go on to Glass, Glastonbury, Glatz and Glauber. The only aspect of it, however, which immediately concerns the present historian is the fact that the citizens it breeds are apt to be grim, dour, persevering, tenacious men; men with red whiskers who know what they want and mean to get it. Such a one was Angus McAllister, head-gardener at Blandings Castle.

For years Angus McAllister had set before himself as his earthly goal the construction of a gravel path through the Castle's famous yew alley. For years he had been bringing the project to the notice of his employer, though in anyone less whiskered the latter's unconcealed loathing would have caused embarrassment. And now, it seemed, he was at it again.

'Gravel path!' Lord Emsworth stiffened through the whole length of his stringy body. Nature, he had always maintained, intended a yew alley to be carpeted with a mossy growth. And, whatever Nature felt about it, he personally was dashed if he was going to have men with Clydeside accents and faces like dissipated potatoes coming along and mutilating that lovely expanse of green velvet. 'Gravel path, indeed! Why not asphalt? Why not a few hoardings with advertisements of liver pills and a filling-station? That's what the man would really like.'

Lord Emsworth felt bitter, and when he felt bitter he could be terribly sarcastic.

'Well, I think it is a very good idea,' said his sister. 'One could walk there in wet weather then. Damp moss is ruinous to shoes.'

Lord Emsworth rose. He could bear no more of this. He left the table, the room and the house and, reaching the yew alley some minutes later, was revolted to find it infested by Angus McAllister in person. The head-gardener was standing gazing at the moss like a high priest of some ancient religion about to stick the gaff into the human sacrifice.

'Morning, McAllister,' said Lord Emsworth coldly.

'Good morrrrning, your lorrudsheep.'

There was a pause. Angus McAllister, extending a foot that looked like a violin-case, pressed it on the moss. The meaning of the gesture was plain. It expressed contempt, dislike, a generally anti-moss spirit: and Lord Emsworth, wincing, surveyed the man unpleasantly through his pince-nez. Though not often given to theological speculation, he was wondering why Providence, if obliged to make head-gardeners, had found it necessary to make them so Scotch. In the case of Angus McAllister, why, going a step further, have made him a human being at all? All the ingredients of a first-class mule simply thrown away. He felt that he might have liked Angus McAllister if he had been a mule.

'I was speaking to her leddyship yesterday.'

'Oh?'

'About the gravel path I was speaking to her leddyship.'

'Oh?'

'Her leddyship likes the notion fine.'

'Indeed! Well ...'

Lord Emsworth's face had turned a lively pink, and he was about to release the blistering words which were forming themselves in his mind when suddenly he caught the head-gardener's eye, and paused. Angus McAllister was looking at him in a peculiar manner, and he knew what that look meant. Just one crack, his eye was saying – in Scotch, of course – just one crack out of you and I tender my resignation. And with a sickening shock it came home to Lord Emsworth how completely he was in this man's clutches.

He shuffled miserably. Yes, he was helpless. Except for that kink about gravel paths, Angus McAlister was a head-gardener in a thousand, and he needed him. He could not do without him. That, unfortunately, had been proved by experiment. Once before, at the time when they were grooming for the Agricultural Show that pumpkin which had subsequently romped home so gallant a winner, he had dared to flout Angus McAllister. And Angus had resigned, and he had been forced to plead – yes, plead – with him to come back. An employer cannot hope to do this sort of thing and still rule with an iron hand. Filled with the coward rage that dares to burn but does not dare to blaze, Lord Emsworth coughed a cough that was undisguisedly a bronchial white flag.

'I'll – er – I'll think it over, McAllister.'

'Mphm.'

'I have to go to the village now. I will see you later.'

'Mphm.'

'Meanwhile, I will – er – think it over.'

'Mphm.'

The task of judging the floral displays in the cottage gardens of the little village of Blandings Parva was one to which Lord Emsworth had looked forward with pleasurable anticipation. It was the sort of job he liked. But now, even though he had managed to give his sister Constance the slip and was free from her threatened society, he approached the task with downcast spirit. It is always unpleasant for a proud man to realize that he is no longer captain of his soul; that he is to all intents and purposes ground beneath the number twelve heel of a Glaswegian head-gardener; and, brooding on this, he judged the cottage gardens with a distrait eye. It was only when he came to the last on his list that anything like animation crept into his demeanour.

This, he perceived, peering over its rickety fence, was not at all a bad little garden. It demanded closer inspection. He unlatched the gate and pottered in. And a dog, dozing behind a water-butt, opened one eye and looked at him. It was one of those hairy, nondescript dogs, and its gaze was cold, wary and suspicious, like that of a stockbroker who thinks someone is going to play the confidence trick on him.

Lord Emsworth did not observe the animal. He had pottered to a bed of wallflowers and now, stooping, he took a sniff at them.

As sniffs go, it was an innocent sniff, but the dog for some reason appeared to read into it criminality of a high order. All the indignant householder in him woke in a flash. The next moment the world had become full of hideous noises, and Lord Emsworth's preoccupation was swept away in a passionate desire to save his ankles from harm.

As these chronicles of Blandings Castle have already shown, he was not at his best with strange dogs. Beyond saying 'Go away, sir!' and leaping to and fro with an agility surprising in one of his years, he had accomplished little in the direction of a reasoned plan of defence when the cottage door opened and a girl came out.

'Hoy!' cried the girl.

And on the instant, at the mere sound of her voice, the mongrel, suspending hostilities, bounded at the new-comer and writhed on his back at her feet with all four legs in the air. The spectacle reminded Lord Emsworth irresistibly of his own behaviour in the presence of Angus McAllister.

He blinked at his preserver. She was a small girl, of uncertain age – possibly twelve or thirteen, though a combination of London fogs and early cares had given her face a sort of wizened motherliness which in some odd way caused his lordship from the first to look on her as belonging to his own generation. She was the type of girl you see in back streets carrying a baby nearly as large as herself and still retaining sufficient energy to lead one little brother by the hand and shout recrimination at another in the distance. Her cheeks shone from recent soaping, and she was dressed in a velveteen frock which was obviously the pick of her wardrobe. Her hair, in defiance of the prevailing mode, she wore drawn tightly back into a short pigtail.

'Er – thank you,' said Lord Emsworth.

'Thank you, sir,' said the girl.

For what she was thanking him, his lordship was not able to gather. Later, as their acquaintance ripened, he was to discover that this strange gratitude was a habit with his new friend. She thanked everybody for everything. At the moment, the mannerism surprised him. He continued to blink at her through his pince-nez.

Lack of practice had rendered Lord Emsworth a little rusty in the art of making conversation to members of the other sex. He sought in his mind for topics.

'Fine day.'

'Yes, sir. Thank you, sir.'

'Are you' – Lord Emsworth furtively consulted his list – 'are you the daughter of – ah – Ebenezer Sprockett?' he asked, thinking, as he had often thought before, what ghastly names some of his tenantry possessed.

'No, sir. I'm from London, sir.'

'Ah? London, eh? Pretty warm it must be there.' He paused. Then, remembering a formula of his youth: 'Er – been out much this Season?'

'No, sir.'

'Everybody out of town now, I suppose? What part of London?'

'Drury Line, sir.'

'What's your name? Eh, what?'

'Gladys, sir. Thank you, sir. This is Ern.'

A small boy had wandered out of the cottage, a rather hard-boiled specimen with freckles, bearing surprisingly in his hand a large and beautiful bunch of flowers. Lord Emsworth bowed courteously and with the addition of this third party to the *tête-à-tête* felt more at his ease.

'How do you do,' he said. 'What pretty flowers.'

With her brother's advent, Gladys, also, had lost diffidence and gained conversational aplomb.

'A treat, ain't they?' she agreed eagerly. 'I got 'em for 'im up at the big 'ahse. Coo! The old josser the plice belongs to didn't arf chase me. 'E found me picking 'em and 'e sharted somefin' at me and come runnin' after me, but I copped 'im on the shin wiv a stone and 'e stopped to rub it and I come away.'

Lord Emsworth might have corrected her impression that Blandings Castle and its gardens belonged to Angus McAllister, but his mind was so filled with admiration and gratitude that he refrained from doing so. He looked at the girl almost reverently. Not content with controlling savage dogs with a mere word, this superwoman actually threw stones at Angus McAllister – a thing which he had never been able to nerve himself to do in an association which had lasted nine years – and, what was more, copped him on the shin with them. What nonsense, Lord Emsworth felt, the papers talked about the Modern Girl. If this was a specimen, the Modern Girl was the highest point the sex had yet reached.

'Ern,' said Gladys, changing the subject, 'is wearin' 'air-oil todiy.'

Lord Emsworth had already observed this and had, indeed, been moving to windward as she spoke.

'For the Feet, ' explained Gladys.

'For the feet?' It seemed unusual.

'For the Feet in the pork this afternoon.'

'Oh, you are going to the Fete?'

'Yes, sir, thank you, sir.'

For the first time, Lord Emsworth found himself regarding that grisly social event with something approaching favour.

'We must look out for one another there,' he said cordially. 'You will remember me again? I shall be wearing' – he gulped – 'a top hat.'

'Ern's going to wear a stror penamaw that's been give 'im.'

Lord Emsworth regarded the lucky young devil with frank envy. He rather fancied he knew that panama. It had been his constant companion for some six years and then had been torn from him by his sister Constance and handed over to the vicar's wife for her rummage-sale.

He sighed.

'Well, good-bye.'

'Good-bye, sir. Thank you, sir.'

Lord Emsworth walked pensively out of the garden and, turning into the little street, encountered Lady Constance.

'Oh, there you are, Clarence.'

'Yes,' said Lord Emsworth, for such was the case.

'Have you finished judging the gardens?'

'Yes.'

'I am just going into the end cottage here. The vicar tells me there is a little girl from London staying there. I want to warn her to behave this afternoon. I have spoken to the others.'

Lord Emsworth drew himself up. His pince-nez were slightly askew, but despite this his gaze was commanding and impressive.

'Well, mind what you say,' he said authoritatively. 'None of your district-visiting stuff, Constance.'

'What do you mean?'

'You know what I mean. I have the greatest respect for the young lady to whom you refer. She behaved on a certain recent occasion – on two recent occasions – with notable gallantry and resource, and I won't have her ballyragged. Understand that!'

The technical title of the orgy which broke out annually on the first Monday in August in the park of Blandings Castle was The Blandings Parva School Treat, and it seemed to Lord Emsworth, wanly watching the proceedings from under the shadow of his top hat, that if this was the sort of thing schools looked on as pleasure he and they were mentally poles apart. A function like the Blandings Parva School Treat blurred his conception of Man as Nature's Final Word.

The decent sheep and cattle to whom this park normally belonged had been hustled away into regions unknown, leaving the smooth expanse of turf to children whose vivacity scared Lord Emsworth and adults who appeared to him to have cast aside all dignity and every other noble quality which goes to make a one hundred per cent. British citizen. Look at Mrs Rossiter over there, for instance, the wife of Jno. Rossiter, Provisions, Groceries and Home-Made Jams. On any other day of the year, when you met her, Mrs Rossiter was a nice, quiet, docile woman who gave at the knees respectfully as you passed. Today, flushed in the face and with her bonnet on one side, she seemed to have gone completely native. She was wandering to and fro drinking lemonade out of a bottle and employing her mouth, when not so occupied, to make a devastating noise with what he believed was termed a squeaker.

The injustice of the thing stung Lord Emsworth. This park was his own private park. What right had people to come and blow squeakers in it? How would Mrs Rossiter like it if one afternoon he suddenly invaded her neat little garden in the High Street and rushed about over her lawn, blowing a squeaker.

And it was always on these occasions so infernally hot. July might have ended in a flurry of snow, but directly the first Monday in August arrived and he had to put on a stiff collar out came the sun, blazing with tropic fury. Of course, admitted Lord Emsworth, for he was a fair-minded man, this cut both ways. The hotter the day, the more quickly his collar lost its starch and ceased to spike him like a javelin. This afternoon, for instance, it had resolved itself almost immediately into something which felt like a wet compress. Severe as were his sufferings, he was compelled to recognize that he was that much ahead of the game.

A masterful figure loomed at his side.

'Clarence!'

Lord Emsworth's mental and spiritual state was now such that not even the advent of his sister Constance could add noticeably to his discomfort.

'Clarence, you look a perfect sight.'

'I know I do. Who wouldn't in a rig-out like this? Why in the name of goodness you always insist . . .'

'Please don't be childish, Clarence. I cannot understand the fuss you make about dressing for once in your life like a reasonable English gentleman and not like a tramp.'

'It's this top hat. It's exciting the children.'

'What on earth do you mean, exciting the children?'

'Well, all I can tell you is that just now, as I was passing the place where they're playing football – Football! In weather like this! – a small boy called out something derogatory and threw a portion of a coconut at it.'

'If you will identify the child,' said Lady Constance warmly, 'I will have him severely punished.'

'How the dickens,' replied his lordship with equal warmth, 'can I identify the child? They all look alike to me. And if I did identify him, I would shake him by the hand. A boy who throws coconuts at top hats is fundamentally sound in his views. And stiff collars . . .'

'Stiff! That's what I came to speak to you about. Are you aware that your collar looks like a rag? Go in and change it at once.'

'But, my dear Constance . . .'

'At once, Clarence. I simply cannot understand a man having so little pride in his appearance. But all your life you have been like that. I remember when we were children . . .'

Lord Emsworth's past was not of such purity that he was prepared to stand and listen to it being lectured on by a sister with a good memory.

'Oh, all right, all right, all right,' he said. 'I'll change it, I'll change it.'

'Well, hurry. They are just starting tea.'

Lord Emsworth quivered.

'Have I got to go into that tea-tent?'

'Of course you have. Don't be so ridiculous. I do wish you would realize your position. As master of Blandings Castle . . .'

A bitter, mirthless laugh from the poor peon thus ludicrously described drowned the rest of the sentence.

It always seemed to Lord Emsworth, in analysing these entertainments, that the August Bank Holiday Saturnalia at Blandings Castle reached a peak of repulsiveness when tea was served in the big marquee. Tea over, the agony abated, to become acute once more at the moment when he stepped to the edge of the platform and cleared his throat and tried to recollect what the deuce he had planned to say to the goggling audience beneath him. After that, it subsided again and passed until the following August.

Conditions during the tea hour, the marquee having stood all day under a blazing sun, were generally such that Shadrach, Meshach and Abednego, had they been there, could have learned something new about burning fiery furnaces. Lord Emsworth, delayed by the revision of his toilet, made his entry when the meal was half over and was pleased to find that his second collar almost instantaneously began to relax its iron grip. That, however, was the only gleam of happiness which was to be vouchsafed him. Once in the tent, it took his experienced eye but a moment to discern that the present feast was eclipsing in frightfulness all its predecessors.

Young Blandings Parva, in its normal form, tended rather

212

to the stolidly bovine than the riotous. In all villages, of course, there must of necessity be an occasional tough egg – in the case of Blandings Parva the names of Willie Drake and Thomas (Rat-Face) Blenkiron spring to the mind – but it was seldom that the local infants offered anything beyond the power of a curate to control. What was giving the present gathering its striking resemblance to a reunion of *sans-culottes* at the height of the French Revolution was the admixture of the Fresh Air London visitors.

About the London child, reared among the tin cans and cabbage stalks of Drury Lane and Clare Market, there is a breezy insouciance which his country cousin lacks. Years of back-chat with annoyed parents and relatives have cured him of any tendency he may have had towards shyness, with the result that when he requires anything he grabs for it, and when he is amused by any slight peculiarity in the personal appearance of members of the governing class he finds no difficulty in translating his thoughts into speech. Already, up and down the long tables, the curate's unfortunate squint was coming in for hearty comment, and the front teeth of one of the school-teachers ran it a close second for popularity. Lord Emsworth was not, as a rule, a man of swift inspiration, but it occurred to him at this juncture that it would be a prudent move to take off his top hat before his little guests observed it and appreciated its humorous possibilities.

The action was not, however, necessary. As he raised his hand a rock cake, singing through the air like a shell, took it off for him.

Lord Emsworth had had sufficient. Even Constance, unreasonable woman though she was, could hardly expect him to stay and beam genially under conditions like this. All civilized laws had obviously gone by the board and Anarchy reigned in the marquee. The curate was doing his best to form a provisional government consisting of himself and the two school-teachers, but there was only one man who could have coped adequately with the situation and that was King Herod, who – regrettably – was not among those present. Feeling like some

213

aristocrat of the old *régime* sneaking away from the tumbril, Lord Emsworth edged to the exit and withdrew.

Outside the marquee the world was quieter, but only comparatively so. What Lord Emsworth craved was solitude, and in all the broad park there seemed to be but one spot where it was to be had. This was a red-tiled shed, standing beside a small pond, used at happier times as a lounge or retiring-room for cattle. Hurrying thither, his lordship had just begun to revel in the cool, cow-scented dimness of its interior when from one of the dark corners, causing him to start and bite his tongue, there came the sound of a subdued sniff.

He turned. This was persecution. With the whole park to mess about in, why should an infernal child invade this one sanctuary of his? He spoke with angry sharpness. He came of a line of warrior ancestors and his fighting blood was up.

'Who's that?'

'Me, sir. Thank you, sir.'

Only one person of Lord Emsworth's acquaintance was capable of expressing gratitude for having been barked at in such a tone. His wrath died away and remorse took its place. He felt like a man who in error has kicked a favourite dog.

'God bless my soul!' he exclaimed. 'What in the world are you doing in a cowshed?'

'Please, sir, I was put.'

'Put? How do you mean, put? Why?'

'For pinching things, sir.'

'Eh? What? Pinching things? Most extraordinary. What did you – er – pinch?'

'Two buns, two jem-sengwiches, two apples and a slicer cake.'

The girl had come out of her corner and was standing correctly at attention. Force of habit had caused her to intone the list of purloined articles in the sing-song voice in which she was wont to recite the multiplication-table at school, but Lord Emsworth could see that she was deeply moved. Tear-stains glistened on her face, and no Emsworth had ever been able to watch unstirred a woman's tears. The ninth Earl was visibly affected.

'Blow your nose,' he said, extending his handkerchief.

'Yes, sir. Thank you, sir.'

'What did you say you had pinched? Two buns . . .'

'. . . Two jem-sengwiches, two apples and a slicer cake.'

'Did you eat them?'

'No, sir. They wasn't for me. They was for Ern.'

'Ern? Oh, ah, yes. Yes, to be sure. For Ern, eh?'

'Yes, sir.'

'But why the dooce couldn't Ern have – er – pinched them for himself? Strong, able-bodied young feller, I mean.'

Lord Emsworth, a member of the old school, did not like this disposition on the part of the modern young man to shirk the dirty work and let the woman pay.

'Ern wasn't allowed to come to the treat, sir.'

'What! Not allowed? Who said he mustn't?'

'The lidy, sir.'

'What lidy?'

'The one that come in just after you'd gorn this morning.'

A fierce snort escaped Lord Emsworth. Constance! What the devil did Constance mean by taking it upon herself to revise his list of guests without so much as a . . . Constance, eh? He snorted again. One of these days Constance would go too far.

'Monstrous!' he cried.

'Yes, sir.'

'High-handed tyranny, by Gad. Did she give any reason?'

'The lidy didn't like Ern biting 'er in the leg, sir.'

'Ern bit her in the leg?'

'Yes, sir. Pliying 'e was a dorg. And the lidy was cross and Ern wasn't allowed to come to the treat, and I told 'im I'd bring 'im back something nice.'

Lord Emsworth breathed heavily. He had not supposed that in these degenerate days a family like this existed. The sister copped Angus McAllister on the shin with stones, the brother bit Constance in the leg . . . It was like listening to some grand old saga of the exploits of heroes and demigods.

'I thought if I didn't 'ave nothing myself it would make it all right.'

'Nothing?' Lord Emsworth started. 'Do you mean to tell me you have not had tea?'

'No, sir. Thank you, sir. I thought if I didn't 'ave none, then it would be all right Ern 'aving what I would 'ave 'ad if I 'ad 'ave 'ad.'

His lordship's head, never strong, swam a little. Then it resumed its equilibrium. He caught her drift.

'God bless my soul!' said Lord Emsworth. 'I never heard anything so monstrous and appalling in my life. Come with me immediately.'

'The lidy said I was to stop 'ere, sir.'

Lord Emsworth gave vent to his loudest snort of the afternoon.

'Confound the lidy!'

'Yes, sir. Thank you, sir.'

Five minutes later Beach, the butler, enjoying a siesta in the housekeeper's room, was roused from his slumbers by the unexpected ringing of a bell. Answering its summons, he found his employer in the library, and with him a surprising young person in a velveteen frock, at the sight of whom his eyebrows quivered and, but for his iron self-restraint, would have risen.

'Beach!'

'Your lordship?'

'This young lady would like some tea.'

'Very good, your lordship.'

'Buns, you know. And apples, and jem – I mean jam-sandwiches, and cake, and that sort of thing.'

'Very good, your lordship.'

'And she has a brother, Beach.'

'Indeed, your lordship?'

'She will want to take some stuff away for him.' Lord Emsworth turned to his guest. 'Ernest would like a little chicken, perhaps?'

'Coo!'

'I beg your pardon?'

'Yes, sir. Thank you, sir.'

'And a slice or two of ham?'

'Yes, sir. Thank you, sir.'

'And – he has no gouty tendency?'

'No, sir. Thank you, sir.'

'Capital! Then a bottle of that new lot of port, Beach. It's some stuff they've sent me down to try,' explained his lordship. 'Nothing special, you understand,' he added apologetically, 'but quite drinkable. I should like your brother's opinion of it. See that all that is put together in a parcel, Beach, and leave it on the table in the hall. We will pick it up as we go out.'

A welcome coolness had crept into the evening air by the time Lord Emsworth and his guest came out of the great door of the castle. Gladys, holding her host's hand and clutching the parcel, sighed contentedly. She had done herself well at the tea-table. Life seemed to have nothing more to offer.

Lord Emsworth did not share this view. His spacious mood had not yet exhausted itself.

'Now, is there anything else you can think of that Ernest would like?' he asked. 'If so, do not hesitate to mention it. Beach, can you think of anything?'

The butler, hovering respectfully, was unable to do so.

'No, your lordship. I ventured to add – on my own responsibility, your lordship – some hard-boiled eggs and a pot of jam to the parcel.'

'Excellent! You are sure there is nothing else?'

A wistful look came into Gladys's eyes.

'Could he 'ave some flarze?'

'Certainly,' said Lord Emsworth. 'Certainly, certainly, certainly. By all means. Just what I was about to suggest my – er – what is flarze?'

Beach, the linguist, interpreted.

'I think the young lady means flowers, your lordship.'

'Yes, sir. Thank you, sir. Flarze.'

'Oh?' said Lord Emsworth. 'Oh? Flarze?' he said slowly. 'Oh, ah, yes. I see. H'm!'

He removed his pince-nez, wiped them thoughtfully, replaced them, and gazed with wrinkling forehead at the gardens that stretched gaily out before him. Flarze! It would be idle to deny that those gardens contained flarze in full measure. They were bright with Achillea, Bignonia Radicans, Campanula, Digitalis, Euphorbia, Funkia, Gypsophila, Helianthus, Iris, Liatris, Monarda, Phlox Drummondi, Salvia, Thalictrum, Vinca and Yucca. But the devil of it was that Angus McAllister would have a fit if they were picked. Across the threshold of this Eden the ginger whiskers of Angus McAllister lay like a flaming sword.

As a general rule, the procedure for getting flowers out of Angus McAllister was as follows. You waited till he was in one of his rare moods of complaisance, then you led the conversation gently round to the subject of interior decoration, and then, choosing your moment, you asked if he could possibly spare a few to be put in vases. The last thing you thought of doing was to charge in and start helping yourself.

'I – er – . . .' said Lord Emsworth.

He stopped. In a sudden blinding flash of clear vision he had seen himself for what he was – the spineless, unspeakably unworthy descendant of ancestors who, though they may have had their faults, had certainly known how to handle employees. It was 'How now, varlet!' and 'Marry come up, thou malapert knave!' in the days of previous Earls of Emsworth. Of course, they had possessed certain advantages which he lacked. It undoubtedly helped a man in his dealings with the domestic staff to have, as they had had, the rights of the high, the middle and the low justice – which meant, broadly, that if you got annoyed with your head-gardener you could immediately divide him into four head-gardeners with a battle-axe and no questions asked – but even so, he realized that they were better men than he was and that, if he allowed craven fear of Angus McAllister to stand in the way of this delightful girl and her charming brother getting all the flowers they required, he was not worthy to be the last of their line.

Lord Emsworth wrestled with his tremors.

'Certainly, certainly, certainly,' he said, though not without a qualm. 'Take as many as you want.'

And so it came about that Angus McAllister, crouched in his potting-shed like some dangerous beast in its den, beheld a sight which first froze his blood and then sent it boiling through his veins. Flitting to and fro through his sacred gardens, picking his sacred flowers, was a small girl in a velveteen frock. And – which brought apoplexy a step closer – it was the same small girl who two days before had copped him on the shin with a stone. The stillness of the summer evening was shattered by a roar that sounded like boilers exploding, and Angus McAllister came out of the potting-shed at forty-five miles per hour.

Gladys did not linger. She was a London child, trained from infancy to bear herself gallantly in the presence of alarms and excursions, but this excursion had been so sudden that it momentarily broke her nerve. With a horrified yelp she scuttled to where Lord Emsworth stood and, hiding behind him, clutched the tails of his morning-coat.

'Oo-er!' said Gladys.

Lord Emsworth was not feeling so frightfully good himself. We have pictured him a few moments back drawing inspiration from the nobility of his ancestors and saying, in effect, 'That for McAllister!' but truth now compels us to admit that this hardy attitude was largely due to the fact that he believed the head-gardener to be a safe quarter of a mile away among the swings and roundabouts of the Fete.

The spectacle of the man charging vengefully down on him with gleaming eyes and bristling whiskers made him feel like a nervous English infantryman at the Battle of Bannockburn. His knees shook and the soul within him quivered.

And then something happened, and the whole aspect of the situation changed.

It was, in itself, quite a trivial thing, but it had an astoundingly stimulating effect on Lord Emsworth's morale. What happened was that Gladys, seeking further protection, slipped at this moment a small, hot hand into his.

219

It was a mute vote of confidence, and Lord Emsworth intended to be worthy of it.

'He's coming,' whispered his lordship's Inferiority Complex agitatedly.

'What of it?' replied Lord Emsworth stoutly.

'Tick him off,' breathed his lordship's ancestors in his other ear.

'Leave it to me,' replied Lord Emsworth.

He drew himself up and adjusted his pince-nez. He felt filled with a cool masterfulness. If the man tendered his resignation, let him tender his damned resignation.

'Well, McAllister?' said Lord Emsworth coldly.

He removed his top hat and brushed it against his sleeve.

'What is the matter, McAllister?'

He replaced his top hat.

'You appear agitated, McAllister.'

He jerked his head militantly. The hat fell off. He let it lie. Freed from its loathsome weight he felt more masterful than ever. It had just needed that to bring him to the top of his form.

'This young lady,' said Lord Emsworth, 'has my full permission to pick all the flowers she wants, McAllister. If you do not see eye to eye with me in this matter, McAllister, say so and we will discuss what you are going to do about it, McAllister. These gardens, McAllister, belong to me, and if you do not – er – appreciate that fact you will, no doubt, be able to find another employer – ah – more in tune with your views. I value your services highly, McAllister, but I will not be dictated to in my own garden, McAllister. Er – dash it,' added his lordship, spoiling the whole effect.

A long moment followed in which Nature stood still, breathless. The Achillea stood still. So did the Bignonia Radicans. So did the Campanula, the Digitalis, the Euphorbia, the Funkia, the Gypsophila, the Helianthus, the Iris, the Liatris, the Monarda, the Phlox Drummondi, the Salvia, the Thalictrum, the Vinca and the Yucca. From far off in the direction of the park there sounded the happy howls of children who were probably breaking things, but even these seemed hushed. The evening breeze had died away.

Angus McAllister stood glowering. His attitude was that of one sorely perplexed. So might the early bird have looked if the worm ear-marked for its breakfast had suddenly turned and snapped at it. It had never occurred to him that his employer would voluntarily suggest that he sought another position, and now that he had suggested it Angus McAllister disliked the idea very much. Blandings Castle was in his bones. Elsewhere, he would feel an exile. He fingered his whiskers, but they gave him no comfort.

He made his decision. Better to cease to be a Napoleon than be a Napoleon in exile.

'Mphm,' said Angus McAllister.

'Oh, and by the way, McAllister,' said Lord Emsworth, 'that matter of the gravel path through the yew alley. I've been thinking it over, and I won't have it. Not on any account. Mutilate my beautiful moss with a beastly gravel path? Make an eyesore of the loveliest spot in one of the finest and oldest gardens in the United Kingdom? Certainly not. Most decidedly not. Try to remember, McAllister, as you work in the gardens of Blandings Castle, that you are not back in Glasgow, laying out recreation grounds. That is all, McAllister. Er – dash it – that is all.'

'Mphm,' said Angus McAllister.

He turned. He walked away. The potting-shed swallowed him up. Nature resumed its breathing. The breeze began to blow again. And all over the gardens birds who had stopped on their high note carried on according to plan.

Lord Emsworth took out his handkerchief and dabbed with it at his forehead. He was shaken, but a novel sense of being a man among men thrilled him. It might seem bravado, but he almost wished – yes, dash it, he almost wished – that his sister Constance would come along and start something while he felt like this.

He had his wish.

'Clarence!'

Yes, there she was, hurrying towards him up the garden path. She, like McAllister, seemed agitated. Something was on her mind.

Vintage Wodehouse

'Clarence!'

'Don't keep saying "Clarence!" as if you were a dashed parrot,' said Lord Emsworth haughtily. 'What the dickens is the matter, Constance?'

'Matter? Do you know what the time is? Do you know that everybody is waiting down there for you to make your speech?'

Lord Emsworth met her eye sternly.

'I do not,' he said. 'And I don't care. I'm not going to make any dashed speech. If you want a speech, let the vicar make it. Or make it yourself. Speech! I never heard such dashed nonsense in my life.' He turned to Gladys. 'Now, my dear,' he said, 'if you will just give me time to get out of these infernal clothes and this ghastly collar and put on something human, we'll go down to the village and have a chat with Ern.'

Blandings Castle (1935)

Bertie's Saviour

*Dogs were usually friendly to Bertie in his later life. But one
recalls Stiffy Byng's Scotch terrier Bartholomew (see page 251
and ff.)*

Stop me if I've told you this before, but once when I was up at
Oxford and chatting on the river bank with a girl called something that's slipped my mind there was a sound of barking and
a great hefty dog of the Hound of the Baskervilles type came
galloping at me, obviously intent on mayhem, its whole aspect
that of a dog that has no use for Woosters. And I was just commending my soul to God and thinking that this was where my
new flannel trousers got about thirty bobs' worth of value bitten out of them, when the girl, waiting till she saw the whites of
its eyes, with extraordinary presence of mind opened a coloured
Japanese umbrella in the animal's face. Upon which, with a
startled exclamation it did three back somersaults and retired
into private life.

Jeeves in the Offing (1960)

Honeysuckle Cottage

*Wodehouse was always sympathetic with best-selling
sentimental female novelists. Also with male writers of
sensational mystery novels. Here B meets A in a fourth
dimension.*

'Do you believe in ghosts?' asked Mr Mulliner abruptly. I
weighed the question thoughtfully. I was a little surprised, for
nothing in our previous conversation had suggested the topic.

'Well,' I replied, 'I don't like them, if that's what you mean.
I was once butted by one as a child.'

'Ghosts. Not goats.'

'Oh, ghosts? Do I believe in ghosts?'

'Exactly.'

'Well, yes – and no.'

'Let me put it another way,' said Mr Mulliner, patiently. 'Do
you believe in haunted houses? Do you believe that it is possible for a malign influence to envelop a place and work a spell
on all who come within its radius?'

I hesitated.

'Well, no – and yes.'

Mr Mulliner sighed a little. He seemed to be wondering if I
was always as bright as this.

'Of course,' I went on, 'one has read stories. Henry James's
Turn of The Screw ...'

'I am not talking about fiction.'

'Well, in real life – Well, look here, I once, as a matter of
fact, did meet a man who knew a fellow ...'

'My distant cousin James Rodman spent some weeks in a
haunted house,' said Mr Mulliner, who, if he has a fault, is not

a very good listener. 'It cost him five thousand pounds. That is to say, he sacrificed five thousand pounds by not remaining there. Did you ever,' he asked, wandering, it seemed to me, from the subject, 'hear of Leila J. Pinckney?'

Naturally I had heard of Leila J. Pinckney. Her death some years ago has diminished her vogue, but at one time it was impossible to pass a book-shop or a railway bookstall without seeing a long row of her novels. I have never myself actually read any of them, but I knew that in her particular line of literature, the Squashily Sentimental, she had always been regarded by those entitled to judge as pre-eminent. The critics usually headed their reviews of her stories with the words:

ANOTHER PINCKNEY

or sometimes, more offensively:

ANOTHER PINCKNEY ! ! !

And once, dealing with, I think, *The Love Which Prevails*, the literary expert of the *Scrutinizer* had compressed his entire critique into the single phrase 'Oh God!'

'Of course,' I said. 'But what about her?'

'She was James Rodman's aunt.'

'Yes?'

'And when she died James found that she had left him five thousand pounds and the house in the country where she had lived for the last twenty years of her life.'

'A very nice little legacy.'

'Twenty years,' repeated Mr Mulliner. 'Grasp that, for it has a vital bearing on what follows. Twenty years, mind you, and Miss Pinckney turned out two novels and twelve short stories regularly every year besides a monthly page of Advice to Young Girls in one of the magazines. That is to say, forty of her novels and no fewer than two hundred and forty of her short stories were written under the roof of Honeysuckle Cottage.'

'A pretty name.'

'A nasty, sloppy name,' said Mr Mulliner severely, 'which

should have warned my distant cousin James from the start. Have you a pencil and a piece of paper?' He scribbled for a while, poring frowningly over columns of figures. 'Yes,' he said, looking up, 'if my calculations are correct, Leila J. Pinckney wrote in all a matter of nine million one hundred and forty thousand words of glutinous sentimentality at Honeysuckle Cottage, and it was a condition of her will that James should reside there for six months in every year. Failing to do this, he was to forfeit the five thousand pounds.'

'It must be great fun making a freak will,' I mused. 'I often wish I was rich enough to do it.'

'This was not a freak will. The conditions are perfectly understandable. James Rodman was a writer of sensational mystery stories, and his aunt Leila had always disapproved of his work. She was a great believer in the influence of environment, and the reason why she inserted that clause in her will was that she wished to compel James to move from London to the country. She considered that living in London hardened him and made his outlook on life sordid. She often asked him if he thought it quite nice to harp so much on sudden death and blackmailers with squints. Surely, she said, there were enough squinting blackmailers in the world without writing about them.

'The fact that Literature meant such different things to these two had, I believe, caused something of a coolness between them, and James had never dreamed that he would be remembered in his aunt's will. For he had never concealed his opinion that Leila J. Pinckney's style of writing revolted him, however dear it might be to her enormous public. He held rigid views on the art of the novel, and always maintained that an artist with a true reverence for his craft should not descend to gooey love stories, but should stick austerely to revolvers, cries in the night, missing papers, mysterious Chinamen and dead bodies – with or without gash in throat. And not even the thought that his aunt had dandled him on her knee as a baby could induce him to stifle his literary conscience to the extent of pretending to enjoy her work. First, last and all the time, James Rodman had held the opinion – and voiced it fearlessly – that Leila J. Pinckney wrote bilge.

'It was a surprise to him, therefore, to find that he had been left this legacy. A pleasant surprise, of course. James was making quite a decent income out of the three novels and eighteen short stories which he produced annually, but an author can always find a use for five thousand pounds. And, as for the cottage, he had actually been looking about for a little place in the country at the very moment when he received the lawyer's letter. In less than a week he was installed at his new residence.'

James's first impressions of Honeysuckle Cottage were, he tells me, wholly favourable. He was delighted with the place. It was a low, rambling, picturesque old house with funny little chimneys and a red roof, placed in the middle of the most charming country. With its oak beams, its trim garden, its trilling birds and its rose-hung porch, it was the ideal spot for a writer. It was just the sort of place, he reflected whimsically, which his aunt had loved to write about in her books. Even the apple-cheeked old housekeeper who attended to his needs might have stepped straight out of one of them.

It seemed to James that his lot had been cast in pleasant places. He had brought down his books, his pipes, and his golf-clubs, and was hard at work finishing the best thing he had ever done. *The Secret Nine* was the title of it; and on the beautiful summer afternoon on which this story opens he was in the study, hammering away at his typewriter, at peace with the world. The machine was running sweetly, the new tobacco he had bought the day before was proving admirable, and he was moving on all six cylinders to the end of a chapter.

He shoved in a fresh sheet of paper, chewed his pipe thoughtfully for a moment, then wrote rapidly:

'For an instant Lester Gage thought that he must have been mistaken. Then the noise came again, faint but unmistakable – a soft scratching on the outer panel.

'His mouth set in a grim line. Silently, like a panther, he made

227

one quick step to the desk, noiselessly opened a drawer, drew out his automatic. After that affair of the poisoned needle, he was taking no chances. Still in dead silence, he tiptoed to the door; then, flinging it suddenly open, he stood there, his weapon poised.

'On the mat stood the most beautiful girl he had ever beheld. A veritable child of Faërie. She eyed him for a moment with a saucy smile; then with a pretty, roguish look of reproof shook a dainty forefinger at him.

' "I believe you've forgotten me, Mr Gage!" she fluted with a mock severity which her eyes belied.'

James stared at the paper dumbly. He was utterly perplexed. He had not had the slightest intention of writing anything like this. To begin with, it was a rule with him, and one which he never broke, to allow no girls to appear in his stories. Sinister landladies, yes, and naturally any amount of adventuresses with foreign accents, but never under any pretext what may be broadly described as girls. A detective story, he maintained, should have no heroine. Heroines only held up the action and tried to flirt with the hero when he should have been busy looking for clues, and then went and let the villain kidnap them by some childishly simple trick. In his writing, James was positively monastic.

And yet here was this creature with her saucy smile and her dainty forefinger horning in at the most important point in the story. It was uncanny.

He looked once more at his scenario. No, the scenario was all right.

In perfectly plain words it stated that what happened when the door opened was that a dying man fell in and after gasping, 'The beetle! Tell Scotland Yard that the blue beetle is –' expired on the hearth-rug, leaving Lester Gage not unnaturally somewhat mystified. Nothing whatever about any beautiful girls.

In a curious mood of irritation, James scratched out the offending passage, wrote in the necessary corrections and put

228

the cover on the machine. It was at this point that he heard William whining.

The only blot on this paradise which James had so far been able to discover was the infernal dog, William. Belonging nominally to the gardener, on the very first morning he had adopted James by acclamation, and he maddened and infuriated James. He had a habit of coming and whining under the window when James was at work. The latter would ignore this as long as he could; then, when the thing became insupportable, would bound out of his chair, to see the animal standing on the gravel, gazing expectantly up at him with a stone in his mouth. William had a weak-minded passion for chasing stones; and on the first day James, in a rash spirit of camaraderie, had flung one for him. Since then James had thrown no more stones; but he had thrown any number of other solids, and the garden was littered with objects ranging from match boxes to a plaster statuette of the young Joseph prophesying before Pharaoh. And still William came and whined, an optimist to the last.

The whining, coming now at a moment when he felt irritable and unsettled, acted on James much as the scratching on the door had acted on Lester Gage. Silently, like a panther, he made one quick step to the mantelpiece, removed from it a china mug bearing the legend A Present From Clacton-on-Sea, and crept to the window.

And as he did so a voice outside said, 'Go away, sir, go away!' and there followed a short, high-pitched bark which was certainly not William's. William was a mixture of Airedale, setter, bull-terrier, and mastiff; and when in vocal mood, favoured the mastiff side of his family.

James peered out. There on the porch stood a girl in blue. She held in her arms a small fluffy white dog, and she was endeavouring to foil the upward movement toward this of the blackguard William. William's mentality had been arrested some years before at the point where he imagined that everything in the world had been created for him to eat. A bone, a boot, a steak, the back wheel of a bicycle – it was all one to William. If it was there he tried to eat it. He had even made a plucky attempt to devour the remains of the young Joseph prophesying before Pharaoh. And it was perfectly plain now that he regarded the curious wriggling object in the girl's arms purely in the light of a snack to keep body and soul together till dinner-time.

'William!' bellowed James.

William looked courteously over his shoulder with eyes that beamed with the pure light of a life's devotion, wagged the whiplike tail which he had inherited from his bull-terrier ancestors and resumed his intent scrutiny of the fluffy dog.

'Oh, please!' cried the girl. 'This great rough dog is frightening poor Toto.'

The man of letters and the man of action do not always go hand in hand, but practice had made James perfect in handling with a swift efficiency any situation that involved William. A moment later that canine moron, having received the present from Clacton in the short ribs, was scuttling round the corner of the house, and James had jumped through the window and was facing the girl.

She was an extraordinarily pretty girl. Very sweet and fragile she looked as she stood there under the honeysuckle with the breeze ruffling a tendril of golden hair that strayed from beneath her coquettish little hat. Her eyes were very big and very blue, her rose-tinted face becomingly flushed. All wasted on James, though. He disliked all girls, and particularly the sweet, droopy type.

'Did you want to see somebody?' he asked stiffly.

'Just the house,' said the girl, 'if it wouldn't be giving any trouble. I do so want to see the room where Miss Pinckney wrote her books. This is where Leila J. Pinckney used to live, isn't it?'

'Yes; I am her nephew. My name is James Rodman.'

'Mine is Rose Maynard.'

James led the way into the house, and she stopped with a cry of delight on the threshold of the morning-room.

'Oh, how too perfect!' she cried. 'So this was her study?'

'Yes.'

'What a wonderful place it would be for you to think in if you were a writer too.'

James held no high opinion of women's literary taste, but nevertheless he was conscious of an unpleasant shock.

'I am a writer,' he said coldly. 'I write detective stories.'

'I – I'm afraid' – she blushed – 'I'm afraid I don't often read detective stories.'

'You no doubt prefer,' said James, still more coldly, 'the sort of thing my aunt used to write.'

'Oh, I love her stories!' cried the girl, clasping her hands ecstatically. 'Don't you?'

'I cannot say that I do.'

'What?'

'They are pure apple-sauce,' said James sternly; 'just nasty blobs of sentimentality, thoroughly untrue to life.'

The girl stared.

'Why, that's just what's so wonderful about them, their trueness to life! You feel they might all have happened. I don't understand what you mean.'

They were walking down the garden now. James held the gate open for her and she passed through into the road.

'Well, for one thing,' he said, 'I decline to believe that a marriage between two young people is invariably preceded by some violent and sensational experience in which they both share.'

'Are you thinking of *Scent o' the Blossom*, where Edgar saves Maud from drowning?'

'I am thinking of every single one of my aunt's books.' He looked at her curiously. He had just got the solution of a mystery which had been puzzling him for some time. Almost from the moment he had set eyes on her she had seemed somehow strangely familiar. It now suddenly came to him why it was that he disliked her so much. 'Do you know,' he said, 'you might be one of my aunt's heroines yourself? You're just the sort of girl she used to love to write about.'

Her face lit up.

'Oh, do you really think so?' She hesitated. 'Do you know

231

what I have been feeling ever since I came here? I've been feeling that you are exactly like one of Miss Pinckney's heroes.'

'No, I say, really!' said James, revolted.

'Oh, but you are! When you jumped through that window it gave me quite a start. You were so exactly like Claude Masterton in *Heather o' the Hills.*'

'I have not read *Heather o' the Hills,*' said James with a shudder.

'He was very strong and quiet, with deep, dark, sad eyes.'

James did not explain that his eyes were sad because her society gave him a pain in the neck. He merely laughed scornfully.

'So now, I suppose,' he said, 'a car will come and knock you down and I shall carry you gently into the house and lay you – Look out!' he cried.

It was too late. She was lying in a little huddled heap at his feet. Round the corner a large automobile had come bowling, keeping with an almost affected precision to the wrong side of the road. It was now receding into the distance, the occupant of the tonneau, a stout red-faced gentleman in a fur coat, leaning out over the back. He had bared his head – not, one fears, as a pretty gesture of respect and regret, but because he was using his hat to hide the number plate.

The dog Toto was unfortunately uninjured.

James carried the girl gently into the house and laid her on the sofa in the morning-room. He rang the bell and the apple-cheeked housekeeper appeared.

'Send for the doctor,' said James. 'There has been an accident.'

The housekeeper bent over the girl.

'Eh, dearie, dearie!' she said. 'Bless her sweet pretty face!'

The gardener, he who technically owned William, was routed out from among the young lettuces and told to fetch Doctor Brady. He separated his bicycle from William, who was making a light meal off the left pedal, and departed on his mission. Doctor Brady arrived and in due course he made his report.

'No bones broken, but a number of nasty bruises. And, of course, the shock. She will have to stay here for some time, Rodman. Can't be moved.'

'Stay here! But she can't! It isn't proper.'

'Your housekeeper will act as a chaperon.'

The doctor sighed. He was a stolid-looking man of middle age with side whiskers.

'A beautiful girl, that, Rodman,' he said.

'I suppose so,' said James.

'A sweet, beautiful girl. An elfin child.'

'A what?' cried James, starting.

This imagery was very foreign to Doctor Brady as he knew him. On the only previous occasion on which they had had any extended conversation, the doctor had talked exclusively about the effect of too much protein on the gastric juices.

'An elfin child; a tender, fairy creature. When I was looking at her just now, Rodman, I nearly broke down. Her little hand lay on the coverlet like some white lily floating on the surface of a still pool, and her dear, trusting eyes gazed up at me.'

He pottered off down the garden, still babbling, and James stood staring after him blankly. And slowly, like some cloud athwart a summer sky, there crept over James's heart the chill shadow of a nameless fear.

It was about a week later that Mr Andrew McKinnon, the senior partner in the well-known firm of literary agents, McKinnon & Gooch, sat in his office in Chancery Lane, frowning thoughtfully over a telegram. He rang the bell.

'Ask Mr Gooch to step in here.' He resumed his study of the telegram. 'Oh, Gooch,' he said when his partner appeared, 'I've just had a curious wire from young Rodman. He seems to want to see me very urgently.'

Mr Gooch read the telegram.

'Written under the influence of some strong mental excitement,' he agreed. 'I wonder why he doesn't come to the office if he wants to see you so badly.'

'He's working very hard, finishing that novel for Prodder &

Wiggs. Can't leave it, I suppose. Well, it's a nice day. If you will look after things here I think I'll motor down and let him give me lunch.'

As Mr McKinnon's car reached the crossroads a mile from Honeysuckle Cottage, he was aware of a gesticulating figure by the hedge. He stopped the car.

'Morning, Rodman.'

'Thank God you've come!' said James. It seemed to Mr Mc-Kinnon that the young man looked paler and thinner. 'Would you mind walking the rest of the way? There's something I want to speak to you about.'

Mr McKinnon alighted; and James, as he glanced at him, felt cheered and encouraged by the very sight of the man. The literary agent was a grim, hardbitten person, to whom, when he called at their offices to arrange terms, editors kept their faces turned so that they might at least retain their back collar studs. There was no sentiment in Andrew McKinnon. Editresses of society papers practised their blandishments on him in vain, and many a publisher had walked screaming in the night, dreaming that he was signing a McKinnon contract.

'Well, Rodman,' he said, 'Prodder & Wiggs have agreed to our terms. I was writing to tell you so when your wire arrived. I had a lot of trouble with them, but it's fixed at twenty per cent., rising to twenty-five, and two hundred pounds advance royalties on day of publication.'

'Good!' said James absently. 'Good! McKinnon, do you remember my aunt, Leila J. Pinckney?'

'Remember her? Why, I was her agent all her life.'

'Of course. Then you know the sort of tripe she wrote.'

'No author,' said Mr McKinnon reprovingly, 'who pulls down a steady twenty thousand pounds a year writes tripe.'

'Well anyway, you know her stuff.'

'Who better?'

'When she died she left me five thousand pounds and her house, Honeysuckle Cottage. I'm living there now. McKinnon, do you believe in haunted houses?'

234

'No.'

'Yet I tell you solemnly that Honeysuckle Cottage is haunted!'

'By your aunt?' said Mr McKinnon, surprised.

'By her influence. There's a malignant spell over the place; a sort of miasma of sentimentalism. Everybody who enters it succumbs.'

'Tut-tut! You mustn't have these fancies.'

'They aren't fancies.'

'You aren't seriously meaning to tell me –'

'Well, how do you account for this? That book you were speaking about, which Prodder & Wiggs are to publish – *The Secret Nine*. Every time I sit down to write it a girl keeps trying to sneak in.'

'Into the room?'

'Into the story.'

'You don't want a love interest in your sort of book,' said Mr McKinnon, shaking his head. 'It delays the action.'

'I know it does. And every day I have to keep shooing this infernal female out. An awful girl, McKinnon. A soppy, soupy, treacly, drooping girl with a roguish smile. This morning she tried to butt in on the scene where Lester Gage is trapped in the den of the mysterious leper.'

'No!'

'She did, I assure you. I had to rewrite three pages before I could get her out of it. And that's not the worst. Do you know, McKinnon, that at this moment I am actually living the plot of a typical Leila J. Pinckney novel in just the setting she always used! And I can see the happy ending coming nearer every day! A week ago a girl was knocked down by a car at my door and I've had to put her up, and every day I realize more clearly that sooner or later I shall ask her to marry me.'

'Don't do it,' said Mr McKinnon, a stout bachelor. 'You're too young to marry.'

'So was Methuselah,' said James, a stouter. 'But all the same I know I'm going to do it. It's the influence of this awful house weighing upon me. I feel like an eggshell in a maelstrom. I am

235

being sucked in by a force too strong for me to resist. This morning I found myself kissing her dog!'

'No!'

'I did! And I loathe the little beast. Yesterday I got up at dawn and plucked a nosegay of flowers for her, wet with the dew.'

'Rodman!'

'It's a fact. I laid them at her door and went downstairs kicking myself all the way. And there in the hall was the apple-cheeked housekeeper regarding me archly. If she didn't murmur "Bless their sweet young hearts!" my ears deceived me.'

'Why don't you pack up and leave?'

'If I do I lose the five thousand pounds.'

'Ah!' said Mr McKinnon.

'I can understand what has happened. It's the same with all haunted houses. My aunt's subliminal ether vibrations have woven themselves into the texture of the place, creating an atmosphere which forces the ego of all who come in contact with it to attune themselves to it. It's either that or something to do with the fourth dimension.'

Mr McKinnon laughed scornfully.

'Tut-tut!' he said again. 'This is pure imagination. What has happened is that you've been working too hard. You'll see this precious atmosphere of yours will have no effect on me.'

'That's exactly why I asked you to come down. I hoped you might break the spell.'

'I will that,' said Mr McKinnon jovially.

The fact that the literary agent spoke little at lunch caused James no apprehension. Mr McKinnon was ever a silent trencherman. From time to time James caught him stealing a glance at the girl, who was well enough to come down to meals now, limping pathetically; but he could read nothing in his face. And yet the mere look of his face was a consolation. It was so solid, so matter of fact, so exactly like an unemotional coconut.

'You've done me good,' said James with a sigh of relief, as he escorted the agent down the garden to his car after lunch,

'I felt all along that I could rely on your rugged common sense. The whole atmosphere of the place seems different now.'

Mr McKinnon did not speak for a moment. He seemed to be plunged in thought.

'Rodman,' he said, as he got into his car, 'I've been thinking over that suggestion of yours of putting a love interest into *The Secret Nine*. I think you're wise. The story needs it. After all, what is there greater in the world than love? Love – love – aye, it's the sweetest word in the language. Put in a heroine and let her marry Lester Gage.'

'If,' said James grimly, 'she does succeed in worming her way in she'll jolly well marry the mysterious leper. But look here, I don't understand –'

'It was seeing that girl that changed me,' proceeded Mr Mc-Kinnon. And as James stared at him aghast, tears suddenly filled his hard-boiled eyes. He openly snuffled. 'Aye, seeing her sitting there under the roses, with all that smell of honeysuckle and all. And the birdies singing so sweet in the garden and the sun lighting up her bonny face. The puir wee lass!' he muttered, dabbing at his eyes. 'The puir bonny wee lass! Rodman,' he said, his voice quivering, 'I've decided that we're being hard on Prodder & Wiggs. Wiggs has had a sickness in his home lately. We mustn't be hard on a man who's had sickness in his home, hey, laddie? No, no! I'm going to take back that contract and alter it to a flat twelve per cent and no advance royalties.'

'What!'

'But you shan't lose by it, Rodman. No, no, you shan't lose by it, my manny. I am going to waive my commission. The puir bonny wee lass!'

The car rolled off down the road. Mr McKinnon, seated in the back, was blowing his nose violently.

'This is the end!' said James.

It is necessary at this point to pause and examine James Rodman's position with an unbiased eye. The average man, unless he puts himself in James's place, will be unable to appreciate it.

James, he will feel, was making a lot of fuss about nothing. Here he was, drawing daily closer and closer to a charming girl with big blue eyes, and surely rather to be envied than pitied.

But we must remember that James was one of Nature's bachelors. And no ordinary man, looking forward dreamily to a little home of his own with a loving wife putting out his slippers and changing the gramophone records, can realize the intensity of the instinct for self-preservation which animates Nature's bachelors in times of peril.

James Rodman had a congenital horror of matrimony. Though a young man, he had allowed himself to develop a great many habits which were as the breath of life to him; and these habits, he knew instinctively, a wife would shoot to pieces within a week of the end of the honeymoon.

James liked to breakfast in bed; and, having breakfasted, to smoke in bed and knock the ashes out on the carpet. What wife would tolerate this practice?

James liked to pass his days in a tennis shirt, grey flannel trousers and slippers. What wife ever rests until she has inclosed her husband in a stiff collar, tight boots and a morning suit and taken him with her to *thés musicales*?

These and a thousand other thoughts of the same kind flashed through the unfortunate young man's mind as the days went by, and every day that passed seemed to draw him nearer to the brink of the chasm. Fate appeared to be taking a malicious pleasure in making things as difficult for him as possible. Now that the girl was well enough to leave her bed, she spent her time sitting in a chair on the sun-sprinkled porch, and James had to read to her – and poetry, at that; and not the jolly, wholesome sort of poetry the boys are turning to nowadays, either – good, honest stuff about sin and gas-works and decaying corpses – but the old-fashioned kind with rhymes in it, dealing almost exclusively with love. The weather, moreover, continued superb. The honeysuckle cast its sweet scent on the gentle breeze; the roses over the porch stirred and nodded; the flowers in the garden were lovelier than ever; the birds sang their little throats sore. And every evening there was a magnificent sunset. It was almost as if Nature were doing it on purpose.

At last James intercepted Doctor Brady as he was leaving after one of his visits and put the thing squarely:

'When is that girl going?'

The doctor patted him on the arm.

'Not yet, Rodman,' he said in a low, understanding voice. 'No need to worry yourself about that. Mustn't be moved for days and days and days – I might almost say weeks and weeks and weeks.'

'Weeks and weeks!' cried James.

'And weeks,' said Doctor Brady. He prodded James roguishly in the abdomen. 'Good luck to you, my boy, good luck to you,' he said.

It was some small consolation to James that the mushy physician immediately afterward tripped over William on his way down the path and broke his stethoscope. When a man is up against it like James every little helps.

He was walking dismally back to the house after this conversation when he was met by the apple-cheeked housekeeper.

'The little lady would like to speak to you, sir,' said the apple-cheeked exhibit, rubbing her hands.

'Would she?' said James hollowly.

'So sweet and pretty she looks, sir – oh, sir, you wouldn't believe! Like a blessed angel sitting there with her dear eyes all a-shining.'

'Don't do it!' cried James with extraordinary vehemence. 'Don't do it!'

He found the girl propped up on the cushions and thought once again how singularly he disliked her. And yet, even as he thought this, some force against which he had to fight madly was whispering to him, 'Go to her and take that little hand! Breathe into that little ear the burning words that will make that little face turn away crimsoned with blushes!' He wiped a bead of perspiration from his forehead and sat down.

239

'Mrs Stick-in-the-Mud — what's her name? — says you want to see me.'

The girl nodded.

'I've had a letter from Uncle Henry. I wrote to him as soon as I was better and told him what had happened, and he is coming here tomorrow morning.'

'Uncle Henry?'

'That's what I call him, but he's really no relation. He is my guardian. He and daddy were officers in the same regiment, and when daddy was killed, fighting on the Afghan frontier, he died in Uncle Henry's arms and with his last breath begged him to take care of me.'

James started. A sudden wild hope had waked in his heart. Years ago, he remembered, he had read a book of his aunt's entitled *Rupert's Legacy*, and in that book —

'I'm engaged to marry him,' said the girl quietly.

'Wow!' shouted James.

'What?' asked the girl, startled.

'Touch of cramp,' said James. He was thrilling all over. That wild hope had been realized.

'It was daddy's dying wish that we should marry,' said the girl.

'And dashed sensible of him, too; dashed sensible,' said James warmly.

'And yet,' she went on, a little wistfully, 'I sometimes wonder —'

'Don't!' said James. 'Don't! You must respect daddy's dying wish. There's nothing like daddy's dying wish; you can't beat it. So he's coming here tomorrow, is he? Capital, capital. To lunch, I suppose? Excellent. I'll run down and tell Mrs Who-Is-It to lay in another chop.'

It was with a gay and uplifted heart that James strolled the garden and smoked his pipe next morning. A great cloud seemed to have rolled itself away from him. Everything was for the best in the best of all possible worlds. He had finished *The Secret Nine* and shipped it off to Mr McKinnon, and now as he strolled there was shaping itself in his mind a corking plot about a man with only half a face who lived in a secret den and terrorised London with a series of shocking murders. And what made them so shocking was the fact that each of the victims, when discovered, was found to have only half a face too. The rest had been chipped off, presumably by a blunt instrument.

The thing was coming out magnificently, when suddenly his attention was diverted by a piercing scream. Out of the bushes fringing the river that ran beside the garden burst the apple-cheeked housekeeper.

'Oh, sir! Oh, sir! Oh, sir!'

'What is it?' demanded James irritably.

'Oh, sir! Oh, sir! Oh, sir!'

'Yes, and then what?'

'The little dog, sir! He's in the river!'

'Well, whistle him to come out.'

'Oh, sir, do come quick! He'll be drowned!'

James followed her through the bushes, taking off his coat as he went. He was saying to himself, 'I will not rescue this dog. I do not like the dog. It is high time he had a bath, and in any case it would be much simpler to stand on the bank and fish for him with a rake. Only an ass out of a Leila J. Pinckney book would dive into a beastly river to save –'

At this point he dived. Toto, alarmed by the splash, swam rapidly for the bank, but James was too quick for him. Grasping him firmly by the neck, he scrambled ashore and ran for the house, followed by the housekeeper.

The girl was seated on the porch. Over her there bent the tall soldierly figure of a man with keen eyes and greying hair. The housekeeper raced up.

'Oh, Miss! Toto! In the river! He saved him! He plunged in and saved him!'

The girl drew a quick breath.

'Gallant, damme! By Jove! By gad! Yes, gallant, by George!' exclaimed the soldierly man.

The girl seemed to wake from a reverie.

'Uncle Henry, this is Mr Rodman. Mr Rodman, my guardian, Colonel Carteret.'

'Proud to meet you, sir,' said the colonel, his honest blue eyes glowing as he fingered his short crisp moustache. 'As fine a thing as I ever heard of, damme!'

'Yes, you are brave – brave,' the girl whispered.

'I am wet – wet,' said James, and went upstairs to change his clothes.

When he came down for lunch, he found to his relief that the girl had decided not to join them, and Colonel Carteret was silent and preoccupied. James, exerting himself in his capacity of host, tried him with the weather, golf, India, the Government, the high cost of living, first-class cricket, the modern dancing craze and murderers he had met, but the other still preserved that strange, absent-minded silence. It was only when the meal was concluded and James had produced cigarettes that he came abruptly out of his trance.

'Rodman,' he said, 'I should like to speak to you.'

'Yes?' said James, thinking it was about time.

'Rodman,' said Colonel Carteret, 'or rather, George – I may call you George?' he added, with a sort of wistful diffidence that had a singular charm.

'Certainly,' replied James, 'if you wish it. Though my name is James.'

'James, eh? Well, well, it amounts to the same thing, eh, what, damme, by gad?' said the colonel with a momentary return to his bluff soldierly manner. 'Well, then, James, I have something that I wish to say to you. Did Miss Maynard – did Rose happen to tell you anything about myself in – er – in connection with herself?'

'She mentioned that you and she were engaged to be married.'

The colonel's tightly drawn lips quivered.

'No longer,' he said.

'What?'

'No, John, my boy.'

'James.'

'No, James, my boy, no longer. While you were upstairs changing your clothes she told me – breaking down, poor child, as she spoke – that she wished our engagement to be at an end.'

242

James half rose from the table, his cheeks blanched.

'You don't mean that!' he gasped.

Colonel Carteret nodded. He was staring out of the window, his fine eyes set in a look of pain.

'But this is nonsense!' cried James. 'This is absurd! She – she mustn't be allowed to chop and change like this. I mean to say, it – it isn't fair –'

'Don't think of me, my boy.'

'I'm not – I mean, did she give any reason?'

'Her eyes did.'

'Her eyes did?'

'Her eyes, when she looked at you on the porch, as you stood there – young, heroic – having just saved the life of the dog she loves. It is you who have won that tender heart, my boy.'

'Now, listen,' protested James, 'you aren't going to sit there and tell me that a girl falls in love with a man just because he saves her dog from drowning?'

'Why, surely,' said Colonel Carteret, surprised. 'What better reason could she have?' He sighed. 'It is the old, old story, my boy. Youth to youth. I am an old man. I should have known – I should have foreseen – yes, youth to youth.'

'You aren't a bit old.'

'Yes, yes.'

'No, no.'

'Yes, yes.'

'Don't keep on saying yes, yes!' cried James, clutching at his hair. 'Besides, she wants a steady old buffer – a steady, sensible man of medium age – to look after her.'

Colonel Carteret shook his head with a gentle smile.

'This is mere quixotry, my boy. It is splendid of you to take this attitude; but no, no.'

'Yes, yes.'

'No, no.' He gripped James's hand for an instant, then rose and walked to the door. 'That is all I wished to say, Tom.'

'James.'

'James. I just thought that you ought to know how matters stood. Go to her, my boy, go to her, and don't let any thought

243

of an old man's broken dream keep you from pouring out what is in your heart. I am an old soldier, lad, an old soldier. I have learned to take the rough with the smooth. But I think – I think I will leave you now. I – I should – should like to be alone for a while. If you need me you will find me in the raspberry bushes.'

He had scarcely gone when James also left the room. He took his hat and stick and walked blindly out of the garden, he knew not whither. His brain was numbed. Then, as his powers of reasoning returned, he told himself that he should have foreseen this ghastly thing. If there was one type of character over which Leila J. Pinckney had been wont to spread herself, it was the pathetic guardian who loves his ward but relinquishes her to the younger man. No wonder the girl had broken off the engagement. An elderly guardian who allowed himself to come within a mile of Honeysuckle Cottage was simply asking for it. And then, as he turned to walk back, a dull defiance gripped James. Why, he asked, should he be put upon in this manner? If the girl liked to throw over this man, why should he be the goat?

He saw his way clearly now. He just couldn't do it, that was all. And if they didn't like it they could lump it.

Full of a new fortitude, he strode in at the gate. A tall, soldierly figure emerged from the raspberry bushes and came to meet him.

'Well?' said Colonel Carteret.

'Well?' said James defiantly.

'Am I to congratulate you?'

James caught his keen blue eye and hesitated. It was not going to be so simple as he had supposed.

'Well – er –' he said.

Into the keen blue eyes there came a look that James had not seen there before. It was the stern, hard look which – probably – had caused men to bestow upon this old soldier the name of Cold-Steel Carteret.

'You have not asked Rose to marry you?'

'Er – no; not yet.'

The keen blue eyes grew keener and bluer.

'Rodman,' said Colonel Carteret in a strange, quiet voice, 'I have known that little girl since she was a tiny child. For years she has been all in all to me. Her father died in my arms and with his last breath bade me see that no harm came to his darling. I have nursed her through mumps, measles – aye, and chicken-pox – and I live but for her happiness.' He paused, with a significance that made James's toes curl. 'Rodman,' he said, 'do you know what I would do to any man who trifled with that little girl's affections?' He reached in his hip pocket and an ugly-looking revolver glittered in the sunlight. 'I would shoot him like a dog.'

'Like a dog?' faltered James.

'Like a dog,' said Colonel Carteret. He took James's arm and turned him towards the house. 'She is on the porch. Go to her. And if –' He broke off. 'But tut!' he said in a kindlier tone. 'I am doing you an injustice, my boy. I know it.'

'Oh, you are,' said James fervently.

'Your heart is in the right place.'

'Oh, absolutely,' said James.

'Then go to her, my boy. Later on you may have something to tell me. You will find me in the strawberry beds.'

It was very cool and fragrant on the porch. Overhead, little breezes played and laughed among the roses. Somewhere in the distance sheep bells tinkled, and in the shrubbery a thrush was singing its evensong.

Seated in her chair behind a wicker table laden with tea things, Rose Maynard watched James as he shambled up the path.

'Tea's ready,' she called gaily. 'Where is Uncle Henry?' A look of pity and distress flitted for a moment over her flower-like face. 'Oh, I – I forgot,' she whispered.

'He is in the strawberry beds,' said James in a low voice.

She nodded unhappily.

'Of course, of course. Oh, why is life like this?' James heard her whisper.

He sat down. He looked at the girl. She was leaning back with closed eyes, and he thought he had never seen such a little squirt in his life. The idea of passing his remaining days in her society revolted him. He was stoutly opposed to the idea of marrying anyone; but if, as happens to the best of us, he ever were compelled to perform the wedding glide, he had always hoped it would be with some lady golf champion who would help him with his putting, and thus, by bringing his handicap down a notch or two, enable him to save something from the wreck, so to speak. But to link his lot with a girl who read his aunt's books and liked them; a girl who could tolerate the presence of the dog Toto; a girl who clapped her hands in pretty, childish joy when she saw a nasturtium in bloom – it was too much. Nevertheless, he took her hand and began to speak.

'Miss Maynard – Rose –'

She opened her eyes and cast them down. A flush had come into her cheeks. The dog Toto at her side sat up and begged for cake, disregarded.

'Let me tell you a story. Once upon a time there was a lonely man who lived in a cottage all by himself –'

He stopped. Was it James Rodman who was talking this bilge?

'Yes?' whispered the girl.

'– but one day there came to him out of nowhere a little fairy princess. She –'

He stopped again, but this time not because of the sheer shame of listening to his own voice. What caused him to interrupt his tale was the fact that at this moment the tea-table suddenly began to rise slowly in the air, tilting as it did so a considerable quantity of hot tea on to the knees of his trousers.

'Ouch!' cried James, leaping.

The table continued to rise, and then fell sideways, revealing the homely countenance of William, who, concealed by the cloth, had been taking a nap beneath it. He moved slowly forward, his eyes on Toto. For many a long day William had been desirous of putting to the test, once and for all, the problem of whether Toto was edible or not. Sometimes he thought yes, at other times no. Now seemed an admirable opportunity for a definite decision. He advanced on the object of his experiment, making a low whistling noise through his nostrils, not unlike a boiling kettle. And Toto, after one long look of incredulous horror, tucked his shapely tail between his legs and, turning, raced for safety. He had laid a course in a bee-line for the open garden gate, and William, shaking a dish of marmalade off his head a little petulantly, galloped ponderously after him. Rose Maynard staggered to her feet.

'Oh, save him!' she cried.

Without a word James added himself to the procession. His interest in Toto was but tepid. What he wanted was to get near enough to William to discuss with him that matter of the tea on his trousers. He reached the road and found that the order of the runners had not changed. For so small a dog, Toto was moving magnificently. A cloud of dust rose as he skidded round the corner. William followed. James followed William.

And so they passed Farmer Birkett's barn, Farmer Giles's cow shed, the place where Farmer Willett's pigsty used to be before the big fire, and the Bunch of Grapes public house, Jno. Biggs propr., licensed to sell tobacco, wines and spirits. And it was as they were turning down the lane that leads past Farmer Robinson's chicken run that Toto, thinking swiftly, bolted abruptly into a small drain pipe.

'William!' roared James, coming up at a canter. He stopped to pluck a branch from the hedge and swooped darkly on.

William had been crouching before the pipe, making a noise like a bassoon into its interior; but now he rose and came beamingly to James. His eyes were aglow with chumminess and affection; and placing his forefeet on James's chest, he licked him three times on the face in rapid succession. And as he did so, something seemed to snap in James. The scales seemed to fall from James's eyes. For the first time he saw William as he really was, the authentic type of dog that saves his master from a frightful peril. A wave of emotion swept over him.

'William!' he muttered. 'William!'

William was making an early supper off a half brick he had found in the road. James stooped and patted him fondly.

'William,' he whispered, 'you knew when the time had come to change the conversation, didn't you, old boy!' He straight-

247

ened himself. 'Come, William,' he said. 'Another four miles and we reach Meadowsweet Junction. Make it snappy and we shall just catch the up express, first stop London.'

William looked up into his face and it seemed to James that he gave a brief nod of comprehension and approval. James turned. Through the trees to the east he could see the red roof of Honeysuckle Cottage, lurking like some evil dragon in ambush. Then, together, man and dog passed silently into the sunset.

That (concluded Mr Mulliner) is the story of my distant cousin James Rodman. As to whether it is true, that, of course, is an open question. I, personally, am of the opinion that it is. There is no doubt that James did go to live at Honeysuckle Cottage and, while there, underwent some experience which has left an ineradicable mark upon him. His eyes today have that unmistakable look which is to be seen only in the eyes of confirmed bachelors whose feet have been dragged to the very brink of the pit and who have gazed at close range into the naked face of matrimony.

And, if further proof be needed, there is William. He is now James's inseparable companion. Would any man be habitually seen in public with a dog like William unless he had some solid cause to be grateful to him – unless they were linked together by some deep and imperishable memory? I think not. Myself, when I observe William coming along the street, I cross the road and look into a shop window till he has passed. I am not a snob, but I dare not risk my position in Society by being seen talking to that curious compound.

Nor is the precaution an unnecessary one. There is about William a shameless absence of appreciation of class distinctions which recalls the worst excesses of the French Revolution. I have seen him with these eyes chivvy a pomeranian belonging to a Baroness in her own right from near the Achilles Statue to within a few yards of the Marble Arch.

And yet James walks daily with him in Piccadilly. It is surely significant.

Meet Mr Mulliner (1927)

The Case Against Sir Gregory

Matchingham Hall, where Sir Gregory Parsloe-Parsloe lives, is much too close to Blandings Castle for the comfort of Lord Emsworth and Galahad. And now the Queen of Matchingham is competing against the Empress of Blandings in the Fat Pigs class.

'Then you look after that pig of yours, Clarence.' The Hon. Galahad spoke earnestly. 'I see what this means. Parsloe's up to his old games, and intends to queer the Empress somehow.'

'Queer her?'

'Nobble her. Or, if he can't do that, steal her.'

'You don't mean that.'

'I do mean it. The man's as slippery as a greased eel. He would nobble his grandmother if it suited his book. Let me tell you I've known young Parsloe for 'hirty years and I solemnly state that if his grandmother was entered in a competition for fat pigs and his commitments made it desirable for him to get her out of the way, he would dope her bran-mash and acorns without a moment's hesitation.'

'God bless my soul!' said Lord Emsworth, deeply impressed.

'Let me tell you a little story about young Parsloe. One or two of us used to meet at the Black Footman in Gossiter Street in the old days – they've pulled it down now – and match our dogs against rats in the room behind the bar. Well, I put my Towser, an admirable beast, up against young Parsloe's Banjo on one occasion for a hundred pounds a side. And when the night came and he was shown the rats, I'm dashed if he didn't just give a long yawn and roll over and go to sleep. I whistled him ... called him ... Towser, Towser ... No good ... Fast

249

asleep. And my firm belief has always been that young Parsloe took him aside just before the contest was to start and gave him about six pounds of steak and onions. Couldn't prove anything, of course, but I sniffed the dog's breath and it was like opening the kitchen door of a Soho chophouse on a summer night. That's the sort of man young Parsloe is.'

'Galahad!'

'Fact. You'll find the story in my book.'

Summer Lightning (1929)

The Machinations of Stiffy Byng

*Of all the delightful hell-raising heroines in Wodehouse . . .
Bobbie Wickham, Nobby Hopwood, Corky Pirbright, Pauline
Stoker, Lottie Blossom and others . . . Stiffy Byng, orphan
niece and ward of bad-tempered Sir Watkyn Bassett, is the
most unscrupulous. In this story Bertie Wooster has come to
Totleigh Towers, Sir Watkyn's place, largely to help his friend
Gussie Fink-Nottle heave his engagement to Madeline Bassett
off the rocks. If those two part brass rags, the danger is that
Madeline will reach for Bertie again (they were briefly engaged
once, through a misunderstanding).*

*Gussie, who had made such an ass of himself when presenting
the prizes to the schoolboys (see page 181 and ff.), and got the
wind up about speaking at his own wedding, and he had consulted Jeeves about it. Jeeves's advice is for Gussie to note down
all the unpleasant facts (how they eat soup . . . that sort of
thing) about all the people whose derision he fears at the
wedding breakfast. Then, Jeeves says, he will learn to despise
them and will make his speech to them in complete confidence.
So Gussie has been writing it all down . . . about Sir Watkyn
Bassett, who will be his own father-in-law by then, about
Roderick Spode, the amateur dictator, and others . . . in a small
notebook.*

*Well, Stiffy gets something in her eye, Gussie gallantly whisks
out his handkerchief to remove it, and Madeline, suddenly
appearing, doesn't like the look of things. Out of Gussie's
pocket, with the handkerchief, comes the notebook, and Stiffy,
the eye-operation over, picks it up.*

*So Bertie, for his own safety and to help Gussie, must try to
get the notebook back from Stiffy.*

But Stiffy had other plans for Bertie when he came to Totleigh Towers. She loves the local curate and, since she intends to be a bishop's wife in the foreseeable future, and since Uncle Watkyn will not approve of her marrying a mere curate, she is plotting to get her uncle to give the Rev. Harold a vicarage with one hand and a blessing on their marriage with the other. And her plot, to those ends, involves Bertie, most painfully.

Just for good measure, Stiffy is also feuding with the local police constable, Oates. And here comes Oates on a bicycle ...

The shades of evening were beginning to fall pretty freely by now, but the visibility was still good enough to enable me to observe that up the road there was approaching a large, stout, moon-faced policeman on a bicycle. And he was, one could see, at peace with all the world. His daily round of tasks may or may not have been completed, but he was obviously off duty for the moment, and his whole attitude was that of a policeman with nothing on his mind but his helmet.

Well, when I tell you that he was riding without his hands, you will gather to what lengths the careless gaiety of this serene slop had spread.

And where the drama came in was that it was patent that his attention had not yet been drawn to the fact that he was being chivvied – in the strong, silent, earnest manner characteristic of this breed of animal – by a fine Aberdeen terrier. There he was, riding comfortably along, sniffing the fragrant evening breeze; and there was the Scottie, all whiskers and eyebrows, haring after him hell-for-leather. As Jeeves said later, when I described the scene to him, the whole situation resembled some great moment in a Greek tragedy, where somebody is stepping high, wide and handsome, quite unconscious that all the while Nemesis is at his heels, and he may be right.

The constable, I say, was riding without his hands: and but for this the disaster, when it occurred, might not have been so complete. I was a bit of a cyclist myself in my youth – I think I have mentioned that I once won a choir boys' handicap at some village sports – and I can testify that when you are riding without your hands, privacy and a complete freedom from interruption are of the essence. The merest suggestion of an unexpected Scottie connecting with the ankle-bone at such a time, and you swoop into a sudden swerve. And, as everybody knows, if the hands are not firmly on the handlebars, a sudden swerve spells a smeller.

And so it happened now. A smeller – and among the finest I have ever been privileged to witness – was what this officer of the law came. One moment he was with us, all merry and bright; the next he was in the ditch, a sort of *macédoine* of arms and legs and wheels, with the terrier standing on the edge, looking down at him with that rather offensive expression of virtuous smugness which I have often noticed on the faces of Aberdeen terriers in their clashes with humanity.

And as he threshed about in the ditch, endeavouring to unscramble himself, a girl came round the corner, an attractive young prune upholstered in heather-mixture tweeds, and I recognized the familiar features of S. Byng.

After what Gussie had said, I ought to have been expecting Stiffy, of course. Seeing an Aberdeen terrier, I should have gathered that it belonged to her. I might have said to myself: If Scotties come, can Stiffy be far behind?

Stiffy was plainly vexed with the policeman. You could see it in her manner. She hooked the crook of her stick over the Scottie's collar and drew him back; then addressed herself to the man, who had now begun to emerge from the ditch like Venus rising from the foam.

'What on earth,' she demanded, 'did you do that for?'

It was no business of mine, of course, but I couldn't help feeling that she might have made a more tactful approach to what threatened to be a difficult and delicate conference. And I could see that the policeman felt the same. There was a good deal of mud on his face, but not enough to hide the wounded expression.

'You might have scared him out of his wits, hurling yourself about like that. Poor old Bartholomew, did the ugly man nearly squash him flat?'

Again I missed the tactful note. In describing this public

253

servant as ugly, she was undoubtedly technically correct. Only if the competition had consisted of Sir Watkyn Bassett, Oofy Prosser of the Drones, and a few more fellows like that, could he have hoped to win to success in a beauty contest. But one doesn't want to rub these things in. Suavity is what you need on these occasions. You can't beat suavity.

The policeman had now lifted himself and bicycle out of the abyss, and was putting the latter through a series of tests, to ascertain the extent of the damage. Satisfied that it was slight, he turned and eyed Stiffy rather as old Bassett had eyed me on the occasion when I had occupied the Bosher Street dock.

'I was proceeding along the public highway,' he began, in a slow, measured tone, as if he were giving evidence in court, 'and the dorg leaped at me in a verlent manner. I was zurled from my bersicle –'

Stiffy seized upon the point like a practised debater.

'Well, you shouldn't ride a bicycle. Bartholomew hates bicycles.'

'I ride a bersicle, miss, because, if I didn't I should have to cover my beat on foot.'

'Do you good. Get some of the fat off you.'

'That,' said the policeman, no mean debater himself, producing a notebook from the recesses of his costume and blowing a water-beetle off it, 'is not the point at tissue. The point at tissue is that this makes twice that the animal has committed an aggravated assault on my person, and I shall have to summons you once more, miss, for being in possession of a savage dorg not under proper control.'

The thrust was a keen one, but Stiffy came back strongly.

'Don't be an ass, Oates. You can't expect a dog to pass up a policeman on a bicycle. It isn't human nature. And I'll bet you started it, anyway. You must have teased him, or something, and I may as well tell you that I intend to fight this case to the House of Lords. I shall call this gentleman as a material witness.' She turned to me, and for the first time became aware that I was no gentleman, but an old friend. 'Oh, hello, Bertie.'

'Hullo, Stiff.'

'When did you get here?'

'Oh, recently.'

'Did you see what happened?'

'Oh, rather. Ringside seat throughout.'

'Well, stand by to be subpoenaed.'

'Right ho.'

The policeman had been taking a sort of inventory and writing it down in the book. He was now in a position to call the score.

'Piecer skin scraped off right knee. Bruise or contusion on left elbow. Scratch on nose. Uniform covered with mud and'll have to go and be cleaned. Also shock – severe. You will receive the summons in due course, miss.'

He mounted his bicycle and rode off, causing the dog Bartholomew to make a passionate bound that nearly unshipped him from the restraining stick. Stiffy stood for a moment looking after him a bit yearningly, like a girl who wished that she had half a brick handy. Then she turned away, and I came straight down to brass tacks.

'Stiffy,' I said, 'passing lightly over all the guff about being charmed to see you again and how well you're looking and all that, have you got a small, brown, leather-covered notebook that Gussie Fink-Nottle dropped in the stable yard yesterday?'

She did not reply, seeming to be musing – no doubt on the recent Oates. I repeated the qeustion, and she came out of the trance.

'Notebook?'

'Small, brown, leather-covered, one.'

'Full of a lot of breezy personal remarks?'

'That's the one.'

'Yes, I've got it.'

I flung the hands heavenwards and uttered a joyful yowl. The dog Bartholomew gave me an unpleasant look and said something under his breath in Gaelic, but I ignored him. A kennel of Aberdeen terriers could have rolled their eyes and bared the wisdom tooth without impairing this ecstatic moment.

'Gosh, what a relief!'

'Does it belong to Gussie Fink-Nottle?'

'Yes.'

'You mean to say that it was Gussie who wrote those really excellent character studies of Roderick Spode and Uncle Watkyn? I wouldn't have thought he had it in him.'

'Nobody would. It's a most interesting story. It appears –'

'Though why anyone should waste time on Spode and Uncle Watkyn when there was Oates simply crying out to be written about, I can't imagine. I don't think I have ever met a man, Bertie, who gets in the hair so consistently as this Eustace Oates. He makes me tired. He goes swanking about on that bicycle of his, simply asking for it, and then complains when he gets it. And why should he discriminate against poor Bartholomew in this sickening way? Every red-blooded dog in the village has had a go at his trousers, and he knows it.'

'Where's that book, Stiffy?' I said, returning to the *res*.

'Never mind about books. Let's stick to Eustace Oates. Do you think he means to summons me?'

I said that, reading between the lines, that was rather the impression I had gathered, and she made what I believe is known as a *moue* ... Is it *moue*? ... Shoving out the lips, I mean, and drawing them quickly back again.

'I'm afraid so, too. There is only one word for Eustace Oates, and that is "malignant". He just goes about seeking whom he may devour. Oh, well, more work for Uncle Watkyn.'

'How do you mean?'

'I shall come up before him.'

'Then he does still operate, even though retired?' I said, remembering with some uneasiness the conversation between this ex-beak and Roderick Spode in the collection-room.

'He is only retired from Bosher Street. You can't choke a man off magistrating, once it's in his blood. He's a Justice of the Peace now. He holds a sort of Star Chamber court in the library. That's where I always come up. I'll be flitting about, doing the flowers, or sitting in my room with a good book, and the butler comes and says I'm wanted in the library. And there's

Uncle Watkyn at the desk, looking like Judge Jeffreys, with Oates to give evidence.'

I could picture the scene. Unpleasant, of course. The sort of thing that casts a gloom over a girl's home life.

'And it always ends the same way, with him putting on the black cap and soaking me. He never listens to a word I say. I don't believe the man understands the ABC of justice.'

'That's how he struck me, when I attended his tribunal.'

'And the worst of it is, he knows just what my allowance is, so he can figure out exactly how much the purse will stand. Twice this year he's skinned me to the bone, each time at the instigation of this man Oates – once for exceeding the speed limit in a built-up area, and once because Bartholomew gave him the teeniest little nip on the ankle.'

I tut-tutted sympathetically, but I was wishing that I could edge the conversation back to that notebook. One so frequently finds in girls a disinclination to stick to the important subject.

'The way Oates went on about it, you would have thought Bartholomew had taken his pound of flesh. And I suppose it's all going to happen again now. I'm fed up with this police persecution. One might as well be in Russia. Don't you loathe policemen, Bertie?'

I was not prepared to go quite so far as this in my attitude towards an, on the whole, excellent body of men.

'Well, not *en masse*, if you understand the expression. I suppose they vary, like other sections of the community, some being full of quiet charm, others not so full. I've met some very decent policemen. With the one on duty outside the Drones I am distinctly chummy. In *re* this Oates of yours, I haven't seen enough of him, of course, to form an opinion.'

'Well, you can take it from me that he's one of the worst. And a bitter retribution awaits him. Do you remember the time you gave me lunch at your flat? You were telling me about how you tried to pinch that policeman's helmet in Leicester Square.'

'That was when I first met your uncle. It was that that brought us together.'

'Well, I didn't think much of it at the time, but the other day it suddenly came back to me, and I said to myself: "Out of the mouths of babes and sucklings!" For months I had been trying to think of a way of getting back at this man, Oates, and you had showed it to me.'

I started. It seemed to me that her words could bear but one interpretation. 'You aren't going to pinch his helmet?'

'Of course not.'

'I think you're wise.'

'It's man's work. I can see that. So I've told Harold to do it. He has often said he would do anything in the world for me, bless him.'

Stiffy's map, as a rule, tends to be rather grave and dreamy, giving the impression that she is thinking deep, beautiful thoughts. Quite misleading, of course. I don't suppose she would recognize a deep, beautiful thought, if you handed it to her on a skewer with tartare sauce. Like Jeeves, she doesn't often smile, but now her lips had parted – ecstatically, I think – I should have to check up with Jeeves – and her eyes were sparkling.

'What a man!' she said. 'We're engaged, you know.'

'Oh, are you?'

'Yes, but don't tell a soul. It's frightfully secret. Uncle Watkyn mustn't know about it till he has been well sweetened.'

'And who is this Harold?'

'The curate down in the village.' She turned to the dog Bartholomew. 'Is lovely kind curate going to pinch bad, ugly policeman's helmet for his muzzer, zen, and make her very very happy?' she said.

Or words to that general trend. I can't do the dialect, of course.

I stared at the young pill, appalled at her moral code, if you could call it that. You know, the more I see of women, the more I think that there ought to be a law. Something has got to be done about this sex, or the whole fabric of Society will collapse, and then what silly asses we shall all look.

'Curate?' I said. 'But, Stiffy, you can't ask a curate to go about pinching policemen's helmets.'

'Why not?'

'Well, it's most unusual. You'll get the poor bird unfrocked.'

'Unfrocked?'

'It's something they do to parsons when they catch them bending. And this will inevitably be the outcome of the frightful task you have appointed to the sainted Harold.'

'I don't see that it's a frightful task.'

'You aren't telling me that it's the sort of thing that comes naturally to curates?'

'Yes, I am. It ought to be right up Harold's street. When he was at Magdalen, before he saw the light, he was the dickens of a chap. Always doing things like that.'

Her mention of Magdalen interested me. It had been my own college.

'Magdalen man, is he? What year? Perhaps I know him.'

'Of course you do. He often speaks of you, and was delighted when I told him you were coming here. Harold Pinker.'

I was astounded.

'Harold Pinker? Old Stinker Pinker? Great Scott! One of my dearest pals. I've often wondered where he had got to. And all the while he had sneaked off and become a curate. It just shows you how true it is that one half of the world doesn't know how the other threequarters lives. Stinker Pinker, by Jove! You really mean that old Stinker now cures souls?'

'Certainly. And jolly well, too. The nibs think very highly of him. Any moment now, he may get a vicarage, and then watch his smoke. He'll be a Bishop some day.'

The excitement of discovering a long-lost buddy waned. I found myself returning to the practical issues. I became grave.

And I'll tell you why I became grave. It was all very well for Stiffy to say that this thing would be right up old Stinker's street. She didn't know him as I did. I watched Harold Pinker through the formative years of his life, and I knew him for what he was – a large, lumbering, Newfoundland puppy of a chap – full of zeal, yes – always doing his best, true; but never quite able to make the grade; a man, in short, who if there was a chance of bungling an enterprise and landing himself in the soup, would snatch at it. At the idea of him being turned on to perform the extraordinarily delicate task of swiping Constable Oates's helmet, the blood froze. He hadn't a chance of getting away with it.

I thought of Stinker, the youth. Built rather on the lines of Roderick Spode, he had played Rugby football not only for his University but also for England, and at the art of hurling an opponent into a mud puddle and jumping on his neck with cleated boots had had few, if any, superiors. If I had wanted someone to help me out with a mad bull, he would have been my first choice. If by some mischance I had found myself trapped in an underground den of the Secret Nine, there was nobody I would rather have seen coming down the chimney than the Rev. Harold Pinker.

But mere thews and sinews do not qualify a man to pinch policemen's helmets. You need finesse.

'He will, will he?' I said. 'A fat lot of bishing he's going to do, if he's caught sneaking helmets from members of his flock.'

'He won't be caught.'

'Of course he'll be caught. At the old Alma Mater he was always caught. He seemed to have no notion whatsoever of going about a thing in a subtle, tactful way. Chuck it, Stiffy. Abandon the whole project.'

'No.'

'Stiffy!'

'No. The show must go on.'

I gave it up. I could see plainly that it would be a mere waste of time to try to argue her out of her girlish daydreams. She had the same type of mind, I perceived, as Roberta Wickham, who once persuaded me to go by night to the bedroom of a fellow guest at a country house and puncture his hot-water bottle with a darning-needle on the end of a stick.

'Well, if it must be, it must be, I suppose,' I said resignedly. 'But at least impress upon him that it is essential, when pinching policemen's helmets, to give a forward shove before applying the upwards lift. Otherwise, the subject's chin catches in the strap. It was to overlooking this vital point that my own downfall in Leicester Square was due. The strap caught, the cop was enabled to turn and clutch, and before I knew what had happened I was in the dock, saying "Yes your Honour" and "No, your Honour" to your Uncle Watkyn.'

I fell into a thoughtful silence, as I brooded on the dark future lying in wait for an old friend. I am not a weak man, but I was beginning to wonder if I had been right in squelching so curtly Jeeves's efforts to get me off on a Round-The-World cruise. Whatever you may say against these excursions – the cramped conditions of shipboard, the possibility of getting mixed up with a crowd of bores, the nuisance of having to go and look at the Taj Mahal – at least there is this to be said in their favour, that you escape the mental agony of watching innocent curates dishing their careers and forfeiting all chance of rising to great heights in the Church by getting caught bonneting their parishioners.

I heaved a sigh, and resumed the conversation.

'So you and Stinker are engaged, are you? Why didn't you tell me when you lunched at the flat?'

'It hadn't happened then. Oh, Bertie, I'm so happy I could bite a grape. At least, I shall be, if we can get Uncle Watkyn thinking along "Bless you, my children" lines.'

'Oh, yes, you were saying, weren't you? About him being sweetened. How do you mean, sweetened?'

'That's what I want to have a talk with you about. You remember what I said in my telegram, about there being something I wanted you to do for me?'

I started. A well-defined uneasiness crept over me. I had forgotten all about that telegram of hers.

'It's something quite simple.'

I doubted it. I mean to say, if her idea of a suitable job for curates was the pinching of policemen's helmets, what sort of an assignment, I could not but ask myself, was she likely to hand to me? It seemed that the moment had come for a bit of in-the-bud-nipping.

'Oh, yes?' I said. 'Well, let me tell you here and now that I'm jolly well not going to do it.'

261

'Yellow, eh?'

'Bright yellow. Like my Aunt Agatha.'

'What's the matter with her?'

'She's got jaundice.'

'Enough to give her jaundice, having a nephew like you. Why, you don't even know what it is.'

'I would prefer not to know.'

'Well, I'm going to tell you.'

'I do not wish to listen.'

'You would rather I unleashed Bartholomew? I notice he has been looking at you in that odd way of his. I don't believe he likes you. He does take sudden dislikes to people.'

The Woosters are brave, but not rash. I allowed her to lead me to the stone wall that bordered the terrace, and we sat down. The evening, I remember, was one of perfect tranquillity, featuring a sort of serene peace. Which just shows you.

'I won't keep you long,' she said. 'It's quite simple and straightforward. I shall have to begin, though, by telling you why we have had to be so dark and secret about the engagement. That's Gussie's fault.'

'What has he done?'

'Just been Gussie, that's all. Just gone about with no chin, goggling through his spectacles and keeping newts in his bedroom. You can understand Uncle Watkyn's feelings. His daughter tells him she is going to get married. "Oh, yes?" he says. "Well, let's have a dekko at the chap." And along rolls Gussie. A nasty jar for a father.'

'Quite.'

'Well, you can't tell me that a time when he is reeling under the blow of having Gussie for a son-in-law is the moment for breaking it to him that I want to marry a curate.'

I saw her point. I recollected Freddie Threepwood telling me that there had been trouble at Blandings about a cousin of his wanting to marry a curate. In that case, I gathered, the strain had been eased by the discovery that the fellow was the heir of a well-to-do Liverpool shipping millionaire; but, as a broad, general rule, parents do not like their daughters marrying curates, and I take it that the same thing applies to uncles with their nieces.

'You've got to face it. Curates are not so hot. So before anything can be done in the way of removing the veil of secrecy, we have got to sell Harold to Uncle Watkyn. If we play our cards properly, I am hoping that he will give him a vicarage which he has in his gift. Then we shall begin to get somewhere.'

I didn't like her use of the word 'we', but I saw what she was driving at, and I was sorry to have to insert a spanner in her hopes and dreams.

'You wish me to put in a word for Stinker? You would like me to draw your uncle aside and tell him what a splendid fellow Stinker is? There is nothing I would enjoy more, my dear Stiffy, but unfortunately we are not on those terms.'

'No, no, nothing like that,'

'Well, I don't see what more I can do.'

'You will,' she said, and again I was conscious of the subtle feeling of uneasiness. I told myself that I must be firm. But I could not but remember Roberta Wickham and the hot-water bottle. A man thinks he is being chilled steel – or adamant, if you prefer the expression, and suddenly the mists clear away and he finds that he has allowed a girl to talk him into something frightful. Samson had the same experience with Delilah.

'Oh?' I said, guardedly.

She paused in order to tickle the dog Bartholomew under the left ear. Then she resumed.

'Just praising Harold to Uncle Watkyn isn't any use. You need something much cleverer than that. You want to engineer some terrifically brainy scheme that will put him over with a bang. I thought I had got it a few days ago. Do you ever read *Milady's Boudoir*?'

'I once contributed an article to it on "What The Well-Dressed Man Is Wearing," but I am not a regular reader. Why?'

'There was a story in it last week about a Duke who wouldn't let his daughter marry the young secretary, so the secretary got a friend of his to take the Duke out on the lake and upset the boat, and then he dived in and saved the Duke, and the Duke said "Right ho." '

I resolved that no time should be lost in quashing this idea.

'Any notion you may have entertained that I am going to take Sir W. Bassett out in a boat and upset him can be dismissed instanter. To start with he wouldn't come out on a lake with me.'

'No. And we haven't a lake. And Harold said that if I was thinking of the pond in the village, I could forget it, as it was much too cold to dive into ponds at this time of year. Harold is funny in some ways.'

'I applaud his sturdy common sense.'

'Then I got an idea from another story. It was about a young lover who gets a friend of his to dress up as a tramp and attack the girl's father, and then he dashes in and rescues him.'

I patted her hand gently.

'The flaw in all these ideas of yours,' I pointed out, 'is that the hero always seems to have a half-witted friend who is eager to place himself in the foulest positions on his behalf. In Stinker's case, that is not so. I am fond of Stinker – you could even go as far as to say that I love him like a brother – but there are sharply defined limits to what I am prepared to do to further his interests.'

'Well, it doesn't matter, because he put the presidential veto on that one too. Something about what the vicar would say if it all came out. But he loves my new one.'

'Oh, you've got a new one?'

'Yes, and it's terrific. The beauty of it is that Harold's part in it is above reproach. A thousand vicars couldn't get the goods on him. The only snag was that he has to have someone working with him, and until I heard you were coming down here I couldn't think who we were to get. But now that you have arrived, all is well.'

'It is, is it? I informed you before, young Byng, and I now inform you again that nothing will induce me to mix myself up with your loathsome schemes.'

'Oh, but, Bertie, you must! We're relying on you. And all

you have to do is practically nothing. Just steal Uncle Watkyn's cow-creamer.'

I don't know what you would have done, if a girl in heather-mixture tweeds had sprung this on you, scarcely eight hours after a mauve-faced aunt had sprung the same. It is possible that you would have reeled. Most chaps would, I imagine. Personally, I was more amused than aghast. Indeed, if memory serves me aright, I laughed. If so, it was just as well, for it was about the last chance I had.

'Oh, yes?' I said. 'Tell me more,' I said, feeling that it would be entertaining to allow the little blighter to run on. 'Steal his cow-creamer, eh?'

'Yes. It's a thing he brought back from London yesterday for his collection. A sort of silver cow with a kind of blotto look on its face. He thinks the world of it. He had it on the table in front of him at dinner last night, and was gassing away about it. And it was then that I got the idea. I thought that if Harold could pinch it, and then bring it back, Uncle Watkyn would be so grateful that he would start spouting vicarages like a geyser. And then I spotted the catch.'

'Oh, there was a catch?'

'Of course. Don't you see? How would Harold be supposed to have got the thing? If a silver cow is in somebody's collection, and it disappears, and next day a curate rolls around with it, that curate has got to do some good, quick explaining. Obviously, it must be made to look like an outside job.'

'I see. You want me to put on a black mask and break in through the window and snitch this *objet d'art* and hand it over to Stinker? I see. I see.'

I spoke with satirical bitterness, and I should have thought that anyone could have seen that satirical bitterness was what I was speaking with, but she merely looked at me with admiration and approval.

'You are clever, Bertie. That's exactly it. Of course, you needn't wear a mask.'

'You don't think it would help me throw myself into the part?' I said with s. b. as before.

'Well, it might. That's up to you. But the great thing is to get through the window. Wear gloves, of course, because of the fingerprints.'

'Of course.'

'Then Harold will be waiting outside, and he will take the thing from you.'

'And after that I go off and do my stretch at Dartmoor?'

'Oh, no. You escape in the struggle, of course.'

'What struggle?'

'And Harold rushes into the house, all over blood –'

'Whose blood?'

'Well, I said yours, and Harold thought his. There have got to be signs of a struggle, to make it more interesting, and my idea was that he should hit you on the nose. But he said the thing would carry greater weight if he was all covered with gore. So how we've left it is that you both hit each other on the nose. And then Harold rouses the house and comes in and shows Uncle Watkyn the cow-creamer and explains what happened, and everything's fine. Because, I mean, Uncle Watkyn couldn't just say "Oh, thanks" and leave it at that, could he? He would be compelled, if he had a spark of decency in him, to cough up that vicarage. Don't you think it's a wonderful scheme, Bertie?'

I rose. My face was cold and hard.

'Most. But I am sorry –'

'You don't mean you won't do it, now that you see that it will cause you practically no inconvenience at all? It would only take about ten minutes of your time.'

'I do mean I won't do it.'

'Well, I think you're a pig.'

'A pig, maybe, but a shrewd, levelheaded pig. I wouldn't touch the project with a bargepole. I tell you I know Stinker. Exactly how he would muck the thing up and get us all landed in the jug, I cannot say, but he would find a way. And now I'll take that book, if you don't mind.'

'What book? Oh, that one of Gussie's.'

'Yes.'

'What do you want it for?'

'I want it,' I said gravely, 'because Gussie is not fit to be in charge of it. He might lose it again, in which event it might fall into the hands of your uncle, in which event he would certainly kick the stuffing out of the Gussie–Madeline wedding arrangements, in which event I would be up against it as few men have ever been up against it before.'

'You?'

'None other.'

'How do you come into it?'

'I will tell you.'

And in a few terse words I outlined for her the events which had taken place at Brinkley Court, the situation which had arisen from those events and the hideous peril which threatened me if Gussie's entry were to be scratched.

'You will understand,' I said, 'that I am implying nothing derogatory to your cousin Madeline, when I say that the idea of being united to her in the bonds of holy wedlock is one that freezes the gizzard. The fact is in no way to her discredit. I should feel just the same about marrying many of the world's noblest women. There are certain females whom one respects, admires, reveres, but only from a distance. If they show signs of attempting to come closer, one is prepared to fight them off with a blackjack. It is to this group that your cousin Madeline belongs. A charming girl, and the ideal mate for Augustus Fink-Nottle, but ants in the pants to Bertram.'

She drank this in.

'I see. Yes, I suppose Madeline is a bit of a Gawd-help-us.'

'The expression "Gawd-help-us" is one which I would not have gone so far as to use myself, for I think a chivalrous man ought to stop somewhere. But since you have brought it up, I admit that it covers the facts.'

'I never realized that that was how things were. No wonder you want that book.'

'Exactly.'

'Well, all this has opened up a new line of thought.'

That grave, dreamy look had come into her face. She massaged the dog Bartholomew's spine with a pensive foot.

'Come on,' I said chafing at the delay. 'Slip it across.'

'Just a moment. I'm trying to straighten it all out in my mind. You know, Bertie, I really ought to take that book to Uncle Watkyn.'

'What!'

'That's what my conscience tells me to do. After all, I owe a lot to him. For years he has been a second father to me. And he ought to know how Gussie feels about him, oughtn't he? I mean to say, a bit tough on the old buster, cherishing what he thinks is a harmless newt-fancier in his bosom, when all the time it's a snake that goes about criticizing the way he drinks soup. However, as you're being so sweet and are going to help Harold and me by stealing that cow-creamer, I suppose I shall have to stretch a point.'

We Woosters are pretty quick. I don't suppose it was more than a couple of minutes before I figured out what she meant. I read her purpose, and shuddered.

She was naming the Price of the Papers. In other words, after being blackmailed by an aunt at breakfast, I was now being blackmailed by a female crony before dinner. Pretty good going, even for this lax post-war world.

'Stiffy!' I cried.

'It's no good saying "Stiffy!" Either you sit in and do your bit, or Uncle Watkyn gets some racy light reading over his morning egg and coffee. Think it over, Bertie.'

She hoisted the dog Bartholomew to his feet, and trickled off towards the house. The last I saw of her was a meaning look, directed at me over her shoulder, and it went through me like a knife.

The Code of the Woosters (1938)

Uncle and Nephew

You remember, Pongo felt this way about his uncle in Uncle
Fred Flits By *(page 172 and ff.)*

Lord Ickenham patted her hand, put his arm about her waist
and kissed her tenderly. Pongo wished he had thought of that
himself. He reflected moodily that this was always the way. In
the course of their previous adventures together, if there had
ever been any kissing or hand-patting or waist-encircling to be
done, it had always been his nimbler uncle who had nipped in
ahead of him and attended to it. He coughed austerely.

Uncle Fred in the Springtime (1939)

The Amazing Hat Mystery

The tactful mediator, or raisonneur, *was a frequent hinge in the Wodehouse plots. It was generally a perilous job to undertake. This time two tactful mediators fail in their jobs and find happiness.*

A Bean was in a nursing-home with a broken leg as a result of trying to drive his sports-model Poppenheim through the Marble Arch instead of round it, and a kindly Crumpet had looked in to give him the gossip of the town. He found him playing halma with the nurse, and he sat down on the bed and took a grape, and the Bean asked what was going on in the great world.

'Well,' said the Crumpet, taking another grape, 'the finest minds in the Drones are still wrestling with the great Hat mystery.'

'What's that?'

'You don't mean you haven't heard about it?'

'Not a word.'

The Crumpet was astounded. He swallowed two grapes at once in surprise.

'Why, London's seething with it. The general concensus of opinion is that it has something to do with the Fourth Dimension. You know how things do. I mean to say, something rummy occurs and you consult some big-brained bird and he wags his head and says "Ah! The Fourth Dimension!" Extraordinary nobody's told you about the great Hat mystery.'

'You're the first visitor I've had. What is it, anyway? What hat?'

'Well, there were two hats. Reading from left to right, Percy Wimbolt's and Nelson Cork's.'

The Bean nodded intelligently.

'I see what you mean. Percy had one, and Nelson had the other.'

'Exactly. Two hats in all. Top hats.'

'What was mysterious about them?'

'Why, Elizabeth Bottsworth and Diana Punter said they didn't fit.'

'Well, hats don't sometimes.'

'But these came from Bodmin's.'

The Bean shot up in bed.

'What?'

'You mustn't excite the patient,' said the nurse, who up to this point had taken no part in the conversation.

'But, dash it, nurse,' cried the Bean, 'you can't have caught what he said. If we are to give credence to his story, Percy Wimbolt and Nelson Cork bought a couple of hats at Bodmin's – at *Bodmin's*, I'll trouble you – and they didn't fit. It isn't possible.'

He spoke with strong emotion, and the Crumpet nodded understandingly. People can say what they please about the modern young man believing in nothing nowadays, but there is one thing every right-minded young man believes in, and that is the infallibility of Bodmin's hats. It is one of the eternal verities. Once admit that it is possible for a Bodmin hat not to fit, and you leave the door open for Doubt, Schism and Chaos generally.

'That's exactly how Percy and Nelson felt, and it was for that reason that they were compelled to take the strong line and they did with E. Bottsworth and D. Punter.'

'They took a strong line, did they?'

'A very strong line.'

'Won't you tell us the whole story from the beginning?' said the nurse.

'Right ho,' said the Crumpet, taking a grape. 'It'll make your head swim.'

'So mysterious?'

'So absolutely dashed uncanny from start to finish.'

*

You must know, to begin with, my dear old nurse (said the Crumpet), that these two blokes, Percy Wimbolt and Nelson Cork, are fellows who have to exercise the most watchful care about their lids, because they are so situated that in their case there can be none of that business of just charging into any old hattery and grabbing the first thing in sight. Percy is one of those large, stout, outsize chaps with a head like a water-melon, while Nelson is built more on the lines of a minor jockey and has a head like a peanut.

You will readily appreciate, therefore, that it requires an artist hand to fit them•properly, and that is why they have always gone to Bodmin. I have heard Percy say that his trust in Bodmin is like the unspotted faith of a young curate in his Bishop and I have no doubt that Nelson would have said the same, if he had thought of it.

It was at Bodmin's door that they ran into each other on the morning when my story begins.

'Hullo,' said Percy. 'You come to buy a hat?'

'Yes,' said Nelson. 'You come to buy a hat?'

'Yes.' Percy glanced cautiously about him, saw that he was alone (except for Nelson, of course) and unobserved, and drew closer and lowered his voice. 'There's a reason!'

'That's rummy,' said Nelson. He, also, spoke in a hushed tone. 'I have a special reason, too.'

Percy looked warily about him again, and lowered his voice another notch.

'Nelson,' he said, 'you know Elizabeth Bottsworth?'

'Intimately,' said Nelson.

'Rather a sound young potato, what?'

'Very much so.'

'Pretty?'

'I've often noticed it.'

'Me, too. She is so small, so sweet, so dainty, so lively, so viv—, what's-the-word? – that a fellow wouldn't be far out in calling her an angel in human shape.'

'Aren't all angels in human shape?'

'Are they?' said Percy, who was a bit foggy on angels. 'Well, be that as it may,' he went on, his cheeks suffused to a certain extent, 'I love that girl, Nelson, and she's coming with me to the first day of Ascot, and I'm relying on this new hat of mine to do just that extra bit that's needed in the way of making her reciprocate my passion. Having only met her so far at country houses, I've never yet flashed upon her in a topper.'

Nelson Cork was staring.

'Well, if that isn't the most remarkable coincidence I ever came across in my puff!' he exclaimed, amazed. 'I'm buying my new hat for exactly the same reason.'

A convulsive start shook Percy's massive frame. His eyes bulged.

'To fascinate Elizabeth Bottsworth?' he cried, beginning to writhe.

'No, no,' said Nelson, soothingly. 'Of course not. Elizabeth and I have always been great friends, but nothing more. What I meant was that I, like you, am counting on this forthcoming topper of mine to put me across with the girl I love.'

Percy stopped writhing.

'Who is she?' he asked, interested.

'Diana Punter, the niece of my godmother, old Ma Punter. It's an odd thing, I've known her all my life – brought up as kids together and so forth – but it's only recently that passion has burgeoned. I now worship that girl, Percy, from the top of her head to the soles of her divine feet.'

Percy looked dubious.

'That's a pretty longish distance, isn't it? Diana Punter is one of my closest friends, and a charming girl in every respect, but isn't she a bit tall for you, old man?'

'My dear chap, that's just what I admire so much about her, her superb statuesqueness. More like a Greek goddess than anything I've struck for years. Besides, she isn't any taller for me than you are for Elizabeth Bottsworth.'

'True,' admitted Percy.

'And, anyway, I love her, blast it, and I don't propose to argue the point. I love her, I love her, I love her, and we are lunching together the first day of Ascot.'

'At Ascot?'

'No. She isn't keen on racing so I shall have to give Ascot a miss.'

'That's Love,' said Percy, awed.

'The binge will take place at my godmother's house in Berkeley Square, and it won't be long after that, I feel, before you see an interesting announcement in the *Morning Post*.'

Percy extended his hand. Nelson grasped it warmly.

'These new hats are pretty well bound to do the trick, I should say, wouldn't you?'

'Infallibly. Where girls are concerned, there is nothing that brings home the gravy like a well-fitting topper.'

'Bodmin must extend himself as never before,' said Percy.

'He certainly must,' said Nelson.

They entered the shop. And Bodmin, having measured them with his own hands, promised that two of his very finest efforts should be at their respective addresses in the course of the next few days.

Now, Percy Wimbolt isn't a chap you would suspect of having nerves, but there is no doubt that in the interval which elapsed before Bodmin was scheduled to deliver he got pretty twittery. He kept having awful visions of some great disaster happening to his new hat: and, as things turned out, these visions came jolly near being fulfilled. It has made Percy feel that he is psychic.

What occurred was this. Owing to these jitters of his, he hadn't been sleeping any too well, and on the morning before Ascot he was up as early as ten-thirty, and he went to his sitting-room window to see what sort of a day it was, and the sight he beheld from that window absolutely froze the blood in his veins.

For there below him, strutting up and down the pavement, were a uniformed little blighter whom he recognized as Bodmin's errand-boy and an equally foul kid in mufti. And balanced on each child's loathsome head was a top hat. Against the railings were leaning a couple of cardboard hat-boxes.

274

Now, considering that Percy had only just woken from a dream in which he had been standing outside the Guildhall in his new hat, receiving the Freedom of the City from the Lord Mayor, and the Lord Mayor had suddenly taken a terrific swipe at the hat with his mace, knocking it into hash, you might have supposed that he would have been hardened to anything. But he wasn't. His reaction was terrific. There was a moment of sort of paralysis, during which he was telling himself that he had always suspected this beastly little boy of Bodmin's of having a low and frivolous outlook and being temperamentally unfitted for his high office: and then he came alive with a jerk and let out probably the juiciest yell the neighbourhood had heard for years.

It stopped the striplings like a high-powered shell. One moment, they had been swanking up and down in a mincing and affected sort of way: the next, the second kid had legged it like a streak and Bodmin's boy was shoving the hats back in the boxes and trying to do it quickly enough to enable him to be elsewhere when Percy should arrive.

And in this he was successful. By the time Percy had got to the front door and opened it, there was nothing to be seen but a hat-box standing on the steps. He took it up to his flat and removed the contents with a gingerly and reverent hand, holding his breath for fear the nap should have got rubbed the wrong way or a dent of any nature been made in the gleaming surface; but apparently all was well. Bodmin's boy might sink to taking hats out of their boxes and fooling about with them, but at least he hadn't gone to the last awful extreme of dropping them.

The lid was O.K. absolutely: and on the following morning Percy, having spent the interval polishing it with stout, assembled the boots, the spats, the trousers, the coat, the flowered waistcoat, the collar, the shirt, the quiet grey tie, and the good old gardenia and set off in a taxi for the house where Elizabeth was staying. And presently he was ringing the bell and being told she would be down in a minute, and eventually down she came, looking perfectly marvellous.

275

'What ho, what ho!' said Percy.

'Hullo, Percy,' said Elizabeth.

Now, naturally, up to this moment Percy had been standing with bared head. At this point, he put the hat on. He wanted her to get the full effect suddenly in a good light. And very strategic, too. I mean to say, it would have been the act of a juggins to have waited till they were in the taxi, because in a taxi all toppers look much alike.

So Percy popped the hat on his head with a meaning glance and stood waiting for the uncontrollable round of applause.

And instead of clapping her little hands in girlish ecstasy and doing Spring dances round him, this young Bottsworth gave a sort of gurgling scream not unlike a coloratura soprano choking on a fish-bone.

Then she blinked and became calmer.

'It's all right,' she said. 'The momentary weakness has passed. Tell me, Percy, when do you open?'

'Open?' said Percy, not having the remotest.

'On the Halls. Aren't you going to sing comic songs on the Music Halls?'

Percy's perplexity deepened.

'Me? No. How? Why? What do you mean?'

'I thought that hat must be part of the make-up and that you were trying it on the dog. I couldn't think of any other reason why you should wear one six sizes too small.'

Percy gasped.

'You aren't suggesting this hat doesn't fit me?'

'It doesn't fit you by a mile.'

'But it's a Bodmin.'

'Call it that if you like. I call it a public outrage.'

Percy was appalled. I mean, naturally. A nice thing for a chap to give his heart to a girl and then find her talking in this hideous, flippant way of sacred subjects.

Then it occurred to him that, living all the time in the country, she might not have learned to appreciate the holy significance of the name Bodmin.

'Listen,' he said gently. 'Let me explain. This hat was made

276

by Bodmin, the world-famous hatter of Vigo Street. He measured me in person and guaranteed a fit.'

'And I nearly had one.'

'And if Bodmin guarantees that a hat shall fit,' proceeded Percy, trying to fight against a sickening sort of feeling that he had been all wrong about this girl, 'it fits. I mean, saying a Bodmin hat doesn't fit is like saying ... well, I can't think of anything awful enough.'

'That hat's awful enough. It's like something out of a two-reel comedy. Pure Chas. Chaplin. I know a joke's a joke, Percy, and I'm as fond of a laugh as anyone, but there is such a thing as cruelty to animals. Imagine the feelings of the horses at Ascot when they see that hat.'

Poets and other literary blokes talk a lot about falling in love at first sight, but it's equally possible to fall out of love just as quickly. One moment, this girl was the be-all and the end-all, as you might say, of Percy Wimbolt's life. The next, she was just a regrettable young blister with whom he wished to hold no further communication. He could stand a good deal from the sex. Insults directed to himself left him unmoved. But he was not prepared to countenance destructive criticism of a Bodmin hat.

'Possibly,' he said, coldly, 'you would prefer to go to this bally race-meeting alone?'

'You bet I'm going alone. You don't suppose I mean to be seen in broad daylight in the paddock at Ascot with a hat like that?'

Percy stepped back and bowed formally.

'Drive on, driver,' he said to the driver, and the driver drove on.

Now, you would say that that was rummy enough. A full-size mystery in itself, you might call it. But wait. Mark the sequel. You haven't heard anything yet.

We now turn to Nelson Cork. Shortly before one-thirty, Nelson had shoved over to Berkeley Square and had lunch with his godmother and Diana Punter, and Diana's manner and deportment had been absolutely all that could have been desired. In fact, so chummy had she been over the cutlets and fruit salad that it seemed to Nelson that, if she was like this now, imagination boggled at the thought of how utterly all over him she would be when he sprang his new hat on her.

So when the meal was concluded and coffee had been drunk and old Lady Punter had gone up to her boudoir with a digestive tablet and a sex-novel, he thought it would be a sound move to invite her to come for a stroll along Bond Street. There was the chance, of course, that she would fall into his arms right in the middle of the pavement: but if that happened, he told himself, they could always get into a cab. So he mooted the saunter, and she checked up, and presently they started off.

And you will scarcely believe this, but they hadn't gone more than half-way along Bruton Street when she suddenly stopped and looked at him in an odd manner.

'I don't want to be personal, Nelson,' she said, 'but really I do think you ought to take the trouble to get measured for your hats.'

If a gas main had exploded beneath Nelson's feet, he could hardly have been more taken aback.

'M-m-m-m . . .' he gasped. He could scarcely believe that he had heard aright.

'It's the only way with a head like yours. I know it's a temptation for a lazy man to go into a shop and just take whatever is offered him, but the result is so sloppy. That thing you're wearing now looks like an extinguisher.'

Nelson was telling himself that he must be strong.

'Are you endeavouring to intimate that this hat does not fit?'

'Can't you feel that it doesn't fit?'

'But it's a Bodmin.'

'I don't know what you mean. It's just an ordinary silk hat.'

'Not at all. It's a Bodmin.'

'I don't know what you are talking about.'

'The point I am trying to drive home,' said Nelson, stiffly, 'is that this hat was constructed under the personal auspices of Jno. Bodmin of Vigo Street.'

'Well, it's too big.'

'It is not too big.'

'I say it's too big.'

'And I say a Bodmin hat cannot be too big.'

'Well, I've got eyes, and I say it is.'

Nelson controlled himself with an effort.

'I would be the last person,' he said, 'to criticize your eye-sight, but on the present occasion you will permit me to say that it has let you down with a considerable bump. Myopia is indicated. Allow me,' said Nelson, hot under the collar, but still dignified, 'to tell you something about Jno. Bodmin, as the name appears new to you. Jno. is the last of a long line of Bodmins, all of whom have made hats assiduously for the nobility and gentry all their lives. Hats are in Jno. Bodmin's blood.'

'I don't . . .'

Nelson held up a restraining hand.

'Over the door of his emporium in Vigo Street the passer-by may read a significant legend. It runs: "Bespoke Hatter To The Royal Family." That means, in simple language adapted to the lay intelligence, that if the King wants a new topper he simply ankles round to Bodmin's and says: "Good morning, Bodmin, we want a topper." He does not ask if it will fit. He takes it for granted that it will fit. He has bespoken Jno. Bodmin, and he trusts him blindly. You don't suppose His Gracious Majesty would bespeak a hatter whose hats did not fit. The whole essence of being a hatter is to make hats that fit, and it is to this end that Jno. Bodmin has strained every nerve for years. And that is why I say again – simply and without heat – This hat is a Bodmin.'

Diana was beginning to get a bit peeved. The blood of the Punters is hot, and very little is required to steam it up. She tapped Bruton Street with a testy foot.

'You always were an obstinate, pig-headed little fiend, Nelson, even as a child. I tell you once more, for the last time, that that hat is too big. If it were not for the fact that I can see a pair of boots and part of a pair of trousers, I should not know that there was a human being under it. I don't care how much you argue. I still think you ought to be ashamed of yourself for coming out in the thing. Even if you don't mind for your own sake, you might have considered the feelings of the pedestrians and traffic.'

Nelson quivered.

'You do, do you?'

'Yes, I do.'

'Oh, you do?'

'I said I did. Didn't you hear me? No, I suppose you could hardly be expected to, with an enormous great hat coming down over your ears.'

'You say this hat comes down over my ears?'

'Right over your ears. It's a mystery to me why you think it worth while to deny it.'

I fear that what follows does not show Nelson Cork in the role of a parfait gentil knight, but in extenuation of his behaviour I must remind you that he and Diana Punter had been brought up as children together, and a dispute between a couple who have shared the same nursery is always liable to degenerate into an exchange of personalities and innuendoes. What starts as an academic discussion on hats turns only too swiftly into a raking up of old sores and a grand parade of family skeletons.

It was so in this case. At the word 'mystery,' Nelson uttered a nasty laugh.

'A mystery, eh? As much a mystery, I suppose, as why your uncle George suddenly left England in the year 1920 without stopping to pack up?'

Diana's eyes flashed. Her foot struck the pavement another shrewd wallop.

'Uncle George,' she said haughtily, 'went abroad for his health.'

'You bet he did,' retorted Nelson. 'He knew what was good for him.'

'Anyway, he wouldn't have worn a hat like that.'

'Where they would have put him if he hadn't been off like a scalded kitten, he wouldn't have worn a hat at all.'

A small groove was now beginning to appear in the paving-stone on which Diana Punter stood.

'Well, Uncle George escaped one thing by going abroad, at any rate,' she said. 'He missed the big scandal about your aunt Clarissa in 1922.'

Nelson clenched his fists.

'The jury gave Aunt Clarissa the benefit of the doubt,' he said hoarsely.

'Well, we all know what that means. It was accompanied, if you recollect, by some very strong remarks from the Bench.'

There was a pause.

'I may be wrong,' said Nelson, 'but I should have thought it ill beseemed a girl whose brother Cyril was warned off the Turf in 1923 to haul up her slacks about other people's Aunt Clarissas.'

'Passing lightly over my brother Cyril in 1924,' rejoined Diana, 'what price your cousin Fred in 1927?'

They glared at one another in silence for a space, each realizing with a pang that the supply of erring relatives had now given out. Diana was still pawing the paving-stone, and Nelson was wondering what on earth he could ever have seen in a girl who, in addition to talking subversive drivel about hats, was eight feet tall and ungainly, to boot.

'While as for your brother-in-law's niece's sister-in-law Muriel . . .' began Diana, suddenly brightening.

Nelson checked her with a gesture.

'I prefer not to continue this discussion,' he said, frigidly.

'It is no pleasure to me,' replied Diana, with equal coldness, 'to have to listen to your vapid gibberings. That's the worst of a man who wears his hat over his mouth – he will talk through it.'

'I bid you a very hearty good afternoon, Miss Punter,' said Nelson.

He strode off without a backward glance.

Now, one advantage of having a row with a girl in Bruton Street is that the Drones is only just round the corner, so that you can pop in and restore the old nervous system with the minimum of trouble. Nelson was round there in what practically amounted to a trice, and the first person he saw was Percy, hunched up over a double and splash.

'Hullo,' said Percy.

'Hullo,' said Nelson.

There was a silence, broken only by the sound of Nelson ordering a mixed vermouth. Percy continued to stare before him like a man who has drained the wine-cup of life to its lees, only to discover a dead mouse at the bottom.

'Nelson,' he said at length, 'what are your views on the Modern Girl?'

'I think she's a mess.'

'I thoroughly agree with you,' said Percy. 'Of course, Diana Punter is a rare exception, but, apart from Diana, I wouldn't give you twopence for the modern girl. She lacks depth and reverence and has no sense of what is fitting. Hats, for example.'

'Exactly. But what do you mean Diana Punter is an exception? She's one of the ring-leaders – the spearhead of the movement, if you like to put it that way. Think,' said Nelson, sipping his vermouth, 'of all the unpleasant qualities of the Modern Girl, add them up, double them, and what have you got? Diana Punter. Let me tell you what took place between me and this Punter only a few minutes ago.'

'No,' said Percy. 'Let me tell you what transpired between me and Elizabeth Bottsworth this morning. Nelson, old man, she said my hat – my Bodmin hat – was too small.'

'You don't mean that?'

'Those were her very words.'

'Well, I'm dashed. Listen. Diana Punter told me my equally Bodmin hat was too large.'

They stared at one another.

'It's the Spirit of something,' said Nelson. 'I don't know what, quite, but of something. You see it on all sides. Something very serious has gone wrong with girls nowadays. There is lawlessness and licence abroad.'

'And here in England, too.'

'Well, naturally, you silly ass,' said Nelson, with some asperity. 'When I said abroad, I didn't mean abroad, I meant abroad.'

He mused for a moment.

'I must say, though,' he continued, 'I am surprised at what you tell me about Elizabeth Bottsworth, and am inclined to think there must have been some mistake. I have always been a warm admirer of Elizabeth.'

'And I have always thought Diana one of the best, and I find it hard to believe that she should have shown up in such a dubious light as you suggest. Probably there was a misunderstanding of some kind.'

'Well, I ticked her off properly, anyway.'

Percy Wimbolt shook his head.

'You shouldn't have done that, Nelson. You may have wounded her feelings. In my case, of course, I had no alternative but to be pretty crisp with Elizabeth.'

Nelson Cork clicked his tongue.

'A pity,' he said. 'Elizabeth is sensitive.'

'So is Diana.'

'Not so sensitive as Elizabeth.'

'I should say, at a venture, about five times as sensitive as Elizabeth. However, we must not quarrel about a point like that, old man. The fact that emerges is that we seem both to have been dashed badly treated. I think I shall toddle home and take an aspirin.'

'Me, too.'

They went off to the cloak-room, where their hats were, and Percy put his on.

'Surely,' he said, 'nobody but a half-witted little pipsqueak who can't see straight would say this was too small?'

'It isn't a bit too small,' said Nelson. 'And take a look at this one. Am I not right in supposing that only a female giantess with straws in her hair and astigmatism in both eyes could say it was too large?'

'It's a lovely fit.'

And the cloak-room waiter, a knowledgeable chap of the name of Robinson, said the same.

'So there you are,' said Nelson.

'Ah, well,' said Percy.

They left the club, and parted at the top of Dover Street.

Now, though he had not said so in so many words, Nelson Cork's heart bled for Percy Wimbolt. He knew the other's fine sensibilities and he could guess how deeply he must have been gashed by this unfortunate breaking-off of diplomatic relations with the girl he loved. For, whatever might have happened, however sorely he might have been wounded, the way Nelson Cork looked at it was that Percy loved Elizabeth Bottsworth in spite of everything. What was required here, felt Nelson, was a tactful mediator – a kindly, sensible friend of both parties who would hitch up his socks and plunge in and heal the breach.

So the moment he had got rid of Percy outside the club he hared round to the house where Elizabeth was staying and was lucky enough to catch her on the front door steps. For, naturally, Elizabeth hadn't gone off to Ascot by herself. Directly Percy was out of sight, she had told the taxi-man to drive her home, and she had been occupying the interval since the painful scene in thinking of things she wished she had said to him and taking her hostess's dog for a run – a Pekinese called Clarkson.

She seemed very pleased to see Nelson, and started to prattle of this and that, her whole demeanour that of a girl who, after having been compelled to associate for a while with the Underworld, has at last found a kindred soul. And the more he listened, the more he wanted to go on listening. And the more he looked at her, the more he felt that a lifetime spent in gazing at Elizabeth Bottsworth would be a lifetime dashed well spent.

There was something about the girl's exquisite petiteness and fragility that appealed to Nelson Cork's depths. After having wasted so much time looking at a female Carnera like Diana Punter, it was a genuine treat to him to be privileged to feast the eyes on one so small and dainty. And, what with one thing and another, he found the most extraordinary difficulty in lugging Percy into the conversation.

They strolled along, chatting. And, mark you, Elizabeth Bottsworth was a girl a fellow could chat with without getting a crick in the neck from goggling up at her, the way you had to do when you took the air with Diana Punter. Nelson realized now that talking to Diana Punter had been like trying to exchange thoughts with a flag-pole sitter. He was surprised that this had never occurred to him before.

'You know, you're looking perfectly ripping, Elizabeth,' he said.

'How funny!' said the girl. 'I was just going to say the same thing about you.'

'Not really?'

'Yes, I was. After some of the gargoyles I've seen today – Percy Wimbolt is an example that springs to the mind – it's such a relief to be with a man who really knows how to turn himself out.'

Now that the Percy *motif* had been introduced, it should have been a simple task for Nelson to turn the talk to the subject of his absent friend. But somehow he didn't. Instead, he just simpered a bit and said: 'Oh, no, I say, really, do you mean that?'

'I do, indeed,' said Elizabeth earnestly. 'It's your hat, principally, I think. I don't know why it is, but ever since a child I have been intensely sensitive to hats, and it has always been a pleasure to me to remember that at the age of five I dropped a pot of jam out of the nursery window on to my Uncle Alexander when he came to visit us in a deerstalker cap with earflaps, as worn by Sherlock Holmes. I consider the hat the final test of a man. Now, yours is perfect. I never saw such a beautiful fit. I can't tell you how much I admire that hat. It gives you quite an ambassadorial look.'

Nelson Cork drew a deep breath. He was tingling from head to foot. It was as if the scales had fallen from his eyes and a new life begun for him.

'I say,' he said, trembling with emotion, 'I wonder if you would mind if I pressed your little hand?'

'Do,' said Elizabeth cordially.

'I will,' said Nelson, and did so. 'And now,' he went on, cling-

285

ing to the fin like glue and hiccoughing a bit, 'how about buzzing off somewhere for a quiet cup of tea? I have a feeling that we have much to say to one another.'

It is odd how often it happens in this world that when there are two chaps and one chap's heart is bleeding for the other chap you find that all the while the second chap's heart is bleeding just as much for the first chap. Both bleeding, I mean to say, not only one. It was so in the case of Nelson Cork and Percy Wimbolt. The moment he had left Nelson, Percy charged straight off in search of Diana Punter with the intention of putting everything right with a few well-chosen words.

Because what he felt was that, although at the actual moment of going to press pique might be putting Nelson off Diana, this would pass off and love come into its own again. All that was required, he considered, was a suave go-between, a genial mutual pal who would pour oil on the troubled w's and generally fix things up.

He found Diana walking round and round Berkeley Square with her chin up, breathing tensely through the nostrils. He drew up alongside and what-hoed, and as she beheld him the cold, hard gleam in her eyes changed to a light of cordiality. She appeared charmed to see him and at once embarked on an animated conversation. And with every word she spoke his conviction deepened that of all the ways of passing a summer afternoon there were none fruitier than having a friendly hike with Diana Punter.

And it was not only her talk that enchanted him. He was equally fascinated by that wonderful physique of hers. When he considered that he had actually wasted several valuable minutes that day conversing with a young shrimp like Elizabeth Bottsworth, he could have kicked himself.

Here, he reflected, as they walked round the square, was a girl whose ear was more or less on a level with a fellow's mouth, so that such observations as he might make were enabled to get from point to point with the least possible delay. Talking to Elizabeth Bottsworth had always been like bellowing down a well in the hope of attracting the attention of one of the smaller infusoria at the bottom. It surprised him that he had been so long in coming to this conclusion.

He was awakened from this reverie by hearing his companion utter the name of Nelson Cork.

'I beg your pardon?' he said.

'I was saying,' said Diana, 'that Nelson Cork is a wretched little undersized blob who, if he were not too lazy to work, would long since have signed up with some good troupe of midgets.'

'Oh, would you say that?'

'I would say more than that,' said Diana firmly. 'I tell you, Percy, that what makes life so ghastly for girls, what causes girls to get grey hair and go into convents, is the fact that it is not always possible for them to avoid being seen in public with men like Nelson Cork. I trust I am not uncharitable. I try to view these things in a broad-minded way, saying to myself that if a man looks like something that has come out from under a flat stone it is his misfortune rather than his fault and that he is more to be pitied than censured. But on one thing I do insist, that such a man does not wantonly aggravate the natural unpleasantness of his appearance by prancing about London in a hat that reaches down to his ankles. I cannot and will not endure being escorted along Bruton Street by a sort of human bacillus the brim of whose hat bumps on the pavement with every step he takes. What I have always said and what I shall always say is that the hat is the acid test. A man who cannot buy the right-sized hat is a man one could never like or trust. Your hat, now, Percy, is exactly right. I have seen a good many hats in my time, but I really do not think that I have ever come across a more perfect specimen of all that a hat should be. Not too large, not too small, fitting snugly to the head like the skin on a sausage. And you have just the kind of head that a silk hat shows off. It gives you a sort of look ... how shall I describe it? ... it conveys the idea of a master of men. Leonine is the word I want. There is something about the way it rests on the brow and the almost imperceptible tilt towards the southeast ...'

Percy Wimbolt was quivering like an Oriental muscle-dancer.

287

Soft music seemed to be playing from the direction of Hay Hill, and Berkeley Square had begun to skip round him on one foot.

He drew a deep breath.

'I say,' he said, 'stop me if you've heard this before, but what I feel we ought to do at this juncture is to dash off somewhere where it's quiet and there aren't so many houses dancing the "Blue Danube" and shove some tea into ourselves. And over the pot and muffins I shall have something very important to say to you.'

'So that,' concluded the Crumpet, taking a grape, 'is how the thing stands; and, in a sense, of course, you could say that it is a satisfactory ending.

'The announcement of Elizabeth's engagement to Nelson Cork appeared in the Press on the same day as that of Diana's projected hitching-up with Percy Wimbolt: and it is pleasant that the happy couples should be so well matched as regards size.

'I mean to say, there will be none of that business of a six-foot girl tripping down the aisle with a five-foot-four man, or a six-feet-two man trying to keep step along the sacred edifice with a four-foot-three girl. This is always good for a laugh from the ringside pews, but it does not make for wedded bliss.

'No, as far as the principals are concerned, we may say that all has ended well. But that doesn't seem to me the important point. What seems to me the important point is this extraordinary baffling mystery of those hats.'

'Absolutely,' said the Bean.

'I mean to say, if Percy's hat really didn't fit, as Elizabeth Bottsworth contended, why should it have registered as a winner with Diana Punter?'

'Absolutely,' said the Bean.

'And, conversely, if Nelson's hat was the total loss which Diana Punter considered it, why, only a brief while later, was it going like a breeze with Elizabeth Bottsworth?'

'Absolutely,' said the Bean.

'The whole thing is utterly inscrutable.'

It was at this point that the nurse gave signs of wishing to catch the Speaker's eye.

'Shall I tell you what I think?'

'Say on, my dear young pillow-smoother.'

'I believe Bodmin's boy must have got those hats mixed. When he was putting them back in the boxes, I mean.'

The Crumpet shook his head, and took a grape.

'And then at the club they got the right ones again.'

The Crumpet smiled indulgently.

'Ingenious,' he said, taking a grape. 'Quite ingenious. But a little far-fetched. No, I prefer to think the whole thing, as I say, has something to do with the Fourth Dimension. I am convinced that that is the true explanation, if our minds could only grasp it.'

'Absolutely,' said the Bean.

Young Men in Spats (1936)

Myra Meets an Old Friend

*Lord Ickenham, in his commoner days, had been, in America,
a cow-puncher, soda-jerker, journalist and prospector. Now
he's a belted earl and proud of it.*

On the knoll overlooking the lake there stood a little sort of
imitation Greek temple, erected by Lord Emsworth's grand-
father in the days when landowners went in for little sort of
imitation Greek temples in their grounds. In front of it there
was a marble bench, and on this bench Myra Schoonmaker
was sitting gazing at the lake with what are called unseeing
eyes.

A footstep on the marble floor brought her out of her reverie
with a jerk. She turned and saw a tall, distinguished-looking
man with grey hair and a jaunty moustache, who smiled at her
affectionately.

'Hullo there, young Myra,' he said.

He spoke as if they were old friends, but she had no recollection of ever having seen him before.

'Who are you?' she said. The question seemed abrupt, and
she wished she had thought of something more polished.

A reproachful look came into his eyes.

'You used to say that when I soaped your back, "Nobody
soaps like you, Uncle Fred," you used to say, and you were
right. I had the knack.'

The years fell away from Myra, and she was a child in her
bath again.

'Well!' she said, squeaking in her emotion.

'I see you remember.'

'Uncle Fred! Fancy meeting you again like this after all

290

these years. Though I suppose I ought to call you Mr Twistleton.'

'You would be making a serious social gaffe, if you did. I've come a long way since we last saw each other. By pluck and industry I've worked my way up the ladder, step by step, to dizzy heights. You may have heard that a Lord Ickenham was expected at the Castle today. I am the Lord Ickenham about whom there has been so much talk. And not one of your humble Barons or Viscounts, mind you, but a belted Earl, with papers to prove it.'

'Like Lord Emsworth?'

'Yes, only brighter.'

'I remember now Father saying something about your having become a big wheel.'

'He in no way overstated it. How is he?'

Service with a Smile (1962)

Pig-Hoo-o-o-o-ey!

People can get almost anything that they want out of Lord Emsworth if they do a good turn for his beloved pig.

Thanks to the publicity given to the matter by *The Bridgnorth, Shifnal, and Albrighton Argus* (with which is incorporated *The Wheat-Growers' Intelligencer and Stock Breeders' Gazette*), the whole world today knows that the silver medal in the Fat Pigs class at the eighty-seventh annual Shropshire Agricultural Show was won by the Earl of Emsworth's black Berkshire sow, Empress of Blandings.

Very few people, however, are aware how near that splendid animal came to missing the coveted honour.

Now it can be told.

This brief chapter of Secret History may be said to have begun on the night of the eighteenth of July, when George Cyril Wellbeloved (twenty-nine), pig-man in the employ of Lord Emsworth, was arrested by Police-Constable Evans of Market Blandings for being drunk and disorderly in the tap-room of the Goat and Feathers. On July the nineteenth, after first offering to apologize, then explaining that it had been his birthday, and finally attempting to prove an alibi, George Cyril was very properly jugged for fourteen days without the option of a fine.

On July the twentieth, Empress of Blandings, always hitherto a hearty and even a boisterous feeder, for the first time on record declined all nourishment. And on the morning of July the twenty-first, the veterinary surgeon called in to diagnose and deal with this strange asceticism, was compelled to confess to Lord Emsworth that the thing was beyond his professional skill.

Let us just see, before proceeding, that we have got these dates correct:

July 18. – Birthday Orgy of Cyril Wellbeloved.

July 19. – Incarceration of Ditto.

July 20. – Pig Lays off the Vitamins.

July 21. – Veterinary Surgeon Baffled.

Right.

The effect of the veterinary surgeon's announcement on Lord Emsworth was overwhelming. As a rule, tne wear and tear of our complex modern life left this vague and amiable peer unscathed. So long as he had sunshine, regular meals, and complete freedom from the society of his younger son Frederick, he was placidly happy. But there were chinks in his armour, and one of these had been pierced this morning. Dazed by the news he stood at the window of the great library of Blandings Castle, looking out with unseeing eyes.

As he stood there, the door opened. Lord Emsworth turned; and having blinked once or twice, as was his habit when confronted suddenly with anything, recognized in the handsome and imperious looking woman who had entered, his sister, Lady Constance Keeble. Her demeanour, like his own, betrayed the deepest agitation.

'Clarence,' she cried, 'an awful thing has happened!'

Lord Emsworth nodded dully. 'I know. He's just told me.'

'What! Has he been here?'

'Only this moment left.'

'Why did you let him go? You must have known I would want to see him.'

'What good would that have done?'

'I could at least have assured him of my sympathy,' said Lady Constance stiffly.

'Yes, I suppose you could,' said Lord Emsworth, having considered the point. 'Not that he deserves any sympathy. The man's an ass.'

'Nothing of the kind. A most intelligent young man, as young men go.'

293

'Young? Would you call him young? Fifty, I should say, if a day.'

'Are you out of your senses? Heacham fifty?'

'Not Heacham. Smithers.'

As frequently happened to her when in conversation with her brother, Lady Constance experienced a swimming sensation.

'Will you kindly tell me, Clarence, in a few simple words, what you imagine we are talking about?'

'I'm talking about Smithers. Empress of Blandings is refusing her food, and Smithers says he can't do anything about it. And he calls himself a vet!'

'Then you haven't heard? Clarence, a dreadful thing has happened. Angela has broken off her engagement to Heacham.'

'And the Agricultural Show on Wednesday week!'

'What on earth has that got to do with it?' demanded Lady Constance, feeling a recurrence of the swimming sensation.

'What has it got to do with it?' said Lord Emsworth warmly. 'My champion sow, with less than ten days to prepare herself for a most searching examination in competition with all the finest pigs in the county, starts refusing her food –'

'Will you stop maundering on about your insufferable pig and give your attention to something that really matters? I tell you that Angela – your niece Angela – has broken off her engagement to Lord Heacham and expresses her intention of marrying that hopeless ne'er-do-well, James Belford.'

'The son of old Belford, the parson?'

'Yes.'

'She can't. He's in America.'

'He is not in America. He is in London.'

'No,' said Lord Emsworth, shaking his head sagely. 'You're wrong. I remember meeting his father two years ago out on the road by Meeker's twenty-acre field, and he distinctly told me the boy was sailing for America the next day. He must be there by this time.'

'Can't you understand? He's come back.'

'Oh? Come back? I see. Come *back*?'

'You know there was once a silly sentimental sort of affair

294

between him and Angela; but a year after he left she became engaged to Heacham and I thought the whole thing was over and done with. And now it seems she met this young man Belford when she was in London last week, and it has started all over again. She tells me she has written to Heacham and broken the engagement.'

There was a silence. Brother and sister remained for a space plunged in thought. Lord Emsworth was the first to speak.

'We've tried acorns,' he said. 'We've tried skim milk. And we've tried potato-peel. But, no, she won't touch them.'

Conscious of two eyes raising blisters on his sensitive skin, he came to himself with a start.

'Absurd! Ridiculous! Preposterous!' he said, hurriedly. 'Breaking the engagement? Pooh! Tush! What nonsense! I'll have a word with that young man. If he thinks he can go about the place playing fast and loose with my niece and jilting her without so much as a –'

'Clarence!'

Lord Emsworth blinked. Something appeared to be wrong, but he could not imagine what. It seemed to him that in his last speech he had struck just the right note – strong, forceful, dignified.

'Eh?'

'It is Angela who has broken the engagement.'

'Oh, Angela?'

'She is infatuated with this man Belford. And the point is, what are we to do about it?'

Lord Emsworth reflected.

'Take a strong line,' he said firmly. 'Stand no nonsense. Don't send 'em a wedding-present.'

There is no doubt that, given time, Lady Constance would have found and uttered some adequately corrosive comment on this imbecile suggestion; but even as she was swelling preparatory to giving tongue, the door opened and a girl came in.

She was a pretty girl, with fair hair and blue eyes which in their softer moments probably reminded all sorts of people of twin lagoons slumbering beneath a southern sky. This, however, was not one of those moments. To Lord Emsworth, as they met his, they looked like something out of an oxy-acetylene blow-pipe; and, as far as he was capable of being disturbed by anything that was not his younger son Frederick, he was disturbed. Angela, it seemed to him, was upset about something; and he was sorry. He liked Angela.

To ease a tense situation, he said:

'Angela, my dear, do you know anything about pigs?'

The girl laughed. One of those sharp, bitter laughs which are so unpleasant just after breakfast.

'Yes, I do. You're one.'

'Me?'

'Yes, you. Aunt Constance says that, if I marry Jimmy, you won't let me have my money.'

'Money? Money?' Lord Emsworth was mildly puzzled. 'What money? You never lent me any money.'

Lady Constance's feelings found vent in a sound like an overheated radiator.

'I believe this absent-mindedness of yours is nothing but a ridiculous pose, Clarence. You know perfectly well that when poor Jane died she left you Angela's trustee.'

'And I can't touch my money without your consent till I'm twenty-five.'

'Well, how old are you?'

'Twenty-one.'

'Then what are you worrying about?' asked Lord Emsworth, surprised. 'No need to worry about it for another four years. God bless my soul, the money is quite safe. It is in excellent securities.'

Angela stamped her foot. An unladylike action, but how much better than kicking an uncle with it, as her lower nature prompted.

'I have told Angela,' explained Lady Constance, 'that, while we naturally cannot force her to marry Lord Heacham, we can at least keep her money from being squandered by this wastrel on whom she proposes to throw herself away.'

'He isn't a wastrel. He's got quite enough money to marry me on, but he wants some capital to buy a partnership in a –'

'He is a wastrel. Wasn't he sent abroad because –'

'That was two years ago. And since then –'

'My dear Angela, you may argue until –'

'I'm not arguing. I'm simply saying that I'm going to marry Jimmy, if we both have to starve in the gutter.'

'What gutter?' asked his lordship, wrenching his errant mind away from thought of acorns.

'Any gutter.'

'Now, please listen to me, Angela.'

It seemed to Lord Emsworth that there was a frightful amount of conversation going on. He had the sensation of having become a mere bit of flotsam upon a tossing sea of female voices. Both his sister and his niece appeared to have much to say, and they were saying it simultaneously and *fortissimo*. He looked wistfully at the door.

It was smoothly done. A twist of the handle, and he was beyond those voices where there was peace. Galloping gaily down the stairs, he charged out into the sunshine.

His gaiety was not long lived. Free at last to concentrate itself on the really serious issues of life, his mind grew sombre and grim. Once more there descended upon him the cloud which had been oppressing his soul before all this Heacham–Angela–Belford business began. Each step that took him nearer the sty where the ailing Empress resided seemed a heavier step than the last. He reached the sty; and, draping himself over the rails, peered moodily at the vast expanse of pig within.

For, even though she had been doing a bit of dieting of late, Empress of Blandings was far from being an ill-nourished animal. She resembled a captive balloon with ears and a tail, and was as nearly circular as a pig can be without bursting. Nevertheless, Lord Emsworth, as he regarded her, mourned and would not be comforted. A few more square meals under her belt, and no pig in all Shropshire could have held its head up in the Empress's presence. And now, just for the lack of those few meals, the supreme animal would probably be relegated to the mean obscurity of an 'Honourably Mentioned'. It was bitter, bitter.

297

He became aware that somebody was speaking to him; and, turning, perceived a solemn man in riding breeches.

'I say,' said the young man.

Lord Emsworth, though he would have preferred solitude, was relieved to find that the intruder was at least one of his own sex. Women are apt to stray off into side-issues, but men are practical and can be relied on to stick to the fundamentals. Besides, young Heacham probably kept pigs himself and might have a useful hint or two up his sleeve.

'I say, I've just ridden over to see if there was anything I could do about this fearful business.'

'Uncommonly kind and thoughtful of you, my dear fellow,' said Lord Emsworth, touched. 'I fear things look very black.'

'It's an absolute mystery to me.'

'To me, too.'

'I mean to say, she was all right last week.'

'She was all right as late as the day before yesterday.'

'Seemed quite cheery and chirpy and all that.'

'Entirely so.'

'And then this happens – out of a blue sky, as you might say.'

'Exactly. It is insoluble. We have done everything possible to tempt her appetite.'

'Her appetite? Is Angela ill?'

'Angela? No, I fancy not. She seemed perfectly well a few minutes ago.'

'You've seen her this morning, then? Did she say anything about this fearful business?'

'No. She was speaking about her money.'

'It's all so dashed unexpected.'

'Like a bolt from the blue,' agreed Lord Emsworth. 'Such a thing has never happened before. I fear the worst. According to the Wolff-Lehmann feeding standards, a pig, if in health, should consume daily nourishment amounting to fifty-seven thousand eight hundred calories, these to consist of proteins four pounds five ounces, carbohydrates twenty-five pounds –'

'What has that got to do with Angela?'

'Angela?'

298

'I came to find out why Angela has broken off our engagement.'

Lord Emsworth marshalled his thoughts. He had a misty idea that he had heard something mentioned about that. It came back to him.

'Ah, yes, of course. She has broken off the engagement, hasn't she? I believe it is because she is in love with someone else. Yes, now that I recollect, that was distinctly stated. The whole thing comes back to me quite clearly. Angela has decided to marry someone else. I knew there was some satisfactory explanation. Tell me, my dear fellow, what are your views on linseed meal.'

'What do you mean, linseed meal?'

'Why, linseed meal,' said Lord Emsworth, not being able to find a better definition. 'As a food for pigs.'

'Oh, curse all pigs!'

'What!' There was a sort of astounded horror in Lord Emsworth's voice. He had never been particularly fond of young Heacham, for he was not a man who took much to his juniors, but he had not supposed him capable of anarchistic sentiments like this. 'What did you say?'

'I said, "Curse all pigs!" You keep talking about pigs. I'm not interested in pigs. I don't want to discuss pigs. Blast and damn every pig in existence!'

Lord Emsworth watched him, as he strode away, with an emotion that was partly indignant and partly relief – indignation that a landowner and a fellow son of Shropshire could have brought himself to utter such words, and relief that one capable of such utterance was not going to marry into his family. He had always in his woollen-headed way been very fond of his niece Angela, and it was nice to think that the child had such solid good sense and so much cool discernment. Many girls of her age would have been carried away by the glamour of young Heacham's position and wealth; but she, divining with an intuition beyond her years that he was unsound on the subject of pigs, had drawn back while there was still time and refused to marry him.

A pleasant glow suffused Lord Emsworth's bosom, to be

frozen out a few moments later as he perceived his sister Constance bearing down upon him. Lady Constance was a beautiful woman, but there were times when the charm of her face was marred by a rather curious expression; and from nursery days onward his lordship had learned that this expression meant trouble. She was wearing it now.

'Clarence,' she said, 'I have had enough of this nonsense of Angela and young Belford. The thing cannot be allowed to go drifting on. You must catch the two o'clock train to London.'

'What! Why?'

'You must see this man Belford and tell him that, if Angela insists on marrying him, she will not have a penny for four years. I shall be greatly surprised if that piece of information does not put an end to the whole business.'

Lord Emsworth scratched meditatively at the Empress's tank-like back. A mutinous expression was on his mild face.

'Don't see why she shouldn't marry the fellow,' he mumbled.

'Marry James Belford?'

'I don't see why not. Seems fond of him and all that.'

'You never have had a grain of sense in your head, Clarence. Angela is going to marry Heacham.'

'Can't stand that man. All wrong about pigs.'

'Clarence, I don't wish to have any more discussion and argument. You will go to London on the two o'clock train. You will see Mr Belford. And you will tell him about Angela's money. Is that quite clear?'

'Oh, all right,' said his lordship moodily. 'All right, all right.'

The emotions of the Earl of Emsworth, as he sat next day facing his luncheon-guest, James Bartholomew Belford, across a table in the main dining-room of the Senior Conservative Club, were not of the liveliest and most agreeable. It was bad enough to be in London at all on such a day of golden sunshine. To be charged, while there, with the task of blighting the romance of two young people for whom he entertained a warm regard was unpleasant to a degree.

For, now that he had given the matter thought, Lord Emsworth recalled that he had always liked this boy Belford. A pleasant lad, with, he remembered now, a healthy fondness for that rural existence which so appealed to himself. By no means the sort of fellow who, in the very presence and hearing of Empress of Blandings, would have spoken disparagingly and with oaths of pigs as a class. It occurred to Lord Emsworth, as it has occurred to so many people, that the distribution of money in this world is all wrong. Why should a man like pig-despising Heacham have a rent roll that ran into tens of thousands, while this very deserving youngster had nothing?

These thoughts not only saddened Lord Emsworth – they embarrassed him. He hated unpleasantness, and it was suddenly borne in upon him that, after he had broken the news that Angela's bit of capital was locked up and not likely to get loose, conversation with his young friend during the remainder of lunch would tend to be somewhat difficult.

He made up his mind to postpone the revelation. During the meal, he decided, he would chat pleasantly of this and that; and then, later, while bidding his guest goodbye, he would spring the thing on him suddenly and dive back into the recesses of the club.

Considerably cheered at having solved a delicate problem with such adroitness, he started to prattle.

'The gardens at Blandings,' he said, 'are looking particularly attractive this summer. My head-gardener, Angus McAllister, is a man with whom I do not always find myself seeing eye to eye, notably in the matter of hollyhocks, on which I consider his views subversive to a degree; but there is no denying that he understands roses. The rose garden –'

'How well I remember that rose garden,' said James Belford, sighing slightly and helping himself to brussels sprouts. 'It was there that Angela and I used to meet on summer mornings.'

Lord Emsworth blinked. This was not an encouraging start, but the Emsworths were a fighting clan. He had another try.

'I have seldom seen such a blaze of colour as was to be witnessed there during the month of July. Both McAllister and I adopted a very strong policy with the slugs and plant lice, with the result that the place was a mass of flourishing Damasks and Ayrshires and –'

'Properly to appreciate roses,' said James Belford, 'you want to see them as a setting for a girl like Angela. With her fair hair gleaming against the green leaves she makes a rose garden seem a veritable Paradise.'

'No doubt,' said Lord Emsworth. 'No doubt. I am glad you liked my rose garden. At Blandings, of course, we have the natural advantage of loamy soil, rich in plant food and humus; but, as I often say to McAllister, and on this point we have never had the slightest disagreement, loamy soil by itself is not enough. You must have manure. If every autumn a liberal mulch of stable manure is spread upon the beds and the coarser parts removed in the spring before the annual forking –'

'Angela tells me,' said James Belford, 'that you have forbidden our marriage.'

Lord Emsworth choked dismally over his chicken. Directness of this kind, he told himself with a pang of self-pity, was the sort of thing young Englishmen picked up in America. Diplomatic circumlocution flourished only in a more leisurely civilization, and in those energetic and forceful surroundings you learned to Talk Quick and Do It Now, and all sorts of uncomfortable things.

'Er – well, yes, now you mention it, I believe some informal decision of that nature was arrived at. You see, my dear fellow, my sister Constance feels rather strongly –'

'I understand. I suppose she thinks I'm a sort of prodigal.'

'No, no, my dear fellow. She never said that. Wastrel was the term she employed.'

'Well, perhaps I did start out in business on those lines. But you can take it from me that when you find yourself employed on a farm in Nebraska belonging to an apple-jack-nourished patriarch with strong views on work and a good vocabulary, you soon develop a certain liveliness.'

'Are you employed on a farm?'

'I was employed on a farm.'

'Pigs?' said Lord Emsworth in a low, eager voice.

'Among other things.'

Lord Emsworth gulped. His fingers clutched at the tablecloth.

'Then perhaps, my dear fellow, you can give me some advice. For the last two days my prize sow, Empress of Blandings, has declined all nourishment. And the Agricultural Show is on Wednesday week. I am distracted with anxiety.'

James Belford frowned thoughtfully.

'What does your pig-man say about it?'

'My pig-man was sent to prison two days ago. Two days!' For the first time the significance of the coincidence struck him. 'You don't think that can have anything to do with the animal's loss of appetite?'

'Certainly. I imagine she is missing him and pining away because he isn't there.'

Lord Emsworth was surprised. He had only a distant acquaintance with George Cyril Wellbeloved, but from what he had seen of him he had not credited him with this fatal allure.

'She probably misses his afternoon call.'

Again his lordship found himself perplexed. He had had no notion that pigs were such sticklers for the formalities of social life.

'His call?'

'He must have had some special call that he used when he wanted her to come to dinner. One of the first things you learn on a farm is hog-calling. Pigs are temperamental. Omit to call them, and they'll starve rather than put on the nose-bag. Call them right, and they will follow you to the ends of the earth with their mouths watering.'

'God bless my soul! Fancy that.'

'A fact, I assure you. These calls vary in different parts of America. In Wisconsin, for example, the words, "Poig, Poig, Poig" bring home – in both the literal and the figurative sense – the bacon. In Illinois, I believe they call "Burp, Burp, Burp," while in Iowa the phrase "Klus, Klus, Klus" is preferred. Proceeding to Minnesota, we find "Peega, Peega, Peega" or, alternatively, "Oink, Oink, Oink," whereas in Milwaukee, so largely inhabited by those of German descent, you will hear the good old Teuton "Komm Schweine, Komm Schweine." Oh, yes, there are all sorts of pig-calls, from the Massachusetts "Phew, Phew, Phew" to the "Loo-ey, Loo-ey, Loo-ey" of Ohio, not counting various local devices such as beating on tin cans with axes or rattling pebbles in a suitcase. I knew a man out in Nebraska who used to call his pigs by tapping on the edge of the trough with his wooden leg.'

'Did he, indeed?'

'But a most unfortunate thing happened. One evening, hearing a woodpecker at the top of a tree, they started shinning up it; and when the man came out he found them all lying there in a circle with their necks broken.'

'This is no time for joking,' said Lord Emsworth, pained.

'I'm not joking. Solid fact. Ask anybody out there.'

Lord Emsworth placed a hand to his throbbing forehead.

'But if there is this wide variety, we have no means of knowing which call Wellbeloved . . .'

'Ah,' said James Belford, 'but wait. I haven't told you all. There is a masterword.'

'A what?'

'Most people don't know it, but I had it straight from the lips of Fred Patzel, the hog-calling champion of the Western States. What a man! I've known him to bring pork chops leaping from their plates. He informed me that, no matter whether an animal has been trained to answer to the Illinois "Burp" or the Minnesota "Oink", it will always give immediate service in response to this magic combination of syllables. It is to the pig world what the Masonic grip is to the human. "Oink" in Illinois or "Burp" in Minnesota, and the animal merely raises its eyebrows and stares coldly. But go to either State and call "Pighoo-oo-ey!" . . .'

The expression on Lord Emsworth's face was that of a drowning man who sees a lifeline.

'Is that the masterword of which you spoke?'

'That's it.'

'Pig –?'

'– hoo-oo-ey.'

'Pig-hoo-o-ey?'

'You haven't got it right. The first syllable should be short and staccato, the second long and rising into a falsetto, high but true.'

'Pig-hoo-o-o-ey.'

'Pig-hoo-o-o-ey.'

'Pig-hoo-o-o-ey!' yodelled Lord Emsworth, flinging his head back and giving tongue in a high, penetrating tenor which caused ninety-three Senior Conservatives, lunching in the vicinity, to congeal into living statues of alarm and disapproval.

'More body to the "hoo",' advised James Belford.

'Pig-hoo-o-o-o-ey!'

The Senior Conservative Club is one of the few places in London where lunchers are not accustomed to getting music with their meals. White-whiskered financiers gazed bleakly at bald-headed politicians, as if asking silently what was to be done about this. Bald-headed politicians stared back at white-whiskered financiers, replying in the language of the eye that they did not know. The general sentiment prevailing was a vague determination to write to the Committee about it.

'Pig-hoo-o-o-ey!' carolled Lord Emsworth. And, as he did so, his eye fell on the clock over the mantelpiece. Its hands pointed to twenty minutes to two.

He started convulsively. The best train in the day for Market Blandings was the one which left Paddington station at two sharp. After that there was nothing till the five-five.

He was not a man who often thought; but, when he did, to think was with him an act. A moment later he was scudding over the carpet, making for the door that led to the broad staircase.

Throughout the room which he had left, the decision to write in strong terms to the Committee was now universal; but from the mind, such as it was, of Lord Emsworth the past, with the single exception of the word 'Pig-hoo-o-o-o-ey!', had been completely blotted.

Whispering the magic syllables, he sped to the cloakroom and retrieved his hat. Murmuring them over and over again, he sprang into a cab. He was still repeating them as the train moved out of the station, and he would doubtless have gone on repeating them all the way to Market Blandings, had he not, as was his invariable practice when travelling by rail, fallen asleep after the first ten minutes of the journey.

The stopping of the train at Swindon Junction woke him with a start. He sat up, wondering, after his usual fashion on these occasions, who and where he was. Memory returned to him, but a memory that was, alas, incomplete. He remembered his name. He remembered that he was on his way home from a visit to London. But what it was that you said to a pig when inviting it to drop in for a bite of dinner he had completely forgotten.

It was the opinion of Lady Constance Keeble, expressed verbally during dinner in the brief intervals when they were alone, and by means of silent telepathy when Beach, the butler, was adding his dignified presence to the proceedings, that her brother Clarence, in his expedition to London to put matters plainly to James Belford, had made an outstanding idiot of himself.

There had been no need whatever to invite the man Belford to lunch; but, having invited him to lunch, to leave him sitting, without having clearly stated that Angela would have no money for four years, was the act of a congenital imbecile. Lady Constance had been aware ever since their childhood days that her brother had about as much sense as a –

Here Beach entered, superintending the bringing-in of the savoury, and she had been obliged to suspend her remarks.

This sort of conversation is never agreeable to a sensitive man, and his lordship had removed himself from the danger zone as soon as he could manage it. He was now seated in the library, sipping port and straining a brain which Nature had never intended for hard exercise in an effort to bring back that word of magic of which his unfortunate habit of sleeping in trains had robbed him.

'Pig –'

He could remember as far as that; but of what avail was a

single syllable? Besides, weak as his memory was, he could recall that the whole gist or nub of the thing lay in the syllable
that followed. The 'pig' was a mere preliminary.

Lord Emsworth finished his port and got up. He felt restless,
stifled. The summer night seemed to call to him like some
silver-voiced swineherd calling to his pig. Possibly, he thought,
a breath of fresh air might stimulate his brain-cells. He wandered downstairs; and, having dug a shocking old slouch hat
out of the cupboard where he hid it to keep his sister Constance
from impounding and burning it, he strode heavily out into the
garden.

He was pottering aimlessly to and fro in the parts adjacent to
the rear of the castle when there appeared in his path a slender
female form. He recognized it without pleasure. Any unbiased
judge would have said that his niece Angela, standing there in
the soft pale light, looked like some dainty spirit of the Moon.
Lord Emsworth was not an unbiased judge. To him Angela
looked like Trouble. The march of civilization has given the
modern girl a vocabulary and an ability to use it which her
grandmother never had. Lord Emsworth would not have
minded meeting Angela's grandmother a bit.

'Is that you, my dear?' he said nervously.

'Yes.'

'I didn't see you at dinner.'

'I didn't want any dinner. The food would have choked me. I
can't eat.'

'It's precisely the same with my pig,' said his lordship. 'Young
Belford tells me –'

Into Angela's queenly disdain there flashed a sudden animation.

'Have you seen Jimmy? What did he say?'

'That's just what I can't remember. It began with the word
"Pig" –'

'But after he had finished talking about you, I mean. Didn't
he say anything about coming down here?'

'Not that I remember.'

'I expect you weren't listening. You've got a very annoying

307

habit, Uncle Clarence,' said Angela maternally, 'of switching your mind off and just going blah when people are talking to you. It gets you very much disliked on all sides. Didn't Jimmy say anything about me?'

'I fancy so. Yes, I am nearly sure he did.'

'Well, what?'

'I cannot remember.'

There was a sharp clicking noise in the darkness. It was caused by Angela's upper front teeth meeting her lower front teeth; and was followed by a sort of wordless exclamation. It seemed only too plain that the love and respect which a niece should have for an uncle were in the present instance at a very low ebb.

'I wish you wouldn't do that,' said Lord Emsworth plaintively.

'Do what?'

'Make clicking noises at me.'

'I will make clicking noises at you. You know perfectly well, Uncle Clarence, that you are behaving like a bohunkus.'

'A what?'

'A bohunkus,' explained his niece coldly, 'is a very inferior sort of worm. Not the kind of worm that you see on lawns, which you can respect, but a really degraded species.'

'I wish you would go in, my dear,' said Lord Emsworth. 'The night air may give you a chill.'

'I won't go in. I came out here to look at the moon and think of Jimmy. What are you doing out here, if it comes to that?'

'I came out here to think. I am greatly exercized about my pig, Empress of Blandings. For two days she has refused her food, and young Belford says she will not eat until she hears the proper call or cry. He very kindly taught it to me, but unfortunately I have forgotten it.'

'I wonder you had the nerve to ask Jimmy to teach you pig-calls, considering the way you're treating him.'

'But –'

'Like a leper, or something. And all I can say is that, if you remember this call of his, and it makes the Empress eat, you ought to be ashamed of yourself if you still refuse to let me marry him.'

'My dear,' said Lord Emsworth earnestly, 'if through young Belford's instrumentality Empress of Blandings is induced to take nourishment once more, there is nothing I will refuse him – nothing.'

'Honour bright?'

'I give you my solemn word.'

'You won't let Aunt Constance bully you out of it?'

Lord Emsworth drew himself up.

'Certainly not,' he said proudly. 'I am always ready to listen to your Aunt Constance's views, but there are certain matters where I claim the right to act according to my own judgement.' He paused and stood musing. 'It began with the word "Pig –" '

From somewhere near at hand music made itself heard. The servants' hall, its day's labour ended, was refreshing itself with the housekeeper's gramophone. To Lord Emsworth the strains were merely an additional annoyance. He was not fond of music. It reminded him of his young son Frederick, a flat but persevering songster both in and out of the bath.

'Yes. I can distinctly recall as much as that. Pig – Pig –'

'WHO –'

Lord Emsworth leaped into the air. It was as if an electric shock had been applied to his person.

'WHO stole my heart away?' howled the gramophone. 'WHO –?'

The peace of the summer night was shattered by a triumphant shout.

'Pig-HOO-o-o-o-ey!'

A window opened. A large, bald head appeared. A dignified voice spoke.

'Who is there? Who is making that noise?'

'Beach!' cried Lord Emsworth. 'Come out here at once.'

'Very good, your lordship.'

And presently the beautiful night was made still more lovely by the added attraction of the butler's presence.

'Beach, listen to this.'

'Very good, your lordship.'

'Pig-hoo-o-o-o-ey!'

'Very good, your lordship.'

'Now you do it.'

'I, your lordship?'

'Yes. It's a way you call pigs.'

'I do not call pigs, your lordship,' said the butler coldly.

'What do you want Beach to do it for?' asked Angela.

'Two heads are better than one. If we both learn it, it will not matter should I forget it again.'

'By Jove, yes! Come on, Beach. Push it over the thorax,' urged the girl eagerly. 'You don't know it, but this is a matter of life and death. At-a-boy, Beach! Inflate the lungs and go it.'

It had been the butler's intention, prefacing his remarks with the statement that he had been in service at the castle for eighteen years, to explain frigidly to Lord Emsworth that it was not his place to stand in the moonlight practising pig-calls. If, he would have gone on to add, his lordship saw the matter from a different angle, then it was his, Beach's, painful duty to tender his resignation, to become effective one month from that day.

But the intervention of Angela made this impossible to a man of chivalry and heart. A paternal fondness for the girl, dating from the days when he had stooped to enacting – and very convincingly, too, for his was a figure that lent itself to the impersonation – the *rôle* of a hippopotamus for her childish amusement, checked the words he would have uttered. She was looking at him with bright eyes, and even the rendering of pig-noises seemed a small sacrifice to make for her sake.

'Very good, your lordship,' he said in a low voice, his face pale and set in the moonlight. 'I shall endeavour to give satisfaction. I would merely advance the suggestion, your lordship, that we move a few steps farther away from the vicinity of the servants' hall. If I were to be overheard by any of the lower domestics, it would weaken my position as a disciplinary force.'

'What chumps we are!' cried Angela, inspired. 'The place to do it is outside the Empress's sty. Then, if it works, we'll see it working.'

Lord Emsworth found this a little abstruse, but after a moment he got it.

'Angela,' he said, 'you are a very intelligent girl. Where you get your brains from, I don't know. Not from my side of the family.'

The bijou residence of the Empress of Blandings looked very snug and attractive in the moonlight. But beneath even the beautiful things of life there is always an underlying sadness. This was supplied in the present instance by a long, low trough, only too plainly full to the brim of succulent mash and acorns. The fast, obviously, was still in progress.

The sty stood some considerable distance from the castle walls, so that there had been ample opportunity for Lord Emsworth to rehearse his little company during the journey. By the time they had ranged themselves against the rails, his two assistants were letter-perfect.

'Now,' said his lordship.

There floated out upon the summer's night a strange composite sound that sent the birds roosting in the trees above shooting off their perches like rockets. Angela's clear soprano rang out like the voice of the village blacksmith's daughter. Lord Emsworth contributed a reedy tenor. And the bass notes of Beach probably did more to startle the birds than any other one item in the programme.

They paused and listened. Inside the Empress's boudoir there sounded the movement of a heavy body. There was an inquiring grunt. The next moment the sacking that covered the doorway was pushed aside, and the noble animal appeared.

'Now!' said Lord Emsworth again.

Once more that musical cry shattered the silence of the night. But it brought no responsive movement from Empress of Blandings. She stood there motionless, her nose elevated, her ears hanging down, her eyes everywhere but on the trough where, by rights, she should now be digging in and getting hers. A chill disappointment crept over Lord Emsworth, to be succeeded by a gust of petulant anger.

'I might have known it,' he said bitterly. 'That young scoundrel was deceiving me. He was playing a joke on me.'

'He wasn't,' cried Angela indignantly. 'Was he, Beach?'

'Not knowing the circumstances, Miss, I cannot venture an opinion.'

'Well, why has it no effect, then?' demanded Lord Emsworth.

'You can't expect it to work right away. We've got her stirred up, haven't we? She's thinking it over, isn't she? Once more will do the trick. Ready, Beach?'

'Quite ready, miss.'

'Then when I say three. And this time, Uncle Clarence, do please for goodness' sake not yowl like you did before. It was enough to put any pig off. Let it come out quite easily and gracefully. Now, then. One, two – three!'

The echoes died away. And as they did so a voice spoke.

'Community singing?'

'Jimmy!' cried Angela, whisking round.

'Hullo, Angela. Hullo, Lord Emsworth. Hullo, Beach.'

'Good evening, sir. Happy to see you once more.'

'Thanks. I'm spending a few days at the Vicarage with my father. I got down here by the five-five.'

Lord Emsworth cut peevishly in upon these civilities.

'Young man,' he said, 'what do you mean by telling me that my pig would respond to that cry? It does nothing of the kind.'

'You can't have done it right.'

'I did it precisely as you instructed me. I have had, moreover, the assistance of Beach here and my niece Angela –'

'Let's hear a sample.'

Lord Emsworth cleared his throat. 'Pig-hoo-o-o-o-ey!'

James Belford shook his head.

'Nothing like it,' he said. 'You want to begin the "Hoo" in a low minor of two quarter notes in four-four time. From this build gradually to a higher note, until at last the voice is soaring in full crescendo, reaching F sharp on the natural scale and dwelling for two retarded half-notes, then breaking into a shower of accidental grace-notes.'

'God bless my soul!' said Lord Emsworth, appalled. 'I shall never be able to do it.'

'Jimmy will do it for you,' said Angela. 'Now that he's engaged to me, he'll be one of the family and always popping about here. He can do it every day till the show is over.'

James Belford nodded.

'I think that would be the wisest plan. It is doubtful if an amateur could ever produce real results. You need a voice that has been trained on the open prairie and that has gathered richness and strength from competing with tornadoes. You need a manly, wind-scorched voice with a suggestion in it of the crackling of corn husks and the whisper of evening breezes in the fodder. Like this!'

Resting his hands on the rail before him, James Belford swelled before their eyes like a young balloon. The muscles on his cheekbones stood out, his forehead became corrugated, his ears seemed to shimmer. Then, at the very height of the tension, he let it go like, as the poet beautifully puts it, the sound of a great Amen.

'PIG-HOOOOO-OOO-OOO-O-O-ey!'

They looked at him, awed. Slowly, fading off across hill and dale, the vast bellow died away. And suddenly, as it died, another, softer sound succeeded it. A sort of gulpy, gurgly, plobby, squishy, woffle-some sound, like a thousand eager men drinking soup in a foreign restaurant. And, as he heard it, Lord Emsworth uttered a cry of rapture.

The Empress was feeding.

Blandings Castle (1935)

A Top Hat Goes Flying

At lunch-time on the first day of the Eton and Harrow cricket match London's clubland is full of top hats. Lord Ickenham is at the Drones, a guest of his long-suffering nephew Pongo. By a lucky chance there is a catapult, and a Brazil nut, to Lord Ickenham's hand, and he sits, waiting for a target, at the open window. Opposite the Drones is the more sedate Demosthenes Club.

The door of the Demosthenes had swung open, and there had come down the steps a tall, stout, florid man of middle age who wore his high silk hat like the plumed helmet of Henry of Navarre. He stood on the pavement looking about him for a taxi-cab – with a sort of haughty impatience, as though he had thought that, when he wanted a taxi-cab, ten thousand must have sprung from their ranks to serve him.

'Tiger on skyline,' said the Egg.

'Complete with topper,' said the Bean. 'Draw that bead without delay, is my advice.'

'Just waiting till I can see the whites of his eyes,' said Lord Ickenham.

Pongo, whose air now was that of a man who has had it drawn to his attention that there is a ticking bomb attached to his coat-tails, repeated his stricken-duck impersonation, putting this time even more feeling into it. Only the fact that he had brilliantined them while making his toilet that morning kept his knotted and combined locks from parting and each particular hair from standing on end like quills upon the fretful porpentine.

'For heaven's sake, Uncle Fred!'

'My boy?'

'You can't pot that bird's hat!'

'Can't?' Lord Ickenham's eyebrows rose. 'A strange word to hear on the lips of one of our proud family. Did our representative at King Arthur's Round Table say "Can't" when told off by the front office to go and rescue damsels in distress from two-headed giants? When Henry the Fifth at Harfleur cried "Once more unto the breach, dear friends, once more, or close the walls up with our English dead", was he damped by hearing the voice of a Twistleton in the background saying he didn't think he would be able to manage it? No! The Twistleton in question, subsequently to do well at the battle of Agincourt, snapped into it with his hair in a braid and was the life and soul of the party. But it may be that you are dubious concerning my ability. Does the old skill still linger, you are asking yourself? You need have no anxiety. Anything William Tell could do I can do better.'

'But it's old Bastable.'

Lord Ickenham had not failed to observe this, but the discovery did nothing to weaken his resolution. Though fond of Sir Raymond Bastable, he found much to disapprove of in him. He considered the eminent barrister pompous, arrogant and far too pleased with himself.

Nor in forming this diagnosis was he in error. There may have been men in London who thought more highly of Sir Raymond Bastable than did Sir Raymond Bastable, but they would have been hard to find, and the sense of being someone set apart from and superior to the rest of the world inevitably breeds arrogance. Sir Raymond's attitude toward those about him – his nephew Cosmo, his butler Peasemarch, his partners at bridge, the waiters at the Demosthenes and, in particular, his sister, Phoebe Wisdom, who kept house for him and was reduced by him to a blob of tearful jelly almost daily – was always that of an irritable tribal god who intends to stand no nonsense from his worshippers and is prepared, should the smoked offering fall in any way short of the highest standard, to say it with thunderbolts. To have his top hat knocked off

315

with a Brazil nut would, in Lord Ickenham's opinion, make him a better, deeper, more lovable man.

'Yes, there he spouts,' he said.

'He's Aunt Jane's brother.'

'Half-brother is the more correct term. Still, as the wise old saying goes, half a brother is better than no bread.'

'Aunt Jane will skin you alive, if she finds out.'

'She won't find out. That is the thought that sustains me. But I must not waste time chatting with you, my dear Pongo, much as I enjoy your conversation. I see a taxi-cab approaching, and if I do not give quick service, my quarry will be gone with the wind. From the way his nostrils are quivering as he sniffs the breeze, I am not sure that he has not already scented me.'

Narrowing his gaze, Lod Ickenham released the guided missile, little knowing, as it sped straight and true to its mark, that he was about to enrich English literature and provide another job of work for a number of deserving printers and compositors.

Yet such was indeed the case. The question of how authors come to write their books is generally one not easily answered. Milton, for instance, asked how he got the idea for *Paradise Lost*, would probably have replied with a vague 'Oh, I don't know, you know. These things sort of pop into one's head, don't you know,' leaving the researcher very much where he was before. But with Sir Raymond Bastable's novel *Cocktail Time* we are on firmer ground. It was directly inspired by the accurate catapultmanship of Pongo Twistleton's Uncle Fred.

Had his aim not been so unerring, had he failed, as he might so well have done, to allow for windage, the book would never have been written.

> *Cocktail Time (1958)*, and you must read it to
> find out why the Brazil nut shot by Uncle Fred
> caused Sir Raymond Bastable to write, under a
> pseudonym, that angry best-selling novel
> *Cocktail Time*.

Tried in the Furnace

It was a surprise to find the stunning Angelica Briscoe still at the vicarage, still unmarried, in Aunts Aren't Gentlemen, which *was published thirty-eight years later than this story.*

The annual smoking-concert of the Drones Club had just come to an end, and it was the unanimous verdict of the little group assembled in the bar for a last quick one that the gem of the evening had been item number six on the programme, the knockabout cross-talk act of Cyril ('Barmy') Fotheringay-Phipps and Reginald ('Pongo') Twistleton-Twistleton. Both Cyril, in the red beard, and Reginald, in the more effective green whiskers, had shown themselves, it was agreed, at the very peak of their form. With sparkling repartee and vigorous by-play they had gripped the audience from the start.

'In fact,' said an Egg, 'it struck me that they were even better than last year. Their art seemed to have deepened somehow.'

A thoughtful Crumpet nodded.

'I noticed the same thing. The fact is, they passed through a soul-testing experience not long ago and it has left its mark upon them. It also dashed nearly wrecked the act. I don't know if any of you fellows are aware of it, but at one time they had definitely decided to scratch the fixture and not give a performance at all.'

'What!'

'Absolutely. They were within a toucher of failing to keep faith with their public. Bad blood had sprung up between them. Also pique and strained relations. They were not on speaking terms.'

His hearers were frankly incredulous. They pointed out that

the friendship between the two artistes had always been a by-word or whatever you called it. A well-read Egg summed it up by saying that they were like Thingummy and What's-his-name.

'Nevertheless,' insisted the Crumpet, 'what I am telling you is straight, official stuff. Two weeks ago, if Barmy had said to Pongo: "Who was that lady I saw you coming down the street with?" Pongo would not have replied: "That was no lady, that was my wife," – he would simply have raised his eyebrows coldly and turned away in a marked manner.'

It was a woman, of course (proceeded the Crumpet) who came between them. Angelica Briscoe was her name, and she was the daughter of the Rev. P. P. Briscoe, who vetted the souls of the local peasantry at a place called Maiden Eggesford down in Somersetshire. This hamlet is about half a dozen miles from the well-known resort, Bridmouth-on-Sea, and it was in the establishment of the Messrs. Thorpe and Widgery, the popular grocers of that town, that Barmy and Pongo first set eyes on the girl.

They had gone to Bridmouth partly for a splash of golf, but principally to be alone and away from distractions, so that they would be able to concentrate on the rehearsing and building-up of this cross-talk act which we have just witnessed. And on the morning of which I speak they had strolled into the Thorpe and Widgery emporium to lay in a few little odds and ends, and there, putting in a bid for five pounds of streaky bacon, was a girl so lovely that they congealed in their tracks. And, as they stood staring, she said to the bloke behind the counter.

'That's the lot. Send them to Miss Angelica Briscoe, The Vicarage, Maiden Eggesford.'

She then pushed off, and Barmy and Pongo, feeling rather as if they had been struck by lightning, bought some sardines and a segment of certified butter in an overwrought sort of way and went out.

They were both pretty quiet for the rest of the day, and after dinner that night Pongo said to Barmy:

318

'I say, Barmy.'

And Barmy said:

'Hullo?'

And Pongo said:

'I say, Barmy, it's a bally nuisance, but I'll have to buzz up to London for a day or two. I've suddenly remembered some spots of business that call for my personal attention. You won't mind my leaving you?'

Barmy could scarcely conceal his bracedness. Within two minutes of seeing that girl, he had made up his mind that somehow or other he must repair to Maiden Eggesford and get to know her, and the problem which had been vexing him all day had been what to do with the body – viz. Pongo's.

'Not a bit,' he said.

'I'll be back as soon as I can.'

'Don't hurry,' said Barmy heartily. 'As a matter of fact, a few days' lay-off will do the act all the good in the world. Any pro. will tell you that the worst thing possible is to over-rehearse. Stay away as long as you like.'

So next morning – it was a Saturday – Pongo climbed on to a train, and in the afternoon Barmy collected his baggage and pushed off to the Goose and Grasshopper at Maiden Eggesford. And, having booked a room there and toddled into the saloon bar for a refresher with the love-light in his eyes, the first thing he saw was Pongo chatting across the counter with the barmaid.

Neither was much bucked. A touch of constraint about sums it up.

'Hullo!' said Barmy.

'Hullo!' said Pongo.

'You here?'

'Yes. You here?'

'Yes.'

'Oh.'

There was a bit of a silence.

'So you didn't go to London' said Barmy.

'No,' said Pongo.

319

'Oh,' said Barmy.

'And you didn't stick on at Bridmouth?' said Pongo.

'No,' said Barmy.

'Oh,' said Pongo.

There was some more silence.

'You came here, I see,' said Pongo.

'Yes,' said Barmy. 'I see *you* came here.'

'Yes,' said Pongo. 'An odd coincidence.'

'Very odd.'

'Well, skin off your nose,' said Pongo.

'Fluff in your latchkey,' said Barmy.

He drained his glass and tried to exhibit a light-hearted non-chalance, but his mood was sombre. He was a chap who could put two and two together and sift and weigh the evidence and all that sort of thing, and it was plain to him that love had brought Pongo also to this hamlet, and he resented the fact. Indeed, it was at this instant, he tells me, that there came to him the first nebulous idea of oiling out of that cross-talk act of theirs. The thought of having to ask a beastly, butting-in blighter like Reginald Twistleton-Twistleton if he was fond of mutton-broth and being compelled to hit him over the head with a rolled-up umbrella when he replied 'No, Mutt and Jeff,' somehow seemed to revolt his finest feelings.

Conversation rather languished after this, and presently Pongo excused himself in a somewhat stiff manner and went upstairs to his room. And it was while Barmy was standing at the counter listening in a distrait kind of way to the barmaid telling him what cucumber did to her digestive organs that a fellow in plus fours entered the bar and Barmy saw that he was wearing the tie of his old school.

Well, you know how it is when you're in some public spot and a stranger comes in wearing the old school tie. You shove a hasty hand over your own and start to sidle out before the chap can spot it and grab you and start gassing. And Barmy was just doing this when the barmaid uttered these sensational words:

'Good evening, Mr Briscoe.'

Barmy stood spellbound. He turned to the barmaid and spoke in a hushed whisper.

'Did you say "Briscoe"?'

'Yes, sir.'

'From the Vicarage?'

'Yes, sir.'

Barmy quivered like a jelly. The thought that he had had the amazing luck to find in the brother of the girl he loved an old schoolmate made him feel boneless. After all, he felt, as he took his hand away from his tie, there is no bond like that of the old school. If you meet one of the dear old school in a public spot, he meant to say, why, you go straight up to him and start fraternizing.

He made a bee-line for the chap's table.

'I say,' he said, 'I see you're wearing a . . .'

The chap's hand had shot up to his tie with a sort of nervous gesture, but he evidently realized that the time had gone by for protective measures. He smiled a bit wryly.

'Have a drink,' he said.

'I've got one, thanks,' said Barmy. 'I'll bring it along to your table, shall I? Such a treat meeting someone from the dear old place, what?'

'Oh, rather.'

'I think I'd have been a bit after your time, wouldn't I?' said Barmy, for the fellow was well stricken in years – twenty-eight, if a day. 'Fotheringay-Phipps is more or less my name. Yours is Briscoe, what?'

'Yes.'

Barmy swallowed a couple of times.

'Er . . . Ah . . . Um . . . I think I saw your sister yesterday in Bridmouth,' he said, blushing prettily.

So scarlet, indeed, did his countenance become that the other regarded him narrowly, and Barmy knew that he had guessed his secret.

'You saw her in Bridmouth yesterday, eh?'

'Yes.'

'And now you're here.'

321

'Er – yes.'

'Well, well,' said the chap, drawing his breath in rather thoughtfully.

There was a pause, during which Barmy's vascular motors continued to do their bit.

'You must meet her,' said the chap.

'I should like to,' said Barmy. 'I only saw her for a moment buying streaky bacon, but she seemed a charming girl.'

'Oh, she is.'

'I scarcely noticed her, of course, but rather attractive she struck me as.'

'Quite.'

'I gave her the merest glance, you understand, but I should say at a venture that she has a great white soul. In fact,' said Barmy, losing his grip altogether, 'you wouldn't be far out in describing her as divine.'

'You must certainly meet her,' said the chap. Then he shook his head. 'No, it wouldn't be any good.'

'Why not?' bleated Barmy.

'Well, I'll tell you,' said the chap. 'You know what girls are. They have their little enthusiasms and it hurts them when people scoff at them. Being a parson's daughter, Angelica is wrapped up at present in the annual village School Treat. I can see at a glance the sort of fellow you are – witty, mordant, ironical. You would get off one of your devastating epigrams at the expense of the School Treat, and, while she might laugh at the wit, she would be deeply wounded by the satire.'

'But I wouldn't dream . . .'

'Ah, but if you didn't, if you spoke approvingly of the School Treat, what then? The next thing that would happen would be that she would be asking you to help her run it. And that would bore you stiff.'

Barmy shook from stem to stern. This was better even than he had hoped.

'You don't mean she would let me help her with the School Treat?'

'Why, you wouldn't do it, would you?'

'I should enjoy it above all things.'

'Well, if that's the way you feel, the matter can easily be arranged. She will be here any moment now to pick me up in her car.'

And, sure enough, not two minutes later there floated through the open window a silvery voice, urging the fellow, who seemed to answer to the name of 'Fathead,' to come out quick, because the voice did not intend to remain there all night.

So the fellow took Barmy out, and there was the girl, sitting in a two-seater. He introduced Barmy. The girl beamed. Barmy beamed. The fellow said that Barmy was anxious to come and help with the School Treat. The girl beamed again. Barmy beamed again. And presently the car drove off, the girl's last words being a reminder that the binge started at two sharp on the Monday.

That night, as they dined together, Barmy and Pongo put in their usual spot of rehearsing. It was their practice to mould and shape the act during meals, as they found that mastication seemed to sharpen their intellect. But tonight it would have been plain to an observant spectator that their hearts were not in it. There was an unmistakable coolness between them. Pongo said he had an aunt who complained of rheumatism, and Barmy said, Well, who wouldn't? And Barmy said his father could not meet his creditors, and Pongo said, Did he want to? But the old fire and sparkle were absent. And they had relapsed into a moody silence when the door opened and the barmaid pushed her head in.

'Miss Briscoe has just sent over a message, Mr Phipps,' said the barmaid. 'She says she would like you to be there a little earlier than two, if you can manage it. One-fifteen, if possible, because there's always so much to do.'

'Oh, right,' said Barmy, a bit rattled, for he had heard the sharp hiss of his companion's in-drawn breath.

'I'll tell her,' said the barmaid.

She withdrew, and Barmy found Pongo's eyes resting on him like a couple of blobs of vitriol.

323

'What's all this?' asked Pongo.

Barmy tried to be airy.

'Oh, it's nothing. Just the local School Treat. The vicar's daughter here – a Miss Briscoe – seems anxious that I should drop round on Monday and help her run it.'

Pongo started to grind his teeth, but he had a chunk of potato in his mouth at that moment and was hampered. But he gripped the table till his knuckles stood out white under the strain.

'Have you been sneaking round behind my back and inflicting your beastly society on Miss Briscoe?' he demanded.

'I do not like your tone, Reginald.'

'Never mind about my tone. I'll attend to my tone. Of all the bally low hounds that ever stepped you are the lowest. So this is what the friendship of years amounts to, is it? You crawl in here and try to cut me out with the girl I love.'

'Well, dash it . . .'

'That is quite enough.'

'But, dash it . . .'

'I wish to hear no more.'

'But, dash it, I love her, too. It's not my fault if you happen to love her, too, is it? I mean to say, if a fellow loves a girl and another fellow loves her, too, you can't expect the fellow who loves the girl to edge out because he happens to be acquainted with the fellow who loves her, too. When it comes to Love, a chap has got to look out for his own interests, hasn't he? You didn't find Romeo or any of those chaps easing away from the girl just to oblige a pal, did you? Certainly not. So I don't see . . .'

'Please!' said Pongo.

A silence fell.

'Might I trouble you to pass the mustard, Fotheringay-Phipps,' said Pongo coldly.

'Certainly, Twistleton-Twistleton,' replied Barmy, with equal hauteur.

It is always unpleasant not to be on speaking terms with an

old friend. To be cooped up alone in a mouldy village pub with an old friend with whom one has ceased to converse is simply rotten. And this is especially so if the day happens to be a Sunday.

Maiden Eggesford, like so many of our rural hamlets, is not at its best and brightest on a Sunday. When you have walked down the main street and looked at the Jubilee Watering-Trough, there is nothing much to do except go home and then come out again and walk down the main street once more and take another look at the Jubilee Watering-Trough. It will give you some rough idea of the state to which Barmy Fotheringay-Phipps had been reduced by the end of the next day when I tell you that the sound of the church bells ringing for evensong brought him out of the Goose and Grasshopper as if he had heard a fire-engine. The thought that at last something was going to happen in Maiden Eggesford in which the Jubilee Watering-Trough *motif* was not stressed, stirred him strangely. He was in his pew in three jumps. And as the service got under way he began to feel curious emotions going on in his bosom.

There is something about evening church in a village in the summer-time that affects the most hard-boiled. They had left the door open, and through it came the scent of lime trees and wallflowers and the distant hum of bees fooling about. And gradually there poured over Barmy a wave of sentiment. As he sat and listened to the First Lesson he became a changed man.

The Lesson was one of those chapters of the Old Testament all about how Abimalech begat Jazzbo and Jazzbo begat Zachariah. And, what with the beauty of the words and the peace of his surroundings, Barmy suddenly began to become conscious of a great remorse.

He had not done the square thing, he told himself, by dear old Pongo. Here was a chap, notoriously one of the best, as sound an egg as ever donned a heliotrope sock, and he was deliberately chiselling him out of the girl he loved. He was doing the dirty on a fellow whom he had been pally with since their Eton jacket days – a bloke who time and again had shared with him his last bar of almond-rock. Was this right? Was this

325

just? Would Abimalech have behaved like that to Jazzbo or – for the matter of that – Jazzbo to Zachariah? The answer, he could not disguise it from himself, was in the negative.

It was a different, stronger Barmy, a changed, chastened Cyril Fotheringay-Phipps, who left the sacred edifice at the conclusion of the vicar's fifty-minute sermon. He had made the great decision. It would play the dickens with his heart and probably render the rest of his life a blank, but nevertheless he would retire from the unseemly struggle and give the girl up to Pongo.

That night, as they cold-suppered together, Barmy cleared his throat and looked across at Pongo with a sad, sweet smile.

'Pongo,' he said.

The other glanced up distantly from his baked potato.

'There is something you wish to say to me, Fotheringay-Phipps?'

'Yes,' said Barmy. 'A short while ago I sent a note to Miss Briscoe, informing her that I shall not be attending the School Treat and mentioned that you will be there in my stead. Take her, Pongo, old man. She is yours. I scratch my nomination.'

Pongo stared. His whole manner changed. It was as if he had been a Trappist monk who had suddenly decided to give Trappism a miss and become one of the boys again.

'But, dash it, this is noble!'

'No, no.'

'But it is! It's ... well, dash it, I hardly know what to say.'

'I hope you will be very, very happy.'

'Thanks, old man.'

'Very, very, very happy.'

'Rather! I should say so. And I'll tell you one thing. In the years to come there will always be a knife and fork for you at our little home. The children shall be taught to call you Uncle Barmy.'

'Thanks,' said Barmy. 'Thanks.'

'Not at all,' said Pongo. 'Not at all.'

At this moment, the barmaid entered with a note for Barmy. He read it and crumpled it up.

'From Her?' asked Pongo.

'Yes.'

'Saying she quite understands, and so forth?'

'Yes.'

Pongo ate a piece of cheese in a meditative manner. He seemed to be pursuing some train of thought.

'I should think,' he said, 'that a fellow who married a clergyman's daughter would get the ceremony performed at cut rates, wouldn't he?'

'Probably.'

'If not absolutely on the nod?'

'I shouldn't wonder.'

'Not,' said Pongo, 'that I am influenced by any consideration like that, of course. My love is pure and flamelike, with no taint of dross. Still, in times like these, every little helps.'

'Quite,' said Barmy. 'Quite.'

He found it hard to control his voice. He had lied to his friend about that note. What Angelica Briscoe had really said in it was that it was quite all right if he wanted to edge out of the School Treat, but that she would require him to take the Village Mothers for their Annual Outing on the same day. There had to be some responsible person with them, and the curate had sprained his ankle tripping over a footstool in the vestry.

Barmy could read between the lines. He saw what this meant. His fatal fascination had done its deadly work, and the girl had become infatuated with him. No other explanation would fit the facts. It was absurd to suppose that she would lightly have selected him for this extraordinarily important assignment. Obviously it was the big event of the village year. Anyone would do to mess about at the School Treat, but Angelica Briscoe would place in charge of the Mothers' Annual Outing only a man she trusted . . . respected . . . loved.

He sighed. What must be, he felt, must be. He had done his conscientious best to retire in favour of his friend, but Fate had been too strong.

*

327

I found it a little difficult (said the Crumpet) to elicit from Barmy exactly what occurred at the annual outing of the Village Mothers of Maiden Eggesford. When telling me the story, he had the air of a man whose old wound is troubling him. It was not, indeed, till the fourth cocktail that he became really communicative. And then, speaking with a kind of stony look in his eye, he gave me a fairly comprehensive account. But even then each word seemed to hurt him in some tender spot.

The proceedings would appear to have opened in a quiet and orderly manner. Sixteen females of advanced years assembled in a motor-coach, and the expedition was seen off from the Vicarage door by the Rev. P. P. Briscoe in person. Under his eye, Barmy tells me, the Beauty Chorus was demure and docile. It was a treat to listen to their murmured responses. As nice and respectable a bunch of mothers, Barmy says, as he had ever struck. His only apprehension at this point, he tells me, was lest the afternoon's proceedings might possibly be a trifle stodgy. He feared a touch of ennui.

He needn't have worried. There was no ennui.

The human cargo, as I say, had started out in a spirit of demureness and docility. But it was amazing what a difference a mere fifty yards of the high road made to these Mothers. No sooner were they out of sight of the Vicarage than they began to effervesce to an almost unbelievable extent. The first intimation Barmy had that the binge was going to be run on lines other than those which he had anticipated, was when a very stout Mother in a pink bonnet and a dress covered with bugles suddenly picked off a passing cyclist with a well-directed tomato, causing him to skid into a ditch. Upon which, all sixteen mothers laughed like fiends in hell, and it was plain that they considered that the proceedings had now been formally opened.

Of course, looking back at it now in a calmer spirit, Barmy tells me that he can realize that there is much to be said in palliation of the exuberance of these ghastly female pimples. When you are shut up all the year round in a place like Maiden Eggesford, with nothing to do but wash underclothing and attend Divine Service, you naturally incline to let yourself go a bit at times of festival and holiday. But at the moment he did not think of this, and his spiritual agony was pretty pronounced.

If there's one thing Barmy hates it's being conspicuous, and conspicuous is precisely what a fellow cannot fail to be when he's in a motor-coach with sixteen women of mature ages who alternate between singing ribald songs and hurling volleys of homely chaff at passers-by. In this connection, he tells me, he is thinking particularly of a Mother in spectacles and a Homburg hat, which she had pinched from the driver of the vehicle, whose prose style appeared to have been modelled on that of Rabelais.

It was a more than usually penetrating sally on the part of this female which at length led him to venture a protest.

'I say! I mean, I say. I say, dash it, you know. I mean, dash it,' said Barmy, feeling, even as he spoke, that the rebuke had not been phrased as neatly as he could have wished.

Still, lame though it had been, it caused a sensation which can only be described as profound. Mother looked at Mother. Eyebrows were raised, breath drawn in censoriously.

'Young man,' said the Mother in the pink bonnet, who seemed to have elected herself forewoman, 'kindly keep your remarks to yourself.'

Another Mother said: 'The idea!' and a third described him as a kill-joy.

'We don't want none of *your* impudence,' said the one in the pink bonnet.

'Ah!' agreed the others.

'A slip of a boy like that!' said the Mother in the Homburg hat, and there was a general laugh, as if the meeting considered that the point had been well taken.

Barmy subsided. He was wishing that he had yielded to the advice of his family and become a curate after coming down from the University. Curates are specially trained to handle this sort of situation. A tough, hard-boiled curate, spitting out of the corner of his mouth, would soon have subdued these mothers, he reflected. He would have played on them as on a stringed instrument – or, rather, as on sixteen stringed instruments. But Barmy, never having taken orders, was helpless.

So helpless, indeed, that when he suddenly discovered that they were heading for Bridmouth-on-Sea he felt that there was nothing he could do about it. From the vicar's own lips he had had it officially that the programme was that the expedition should drive to the neighbouring village of Bottsford Mortimer, where there were the ruins of an old abbey, replete with interest; lunch among the ruins; visit the local museum (founded and presented to the village by the late Sir Wandesbury Pott, J.P.); and, after filling in with a bit of knitting, return home. And now the whole trend of the party appeared to be towards the Amusement Park on the Bridmouth pier. And, though Barmy's whole soul shuddered at the thought of these sixteen Bacchantes let loose in an Amusement Park, he hadn't the nerve to say a word.

It was at about this point, he tells me, that a vision rose before him of Pongo happily loafing through the summer afternoon amidst the placid joys of the School Treat.

Of what happened at the Amusement Park Barmy asked me to be content with the sketchiest of outlines. He said that even now he could not bear to let his memory dwell upon it. He confessed himself perplexed by the psychology of the thing. These Mothers, he said, must have had mothers of their own and at those mothers' knees must have learned years ago the difference between right and wrong, and yet ... Well, what he was thinking of particularly, he said, was what occurred on the Bump the Bumps apparatus. He refused to specify exactly, but he said that there was one woman in a puce mantle who definitely seemed to be living for pleasure alone.

It was a little unpleasantness with the proprietor of this concern that eventually led the expedition leaving the Amusement Park and going down to the beach. Some purely technical point of finance, I understand – he claiming that a Mother in bombazine had had eleven rides and only paid once. It resulted in Barmy getting lugged into a brawl and rather roughly handled – which was particularly unfortunate, because the bombazined Mother explained on their way down to the beach that the whole thing had been due to a misunderstanding. In actual fact, what had really happened was that she had had twelve rides and paid twice.

However, he was so glad to get his little troupe out of the place that he counted an eye well blacked as the price of deliverance, and his spirits, he tells me, had definitely risen when suddenly the sixteen Mothers gave a simultaneous whoop and made for a sailing-boat which was waiting to be hired, sweeping him along with them. And the next moment they were off across the bay, bowling along before a nippy breeze which, naturally, cheesed it abruptly as soon as it had landed them far enough away from shore to make things interesting for the unfortunate blighter who had to take to the oars.

This, of course, was poor old Barmy. There was a man in charge of the boat, but he, though but a rough, untutored salt, had enough sense not to let himself in for a job like rowing this Noah's Ark home. Barmy did put it up to him tentatively, but the fellow said that he had to attend to the steering, and when Barmy said that he, Barmy, knew how to steer, the fellow said that he, the fellow, could not entrust a valuable boat to an amateur. After which, he lit his pipe and lolled back in the stern sheets with rather the air of an ancient Roman banqueter making himself cosy among the cushions. And Barmy, attaching himself to a couple of oars of about the size of those served out to galley-slaves in the old trireme days, started to put his back into it.

For a chap who hadn't rowed anything except a light canoe since he was up at Oxford, he considers he did dashed well, especially when you take into account the fact that he was much hampered by the Mothers. They would insist on singing that thing about 'Give yourself a pat on the back,' and, apart from the fact that Barmy considered that something on the lines of the Volga Boat-Song would have been far more fitting, it was a tune it was pretty hard to keep time to. Seven times he caught crabs, and seven times those sixteen Mothers stopped singing and guffawed like one Mother. All in all, a most painful experience. Add the fact that the first thing the females did on hitting the old Homeland again was to get up an informal dance on the sands and that the ride home in the quiet evenfall was more or less a repetition of the journey out, and you will agree with me that Barmy, as he eventually tottered into the saloon bar of the Goose and Grasshopper, had earned the frothing tankard which he now proceeded to order.

He had just sucked it down and was signalling for another, when the door of the saloon bar opened and in came Pongo.

If Barmy had been less preoccupied with his own troubles he would have seen that Pongo was in poorish shape. His collar was torn, his hair dishevelled. There were streaks of chocolate down his face and half a jam sandwich attached to the back of his coat. And so moved was he at seeing Barmy that he started ticking him off before he had so much as ordered a gin and ginger.

'A nice thing you let me in for!' said Pongo. 'A jolly job you shoved off on me!'

Barmy was feeling a little better after his ingurgitations, and he was able to speak.

'What are you talking about?'

'I am talking about School Treats,' replied Pongo, with an intense bitterness. 'I am talking about seas of children, all with sticky hands, who rubbed those hands on me. I am talking ... Oh, it's no good your gaping like a diseased fish, Fotheringay-Phipps. You know dashed well that you planned the whole thing. Your cunning fiend's brain formulated the entire devilish scheme. You engineered the bally outrage for your own foul purposes, to queer me with Angelica. You thought that when a girl sees a man blindfolded and smacked with rolled-up newspapers by smelly children she can never feel the same to him again. Ha!' said Pongo, at last ordering his gin and ginger.

Barmy was stunned, of course, by this violent attack, but he retained enough of the nice sense of propriety of the Fotheringay–Phippses to realize that this discussion could not be continued in public. Already the barmaid's ears had begun to work loose at the roots as she pricked them up.

'I don't know what the dickens you're talking about,' he said, but bring your drink up to my room and we'll go into the matter there. We cannot bandy a woman's name in a saloon bar.'

'Who's bandying a woman's name?'

'You are. You bandied it only half a second ago. If you don't call what you said bandying, there are finer-minded men who do.'

So they went upstairs, and Barmy shut the door.

'Now, then,' he said. 'What's all this drivel?'

'I've told you.'

'Tell me again.'

'I will.'

'Right ho. One moment.'

Barmy went to the door and opened it sharply. There came the unmistakable sound of a barmaid falling downstairs. He closed the door again.

'Now, then,' he said.

Pongo drained his gin and ginger.

'Of all the dirty tricks one man ever played on another,' he began, 'your sneaking out of that School Treat and letting me in for it is one which the verdict of history will undoubtedly rank the dirtiest. I can read you now like a book, Fotheringay-Phipps. Your motive is crystal-clear to me. You knew at what a disadvantage a man appears at a School Treat, and you saw to it that I and not you should be the poor mutt to get smeared with chocolate and sloshed with newspapers before the eyes of Angelica Briscoe. And I believed you when you handed me all that drip about yielding your claim and what not. My gosh!'

For an instant, as he heard these words, stupefaction rendered Barmy speechless. Then he found his tongue. His generous soul was seething with indignation at the thought of how his altruism, his great sacrifice, had been misinterpreted.

'What absolute rot!' he cried. 'I never heard such bilge in ny life. My motives in sending you to that School Treat instead of me were unmixedly chivalrous. I did it simply and solely to enable you to ingratiate yourself with the girl, not reflecting that it was out of the question that she should ever love a pop-eyed, pimply-faced poop like you.'

Pongo started.

'Pop-eyed?'

'Pop-eyed was what I said.'

'Pimply-faced?'

'Pimply-faced was the term I employed.'

'Poop?'

'Poop was the expression with which I concluded. If you want to know the real obstacle in the way of any wooing you may do now or in the years to come, Twistleton-Twistleton, it is this – that you entirely lack sex-appeal and look like nothing on earth. A girl of the sweet, sensitive nature of Angelica Briscoe does not have to see you smeared with chocolate to recoil from you with loathing. She does it automatically, and she does it on her head.'

'Is that so?'

'That is so.'

'Oh, let me inform you that in spite of what happened, in spite of the fact that she has seen me at my worst, there is something within me that tells me that Angelica Briscoe loves me and will one day be mine.'

'Mine, you mean. I can read the message in a girl's shy, drooping eyes, Twistleton-Twistleton, and I am prepared to give you odds of eleven to four that before the year is out I shall be walking down the aisle with Angelica Fotheringay-Phipps on my arm. I will go further. Thirty-three to eight.'

'What in?'

'Tenners.'

'Done.'

It was at this moment that the door opened.

'Excuse me, gentlemen,' said the barmaid.

The two rivals glared at the intruder. She was a well-nourished girl with a kind face. She was rubbing her left leg, which appeared to be paining her. The staircases are steep at the Goose and Grasshopper.

'You'll excuse me muscling in like this, gentlemen,' said the barmaid, or words to that effect, 'but I happened inadvertently to overhear your conversation, and I feel it my duty to put you straight on an important point of fact. Gentlemen, all bets are off. Miss Angelica Briscoe is already engaged to be married.'

You can readily conceive the effect of this announcement. Pongo biffed down into the only chair, and Barmy staggered against the wash-hand stand.

'What!' said Pongo.

'What!' said Barmy.

The barmaid turned to Barmy.

'Yes, sir. To the gentleman you were talking to in my bar the afternoon you arrived.'

Her initial observation had made Barmy feel as if he had been punched in the wind by sixteen Mothers, but at this addendum he was able to pull himself together.

'Don't be an ass, my dear old barmaid,' he said. 'That was Miss Briscoe's brother.'

'No, sir.'

'But his name was Briscoe, and you told me he was at the Vicarage.'

'Yes, sir. He spends a good deal of time at the Vicarage, being the young lady's second cousin, and engaged to her since last Christmas!'

Barmy eyed her sternly. He was deeply moved.

'Why did you not inform me of this earlier, you chump of a barmaid? With your gift for listening at doors you must long since have become aware that this gentleman here and myself were deeply enamoured of Miss Briscoe. And yet you kept these facts under your hat, causing us to waste our time and experience the utmost alarm and despondency. Do you realize, barmaid, that, had you spoken sooner, my friend here would not have been subjected to nameless indignities at the School Treat . . .'

'Yes, sir. It was the School Treat that Mr Briscoe was so bent on not having to go to, which he would have had to have done, Miss Angelica insisting. He had a terrible time there last year, poor gentleman. He was telling me about it. And that was why he asked me as a particular favour not to mention that he was engaged to Miss Briscoe, because he said that, if he played his

335

cards properly and a little secrecy and silence were observed in the proper quarters, there was a mug staying at the inn that he thought he could get to go instead of him. It would have done you good, sir, to have seen the way his face lit up as he said it. He's a very nice gentleman, Mr Briscoe, and we're all very fond of him. Well, I mustn't stay talking here, sir. I've got my bar to see to.'

She withdrew, and for some minutes there was silence in the room. It was Barmy who was the first to break it.

'After all, we still have our Art,' said Barmy.

He crossed the room and patted Pongo on the shoulder.

'Of course, it's a nasty shock, old man . . .'

Pongo had raised his face from his hands and was fumbling for his cigarette-case. There was a look in his eyes as if he had just wakened from a dream.

'Well, *is* it?' he said. 'You've got to look at these things from every angle. Is a girl who can deliberately allow a man to go through the horrors of a School Treat worth bothering about?'

Barmy started.

'I never thought of that. Or a girl, for that matter, who could callously throw a fellow to the Village Mothers.'

'Remind me some time to tell you about a game called "Is Mr Smith At Home?" where you put your head in a sack and the younger generation jab you with sticks.'

'And don't let me forget to tell you about that Mother in the puce mantle on the Bump the Bumps.'

'There was a kid called Horace . . .'

'There was a Mother in a Homburg hat . . .'

'The fact is,' said Pongo, 'we have allowed ourselves to lose our sober judgement over a girl whose idea of a mate is a mere "Hey, you," to be ordered hither and thither at her will, and who will unleash the juvenile population of her native village upon him without so much as a pang of pity – in a word, a parson's daughter. If you want to know the secret of a happy and successful life, Barmy, old man, it is this: Keep away from parsons' daughters.'

'Right away,' agreed Barmy. 'How do you react to hiring a car and pushing off to the metropolis at once?'

'I am all for it. And if we're to give of our best on the evening of the eleventh *prox.* we ought to start rehearsing again immediately.'

'We certainly ought.'

'We haven't any too much time, as it is.'

'We certainly haven't. I've got an aunt who complains of rheumatism.'

'Well, who wouldn't? My father can't meet his creditors.'

'Does he want to? My uncle Joe's in very low water just now.'

'Too bad. What's he doing?'

'Teaching swimming. Listen, Pongo,' said Barmy, 'I've been thinking. You take the green whiskers this year.'

'No, no.'

'Yes, really. I mean it. If I've said it to myself once, I've said it a hundred times – good old Pongo simply must have the green whiskers this year.'

'Barmy!'

'Pongo!'

They clasped hands. Tried in the furnace, their friendship had emerged strong and true. Cyril Fotheringay-Phipps and Reginald Twistleton-Twistleton were themselves again.

Young Men in Spats (*1936*)

Gally and Sue

The Hon. Galahad Threepwood had never married. Years and years ago he had wanted to marry Dolly Henderson, the Tivoli girl. But his father had put a stop to that by shipping Gally off to South Africa. And now Ronnie Fish, son of one of Gally's many formidable sisters, has fallen in love with Sue Brown, a chorus girl, daughter of dear, departed Dolly. Galahad is determined that, unworthy though his nephew may seem, his marriage to Sue shall not be prevented.

Cooled by the shade of the cedar, refreshed by the contents of the amber glass in which ice tinkled so musically when he lifted it to his lips, the Hon. Galahad had achieved a Nirvana-like repose. Storms might be raging elsewhere in the grounds of Blandings Castle, but there on the lawn there was peace – the perfect unruffled peace which in this world seems to come only to those who have done nothing whatever to deserve it.

The Hon. Galahad Threepwood, in his fifty-seventh year, was a dapper little gentleman on whose grey but still thickly-covered head the weight of a consistently misspent life rested lightly. His flannel suit sat jauntily upon his wiry frame, a black-rimmed monocle gleamed jauntily in his eye. Everything about this Musketeer of the nineties was jaunty. It was a standing mystery to all who knew him that one who had had such an extraordinarily good time all his life should, in the evening of that life, be so superbly robust. Wan contemporaries who had once painted a gaslit London red in his company and were now doomed to an existence of dry toast, Vichy water, and German cure resorts felt very strongly on this point. A man of his antecedents, they considered, ought by rights to be rounding off his career in a bath-chair instead of flitting about the place, still chaffing head waiters as of old and calling for the wine list without a tremor.

A little cock-sparrow of a man. One of the Old Guard which dies but does not surrender. Sitting there under the cedar, he looked as if he were just making ready to go to some dance-hall of the days when dance-halls were dance-halls, from which in the quiet dawn it would take at least three waiters, two commissionaires and a policeman to eject him . . .

Sue crossed the turf to where the Hon. Galahad sat.

The author of the Reminiscences scanned her affectionately through his monocle. Amazing, he was thinking, how like her mother she was. He noticed it more every day. Dolly's walk, and just that way of tilting her chin and smiling at you that Dolly had had. For an instant the years fell away from the Hon. Galahad Threepwood, and something that was not of this world went whispering through the garden.

Sue stood looking down at him. She placed a maternal finger on top of his head, and began to twist the grey hair round it.

'Well, young Gally.'

'Well, young Sue.'

'You look very comfortable.'

'I am comfortable.'

'You won't be long. The luncheon gong will be going in a minute.'

The Hon. Galahad sighed. There was always something, he reflected.

'What a curse meals are! Don't let's go in.'

'I'm going in, all right. My good child, I'm starving.'

'Pure imagination.'

'Do you mean to say you're not hungry, Gally?'

'Of course I'm not. No healthy person really needs food. If people would only stick to drinking, doctors would go out of business. I can state you a case that proves it. Old Freddie Potts in the year '98.'

'Old Freddie Potts in the year '98, did you say, Mister Bones?'

339

'Old Freddie Potts in the year '98,' repeated the Hon. Galahad firmly. 'He lived almost entirely on Scotch whisky, and in the year '98 this prudent habit saved him from an exceedingly unpleasant attack of hedgehog poisoning.'

'What poisoning?'

'Hedgehog poisoning. It was down in the south of France that it happened. Freddie had gone to stay with his brother Eustace at his villa at Grasse. Practically a teetotaller, this brother, and in consequence passionately addicted to food.'

'Still, I can't see why he wanted to eat hedgehogs.'

'He did not want to eat hedgehogs. Nothing was farther from his intentions. But on the second day of old Freddie's visit he gave his chef twenty francs to go to market and buy a chicken for dinner, and the chef, wandering along, happened to see a dead hedgehog lying in the road. It had been there some days, as a matter of fact, but this was the first time he had noticed it. So, feeling that here was where he pouched twenty francs ...'

'I wish you wouldn't tell me stories like this just before lunch.'

'If it puts you off your food, so much the better. Bring the roses to your cheeks. Well, as I was saying, the chef, who was a thrifty sort of chap and knew that he could make a dainty dish out of his old grandmother, if allowed to mess about with a few sauces, added the twenty francs to his savings and gave Freddie and Eustace the hedgehog next day *en casserole*. Mark the sequel. At two-thirty prompt, Eustace, the teetotaller, turned nile-green, started groaning like a lost soul, and continued to do so for the remainder of the week, when he was pronounced out of danger. Freddie, on the other hand, his system having been healthfully pickled in alcohol, throve on the dish and finished it up cold next day.'

'I call that the most disgusting story I ever heard.'

'The most moral story you ever heard. If I had my way, it would be carved up in letters of gold over the door of every school and college in the kingdom, as a warning to the young.'

Summer Lightning (1929)

Two Good Dinners at Blandings Castle

The opening and close of a Blandings novel. Much happens in the intervening two hundred-odd pages, and Galahad Threepwood, illustrious member of the old Pelican Club, has engineered happy endings for all.

The summer day was drawing to a close and dusk had fallen on Blandings Castle, shrouding from view the ancient battlements, dulling the silver surface of the lake and causing Lord Emsworth's supreme Berkshire sow Empress of Blandings to leave the open air portion of her sty and withdraw into the covered shed where she did her sleeping. A dedicated believer in the maxim of early to bed and early to rise, she always turned in at about this time. Only by getting its regular eight hours can a pig keep up to the mark and preserve that schoolgirl complexion.

Deprived of her society, which he had been enjoying since shortly after lunch, Clarence, ninth Earl of Emsworth, the seigneur of this favoured realm, pottered dreamily back to the house, pottered dreamily to the great library which was one of its features, and had just pottered dreamily to his favourite chair, when Beach, his butler, entered bearing a laden tray. He gave it a vague stare which had so often incurred the censure – 'Oh, for goodness sake, Clarence, don't stand there looking like a goldfish' – of his sisters, Constance, Dora, Charlotte, Julia and Hermione.

'Eh?' he said. 'What?' he added.

'Your dinner, m'lord.'

Lord Emsworth's face cleared. He was telling himself that he might have known that there would be some simple explanation for that tray. Trust Beach to have everything under control . . .

'That stuff smells good, Beach. What is it?'

'Leg of lamb, m'lord, with boiled potatoes.'

Lord Emsworth received the information with a gratified nod. Good plain English fare. How different, he was thinking, from the bad old era when his sister Constance had been the Führer of Blandings Castle. Under her regime dinner would have meant dressing and sitting down, probably with a lot of frightful guests, to a series of ghastly dishes with French names, and fuss beyond belief if one happened to swallow one's front shirt stud and substituted for it a brass paper-fastener.

'And,' Beach added, for he was a man who liked to be scrupulously accurate, 'spinach.'

'Capital, capital. And to follow?'

'Roly-poly pudding, m'lord.'

'Excellent. With plenty of jam, I hope?'

'Yes, m'lord. I instructed Mrs Willoughby –'

'Who is Mrs Willoughby?'

'The Cook, m'lord.'

'I thought her name was Perkins.'

'No, m'lord, Willoughby. I instructed her to be careful that there was no stint.'

'Thank you, Beach. Are you fond of roly-poly pudding?'

'Yes, m'lord.'

'With plenty of jam?'

'Yes, m'lord.'

'It's quite essential, I always feel. Unless there is lots of jam roly-poly pudding is not worth eating. All right. Bring it when I ring, will you?'

'Very good, m'lord.'

Left alone, Lord Emsworth attacked his good plain English fare with gusto, musing as he did on the stupendous improvement in conditions at the castle since his sister Constance had married that American fellow James Schoonmaker and gone to live in New York.

*

Another summer day was drawing to a close, and dusk had fallen once more on Blandings Castle. The Empress had turned in. Chauffeur Voules was playing his harmonica. The stable cat was having a quick wash and brush up before starting on its night out. And in the kitchen Mrs Willoughby, the cook, was putting the final touches on the well-jammed roly-poly pudding which Beach would soon be taking to the library, where Gally and Lord Emsworth were enjoying their dinner of good plain English fare.

Through the open window the scent of stocks and tobacco plant floated in, competing with the aroma of the leg of lamb, the boiled potatoes and the spinach with which dinner had begun. Beach brought in the roly-poly pudding and withdrew, and Lord Emsworth heaved a contented sigh. In Lady Constance's time it would have made his stiff shirt front go pop, but now it merely stirred the bosom of his shooting coat with the holes in the elbows. His toes wriggled sensuously inside his bedroom slippers.

'This is very pleasant, Galahad,' he said, and Gally endorsed the sentiment.

'I was thinking the same thing, Clarence. No Connie, no Dunstable. Peace, perfect peace with loved ones far away, as one might say. I'm sorry I'm leaving.'

'You must, I suppose?'

'I doubt if the marriage would be legal without me.'

'Someone you know is being married?'

'My godson.'

'I've never met him, have I?'

'Certainly you have. The chap who falls downstairs.'

'Ah yes. Who is he marrying?'

'Linda Gilpin.'

'Who is Linda Gilpin?'

'The girl who kisses him after he's fallen downstairs. I am to be Johnny's best man.'

'Who –'

'Yes, I see I'm confusing you, Clarence. Johnny and my godson are one and the same. All straight now?'

'Perfectly, perfectly. Your godson Johnny is marrying Linda Gilpin.'

'You put it in a nutshell. And I have to be there when the firing squad assembles. Furthermore, Trout and Vanessa Polk insist on me dining with them before they go off on their honeymoon.'

'Who is Trout?'

'The chap who has married Vanessa Polk.'

'Who is Vanessa Polk?'

'The girl who has married Trout. They've both married each other, and they're going for the honeymoon to Nassau.'

'That's where the Falls are, isn't it? People go over them in barrels, which is a thing I don't suppose many young couples would care to do. But no doubt Mr and Mrs Trout will find some other way of passing the time. Vanessa Polk, did you say? Wasn't she staying here?'

'That's right, and so was Trout.'

'I thought the names were familiar. Nice girl. Very sound on pigs. I hope she will be very happy.'

'I'm sure she will.'

'And I hope your godson will be very happy.'

'Have no uneasiness about that. He loves his popsy.'

'I thought you said her name was Linda.'

'Popsy is the generic term. By the way, did Connie confide in you much while she was here?'

'Not very much.'

'Then you probably don't know that serious obstacles had to be surmounted before the Johnny–Linda Gilpin merger could be put through. It was touch and go for quite a time. Snags arose. Tricky corners had to be rounded. It was only at long last that they were given the green light. But all that's over now. It makes me feel as if I were sitting in at the end of a play, one of those charming delicate things the French do so well. You know the sort of thing I mean – lightly sentimental, the smile following the tear. I am having my dinner. The storm is over, there is sunlight in my heart. I have a glass of wine and sit thinking of what has passed. And now we want something to bring down the curtain. A toast is indicated. Let us drink to the Pelican Club, under whose gentle tuition I learned to keep cool, stiffen the upper lip and always think a shade quicker than the next man. To the Pelican Club,' said Gally, raising his glass.

'To the Pelican Club,' said Lord Emsworth, raising his. 'What is the Pelican Club, Galahad?'

'God bless you, Clarence,' said Gally. 'Have some more roly-poly pudding.'

A Pelican at Blandings (1969)

Valley Fields the Blest

*Mr Cornelius, of The Nook, Valley Fields, has just offered to
lend Freddie Widgeon the £3,000 he needs to buy a share in a
tea plantation in Kenya . . . and to marry Sally Foster. Valley
Fields is a garden suburb area of London that features in many
of Wodehouse's books. It is undoubtedly the Dulwich of his
schooldays. Freddie is not the first Drones Club type to come
and live temporarily in Valley Fields, to escape creditors or
aunts or other menaces.*

'I should be able to pay you back in the course of time, but I
don't like the idea of you risking all your life's savings like this.'

Mr Cornelius's beard stirred as if a passing breeze had ruffled
it.

'These are not my life savings, Mr Widgeon. I think I have
spoken to you of my brother Charles?'

'The one who's living in America?'

'The one who was living in America,' corrected Mr Cornelius.
'He passed away a few days ago. He fell out of his aeroplane.'

'No, really? I say, I'm awfully sorry.'

'I also. I was very fond of Charles, and he of me. He frequently urged me to give up my business and come and join
him in New York, but it would have meant leaving Valley
Fields, and I always declined. The reason I have brought his
name up in the conversation is that he left me his entire fortune, amounting, the lawyers tell me, to between three and four
million dollars.'

'What!'

'So they say.'

'Well, fry me for an onion!'

'The will is not yet probated, but the lawyers are in a position to advance me any sums I may require, however large, so you can rest assured that there will be no difficulty over a trivial demand like three thousand pounds.'

'Trivial?'

'A mere bagatelle. So you see that I can well afford to lend you a helping hand, and, as I told you before, it will be a pleasure.'

Freddie drew a deep breath. Mr Cornelius, his rabbits and the garden of The Nook seemed to him to be executing a spirited version of the dance, so popular in the twenties, known as the shimmy.

'Cornelius,' he said, 'you would probably object, if I kissed you, so I won't, but may I say . . . No, words fail me. My gosh, you're wonderful! You've saved two human lives from the soup, and you can quote me as stating this, that if ever an angel in human shape . . . No, as I said, words fail me.'

Mr Cornelius, who had been smiling – at least, so thought Freddie, for his beard had been in a constant state of agitation – became grave.

'There is just one thing, Mr Widgeon. You must not mention a word of this to anyone, except of course Miss Foster, in whom you will naturally have to confide. But you must swear her to secrecy.'

'I'll see that her lips are sealed all right. But why?'

'This must never reach Mrs Cornelius's ears.'

'Hasn't it?'

'Fortunately, no.'

'You mean she doesn't know? You haven't told her about these pennies from heaven?'

'I have not, and I do not intend to, Mr Widgeon,' said Mr Cornelius, graver than ever, 'have you any conception of what would happen, were my wife to learn that I was a millionaire? Do you think I should be allowed to go on living in Valley Fields, the place I love, and continue to be a house agent, the work I love? Do you suppose I should be permitted to keep my old friends, like Mr Wrenn of San Rafael, with whom I play chess on Saturdays, and feed rabbits in my shirt sleeves? No, I should be whisked off to a flat in Mayfair, I should have to spend long months in the south of France, a butler would be engaged and I should have to dress for dinner every night. I should have to join a London club, take a box at the opera, learn to play polo,' said Mr Cornelius, allowing his morbid fancy to run away with him a little. 'The best of women are not proof against sudden wealth. Mrs Cornelius is perfectly happy and contented in the surroundings to which she has always been accustomed – she was a Miss Bulstrode of Happy Haven at the time of our marriage – and I intend that she shall remain happy and contented.'

Ice in the Bedroom (*1961*)

Romance at Droitgate Spa

In the snobbish world of invalids, a mere gout-sufferer suddenly makes the social grade.

When young Freddie Fitch-Fitch went down to Droitgate Spa, that celebrated cure resort in the west of England, to ask his uncle and trustee, Major-General Sir Aylmer Bastable, to release his capital in order that he might marry Annabel Purvis, he was fully alive to the fact that the interview might prove a disagreeable one. However, his great love bore him on, and he made the journey and was shown into the room where the old man sat nursing a gouty foot.

'Hullo-ullo-ullo, uncle,' he cried, for it was always his policy on these occasions to be buoyant till thrown out. 'Good morning, good morning, good morning.'

'Gaw!' said Sir Aylmer, with a sort of long, shuddering sigh. 'It's you, is it?'

And he muttered something which Freddie did not quite catch, though he was able to detect the words 'last straw.'

Freddie's heart sank a little. He could see that his flesh and blood was in a difficult mood, and he guessed what must have happened. No doubt Sir Aylmer had been to the Pump Room earlier in the day to take the waters, and while there had met and been high-hatted by some swell whom the doctors had twice given up for dead. These snobs, he knew, were always snubbing the unfortunate old man.

On coming to settle in Droitgate Spa, Sir Aylmer Bastable had a humiliating shock. The head of a fine old family and the possessor of a distinguished military record, he had expected on his arrival to be received with open arms by the best people and welcomed immediately into the inner set. But when it was discovered that all he had wrong with him was a touch of gout in the right foot, he found himself cold-shouldered by the men who mattered and thrust back on the society of the asthma patients and the fellows with slight liver trouble.

For though few people are aware of it – so true is it that half the world does not know how the other half lives – there is no section of the community in which class-consciousness is so rampant as among invalids. The ancient Spartans, one gathers, were far from cordial towards their Helots, and the French aristocrat of pre-Revolution days tended to be a little stand-offish with his tenantry, but their attitude was almost back-slapping compared with that of – let us say – the man who has been out in Switzerland taking insulin for his diabetes towards one who is simply undergoing treatment from the village doctor for an ingrowing toenail. And this is particularly so, of course, in those places where invalids collect in gangs – Baden-Baden, for example, or Hot Springs, Virginia, or, as in Sir Aylmer's case, Droitgate Spa.

In such resorts the atmosphere is almost unbelievably cliquy. The old aristocracy, the top-notchers with maladies that get written up in the medical journals, keep themselves to themselves pretty rigidly, and have a very short way with the smaller fry.

It was this that had soured Sir Aylmer Bastable's once sunny disposition and caused him now to glare at Freddie with an unfriendly eye.

'Well,' he said, 'what do you want?'

'Oh, I just looked in,' said Freddie. 'How's everything?'

'Rotten,' replied Sir Aylmer. 'I've just lost my nurse.'

'Dead?'

'Worse. Married. The cloth-headed girl has gone off and got spliced to one of the *canaille* – a chap who's never even had so much as athlete's foot. She must be crazy.'

'Still, one sees her point of view.'

'No, one doesn't.'

'I mean,' said Freddie, who felt strongly on this subject, 'it's love that makes the world go round.'

'It isn't anything of the kind,' said Sir Aylmer. Like so many fine old soldiers, he was inclined to be a little literal-minded. 'I never heard such dashed silly nonsense in my life. What makes the world go round is ... Well, I've forgotten at the moment, but it certainly isn't love. How the dooce could it?'

'Oh, right-ho. I see what you mean,' said Freddie. 'But put it another way. Love conquers all. Love's all right. Take it from me.'

The old man looked at him sharply.

'Are you in love?'

'Madly.'

'Of all the young cuckoos! And I suppose you've come to ask for money to get married on?'

'Not at all. I just popped round to see how you were. Still, as the subject has happened to crop up –'

Sir Aylmer brooded for a moment, snorting in an undertone.

'Who's the girl?' he demanded.

Freddie coughed, and fumbled with his collar. The crux of the situation, he realized, had now been reached. He had feared from the first that this was where the good old snag might conceivably sidle into the picture. For his Annabel was of humble station, and he knew how rigid were his relative's views on the importance of birth. No bigger snob ever swallowed a salicylate pill.

'Well, as a matter of fact,' he said, 'she's a conjurer's stooge.'

'A *what*?'

'A conjurer's assistant, don't you know. I saw her first at a charity matinée. She was abetting a bloke called The Great Boloni.'

'In what sense, abetting?'

'Well, she stood there up-stage, don't you know, and every now and then she would skip down-stage, hand this chap a bowl of goldfish or something, beam at the audience, do a sort of dance step and skip back again. You know the kind of thing.'

A dark frown had come into Sir Aylmer's face.

351

Vintage Wodehouse

'I do,' he said grimly. 'My only nephew has been ensnared by a bally, beaming goldfish-hander! Ha!'

'I wouldn't call it ensnared exactly,' said Freddie deferentially.

'I would,' said Sir Aylmer. 'Get out of here.'

'Right,' said Freddie, and caught the 2.35 express back to London. And it was during the journey that an idea flashed upon him.

The last of the Fitch-Fitches was not a great student of literature, but he occasionally dipped into a magazine: and everybody who has ever dipped into a magazine has read a story about a hard-hearted old man who won't accept the hero's girl at any price, so what do they do but plant her on him without telling him who she is and, by Jove, he falls under her spell completely, and then they tear off their whiskers and there they are. There was a story of this nature in the magazine which Freddie had purchased at the bookstall at Droitgate Spa Station, and, as he read it, he remembered what his uncle had told him about his nurse handing in her portfolio.

By the time the train checked in at Paddington, his plans were fully formed.

'Listen,' he said to Annabel Purvis, who had met him at the terminus, and Annabel said: 'What?'

'Listen,' said Freddie, and Annabel again said: 'What?'

'Listen,' said Fredie, clasping her arm tenderly and steering her off in the direction of the refreshment-room, where it was his intention to have a quick one. 'To a certain extent I am compelled to admit that my expedition has been a wash-out . . .'

Annabel caught her breath sharply.

'No blessing?'

'No blessing.'

'And no money?'

'No money. The old boy ran entirely true to stable form. He listened to what I had to say, snorted in an unpleasant manner and threw me out. The old routine. But what I'm working round to is that the skies are still bright and the blue bird on the job. I have a scheme. Could you be a nurse?'

352

'I used to nurse my Uncle Joe.'

'Then you shall nurse my Uncle Aylmer. The present incumbent, he tells me, has just tuned out, and he needs a successor. I will phone him that I am dispatching immediately a red-hot nurse whom he will find just the same as Mother makes, and you shall go down to Droitgate Spa and ingratiate yourself.'

'But how?'

'Why, cluster round him. Smooth his pillow. Bring him cooling drinks. Coo to him, and give him the old oil. Tell him you are of gentle birth, if that's the expression I want. And when the time is ripe, when you have entwined yourself about his heart and he looks upon you as a daughter, shoot me a wire and I'll come down and fall in love with you and he will give us his consent, blessing and the stuff. I guarantee this plan. It works.'

So Annabel went to Droitgate Spa, and about three weeks later a telegram arrived for Freddie, running as follows:

Have ingratiated self. Come at once. Love and kisses. Annabel.

Within an hour of its arrival, Freddie was on his way to Podagra Lodge, his uncle's residence.

He found Sir Aylmer in his study. Annabel was sitting by his side, reading aloud to him from a recently published monograph on certain obscure ailments of the medulla oblongata. For the old man, though a mere gout patient, had pathetic aspirations towards higher things. There was a cooling drink on the table, and, as Freddie entered, the girl paused in her reading to smooth her employer's pillow.

'Gaw!' said Sir Aylmer. 'You again?'

'Here I am,' said Freddie.

'Well, by an extraordinary chance, I'm glad to see you. Leave us for a moment, Miss Purvis. I wish to speak to my nephew here, such as he is, on a serious and private matter. Did you notice that girl?' he said, as the door closed.

'I did, indeed.'

'Pretty.'

'An eyeful.'

'And as good,' said Sir Aylmer, 'as she is beautiful. You

353

should see her smooth pillows. And what a cooling drink she mixes! Excellent family, too, I understand. Her father is a colonel. Or, rather, was. He's dead.'

'Ah, well, all flesh is as grass.'

'No, it isn't. It's nothing of the kind. The two things are entirely different. I've seen flesh and I've seen grass. No resemblance whatever. However, that is not the point at issue. What I wanted to say was that if you were not a damn fool, that's the sort of girl you would be in love with.'

'I am.'

'A damn fool?'

'No. In love with that girl.'

'What! You have fallen in love with Miss Purvis? Already?'

'I have.'

'Well, that's the quickest thing I ever saw. What about your beaming goldfish?'

'Oh, that's all over. A mere passing boyish fancy.'

Sir Aylmer took a deep swig at his cooling drink, and regarded him in silence for a moment.

'Well,' he said, at length, breathing heavily, 'if that's the airy, casual way in which you treat life's most sacred emotions, the sooner you are safely married and settled down, the better. If you're allowed to run around loose much longer, indulging those boyish fancies of yours, I foresee the breach of promise case of the century. However, I'm not saying I'm not relieved. I am relieved. I suppose she wore tights, this goldfish girl?'

'Pink.'

'Disgusting. Thank God it's all over. Very good, then. You are free, I understand, to have a pop at Miss Purvis. Do you propose to do so?'

'I do.'

'Excellent. You get that sweet, refined, most-suitable-in-all-respects girl to marry you, and I'll hand over that money of yours, every penny of it.'

'I will start at once.'

'Heaven speed your wooing,' said Sir Aylmer.

And ten minutes later Freddie was able to inform his uncle

that his whirlwind courtship had been successful, and Sir Aylmer said that when he had asked Heaven to speed his wooing he had had no notion that it would speed it to quite that extent. He congratulated Freddie and said he hoped that he appreciated his good fortune, and Freddie said he certainly did, because his love was like a red, red rose, and Sir Aylmer said 'No, she wasn't,' and when Freddie added that he was walking on air Sir Aylmer said he couldn't be – the thing was physically impossible.

However, he gave his blessing and promised to release Freddie's capital as soon as the necessary papers were drawn up, and Freddie went back to London to see his lawyer about this.

His mood, as the train sped through the quiet countryside, was one of perfect tranquillity and happiness. It seemed to him that his troubles were now definitely ended. He looked down the vista of the years and saw nothing but joy and sunshine. If somebody had told Frederick Fitch-Fitch at that moment that even now a V-shaped depression was coming along which would shortly blacken the skies and lower the general temperature to freezing-point, he would not have believed him.

Nor when, two days later, as he sat in his club, he was informed that a Mr Rackstraw was waiting to see him in the small smoking-room, did he have an inkling that here was the V-shaped depression in person. His heart was still light as he went down the passage, wondering idly, for the name was unfamiliar to him, who this Mr Rackstraw might be. He entered the room, and found there a tall, thin man with pointed black moustaches who was pacing up and down, nervously taking rabbits out of his top-hat as he walked.

'Mr Rackstraw?'

His visitor spun round, dropping a rabbit. He gazed at Freddie piercingly. He had bright, glittering, sinister eyes.

'That is my name, Mortimer Rackstraw.'

Freddie's mind had flown back to the charity matinée at which he had first seen Annabel, and he recognized the fellow now.

355

'The Great Boloni, surely?'

'I call myself that professionally. So you are Mr Fitch? So *you* are Mr Fitch? Ha! Fiend!'

'Eh?'

'I am not mistaken. You are Frederick Fitch?'

'Frederick Fitch-Fitch.'

'I beg your pardon. In that case, I should have said "Fiend! Fiend!"'

He produced a pack of cards and asked Freddie to take one – any one – and memorize it and put it back. Freddie did so absently. He was considerably fogged. He could make nothing of all this.

'How do you mean – Fiend-Fiend?' he asked.

The other sneered unpleasantly.

'Cad!' he said, twirling his moustache.

'Cad?' said Freddie, mystified.

'Yes, sir. Cad. You have stolen the girl I love.'

'I don't understand.'

'Then you must be a perfect ass. It's quite simple, isn't it? I can't put it any plainer, can I? I say you have stolen ... Well, look here,' said Mortimer Rackstraw. 'Suppose this top-hat is me. This rabbit,' he went on, producing it from the lining, 'is the girl I love. You come along and – presto – the rabbit vanishes.'

'It's up your sleeve.'

'It is not up my sleeve. And if it were, if I had a thousand sleeves and rabbits up every one of them, that would not alter the fact that you have treacherously robbed me of Annabel Purvis.'

Freddie began to see daylight. He was able to appreciate the other's emotion. 'So you love Annabel, too?'

'I do.'

'I don't wonder. Nice girl, what? I see, I see. You worshipped her in secret, never telling your love.'

'I did tell my love. We were engaged.'

'Engaged?'

'Certainly. And this morning I get a letter from her saying

356

that it's all off, because she has changed her mind and is going to marry you. She has thrown me over.'

'Oh, ah? Well, I'm frightfully sorry – deepest sympathy, and all that, but I don't see what's to be done about it, what?'

'I do. There still remains – revenge.'

'Oh, I say, dash it! You aren't going to be stuffy about it?'

'I am going to be stuffy about it. For the moment you triumph. But do not imagine that this is the end. You have not heard the last of me. Not by any means. You may have stolen the woman I love with your underhand chicanery, but I'll fix you.'

'How?'

'Never mind how. You will find out how quite soon enough. A nasty jolt you're going to get, my good fiend, and almost immediately. As sure,' said Mortimer Rackstraw, illustrating by drawing one from Freddie's back hair, 'as eggs are eggs. I wish you a very good afternoon.'

He took up his top-hat, which in his emotion he had allowed to fall to the ground, brushed it on his coat-sleeve, extracted from it a cage of love-birds and strode out.

A moment later, he returned, bowed a few times to right and left and was gone again.

To say that Freddie did not feel a little uneasy as the result of this scene would be untrue. There had been something in the confident manner in which the other had spoken of revenging himself that he had not at all liked. The words had had a sinister ring, and all through the rest of the day he pondered thoughtfully, wondering what a man so trained in the art of having things up his sleeve might have up it now. It was in meditative mood that he dined, and only on the following morning did his equanimity return to him.

Able, now that he had slept on it, to review the disturbing conversation in its proper perspective, he came to the conclusion that the fellow's threats had been mere bluff. What, after all, he asked himself, could this conjurer do? It was not as if they had been living in the Middle Ages, when chaps of that

357

sort used to put spells on you and change you into things.

No, he decided, it was mere bluff, and with his complacency completely restored had just lighted a cigarette and fallen to dreaming of the girl he loved, when a telegram was brought to him.

It ran as follows:

Come at once. All lost. Ruin stares face. Love and kisses. Annabel.

Half an hour later he was in the train, speeding towards Droitgate Spa.

It had been Freddie's intention, on entering the train, to devote the journey to earnest meditation. But, as always happens when one wishes to concentrate and brood during a railway journey, he found himself closeted with a talkative fellow-traveller.

The one who interrupted Freddie's thought was a flabby, puffy man of middle age, wearing a red waistcoat, brown shoes, a morning coat and a bowler hat. With such a Grade A bounder, even had his mind been at rest, Freddie would have had little in common, and he sat chafing while the prismatic fellow prattled on. Nearly an hour passed before he was freed from the infliction of the other's conversation, but eventually the man's head began to nod, and presently he was snoring and Freddie was able to give himself up to his reverie.

His thoughts became less and less agreeable as the train rolled on. And what rendered his mental distress so particularly acute was the lack of detail in Annabel's telegram. It seemed to him to offer so wide a field for uncomfortable speculation.

'All lost,' for instance. A man could do a lot of thinking about a phrase like that. And 'Ruin stares face.' Why, he asked himself, did ruin stare face? While commending Annabel's thriftiness in keeping the thing down to twelve words, he could not help wishing that she could have brought herself to spring another twopence and be more lucid.

But of one thing he felt certain. All this had something to do with his recent visitor. Behind that mystic telegram he seemed to see the hand of Mortimer Rackstraw, that hand whose quickness deceived the eye, and he knew that in lightly dismissing the other as a negligible force he had been too sanguine.

By the time he reached Podagra Lodge, the nervous strain had become almost intolerable. As he rang the bell he was quivering like some jelly set before a diet-patient, and the sight of Annabel's face as she opened the door did nothing to alleviate his perturbation. The girl was obviously all of a twitter.

'Oh, Freddie!' she cried. 'The worst has happened.'

Freddie gulped.

'Rackstraw?'

'Yes,' said Annabel. 'But how did you know about him?'

'He came to see me, bubbling over a good deal with veiled menaces and what not,' explained Freddie. He frowned, and eyed her closely. 'Why didn't you tell me you had been engaged to that bird?'

'I didn't think you would be interested. It was just a passing girlish fancy.'

'You're sure? You didn't really love this blighted prestidigitator?'

'No, no. I was dazzled for a while, as any girl might have been, when he sawed me in half, but then you came along and I saw that I had been mistaken, and that you were the only man in the world for me.'

'Good egg,' said Freddie, relieved.

He kissed her fondly and, as he did so, there came to his ears the sound of rhythmic hammering from somewhere below.

'What's that?' he asked.

Annabel wrung her hands.

'It's Mortimer!'

'Is he here?'

'Yes. He arrived on the one-fifteen. I locked him in the cellar.'

'Why?'

'To stop him going to the Pump Room.'

'Why shouldn't he go to the Pump Room?'

359

'Because Sir Aylmer has gone there to listen to the band, and they must not meet. If they do, we are lost. Mortimer has hatched a fearful plot.'

Freddie's heart seemed to buckle under within him. He had tried to be optimistic, but all along he had known that Mortimer Rackstraw would hatch some fearful plot. He could have put his shirt on it. A born hatcher.

'What plot?'

Annabel wrung her hands again.

'He means to introduce Sir Aylmer to my Uncle Joe. He wired to Uncle Joe to come to Droitgate Spa. He had arranged to meet him at the Pump Room, and then he was going to introduce him to Sir Aylmer.'

Freddie was a little fogged. It did not seem to him much of a plot.

'Now that I can never be his, all he wants is to make himself unpleasant and prevent our marriage. And he knows that Sir Aylmer will never consent to your marrying me if he finds out that I have an uncle like Uncle Joe.'

Freddie ceased to be fogged. He saw the whole devilish scheme now – a scheme worthy of the subtle brain that could put the ace of spades back in the pack, shuffle, cut three times, and then produce it from the inside of a lemon.

'Is he so frightful?' he quavered.

'Look,' said Annabel simply. She took a photograph from her bosom and extended it towards him with a trembling hand. 'That is Uncle Joe, taken in the lodge regalia of a Grand Exalted Periwinkle of the Mystic Order of Whelks.'

Freddie glanced at the photograph and started back with a hoarse cry. Annabel nodded sadly.

'Yes,' she said. 'That is how he takes most people. The only faint hope I have is that he won't have been able to come. But if he has –'

'He has,' cried Freddie, who had been fighting for breath. 'We travelled down in the train together.'

'What?'

'Yes. He must be waiting at the Pump Room now.'

'And at any moment Mortimer will break his way out of the cellar. The door is not strong. What shall we do?'

'There is only one thing to do. I have all the papers ...'

'You have no time to read now.'

'The legal papers, the ones my uncle has to sign in order to release my money. There is just a chance that if I rush to the Pump Room I may get him to put his name on the dotted line before the worst happens.'

'Then rush,' cried Annabel.

'I will,' said Freddie.

He kissed her quickly, grabbed his hat, and was off the mark like a jack rabbit.

A man who is endeavouring to lower the record for the distance between Podagra Lodge, which is in Arterio-Sclerosis Avenue, and the Droitgate Spa Pump Room has little leisure for thinking, but Freddie managed to put in a certain amount as his feet skimmed the pavement. And the trend of his thought was such as to give renewed vigour to his legs. He could scarcely have moved more rapidly if he had been a character in a two-reel film with the police after him.

And there was need for speed. Beyond a question, Annabel had been right when she had said that Sir Aylmer would never consent to their union if he found out that she had an uncle like her Uncle Joe. Uncle Joe would get right in amongst him. Let them but meet, and nothing was more certain than that the haughty old man would veto the proposed nuptials.

A final burst of speed took him panting up the Pump Room steps and into the rotunda where all that was best and most refined in Droitgate Spa was accustomed to assemble of an afternoon and listen to the band. He saw Sir Aylmer in a distant seat and hurried towards him.

'Gaw!' said Sir Aylmer. 'You?'

Freddie could only nod.

'Well, stop puffing like that and sit down,' said Sir Aylmer. 'They're just going to play "Poet and Peasant".'

Freddie recovered his breath.

361

'Uncle,' he began. But it was too late. Even as he spoke, the conductor's baton fell and Sir Aylmer's face assumed that reverent, doughlike expression of attention so familiar in the rotundas of cure resorts.

'S'h,' he said.

Of all the uncounted millions who in their time have listened to bands playing 'Poet and Peasant', few can ever have listened with such a restless impatience as did Frederick Fitch-Fitch on this occasion. Time was flying. Every second was precious. At any moment disaster might befall. And the band went on playing as if it had taken on a life-job. It seemed to him an eternity before the final oom-pom-pa.

'Uncle,' he cried, as the echoes died away.

'S'h,' said Sir Aylmer testily, and Freddie, with a dull despair, perceived that they were going to get an encore.

Of all the far-flung myriads who year in and year out have listened to bands playing the overture 'Raymond' few can ever have chafed as did Frederick Fitch-Fitch now. This suspense was unmanning him, this delay was torture. He took the papers and a fountain-pen from his pocket and toyed with them nervously. He wondered dully as he sat there how the opera 'Raymond' had ever managed to get itself performed, if the overture was as long as this. They must have rushed it through in the last five minutes of the evening as the audience groped for its hats and wraps.

But there is an end to all things, even to the overture from 'Raymond'. Just as the weariest river winds somewhere safe to sea, so does this overture eventually finish. And when it did, when the last notes faded into silence and the conductor stood bowing and smiling with that cool assumption, common to all conductors, that it is they and not the perspiring orchestra who have been doing the work, he started again.

'Uncle,' he said, 'may I trouble you for a moment? ... These papers.'

Sir Aylmer cocked an eye at the documents.

'What papers are those?'

'The ones you have to sign, releasing my capital.'

'Oh, those,' said Sir Aylmer genially. The music had plainly mellowed him. 'Of course, yes. Certainly, certainly. Give me . . .'

He broke off, and Freddie saw that he was looking at a distinguished, silvery-haired man with thin, refined features, who was sauntering by.

'Afternoon, Rumbelow,' he said.

There was an unmistakable note of obsequiousness in Sir Aylmer's voice. His voice had become pink, and he was shuffling his feet and twiddling his fingers. The man to whom he had spoken paused and looked down. Seeing who it was that accosted him, he raised a silvery eyebrow. His manner was undisguisedly supercilious.

'Ah, Bastable,' he said distantly.

A duller man than Sir Aylmer Bastable could not have failed to detect the cold hauteur in his voice. Freddie saw the flush on his uncle's face deepen. Sir Aylmer mumbled something about hoping that the distinguished-looking man was feeling better today.

'Worse,' replied the other curtly. 'Much worse. The doctors are baffled. Mine is a very complicated case.' He paused for a moment, and his delicately chiselled lip curled in a sneer. 'And how is the gout, Bastable? Gout! Ha, ha!'

Without waiting for a reply, he passed on and joined a group that stood chatting close by. Sir Aylmer choked down a mortified oath.

'Snob!' he muttered. 'Thinks he's everybody just because he's got talengiectasis. I don't see what's so wonderful about having talengiectasis. Anybody could have . . . What on earth are you doing? What the devil's all this you're waving under my nose? Papers? Papers? I don't want any papers. Take them away, sir!'

And before Freddie could burst into the impassioned plea which trembled on his lips, a commotion in the doorway distracted his attention. His heart missed a beat, and he sat there, frozen.

On the threshold stood Mortimer Rackstraw. He was making some inquiry of an attendant, and Freddie could guess only too well what that inquiry was. Mortimer Rackstraw was asking which of those present was Major-General Sir Aylmer Bastable. Attached to his arm, obviously pleading with him and appealing to his better self, Annabel Purvis gazed up into his face with tear-filled eyes.

A moment later, the conjurer strode up, still towing the girl. He halted before Sir Aylmer and threw Annabel aside like a soiled glove. His face was cold and hard and remorseless. With one hand he was juggling mechanically with two billiard balls and a bouquet of roses.

'Sir Aylmer Bastable?'

'Yes.'

"I forbid the banns.'

'What banns?'

'Their banns,' said Mortimer Rackstraw, removing from his lips the hand with which he had been coldly curling his moustache and jerking it in the direction of Annabel and Freddie, who stood clasped in each other's arms, waiting for they knew not what.

'They're not up yet,' said Annabel.

The conjurer seemed a little taken aback.

'Oh?' he said. 'Well, when they are, I forbid them. And so will you, Sir Aylmer, when you hear all.'

Sir Aylmer puffed.

'Who is this tight bounder?' he asked irritably.

Mortimer Rackstraw shook his head and took the two of clubs from it.

'A bounder, maybe,' he said, 'but not tight. I have come here, Sir Aylmer, in a spirit of altruism to warn you that if you allow your nephew to marry this girl the grand old name of Bastable will be mud.'

Sir Aylmer started.

'Mud?'

'Mud. She comes from the very dregs of society.'

'I don't,' cried Annabel.

'Of course she doesn't,' cried Freddie.

'Certainly she does not,' assented Sir Aylmer warmly. 'She told me herself that her father was a colonel.'

Mortimer Rackstraw uttered a short, sneering laugh and took an egg from his left elbow.

'She did, eh? Did she add that he was a colonel in the Salvation Army?'

'What?'

'And that before he saw the light he was a Silver Ring bookie, known to all the heads as Rat-Faced Rupert, the Bermondsey Twister?'

'Good God!'

Sir Aylmer turned to the girl with an awful frown.

'Is this true?'

'Of course it's true,' said Mortimer Rackstraw. 'And if you want further proof of her unfitness to be your nephew's bride, just take a look at her Uncle Joe, who is now entering left-centre.'

And Freddie, listless now and without hope, saw that his companion of the train was advancing towards them. He heard Sir Aylmer gasp and was aware that Annabel had stiffened in his arms. He was not surprised. The sun, filtering through the glass of the rotunda lit up the man's flabby puffiness, his morning coat, his red waistcoat and his brown shoes, and rarely if ever, thought Freddie, could the sun of Droitgate Spa have shone on a more ghastly outsider.

There was nothing, however, in the newcomer's demeanour to suggest that he felt himself out of place in these refined surroundings. His manner had an easy self-confidence. He sauntered up and without *gêne* slapped the conjurer on the back and patted Annabel on the shoulder.

' 'Ullo, Mort. 'Ullo, Annie, my dear.'

Sir Aylmer, who had blinked, staggered and finally recovered himself, spoke in a voice of thunder.

'You, sir! Is this true?'

'What's that, old cock?'

'Are you this girl's uncle?'

'That's right.'

'Gaw!' said Sir Aylmer.

He would have spoken further, but at this point the band burst into 'Pomp and Circumstance', and conversation was temporarily suspended. When it became possible once more for the human voice to make itself heard, it was Annabel's Uncle Joe who took the floor. He had recognized Freddie.

'Why, I've met you,' he said. 'We travelled down in the train together. Who's this young feller, Annie, that's huggin' and squeezin' you?'

'He is the man I am going to marry,' said Annabel.

'He is not the man you are going to marry,' said Sir Aylmer.

'Yes, I am the man she is going to marry,' said Freddie.

'No, you're not the man she is going to marry,' said Mortimer Rackstraw.

Annabel's Uncle Joe seemed puzzled. He appeared not to know what to make of this conflict of opinion.

'Well, settle it among yourselves,' he said genially. 'All I know is that whoever does marry you, Annie, is going to get a good wife.'

'That's me,' said Freddie.

'No, it isn't,' said Sir Aylmer.

'Yes, it is,' said Annabel.

'No, it's not,' said Mortimer Rackstraw.

'Because I'm sure no man,' proceeded Uncle Joe, 'ever had a better niece. I've never forgotten the way you used to come and smooth my pillow and bring me cooling drinks when I was in the hospital.'

There was the sound of a sharp intake of breath. Sir Aylmer, who was saying, 'It isn't, it isn't, it isn't,' had broken off abruptly.

'Hospital?' he said. 'Were you ever in a hospital?'

Mr Boffin laughed indulgently.

'Was I ever in a hospital! That's a good 'un. That would make the boys on the Medical Council giggle. Ask them at St Luke's if Joe Boffin was ever in a hospital. Ask them at St Christopher's. Why, I've spent most of my life in hospitals. Started as a child with Congenital Pyloric Hypertrophy of the Stomach and never looked back.'

Sir Aylmer was trembling violently. A look of awe had come into his face, the look which a small boy wears when he sees a heavyweight champion of the world.

'Did you say your name was Joe Boffin?'

'That's right.'

'Not *the* Joe Boffin? Not the man there was that interview with in the Christmas number of *The Lancet*?'

'That's me.'

Sir Aylmer started forward impulsively.

'May I shake your hand?'

'Put it there.'

'I am proud to meet you, Mr Boffin. I am one of your greatest admirers.'

'Nice of you to say so, ol' man.'

'Your career has been an inspiration to me. Is it really true that you have Thrombosis of the Heart *and* Vesicular Emphysema of the Lungs?'

'That's right.'

'And that your temperature once went up to 107.5?'

'Twice. When I had Hyperpyrexia.'

Sir Aylmer sighed.

'The best I've ever done is 102.2.'

Joe Boffin patted him on the back.

'Well, that's not bad,' he said. 'Not bad at all.'

'Excuse me,' said a well-bred voice.

It was the distinguished-looking man with the silvery hair who had approached them, the man Sir Aylmer had addressed as Rumbelow. His manner was diffident. Behind him stood an eager group, staring and twiddling their fingers.

'Excuse me, my dear Bastable, for intruding on a private conversation, but I fancied ... and my friends fancied ...'

'We all fancied,' said the group.

'That we overheard the name Boffin. Can it be, sir, that you are Mr *Joseph* Boffin?'

'That's right.'

'Boffin of St Luke's?'

'That's right.'

The silvery-haired man seemed overcome by a sudden shyness. He giggled nervously.

'Then may we say – my friends and I – how much ... We felt we would just like ... Unwarrantable intrusion, of course,

367

but we are all such great admirers. I suppose you have to go through a good deal of this sort of thing, Mr Boffin. . . . People coming up to you, I mean, and . . . Perfect strangers, I mean to say . . .'

'Quite all right, old man, quite all right. Always glad to meet the fans.'

'Then may I introduce myself. I am Lord Rumbelow. These are my friends, the Duke of Mull, the Marquis of Peckham, Lord Percy . . .'

' 'Ow are you, 'ow are you? Come and join us, boys. My niece Miss Purvis.'

'Charmed.'

'The young chap she's going to marry.'

'How do you do?'

'And his uncle, Sir Aylmer Bastable.'

All heads were turned towards the Major-General. Lord Rumbelow spoke in awed voice.

'Is it really so, Bastable? Your nephew is actually going to marry Mr Boffin's niece? I congratulate you, my dear fellow. A most signal honour.' A touch of embarrassment came into his manner. He coughed. 'We were just talking about you, oddly enough, Bastable, my friends and I. Saying what a pity it was that we saw so little of you. And we were wondering – it was the Duke's suggestion – if you would care to become a member of a little club we have – quite a small affair – rather exclusive, we like to feel – the Twelve Jolly Stretcher-Cases . . .

'My dear Rumbelow!'

'We have felt for a long time that our company was incomplete without you. So you will join us? Capital, capital! Perhaps you will look in there tonight? Mr Boffin, of course,' he went on deprecatingly, 'would, I am afraid, hardly condescend to allow himself to be entertained by so humble a little circle. Otherwise –'

Joe Boffin slapped him affably on the back.

'My dear feller, I'd be delighted. There's nothing stuck-up about me.'

'Well, really! I hardly know what to say . . .'

'We can't all be Joe Boffins. That's the way I look at it.'

'The true democratic spirit.'

'Why I was best man at a chap's wedding last week, and all he'd got was emotional dermatitis.'

'Amazing! Then you and Sir Aylmer will be with us tonight? Delighted. We can give you a bottle of lung tonic which I think you will appreciate. We pride ourselves on our cellar.'

A babble of happy chatter had broken out, almost drowning the band, and Mr Boffin, opening his waistcoat, was showing the Duke of Mull the scar left by his first operation. Sir Aylmer, watching them with throbbing heart, was dizzily aware of a fountain-pen being thrust into his hand.

'Eh?' he said. 'What? What's this? What, what?'

'The papers,' said Freddie. 'The merry old documents in the case. You sign here, where my thumb is.'

'Eh? What? Eh? Ah, yes, to be sure. Yes, yes, yes,' said Sir Aylmer, absently affixing his signature.

'Thank you, uncle, a thousand . . .'

'Quite, quite. But don't bother me now, my boy. Busy. Got a lot to talk about to those friends of mine. Take the girl away and give her a sulphur water.'

And, brushing aside Mortimer Rackstraw, who was offering him a pack of cards, he joined the group about Joe Boffin. Freddie clasped Annabel in a fond embrace. Mortimer Rackstraw stood glaring for a moment, twisting his moustache. Then he took the flags of all nations from Annabel's back hair and, with a despairing gesture, strode from the room.

Eggs, Beans and Crumpets (1940)

Introducing Percy Pilbeam

*Percy Pilbeam, Oofy Prosser, Ogden Ford, Aubrey Upjohn,
the Princess Dwornitschek, the Duke of Dunstable . . . there
aren't many real stinkers in all the Wodehouse works. But
Pilbeam probably deserves to head the short list, and he turns
up in several of the novels. Galahad never did get at him with
a horsewhip for what he had written about him in* Society Spice
*('I may tell you,' Pilbeam said later to Sir Gregory Parsloe,
'that it was foreign to the editorial policy of* Society Spice *ever
to meet visitors who called with horsewhips'). Pity. Ronnie
Fish never did get at Pilbeam for making a pass at Sue Brown.
Pilbeam ran too fast. Pity.*

If you go up Beeston Street in the south-western postal division
of London and follow the pavement on the right-hand side,
you come to a blind alley called Hayling Court. If you enter
the first building on the left of this blind alley and mount a
flight of stairs, you find yourself facing a door, on the ground-
glass of which is the legend:

ARGUS
ENQUIRY
AGENCY
LTD

and below it, to one side, the smaller legend

P. FROBISHER PILBEAM, MGR

And if, at about the hour when Ronnie Fish had stepped into
his two-seater in the garage of Blandings Castle, you had

opened this door and gone in and succeeded in convincing the gentlemanly office-boy that yours was a *bona fide* visit, having nothing to do with the sale of life insurance, proprietary medicines or handsomely bound sets of Dumas, you would have been admitted to the august presence of the Mgr himself. P. Frobisher Pilbeam was seated at his desk, reading a telegram which had arrived during his absence at lunch.

This is peculiarly an age of young men starting out in business for themselves; of rare, unfettered spirits chafing at the bonds of employment and refusing to spend their lives working forty-eight weeks in the year for a salary. Quite early in his career Pilbeam had seen where the big money lay, and decided to go after it.

As editor of that celebrated weekly scandal-sheet, *Society Spice*, Percy Pilbeam had had exceptional opportunities of discovering in good time the true bent of his genius: with the result that, after three years of nosing out people's discreditable secrets on behalf of the Mammoth Publishing Company, his employers, he had come to the conclusion that a man of his gifts would be doing far better for himself nosing out such secrets on his own behalf. Considerably to the indignation of Lord Tilbury, the Mammoth's guiding spirit, he had borrowed some capital, handed in his portfolio, and was now in an extremely agreeable financial position.

The telegram over which he sat brooding with wrinkled forehead was just the sort of telegram an Enquiry agent ought to have been delighted to receive, being thoroughly cryptic and consequently a pleasing challenge of his astuteness as a detective, but Percy Pilbeam, in his ten minutes' acquaintance with it, had come to dislike it heartily. He preferred his telegrams easier.

It ran as follows:

Be sure send best man investigate big robbery.

It was unsigned.

What made the thing particularly annoying was that it was so tantalizing. A big robbery probably meant jewels, with a correspondingly big fee attached to their recovery. But you

371

cannot scour England at random, asking people if they have had a big robbery in their neighbourhood.

Reluctantly, he gave the problem up; and, producing a pocket mirror, began with the aid of a pen nib to curl his small and revolting moustache. His thoughts had drifted now to Sue. They were not altogether sunny thoughts, for the difficulty of making Sue's acquaintance was beginning to irk Percy Pilbeam. He had written her notes. He had sent her flowers. And nothing had happened. She ignored the notes, and what she did with the the flowers he did not know. She certainly never thanked him for them.

Brooding upon these matters, he was interrupted by the opening of the door. The gentlemanly office-boy entered. Pilbeam looked up, annoyed.

'How many times have I told you not to come in here without knocking?' he asked sternly.

The office-boy reflected.

'Seven,' he replied.

'What would you have done if I had been in conference with an important client?'

'Gone out again,' said the office-boy. Working in a Private Enquiry Agency, you drop into the knack of solving problems.

'Well, go out now.'

'Very good, sir. I merely wished to say that, while you were absent at lunch, a gentleman called.'

'Eh? Who was he?'

The office-boy, who liked atmosphere, and hoped some day to be promoted to the company of Mr Murphy and Mr Jones, the two active assistants who had their lair on the ground floor, thought for a moment of saying that, beyond the obvious facts that the caller was a Freemason, left-handed, a vegetarian and a traveller in the East, he had made no deductions from his appearance. He perceived, however, that his employer was not in the vein for that sort of thing.

'A Mr Carmody, sir. Mr Hugo Carmody.'

'Ah!' Pilbeam displayed interest. 'Did he say he would call again?'

'He mentioned the possibility, sir.'

'Well, if he does, inform Mr Murphy and tell him to be ready when I ring.'

The office-boy retired, and Pilbeam returned to his thoughts of Sue. He was quite certain now that he did not like her attitude. Her attitude wounded him. Another thing he deplored was the reluctance of stage-door keepers to reveal the private addresses of the personnel of the company. Really, there seemed to be no way of getting to know the girl at all.

Eight respectful knocks sounded on the door. The office-boy, though occasionally forgetful, was conscientious. He had restored the average.

'Well?'

'Mr Carmody to see you, sir.'

Pilbeam once more relegated Sue to the hinterland of his mind. Business was business.

'Show him in.'

'This way, sir,' said the office-boy with a graceful courtliness which, even taking into account the fact that he suffered from adenoids, had an old-world flavour, and Hugo sauntered across the threshold.

Hugo felt, and was looking, quietly happy. He seemed to bring the sunshine with him. Nobody could have been more wholeheartedly attached than he to Blandings Castle and the society of his Millicent but he was finding London, revisited, singularly attractive.

'And this, if I mistake not, Watson, is our client now,' said Hugo genially.

Such was his feeling of universal benevolence that he embraced with his goodwill even the repellent-looking young man who had risen from the desk. Percy Pilbeam's eyes were too small and too close together and he marcelled his hair in a manner distressing to right-thinking people, but today he had to be lumped in with the rest of the species as a man and a brother, so Hugo bestowed a dazzling smile upon him. He still thought Pilbeam should not have been wearing pimples with a red tie. One or the other if he liked. But not both. Nevertheless he smiled upon him.

'Fine day,' he said.

'Quite,' said Pilbeam.

'Very jolly, the smell of the asphalt and carbonic gas.'

'Quite.'

'Some people might call London a shade on the stuffy side on an afternoon like this. But not Hugo Carmody.'

'No?'

'No. H. Carmody finds it just what the doctor ordered.' He sat down. 'Well, sleuth,' he said, 'to business. I called before lunch, but you were out.'

'Yes.'

'But here I am again. And I suppose you want to know what I've come about?'

'When you're ready to get round to it,' said Pilbeam patiently.

Hugo stretched his long legs comfortably.

'Well, I know you detective blokes always want a fellow to begin at the beginning and omit no detail, for there is no saying how important some seemingly trivial fact may be. Omitting birth and early education then, I am at the moment private secretary to Lord Emsworth, at Blandings Castle, in Shropshire. And,' said Hugo, 'I maintain, a jolly good secretary. Others may think differently, but that is my view.'

'Blandings Castle?'

A thought had struck the proprietor of the Argus Enquiry Agency. He fumbled in his desk and produced the mysterious telegram. Yes, as he had fancied, it had been handed in at a place called Market Blandings.

'Do you know anything about this?' he asked pushing it across the desk.

Hugo glanced at the document.

'The old boy must have sent that after I left,' he said. 'The absence of signature is, no doubt, due to mental stress. Lord Emsworth is greatly perturbed. A-twitter. Shaken to the core, you might say.'

'About this robbery?'

'Exactly. It has got right in amongst him.'

Pilbeam reached for pen and paper. There was a stern, set, bloodhound sort of look in his eyes.

'Kindly give me the details.'

Hugo pondered a moment.

'It was a dark and stormy night ... No, I'm a liar. The moon was riding serenely in the sky ...'

'This big robbery? Tell me about it.'

Hugo raised his eyebrows.

'Big?'

'The telegram says "big." '

'These telegraph-operators will try to make sense. You can't stop them editing. The word should be "pig." Lord Emsworth's pig has been stolen!'

'Pig!' cried Percy Pilbeam.

Hugo looked at him a little anxiously.

'You know what a pig is, surely? If not, I'm afraid there is a good deal of tedious spade work ahead of us.'

Summer Lightning (1929)

Bramley is So Bracing

When, in the happy ending of the 1961 novel Ice in the
Bedroom, *Freddie Widgeon is on his way to the altar, and
Kenya, with Sally Foster, you think how lucky he was to have
failed in all his scores of earlier passionate courtships:
especially his courtship of the Hon. Mavis Peasmarch. Of
Mavis Peasmarch a Drones character had said*

*'You needn't let it get about, of course, but that girl, to my
certain knowledge, plays the organ in the local church and may
often be seen taking soup to the deserving villagers with many
a gracious word.'*

*Bingo Little, whose baby Freddie purloins in this story, had
had almost as many rejections as Freddie in his pursuits of
girls. But then he met Rosie M. Banks, the best-selling novelist,
and they married. Of all the recurrent characters they are
among the very few couples who specifically get married
between one story and the next, have issue . . . to wit the
Algernon Aubrey of this story that follows.*

A general meeting had been called at the Drones to decide on
the venue for the club's annual golf rally, and the school of
thought that favoured Bramley-on-Sea was beginning to make
headway when Freddie Widgeon took the floor. In a speech
of impassioned eloquence he warned his hearers not to go within fifty miles of the beastly place. And so vivid was the impression he conveyed of Bramley-on-Sea as a spot where the
law of the jungle prevailed and anything could happen to anybody that the voters were swayed like reeds and the counter
proposal of Cooden Beach was accepted almost unanimously.

His warmth excited comment at the bar.

'Freddie doesn't like Bramley,' said an acute Egg, who had been thinking it over with the assistance of a pink gin.

'Possibly,' suggested a Bean, 'because he was at school there when he was a kid.'

The Crumpet who had joined the group shook his head.

'No, it wasn't that,' he said. 'Poor old Freddie had a very painful experience at Bramley recently, culminating in his getting the raspberry from the girl he loved.'

'What, again?'

'Yes. It's curious about Freddie,' said the Crumpet, sipping a thoughtful martini. 'He rarely fails to click, but he never seems able to go on clicking. A whale at the Boy Meets Girl stuff, he is unfortunately equally unerring at the Boy Loses Girl.'

'Which of the troupe was it who gave him the air this time?' asked an interested Pieface.

'Mavis Peasmarch. Lord Bodsham's daughter.'

'But, dash it,' protested the Pieface, 'that can't be right. She returned him to store ages ago. You told us about it yourself. That time in New York when he got mixed up with the female in the pink négligé picked out with ultramarine lovebirds.'

The Crumpet nodded.

'Quite true. He was, as you say, handed his portfolio on that occasion. But Freddie is a pretty gifted explainer, if you give him time to mould and shape his story, and on their return to England he appears to have squared himself somehow. She took him on again – on appro., as it were. The idea was that if he proved himself steady and serious, those wedding bells would ring out. If not, not a tinkle.

'Such was the position of affairs when he learned from this Peasmarch that she and her father were proposing to park themselves for the summer months at the Hotel Magnifique at Bramley-on-Sea.'

Freddie's instant reaction to the news was, of course (said the Crumpet), an urge to wangle a visit there himself, and he devoted the whole force of his intellect to trying to think how this

377

could be done. He shrank from spending good money on a hotel, but on the other hand his proud soul scorned a boarding-house, and what they call an *impasse* might have resulted, had he not discovered that Bingo Little and Mrs Bingo had taken a shack at Bramley in order that the Bingo baby should get its whack of ozone. Bramley, as I dare say you have seen mentioned on the posters, is so bracing, and if you are a parent you have to think of these things. Brace the baby, and you are that much ahead of the game.

To cadge an invitation was with Freddie the work of a moment, and a few days later he arrived with the suitcase and two-seater, deposited the former, garaged the latter, kissed the baby and settled in.

Many fellows might have objected to the presence on the premises of a bib-and-bottle juvenile, but Freddie has always been a good mixer, and he and this infant hit it off from the start like a couple of sailors on shore leave. It became a regular thing with him to take the half-portion down to the beach and stand by while it mucked about with its spade and bucket. And it was as he was acting as master of the revels one sunny day that there came ambling along a well-nourished girl with golden hair, who passed and scrutinized the Bingo issue with a genial smile.

'Is the baby building a sand castle?' she said.

'Well, yes and no,' replied Freddie civilly. 'It thinks it is, but if you ask me, little of a constructive nature will result.'

'Still, so long as it's happy.'

'Oh, quite.'

'Nice day.'

'Beautiful.'

'Could you tell me the correct time?'

'Precisely eleven.'

'Coo!' said the girl. 'I must hurry, or I shall be late. I'm meeting a gentleman friend of mine on the pier at half-past ten.'

And that was that. I mean, just one of those casual encounters which are so common at the seashore, with not a word spoken on either side that could bring the blush of shame to the cheek of modesty. I stress this, because this substantial blonde was to become entangled in Freddie's affairs and I want to make it clear at the outset that from start to finish he was as pure as the driven snow. Sir Galahad could have taken his correspondence course.

It was about a couple of days after this that a picture post-card, forwarded from his London address, informed him that Mavis and her father were already in residence at the Magnifique, and he dashed into the two-seater and drove round there with a beating heart. It was his intention to take the loved one for a spin, followed by a spot of tea at some wayside shoppe.

This project, however, was rendered null and void by the fact that she was out. Old Bodsham, receiving Freddie in the suite, told him that she had gone to take her little brother back to his school.

'We had him for lunch,' said the Bod.

'No, did you?' said Freddie. 'A bit indigestible, what?' He laughed heartily for some moments at his ready wit; then, seeing the gag had not got across, cheesed it. He remembered now that there had always been something a bit Wednesday-matineeish about the fifth Earl of Bodsham. An austere man, known to his circle of acquaintants as The Curse of the Eastern Counties. 'He's at school here, is he?'

'At St Asaph's. An establishment conducted by an old college friend of mine, the Rev. Aubrey Upjohn.'

'Good Lord!' said Freddie, feeling what a small world it was. 'I used to be at St Asaph's.'

'Indeed?'

'Absolutely. I served a three years' sentence there before going on to Eton. Well, I'll be pushing along, then. Give Mavis my love, will you, and say I'll be round bright and early in the morning.'

He buzzed off and hopped into the car again, and for the space of half an hour or so drove about Bramley, feeling a bit at a loose end. And he was passing through a spot called Marina Crescent, a sort of jungle of boarding-houses, when he became aware that stirring things were happening in his immediate vicinity.

Along the road towards him there had been approaching a well-nourished girl with golden hair. I don't suppose he had noticed her – or, if he had, it was merely to say to himself 'Ah, the substantial blonde I met on the beach the other morning' and dismiss her from his thoughts. But at this moment she suddenly thrust herself on his attention by breaking into a rapid gallop, and at the same time a hoarse cry rent the air, not unlike that of a lion of the desert scenting its prey, and Freddie perceived charging out of a side street an elderly man with whiskers, who looked as if he might be a retired sea captain or a drysalter or something.

The spectacle perplexed him. He had always known that Bramley was bracing, but he had never supposed that it was as bracing as all this. And he had pulled up in order to get a better view, when the substantial blonde, putting on a burst of speed in the straight, reached the car and hurled herself into it.

'Quick!' she said.

'Quick?' said Freddie. He was puzzled. 'In what sense do you use the word "Quick"?' he asked, and was about to go further into the thing when the whiskered bird came dashing up and scooped the girl out of the car as if she had been a winkle and his hand a pin.

The girl grabbed hold of Freddie, and Freddie grabbed hold of the steering wheel, and the whiskered bird continued to freeze on to the girl, and for a while the human chain carried on along these lines. Then there was a rending sound, and the girl and Freddie came apart.

The whiskered bozo regarded him balefully.

'If we weren't in a public place,' he said, 'I would horsewhip you. If I had a horsewhip.'

And with these words he dragged the well-nourished girl from the scene, leaving Freddie, as you may well suppose, quite a bit perturbed and a long way from grasping the inner meaning.

The recent fracas had left him half in and half out of the car, and he completed the process by alighting. He had an idea that the whiskered ancient might have scratched his paint. But fortunately everything was all right, and he was leaning against the bonnet, smoking a soothing cigarette, when Mavis Peasmarch spoke behind him.

'Frederick!' she said.

Freddie tells me that at the sound of that loved voice he sprang six feet straight up in the air, but I imagine this to be an exaggeration. About eighteen inches, probably. Still, he sprang quite high enough to cause those leaning out of the windows of Marina Crescent to fall into the error of supposing him to be an adagio dancer practising a new step.

'Oh, hullo, darling!' he said.

He tried to speak in a gay and debonair manner, but he could not but recognize that he had missed his objective by a mile. Gazing at Mavis Peasmarch, he noted about her a sort of rigidity which he didn't like. Her eyes were stern and cold, and her lips tightly set. Mavis had inherited from her father that austere Puritanism which makes the old boy so avoided by the County, and this she was now exuding at every pore.

'So there you are!' he said, still having a stab at the gay and debonair.

'Yes,' said Mavis Peasmarch.

'I'm here, too,' said Freddie.

'So I see,' said Mavis Peasmarch.

'I'm staying with a pal. I thought I'd come here and surprise you.'

'You have,' said Mavis Peasmarch. She gave a sniff that sounded like a nor'easter ripping the sails of a stricken vessel. 'Frederick what does this mean?'

'Eh?'

'That girl.'

'Oh, that *girl*?' said Freddie. 'Yes, I see what you mean. You are speaking of that girl. Most extraordinary, wasn't it?'

'Most.'

'She jumped into my car, did you notice?'

'I did. An old friend?'

'No, no. A stranger, and practically total, at that.'

'Oh?' said Mavis Peasmarch, and let go another sniff that went echoing down the street. 'Who was the old man?'

'I don't know. Another stranger, even more total.'

'He said he wanted to horsewhip you.'

'Yes, I heard him. Dashed familiar.'

'Why did he want to horsewhip you?'

'Ah, there you've got me. The man's thought processes are a sealed book to me.'

'The impression I received was that he resented your having made his daughter the plaything of an idle hour.'

'But I didn't. As a matter of fact, I haven't had much spare time since I got here.'

'Oh?'

'The solution that suggests itself to me is that we have stumbled up against one of those E. Phillips Oppenheim situations. Yes, that would explain the whole thing. Here's how I figure it out. The girl is an international spy. She got hold of the plans of the fortifications and was taking them to an accomplice, when along came the whiskered bird, a secret service man. You could see those whiskers were a disguise. He thought I was the accomplice.'

'Oh?'

'How's your brother Wilfred?' asked Freddie, changing the subject.

'Will you please drive me to my hotel?' said Mavis, changing it again.

'Oh, right,' said Freddie. 'Right.'

That night, Freddie lay awake, ill at ease. There had been something in the adored object's manner, when he dropped her at the hotel, which made him speculate as to whether that explanation of his had got over quite so solidly as he had hoped. He had suggested coming in and having a cosy chat, and she had said No, please, I have a headache. He had said how well she was looking, and she had said Oh? And when he had asked her if she loved her little Freddie, she had made no audible response.

All in all, it looked to Freddie as if what is technically called a lover's tiff had set in with a good deal of severity, and as he lay tossing on his pillow he pondered quite a bit on how this could be adjusted.

What was needed here, he felt, was a gesture – some spectacular performance on his part which would prove that his heart was in the right place.

But what spectacular performance?

He toyed with the idea of saving Mavis from drowning, only to dismiss it when he remembered that on the rare occasions when she took a dip in the salty she never went in above the waist.

He thought of rescuing old Bodsham from a burning building. But how to procure that burning building? He couldn't just set a match to the Hotel Magnifique and expect it to go up in flames.

And then, working through the family, he came to little Wilfred, and immediately got a Grade-A inspiration. It was via Wilfred that he must oil back into Mavis's esteem. And it could be done, he saw, by going to St Asaph's and asking the Rev. Aubrey Upjohn to give the school a half-holiday. This kindly act would put him right back in the money.

He could picture the scene. Wilfred would come bounding in to tea one afternoon. 'Coo!' Mavis would explain. 'What on earth are you doing here? Have you run away from school?' 'No,' Wilfred would reply, 'the school has run away from me. In other words, thanks to Freddie Widgeon, that prince of square-shooters, we have been given a half-holiday.' 'Well, I'm blowed!' Mavis would ejaculate. 'Heaven bless Freddie Widgeon! I had a feeling all along that I'd been misjudging that bird.'

At this point, Freddie fell asleep.

Often, when you come to important decisions overnight, you find after sleeping on them that they are a bit blue around the edges. But morning, when it came, found Freddie still resolved to go through with his day's good deed. If, however, I were to tell you that he liked the prospect, I should be deceiving you. It is not too much to say that he quailed at it. Years had passed since his knickerbocker days but the Rev. Aubrey Upjohn was still green in his memory. A man spiritually akin to Simon Legree and the late Captain Bligh of the *Bounty*, with whose disciplinary methods his own had much in common, he had made a deep impression on Freddie's plastic mind, and the thought of breezing in and trying to sting him for a half-holiday was one that froze the blood more than a bit.

But two things bore him on: (a) his great love, and (b) the fact that it suddenly occurred to him that he could obtain a powerful talking point by borrowing Bingo's baby and taking it along with him.

Schoolmasters, he knew, are always anxious to build for the future. To them the infant of today is the pupil at so much per of tomorrow. It would strengthen his strategic position enormously if he dangled Bingo's baby before the man's eyes and said: 'Upjohn, I can swing a bit of custom your way. My influence with the parents of this child is stupendous. Treat me right, and down it goes on your waiting list.' It would make all the difference.

So, waiting till Bingo's back and Mrs Bingo's back were turned, he scooped up Junior and started out. And presently he was ringing the front door bell of St Asaph's, the younger generation over his arm, concealed beneath a light overcoat. The parlourmaid showed him into the study, and he was left there to drink in the details of the well-remembered room which he had not seen for so many years.

Now, it so happened that he had hit the place at the moment when the Rev. Aubrey was taking the senior class in Bible history, and when a headmaster has got his teeth into a senior class he does not readily sheathe the sword. There was consequently a longish wait, and as the minutes passed Freddie began to find the atmosphere of the study distinctly oppressive.

The last time he had been in this room, you see, the set-up had been a bit embarrassing. He had been bending over a chair, while the Rev. Aubrey Upjohn, strongly posted in his rear, stood measuring the distance with half-closed eyes, preparatory to bringing the old malacca down on his upturned trousers' seat. And memories like this bring with them a touch of sadness.

Outside the French window the sun was shining, and it seemed to Freddie that what was needed to dissipate the feeling of depression from which he had begun to suffer was a stroll in the garden with a cigarette. He sauntered out, accordingly, and had paced the length of the grounds and was gazing idly over the fence at the end of them, when he perceived that beyond this fence a certain liveliness was in progress.

He was looking into a small garden, at the back of which was a house. And at an upper window of this house was a girl. She was waving her arms at him.

It is never easy to convey every shade of your meaning by waving your arms at a distance of forty yards, and Freddie not unnaturally missed quite a good deal of the gist. Actually, what the girl was trying to tell him was that she had recently met at the bandstand on the pier a man called George Perkins, employed in a London firm of bookmakers doing business under the trade name of Joe Sprockett; that a mutual fondness for the Overture to *Zampa* had drawn them together; that she had become deeply enamoured of him; that her tender sentiments had been fully reciprocated; that her father, who belonged to a religious sect which disapproved of bookmakers, had refused to sanction the match or even to be introduced to the above Perkins; that he – her father – had intercepted a note from the devout lover, arranging for a meeting at the latter's boarding-house (10, Marina Crescent) and a quick wedding at the local registrar's; and that he – she was still alluding to her father – had now locked her in her room until, in his phrase, she should come to her senses. And what she wanted Freddie to do was let her out. Because good old George was waiting at 10, Marina Crescent with the licence, and if she could only link up with him they could put the thing through promptly.

Freddie, as I say, did not get quite all of this, but he got enough of it to show him that here was a damsel in distress, and he was stirred to his foundations. He had not thought that this sort of thing happened outside the thrillers, and even there he had supposed it to be confined to moated castles. And this wasn't a moated castle by any means. It was a two-storey desirable residence with a slate roof, standing in park-like grounds extending to upwards of a quarter of an acre. It looked the sort of place that might belong to a retired sea captain or possibly a drysalter.

Full of the old knight-errant spirit, for he has always been a pushover for damsels in distress, he leaped the fence with sparkling eyes. And it was only when he was standing beneath the window that he recognized in the girl who was goggling at him through the glass like some rare fish in an aquarium his old acquaintance, the substantial blonde.

The sight cooled him off considerably. He is rather a superstitious sort of chap, and he had begun to feel that this billowy curver wasn't lucky for him. He remembered now that a gipsy had once warned him to beware of a fair woman, and for a moment it was touch and go whether he wouldn't turn away and ignore the whole unpleasant affair. However, the old knight-errant spirit was doing its stuff, and he decided to carry on as planned. Gathering from a quick twist of her eyebrows that the key was in the outside of the door, he nipped in through the sitting-room window, raced upstairs and did the needful. And a moment later she was emerging like a cork out of a bottle and shooting down the stairs. She whizzed into the sitting-room and whizzed through the window, and he whizzed after her. And the first thing he saw as he came skimming over the sill was her galloping round the lawn, closely attended by the whiskered bloke who had scooped her out of the car in Marina Crescent. He had a three-pronged fork in his possession and was whacking at her with the handle, getting a bull's-eye at about every second shot.

It came as a great surprise to Freddie, for he had distinctly understood from the way the girl had twiddled her fingers that her father was at the croquet club, and for a moment he paused, uncertain what to do.

He decided to withdraw. No chivalrous man likes to see a woman in receipt of a series of juicy ones with a fork handle, but the thing seemed to him one of those purely family disputes which can only be threshed out between father and daughter. He had started to edge away, accordingly, when the whiskered bloke observed him and came charging in his direction, shouting the old drysalters' battle cry. One can follow his train of thought, of course. He supposed Freddie to be George Perkins, the lovelorn bookie, and wished to see the colour of his insides. With a good deal of emotion, Freddie saw that he was now holding the fork by the handle.

Exactly what the harvest would have been, had nothing occurred to interfere with the old man's plans, it is hard to say. But by great good fortune he tripped over a flower-pot while he was still out of jabbing distance and came an impressive purler. And before he could get right side up again, Freddie had seized the girl, hurled her over the fence, leaped the fence himself and started lugging her across the grounds of St Asaph's to his car, which he had left at the front door.

The going had been so good, and the substantial blonde was in such indifferent condition, that even when they were in the car and bowling off little came through in the way of conversation. The substantial blonde, having gasped out a request that he drive her to 10, Marina Crescent, lay back panting, and was still panting when they reached journey's end. He decanted her and drove off. And it was as he drove off that he became aware of something missing. Something he should have had on his person was not on his person.

He mused.

His cigarette case?

No, he had his cigarette case.

His hat?

No, he had his hat.

His small change? . . .

And then he remembered. Bingo's baby. He had left it chewing a bit of indiarubber in the Rev. Aubrey Upjohn's study.

*

Well, with his nervous system still all churned up by his recent experiences, an interview with his old preceptor was not a thing to which he looked forward with anything in the nature of ecstasy, but he's a pretty clear-thinking chap, and he realized that you can't go strewing babies all over the place and just leave them. So he went back to St Asaph's and trotted round to the study window. And there inside was the Rev. Aubrey, pacing the floor in a manner which the most vapid and irreflective observer would have recognized as distraught.

I suppose practically the last thing an unmarried schoolmaster wants to find in his sanctum is an unexplained baby, apparently come for an extended visit; and the Rev. Aubrey Upjohn, on entering the study shortly after Freddie had left it and noting contents, had sustained a shock of no slight order. He viewed the situation with frank concern.

And he was turning to pace the floor again, when he got another shock. He had hoped to be alone, to think this thing over from every angle, and there was a young man watching him from the window. On this young man's face there was what seemed to him a sneering grin. It was really an ingratiating smile, of course, but you couldn't expect a man in the Rev. Aubrey's frame of mind to know that.

'Oh, hullo,' said Freddie. 'You remember me, don't you?'

'No, I do not remember you,' cried the Rev. Aubrey. 'Go away.'

Freddie broadened the ingratiating smile an inch or two.

'Former pupil. Name of Widgeon.'

The Rev. Aubrey passed a weary hand over his brow. One can understand how he must have felt. First this frightful blow, I mean to say, and on top of that the re-entry into his life of a chap he hoped he'd seen the last of years and years ago.

'Yes,' he said, in a low, toneless voice. 'Yes, I remember you, Widgeon.'

'F. F.'

'F., as you say, F. What do you want?'

'I came back for my baby,' said Freddie, like an apologetic plumber.

The Rev. Aubrey started.

'Is this your baby?'

'Well, technically, no. On loan, merely. Some time ago, my pal Bingo Little married Rosie M. Banks, the well-known female novelist. This is what you might call the upshot.'

The Rev. Aubrey seemed to be struggling with some powerful emotion.

'Then it was you who left this baby in my study?'

'Yes. You see –'

'Ha!' said the Rev. Aubrey, and went off with a pop, as if suffering from spontaneous combustion.

'Yes. You see –'

'Ha!' said the Rev. Aubrey, and went off with a pop, as if suffering from spontaneous combustion.

Freddie tells me that few things have impressed him more than the address to which he now listened. He didn't like it, but it extorted a grudging admiration. Here was this man, he meant to say, unable as a clerk in Holy Orders to use any of the words which would have been at the disposal of a layman, and yet by sheer force of character rising triumphantly over the handicap. Without saying a thing that couldn't have been said in the strictest drawing-room, the Rev. Aubrey Upjohn contrived to produce in Freddie the illusion that he had had a falling out with the bucko mate of a tramp steamer. And every word he uttered made it more difficult to work the conversation round to the subject of half-holidays.

Long before he had reached his 'thirdly', Freddie was feeling as if he had been chewed up by powerful machinery, and when he was at length permitted to back out, he felt that he had had a merciful escape. For quite a while it had seemed more than likely that he was going to be requested to bend over that chair again. And such was the Rev. Aubrey's magnetic personality that he would have done it, he tells me, like a shot.

Much shaken, he drove back to the Bingo residence, and the first thing he saw on arriving there was Bingo standing on the steps, looking bereaved to the gills.

'Freddie,' yipped Bingo, 'have you seen Algernon?'

Freddie's mind was not at its clearest.

'No,' he said. 'I don't think I've run across him. Algernon who? Pal of yours? Nice chap?'

Bingo hopped like the high hills.

'My baby, you ass.'

'Oh, the good old baby? Yes, I've got him.'

'Six hundred and fifty-seven curses!' said Bingo. 'What the devil did you want to go dashing off with him for? Do you realize we've been hunting for him all the morning?'

'You wanted him for something special?'

'I was just going to notify the police and have dragnets spread.'

Freddie could see that an apology was in order.

'I'm sorry,' he said. 'Still, all's well that ends well. Here he is. Oh no, he isn't,' he added, having made a quick inspection of the interior of the car. 'I say, this is most unfortunate. I seem to have left him again.'

'Left him?'

'What with all the talk that was going on, he slipped my mind. But I can give you his address. Care of the Rev. Aubrey Upjohn, St Asaph's, Mafeking Road, Bramley-on-Sea. All you have to do is step round at your leisure and collect him. I say, is lunch ready?'

'Lunch?' Bingo laughed a hideous, mirthless laugh. At least, that's what Freddie thinks it was. It sounded like a bursting tyre. 'A fat lot of lunch you're going to get. The cook's got hysterics, the kichen-maid's got hysterics, and so have the parlourmaid and the housemaid. Rosie started having hysterics as early as eleven-thirty, and is now in bed with an ice pack. When she finds out about this, I wouldn't be in your shoes for a million quid. Two million,' added Bingo. 'Or, rather, three.'

This was an aspect of the matter which had not occurred to Freddie. He saw that there was a good deal in it.

'Do you know, Bingo,' he said, 'I believe I ought to be getting back to London today.'

'I would.'

'Several things I've got to do there, several most important things. I dare say, if I whipped back to town, you could send my luggage after me?'

'A pleasure.'

'Thanks,' said Freddie. 'You won't forget the address, will you? St Asaph's, Mafeking Road. Mention my name, and say you've come for the baby I inadvertently left in the study. And now, I think, I ought to be getting round to see Mavis. She'll be wondering what has become of me.'

He tooled off, and a few minutes later was entering the lobby of the Hotel Magnifique. The first thing he saw was Mavis and her father standing by a potted palm.

'Hullo, hullo,' he said, toddling up.

'Ah, Frederick,' said old Bodsham.

I don't know if you remember when I was telling you about that time in New York, my mentioning that at a rather sticky point in the proceedings Freddie had noticed that old Bodsham was looking like a codfish with something on its mind. The same conditions prevailed now.

'Frederick,' proceeded the Bod, 'Mavis has been telling me a most unpleasant story.'

Freddie hardly knew what to say to this. He was just throwing a few sentences together in his mind about the modern girl being sound at heart despite her freedom of speech, and how there isn't really any harm in it if she occasionally gets off one from the smoking room – tolerant, broad-minded stuff, if you know what I mean – when old Bodsham resumed.

'She tells me you have become entangled with a young woman with golden hair.'

'A fat young woman with golden hair,' added Mavis, specifying more exactly.

Freddie waved his arms passionately, like a semaphore.

'Nothing in it,' he cried. 'Nothing whatever. The whole thing greatly exaggerated. Mavis,' he said, 'I am surprised and considerably pained. I should have thought that you would have had more trust in me. Kind hearts are more than coronets and simple faith than Norman blood,' he went on, for he had always remembered that gag after having to write it out two hundred times at school for loosing off a stink bomb in the form-room. 'I told you she was a total stranger.'

'Then how does it happen that you were driving her through the streets of Bramley in your car this morning?' said old Bodsham.

'Yes,' said Mavis. 'That is what I want to know.'

'It is a point,' said old Bodsham, upon which we would both be glad to receive information.'

Catch Freddie at a moment like this, and you catch him at his best. His heart, leaping from its moorings, had loosened one of his front teeth, but there was absolutely nothing in his manner to indicate it. His eyes, as he stared at them, were those of a spotless bimbo cruelly wronged by a monstrous accusation.

'Me?' he said incredulously.

'You,' said old Bodsham.

'I saw you myself,' said Mavis.

I doubt if there is another member of this club who could have uttered at this juncture the light, careless laugh that Freddie did.

'What an extraordinary thing,' he said. 'One can only suppose that there must be somebody in this resort who resembles me so closely in appearance that the keenest eye is deceived. I assure you, Bod – I mean, Lord Bodsham – and you, Mavis – that my morning has been far too full to permit of my giving joy rides to blondes, even if the mere thought of doing so wouldn't have sickened me to the very soul. The idea having crossed my mind that little Wilfred would appreciate it, I went to St Asaph's to ask the Rev. Aubrey Upjohn to give the school a half-holiday. I want no thanks, of course. I merely mention the matter to show how ridiculous this idea of yours is that I was buzzing about with blondes in my two-seater. The Rev. Aubrey will tell you that I was in conference with him for the dickens of a time. After which, I was in conference with my friend, Bingo Little. And after that I came here.'

There was a silence.

'Odd,' said the Bod.

'Very odd,' said Mavis.

They were very plainly rattled. And Freddie was just beginning to have that feeling, than which few are pleasanter, of having got away with it in the teeth of fearful odds, when the revolving door of the hotel moved as if impelled by some irresistible force, and through it came a bulging figure in mauve, surmounted by golden hair. Reading from left to right, the substantial blonde.

'Coo!' she exclaimed, sighting Freddie. 'There you are, ducky! Excuse me half a jiff,' she added to Mavis and the Bod, who had rocked back on their heels at the sight of her, and she linked her arm in Freddie's and drew him aside.

'I hadn't time to thank you before,' she said. 'Besides being too out of breath. Papa is very nippy on his feet, and it takes it out of a girl, trying to dodge a fork handle. What luck finding you here like this. My gentleman friend and I were married at the registrar's just after I left you, and we're having the wedding breakfast here. And if it hadn't been for you, there wouldn't have been a wedding breakfast. I can't tell you how grateful I am.'

And, as if feeling that actions speak louder than words, she flung her arms about Freddie and kissed him heartily. She then buzzed off to the ladies' room to powder her nose, leaving Freddie rooted to the spot.

He didn't, however, remain rooted long. After one quick glance at Mavis and old Bodsham, he was off like a streak to the nearest exit. That glance, quick though it had been, had shown him that this was the end. The Bod was looking at Mavis, and Mavis was looking at the Bod. And then they both turned and looked at him, and there was that in their eyes which told him, as I say, that it was the finish. Good explainer though he is, there were some things which he knew he could not explain, and this was one of them.

That is why, if our annual tournament had been held this year at Bramley-on-Sea, you would not have found Frederick Widgeon in the ranks, playing to his handicap of twenty-four.

He makes no secret of the fact that he is permanently through with Bramley-on-Sea. If it wants to brace anybody, let it jolly well brace somebody else, about sums up what he feels.

Nothing Serious (1950)

Young Villain

All the important children in Wodehouse's books are splendid monsters of misrule. We love them all, even Edwin the Boy Scout, who gets his behind booted by both Boko Fittleworth and Bertie Wooster (Joy in the Morning).

No, I take that back. Not all the children are lovable. Not Huxley Winkworth, and not Ogden Ford, the fat, chain-smoking 14-year-old American boy (son of a millionaire and thus a ripe target for the kidnappers) who is enrolled at an English preparatory school.

Here Wodehouse tells us how The Little Nugget *came to be written, and what he himself thought of Ogden Ford.*

Between the years 1910 and 1913, when this book was written, there was a close resemblance between me and Shakespeare. He had the edge on me as far as writing was concerned, but we had this in common, that both of us required a helping hand to get us started. He could never get rolling without what are politely called his 'sources', while I would sit for hours in my Greenwich Village hotel room, staring at my typewriter in the hope that it would give me a plot for a story and eventually having to go and see Bob Davis. He was the editor of I don't know how many pulp magazines and, as I have recorded elsewhere, would always supply our little circle of hacks with ideas, if requested. You went to his office in the Flatiron Building, where he sat up to his neck in proofs, contributions etc, and said you wanted a plot, and he gave you one, and you went away and wrote it, and he bought it and paid you the thirty-five dollars or whatever it was. (The magazines he edited were owned by a Mr Munsey, whose ideas on payment were not lavish. One of our crowd sold Bob a seventy-thousand word serial. He got $125 for it.)

The trouble with Bob as a collaborator was that he was never very coherent. He was bubbling over with ideas, but he found a difficulty in making them clear to one who, like me, had been dropped on the head as a baby and was not what you would call bright. Many years after I had graduated from the pulps I read a thing in the *New Yorker* by Russell Maloney where Shakespeare is supposed to be giving Ben Jonson an outline of the play he is working on, and I thought to myself 'Why, that's Bob'. It ran as follows:

'Well, Ben, the central character is this guy, see. He's in love with this girl, see, but her old man doesn't think he's on the level, see, so he tells her – wait a minute, I better start at the beginning. Well, he's come home to be at his mother's wedding, her second wedding. His father's dead. So he sees a ghost and it turns out to be his father and he says that his stepfather, the one that's just married his mother, killed him. I forgot to say that these two guys are brothers. *Which* two guys? The guy that's married his mother and the ghost, of course. Well, I ought to explain that all through the play it looks as if the guy might be crazy, only sometimes it looks as if he wasn't crazy. It's never decided. So he puts on a play and the stepfather yells "Lights! Lights!", and that tips the guy off that he poisoned his father.'

Yes, I thought as I read, that might have been Bob giving me the plot of *The Little Nugget*. He talked for half an hour, but all I returned to Greenwich Village with was a confused recollection that there was this American millionaire – see – and these kidnappers are after his son to kidnap him – see – and there's a girl, of course, and a hero, and the hero's trying to kidnap the kid for the kid's mother and the girl's trying to stop him getting kidnapped and the kidnappers come to the place and all hell breaks loose, and be sure to make the kid sympathetic and touching, you know the sort of thing – blue eyes, golden hair and all that, and now for God's sake get out of here, I'm busy.

So I got out of there and found that I was able to start writing, as always happened after a visit to Bob. The final result was almost entirely my own unaided work, but without him I would never have got off the ground.

He accepted the story, though I think he must have been a little disappointed in Ogden, who may for all I know have had golden hair, but whose best friends could not have called him sympathetic and touching. I used him again in a book called *Piccadilly Jim,* and he was just as repulsive there as he had been in *The Little Nugget.* I should imagine that, when he grows up, if he is ever allowed to, he will be the sort of man who kicks dogs, grinds the face of the poor and takes three hours for lunch at expensive restaurants. He was not drawn from any boy of my acquaintance.

From a Preface to a recent re-issue of Wodehouse's 1913 novel,
The Little Nugget

The Plot So Far

Author of nearly a hundred books and with publishers courting him in almost every country in the world, Wodehouse was fairly polite about publishers in his books.

In his office on the premises of Popgood and Grooly, publishers of the Book Beautiful, Madison Avenue, New York, Cyril Grooly, the firm's junior partner, was practising putts into a tooth glass and doing rather badly even for one with a twenty-four handicap, when Patricia Binstead, Mr Popgood's secretary, entered, and dropping his putter he folded her in a close embrace. This was not because all American publishers are warmhearted impulsive men and she a very attractive girl, but because they had recently become betrothed. On his return from his summer vacation at Paradise Valley, due to begin this afternoon, they would step along to some convenient church and become man, if you can call someone with a twenty-four handicap a man, and wife.

Opening paragraph of 'Sleepy Time' in *Plum Pie*

The Talks to America on the German Radio in 1941

In 1934 Ethel Wodehouse bought Low Wood, a villa in 'The Forest' above Le Touquet in Northern France. It was the only home the Wodehouses owned, and they were there when the German armies swept into France in May 1940. In July, after two undisturbed months, British civilian males under the age of 60 in the Pas de Calais were sent off to internment. These included Wodehouse, who was going to be 59 in October and would be due for release the following October 1941.

Largely through American pressure, Wodehouse was released in June 1941, four months early, and his voice was heard, in five cheerful talks on the German radio, short wave to America, in June and July. He had made the recordings, at the suggestion of a man in the German Foreign Office whom he had met in Berlin, thinking that they would be played on one of the regular transmissions that the American networks, N.B.C. and C.B.S., made from Berlin. (America was, of course, neutral then: not to be at war with Germany for another six months.)

It was a bad time for an Englishman to be giving funny talks to America about his experiences as a prisoner in Germany. Very few people in England heard the talks (they went out at 4 a.m. British time). All people knew was that Wodehouse was broadcasting on the German radio, and they assumed he was putting out hot propaganda for the Nazis and had been released for this purpose.

In fact the talks were completely innocent. But they were completely mistimed.

Wodehouse came in for a storm of abuse in English newspapers, and a Daily Mirror journalist, William Connor, was *briefed by the Minister of Information, Duff Cooper, to broad-cast a bitter attack on Wodehouse on the B.B.C. (The B.B.C. didn't like the idea, or Connor's ranting script. But they had to let it go.) Such is the nature of war and propaganda that Wode-house's Berlin broadcasts did him irreparable harm. For every one person in England who heard his talks on the radio, or read the scripts of them (not published till thirteen years later), twenty had heard and remembered the cheap and ugly things Connor had said.*

Wodehouse never came back to England, and he did not re-ceive his knighthood till he was 93, three merciful months before his death.

Here are some of the things he said in the broadcasts:

(*At the Kommandatur in Le Touquet, when he learnt that he had to go off to internment*) My emotions were very much those of the man in the dock when the Judge, reaching for the black cap, begins, 'Well, prisoner at the bar, it's been nice knowing you . . .' the room swam before my eyes. I seemed to be surrounded by German soldiers, all doing the shimmy . . .

In the end the only thing of importance I left behind was my passport, which was the thing I ought to have packed first. The internee is always being told to show his passport, and if he has not got one, the authorities tend to look squiggle-eyed. I had never really appreciated what class distinction can be till I became an internee without a passport, thereby achieving a social position somewhere in between a wharf-rat and the man the police have detained for questioning in connection with the smash-and-grab raid.

(*His cell in a French prison*) The décor is in the stark modern style. The only pictures on the walls, which are of white-washed stone, are those drawn from time to time by French convicts, boldly executed pencil sketches very much in the vein which you would expect from French convicts, whose mental trend is seldom or never prudish. Most of those in Number 44 had been executed by an artist signing himself 'Simon le Kid de Metz'. His line work was firm and good. The general effect was like finding oneself enclosed in a bound volume of *La Vie Parisienne* ...

Cartmell (*the Le Touquet piano-tuner*) had no pianos to tune and a piano-tuner suddenly deprived of pianos is like a tiger whose medical adviser has put it on a vegetarian diet ...

(*At Liège*) Parades took place at eight in the morning and eight in the evening, and as far as they were concerned I did not object to having to stand for fifty minutes or so, for they provided solid entertainment for the thoughtful mind.

You might think that fifty minutes was rather a long time for eight hundred men to get themselves counted; but you would have understood if you had seen us in action. I don't know why it was, but we could never get the knack of parading. We meant well, but we just didn't seem able to click. It was the same at Huy and in the early days at Tost, though there we never managed to reach quite the same heights of pure delirium. To catch us at our best you would have had to catch us at Liège.

The proceedings would begin with the Sergeant telling us to form fives, whereupon some of us would form fours, some sixes, and others eights. I think our idea was that the great thing was to form something promptly and zealously, without bothering about trivial technicalities. You could see that we were zealous by the way those who had formed sixes, when rebuked, immediately formed fours, while those who had formed fours instantly formed sixes. Nobody could accuse us of not trying to enter into the spirit of the thing.

At long last, we would manage to get into fives, and a very pretty picture we made, too. But was this the end? Far from it. It was not an end but a beginning. What happened was that Old Bill in Row 20 would catch sight of Old George in Row 42 and disorganize our whole formation by shuffling across to ask him if he had heard the one about the travelling salesman.

Time marches on. Presently Old Bill, having had a good laugh with Old George, decides to shuffle back, only to find that his place has been filled up like a hole by the rising tide. This puzzles him for a moment, but a solution soon presents itself. He forms up as the seventh man of a row, just behind Old Perce, who has been over chatting with Old Fred, and has just come back and lined up as number six. The Corporal would then begin to count.

He generally counted us about five times before he saw what was getting his figures wrong. When he did, he cut Bill and Perce out of the flock and chivvied them around for awhile, and after a good deal of shouting, order and symmetry were restored.

But was this the end? Again, no. The Corporal, assisted now by a French interpreter, walks the length of the ranks, counting. Then he walks back, still counting. Then he gets behind us and counts again. ('If I have enough money after this war is over,' said Internee Sandy Youl to me on one of these occasions – we were numbers seven and eight of our row of five – 'I am going to buy a German soldier and keep him in the garden and count him six times a day.')

Something seems to be wrong. There is a long stage wait. The Corporal and the Interpreter have stepped aside and are talking to the Sergeant. The word goes round that we are one short, and people begin to ask 'Where's Old Joe?' It seems that nobody has seen him since breakfast, and we discuss the matter with animation. Can it be that Old Joe has escaped? Perhaps the gaoler's daughter smuggled him in a file in a meat pie?

No, here comes Old Joe, who has been having a quiet smoke at the other end of the yard. He comes strolling along with a cigarette hanging from his lower lip, and eyes us in an indulgent sort of way, as who should say 'Hullo, boys, playing soldiers? May I join in?' He is thoroughly cursed, in German by the Sergeant and Corporal, in French by the Interpreter, and in English by us, and takes his place in the ranks.

The mathematicians among us now feel pretty hopeful. They figure it out that if we were one short before Old Joe's arrival, now that we are plus Old Joe we should come out exactly right. It looks as if at the most one more count from right to left, one more count from left to right and one more count from behind ought to do the trick.

Picture our chagrin and disappointment, accordingly, when we discover, after all this has happened, that we are now *six* short. That is to say, so far from gaining by Old Joe very decently consenting to join the parade, we have received a most serious set-back.

The Sergeant calls for another conference, a sort of General Meeting this time, for the Room Wardens are invited to attend it, and they all stand to one side with their heads together. We cannot hear what they are saying, but we can see the Sergeant's wide gesticulations, and we know that what he is telling the Board is that this looks like funny business to *him*.

'Don't tell me,' he says, 'that six internees can just vanish into thin air.'

'Seven,' says the Corporal with a deferential cough.

The Sergeant dashes back with popping eyes and skims along the ranks.

'You'll think me cuckoo,' he says, coming back, 'but I believe it's eight.'

'Or, rather, nine,' says the Corporal, who, too, has not been idle. 'May I make a suggestion?'

'Do, Heinrich. One welcomes the fresh mind.'

'Let's count' em' says the Corporal.

So we are counted again and the official score is issued. Eight short of the figure.

'Did you ever see the Indian rope trick?' asked the Corporal, making conversation to bridge over an awkward pause. But the Sergeant is not listening. He is trying to think what to do, what to do. If we are going to melt away at this rate, he is saying to himself, it will not be long before he is down to his last internee. Eventually, he announces that we are to return to our dormitories, where the Room Wardens will check us up.

My dormitory is so anxious to please that it gets a large sheet of cardboard and writes on it in chalk the words:

which our linguist assures us means 'Twenty men, all present and correct,' and when the whistle blows for the renewal of the parade we exhibit this.

It doesn't get a smile out of Teacher, which is disappointing, for we feel that short of giving him a red apple we couldn't have done much more for him. After a lot more counting, just when the situation seems to be at a deadlock, with no hope of finding a formula, the Interpreter, who has his inspired moments, says, 'How about the men in hospital?'

These prove to be eight in number, and we are dismissed. We have spent a pleasant and instructive fifty minutes and learned much about the Human Comedy.

The Citadel of Huy (*where they were temporarily incarcerated*) is one of the show places of Belgium. It was actually built, I believe, as late as the Napoleonic wars, but its atmosphere is purely medieval. It is the sort of place which they used to advertise in the Middle Ages as 'Would suit robber baron' ...

(*In the train between Huy and Tost*) One had the choice between trying to sleep sitting upright, and leaning forward with one's elbows on one's knees, in which case one bumped one's head against that of the man opposite. I had never realized the full meaning of the expression 'a hard-headed Yorkshireman' till my frontal bone kept colliding with that of Charlie Webb, who was born and raised in that county ...

In a little brochure I am preparing entitled 'Stone Floors I have Slept On', this one at Tost will be signalled out for special mention. I do not accuse the German authorities of having deliberately iced it, but the illusion of being a pound of butter in a refrigerator was extraordinarily strong and it grew as the night wore on.

One great improvement at Tost, from my viewpoint, was that

men of fifty and over were not liable for fatigues – in other words, the dirty work. I don't know anything that so braces one up on a cold winter's morning, with an Upper Silesian blizzard doing its stuff, as to light one's pipe and look out of the window and watch a gang of younger men shovelling snow. It makes you realize what the man meant who said that Age has its pleasures as well as Youth.

> *The five talks were published complete in the magazine*
> Encounter *in 1954 and in the* Penguin *edition*
> *of* Performing Flea *(1956): nowhere else yet.*

FOR THE BEST IN PAPERBACKS, LOOK FOR THE

In every corner of the world, on every subject under the sun, Penguin represents quality and variety – the very best in publishing today.

For complete information about books available from Penguin – including Pelicans, Puffins, Peregrines and Penguin Classics – and how to order them, write to us at the appropriate address below. Please note that for copyright reasons the selection of books varies from country to country.

In the United Kingdom: For a complete list of books available from Penguin in the U.K., please write to *Dept E.P., Penguin Books Ltd, Harmondsworth, Middlesex, UB7 0DA*

In the United States: For a complete list of books available from Penguin in the U.S., please write to *Dept BA, Penguin, 299 Murray Hill Parkway, East Rutherford, New Jersey 07073*

In Canada: For a complete list of books available from Penguin in Canada, please write to *Penguin Books Canada Ltd, 2801 John Street, Markham, Ontario L3R 1B4*

In Australia: For a complete list of books available from Penguin in Australia, please write to the *Marketing Department, Penguin Books Australia Ltd, P.O. Box 257, Ringwood, Victoria 3134*

In New Zealand: For a complete list of books available from Penguin in New Zealand, please write to the *Marketing Department, Penguin Books (NZ) Ltd, Private Bag, Takapuna, Auckland 9*

In India: For a complete list of books available from Penguin, please write to *Penguin Overseas Ltd, 706 Eros Apartments, 56 Nehru Place, New Delhi, 110019*

In Holland: For a complete list of books available from Penguin in Holland, please write to *Penguin Books Nederland B.V., Postbus 195, NL–1380AD Weesp, Netherlands*

In Germany: For a complete list of books available from Penguin, please write to *Penguin Books Ltd, Friedrichstrasse 10 – 12, D–6000 Frankfurt Main 1, Federal Republic of Germany*

In Spain: For a complete list of books available from Penguin in Spain, please write to *Longman Penguin España, Calle San Nicolas 15, E–28013 Madrid, Spain*